Vanity Project

André Spiteri

First published by Maverick Words Ltd 2024

First edition

ISBN: 978-1-7384480-2-9

Author's Note

Like *Back From The Dead*, *Vanity Project* is set in the fictional Scottish city of Strathburgh, and takes place a few months after the former story ends.

But while I do make passing references to some of the events in *Back From The Dead* – and a few characters and settings reappear briefly – *Vanity Project* is a stand-alone novel. You don't need to have read *Back From The Dead* to follow the story.

I should warn you that *Vanity Project* tackles heavy subject-matter: addiction, domestic abuse, grief, suicide, and transphobia. If you find these themes upsetting, you might want to give it a miss.

AS

Prologue

I didn't mean to kill him. Honest.

I genuinely thought I could make him see sense. Persuade him it would be better for the both of us if he dropped it.

More fool me.

He shook his head deliberately. First one side. Then the other. And then he fixed me with bloodshot eyes and shambled forward – so close I could smell his rancid morning breath – as he made a clumsy attempt to grab my wrist.

I staggered backward, my heart jackhammering in my chest, just as his hand closed over empty air. Suddenly, showing up unannounced and trying to reason with him didn't seem like such a good idea after all. What had possessed me? Why had I come here, to his house, where he'd have a natural advantage?

'The terms have changed,' he said. Although he slurred his words slightly, his tone brooked no argument. 'You don't get to call the shots. Not anymore.'

My throat bobbed up and down, and a sour taste flooded my mouth. My facial muscles wrestled with the terror that threatened to take control of my features. 'Oh, really?' I sneered, doing my best to infuse my words with a confidence I didn't feel. 'Last time I checked, you work for me, not the other way round.'

He recoiled as if I'd slapped him, then bared his teeth like a rabid dog. A tendril of white foam gathered at the corner of his mouth. He wiped it away absently with the back of his hand.

'You've some brass neck. Coming here, making threats,' he spat. 'Who do you think you are?'

That's when I knew I'd flushed away any chance I might've had of bringing him back onside. Not that they were great odds to begin with.

We eyed each other, two duellists waiting for the right moment to draw their weapons. I noticed for the first time that his expensively barbered hair, which was standing every which way in sleep-induced whorls, was dry and lifeless, shot through with white. His cheeks were hollower than I remembered them. His mouth drawn. The grey tracksuit bottoms and black T-shirt he'd worn to bed hung off his gaunt frame.

The silence lay thick around us. Poisonous with hostility. He looked me up and down. Defiant. Scornful. His right eyelid twitched as he shattered the moment with a booming laugh that echoed around the kitchen.

I dug my nails into the soft flesh of my palms, drawing blood but barely feeling the pain. The island's quartz countertop grazed my lower back. I cursed myself as I realised I'd made that most basic of basic mistakes: I'd let myself get cornered. What if he decided to go from words to actions?

'Do as I say, and you'll have nothing to worry about,' he repeated in his groggy voice. 'I'll even let this conversation slide.' He smiled magnanimously. It made him look like a skull covered in skin-coloured tissue paper.

'It's a non-starter,' I shot back through gritted teeth. 'How dare you?'

My voice cracked on the last syllable. My hands shook. I balled my fists tighter.

'Ah.' He scoffed. 'There it is.' Contempt dripped from every word. 'You don't think things through, and then you act all surprised when they don't go your way. Because nothing's ever your fault, is it?'

He scrunched up his face. Raised his voice in a mock falsetto. '"Oh no! Woe is me! Everyone's out to get me."'

I tried to explain he was the one in the wrong. He'd gone off-script. Turned against me when we were supposed to be pulling the same rope. And now he was going to throw it in my face?

But the words wouldn't come. My mouth was too dry. My throat too constricted. The only sound I could manage was a pathetic blubber.

But alongside the fear – fear for what would happen if he made good on his threat – a small flame burned. It was only a matter of time until my rage grew out of control and started spreading unchecked, consuming everything in its wake.

'Fuck off,' he said.

In retrospect, I should've done as he asked. Left and regrouped. Came back at it fresh, with a better plan.

Knowing what I do now, I wonder if perhaps everything would've sorted itself out.

Except, hindsight is twenty-twenty, isn't it? In the moment, the prospect of scurrying away with my tail between my legs was too humiliating to contemplate. He'd raised the stakes too high, and backing down would have piled several tonnes of insult onto a festering injury.

So there we were. The challenge was out. The stakes raised even further.

He straightened his back. Held my gaze.

'We'll see what your colleagues think when I tell them the truth about you,' he said, crossing his hands across his chest. 'And show them the evidence.'

My eyes widened. An automatic reaction I couldn't have stopped if I'd tried.

'Och, aye,' he continued, pressing his advantage. 'I have receipts.'

'You wouldn't dare!' I said. 'It would be as bad for you as it would be for me. Worse.'

'You're assuming I give a shit,' he fired back.

Except a shadow passed across his face. Sorrow? Fear? What wasn't he telling me?

He took another shambling step forward. Tottered on the edge of balance. Regained his footing. Pointed a stubby finger in my face. There were several dark, ridged lines across the nail.

'Try me,' he whispered.

They say it takes a special kind of person to look another human being in the eye and watch the life ebb out of them. But I disagree. Anyone who says they don't have it in them to commit murder simply hasn't found themselves in dire enough circumstances.

Standing in that kitchen, the countertop's sharp edges rubbing the tender flesh of my lower back raw, his finger inches away from my eye and his sickening breath turning my stomach, there was only one choice open to me.

Of that, I've absolutely no doubt.

Chapter One

Friday, 5 January 2024

Detective Inspector Brian Brandon stared into the bathroom mirror, but a stranger stared back at him.

Three weeks of forced leave, and he didn't recognise himself anymore. His wavy salt-and-pepper hair was frizzy, thinning on top, and appeared far heavier on the salt than it had been that morning when he'd checked himself in the hallway before leaving for East Strathburgh Police Station to plead his case. His face was pasty and puffy. Careworn. The face of a man who has had too much time on his hands and far too little to fill it with for much longer than is healthy. The knot of his blue paisley tie constricted his fleshy neck, which was spilling over the collar of his white poplin shirt. A shirt with a tailored fit that, through some process he vaguely understood but couldn't quite fathom, had become too tailored in all the wrong places.

He closed his eyes and held onto the sink with both hands, a captain steering his ship through a thicket of fog.

'I'm fine, sir. I assure you,' he'd told – practically begged – DCI Lowe five minutes earlier. 'Champing at the bit. Raring to go.'

What he hadn't told Lowe was that he wasn't sure how much longer he could trust himself to keep his head without work to occupy him. His thoughts were racing at breakneck pace, taking him places he'd rather not visit for fear he'd want to remain there. Permanently.

Lowe had given him a long, appraising look from beneath his legendarily bushy black eyebrows and leaned forward in his faux-leather office chair. Brian, standing in front of Lowe's cluttered glass and brushed-aluminium desk, had shifted his weight uncomfortably from one foot to the other, like he needed to go to the lavvy.

'It's too soon, Brian,' Lowe had said, steepling his fingers under his non-existent chin.

'It's been long enough,' Brian had insisted. 'I'm polis. It's what I do. This kind of thing... it's...' He'd waved his hand around, looking for the right words. 'It's par for the course in our line of work,' he'd ended flatly.

Lowe had raised his eyebrows. One of the hairs was sticking out at an obtuse angle, giving him an oddly comical look.

'Have you spoken to somebody?' Lowe had asked. His tone was gentle. Fatherly. But there was steel in his eyes. 'It helps. What you've been through—'

'I'm fine,' Brian repeated, a tad more forcefully than he'd intended.

He'd stopped, then. Taken a breath. Held Lowe's eyes with an earnest gaze.

'Look,' Brian had said. 'Try me. That's all I'm asking. If I can't hack it, I'll be the first to tell you. No need to worry about that. We're understaffed as it is. So what do you have to lose?'

Lowe had sighed then. A deep, heavy sound that Brian hadn't been sure what to make of. Was Lowe about to relent? Had he managed to wear him down?

'Let me think about it,' he'd said at last, weighing every word.

'But—'

'*I said*, let me think about it,' Lowe snapped. 'Take the win.'

Brian had pushed down several smart retorts and nodded deferentially.

'Thank you, sir,' he'd said finally, trying not to grit his teeth.

Now, standing in front of a rust-spotted mirror in the lads' lavvy across the hall from Lowe's office, a grey shadow toyed with the edges of his field of vision, and he opened his eyes before it could take on a more substantial form. His thoughts turned to home. To the bottle of Monkey Shoulder in the cupboard under the sink. He pushed them away. Opened the cold tap. Splashed his face. The freezing water jolted him.

Aye, that was better. Once he got back to his flat and peeled off this ill-fitting suit, maybe he'd go for a run. Clear the cobwebs. Put himself on the road to well-being and prove to Lowe he was walking the talk.

He turned the tap off, pulled a bunch of paper towels

from the dispenser and patted his face dry. Then he took a deep breath. Steeled himself. Walked out of the lavvy, through the corridor, toward the carpeted stairs that led to the station's entrance, and the parking area outside.

'DI Brandon!'

Lowe's voice, calling him from his office doorway, stopped him mid-stride. Brian's heart skipped a beat.

'Come back here, will you?' his senior officer added and strode back into his office without waiting for a reply.

Brian followed, his stomach clenching. 'Sir?' he asked from the doorway.

Lowe gave him another one of his appraising looks. His unblinking stare made him feel vulnerable. Naked.

'Fine,' he said, after a pause that felt like it had gone on for hours. 'You're right. We're stretched thin and I can't spare one of my more experienced DIs.'

Brian's knees almost buckled with relief. His lips curved into a smile.

'Does that mean—?'

Lowe lifted a hand, palm outward, in a silencing gesture.

'Just so we're clear,' Lowe continued, 'I'll be watching you like a hawk. The second I sense you're not up to the job, I'm putting you back on forced leave, you hear?'

'Loud and clear,' Brian said, with feeling.

A brief memory flashed. 3 a.m. Two days earlier. A half-empty bottle of Monkey Shoulder standing on the coffee table. Hunched on the sofa in a frayed terry-cloth robe, counting out how many Nytol one-a-day tablets he'd managed to scrounge from his medicine cabinet and wondering what would happen if he took them all. Washed them down with long gulps of the water of life.

Something prickled behind Brian's eyes.

'I won't let you down, sir,' he said, hoping his voice didn't sound as shaky as he felt.

'Let's hope so, Brian,' Lowe said, turning his gaze to his laptop – a sign Brian was being dismissed. 'Let's hope so.'

Chapter Two

Monday, 8 January 2024

SEVENTY-FIVE HOURS, THREE MINUTES, AND THIRTY-four seconds.

That's how long it took for the first murder case since Lowe's reprieve to land on Brian's desk. He'd counted. A testament to how desperate he'd been to put an end to the downward spiral of self-reflection that consumed him when he wasn't in an alcohol-induced stupor.

Strathburgh enjoyed a reputation as a postcard-perfect city, and – with the exception of a brief period of madness in 2023 when a gang war boiled over and twelve civilians, including four high-school children, were killed in two shootings and an arson attack – consistently ranked as one of the safest places in the nation. But the Italians have it right. *Tutto il mondo é paese* – the world is a village. It doesn't matter where you go. Inevitably, you'll find people who do unspeakable things to each other. And, great crime stats or not, Strathburgh was no exception. Beneath the serene, welcoming façade, there was a stubbornly resilient violent streak.

These thoughts were swirling around in Brian's head as he arrived at the crime scene and eased his police-issue chrome-blue Focus behind the forensics van that had parked on the pavement so as not to block the flow of traffic through the narrow street. The neighbourhood, an unassuming suburb north-east of the River Strath, was dotted with cookie-cutter, weathered but well-maintained brown pebble-dash terraces. The kind of place the well-to-do settled for while they waited to climb up the next rung on the property ladder, and certainly not the kind of place you'd expect to get murdered.

Brian killed the engine, unbuckled his seat belt and stared out the windscreen at the two-storey end-of-terrace to his left. The windows, which gleamed even on this overcast January afternoon, were a modern shade of anthracite that matched the wrought-iron gate and offset the bright yellow front door. The small, rectangular flagstoned front garden was bordered with a neatly manicured hedge, and to the left, a water feature spouted a thin stream that trickled down through a series of imitation concrete bowls. On the front door's left jamb, at eye level, there was a Ring doorbell.

The house would've been completely nondescript, a carbon copy of any other house in any other middle-class street in the city, had it not been for the white-and-blue police cordon and the swarm of besuited scene of crime officers converging on it.

Brian took a deep breath and exhaled slowly. He'd been gung-ho for the entire fifteen-minute drive from the station, jacked up on the good kind of adrenaline, ready and willing to roll up his sleeves and get to work piecing together the puzzle that would crack this case. But, now that he was about to attend a murder scene for the first time since ... No, he wouldn't allow his mind to think of it. But since... then, he couldn't help but feel a thread of nervousness worm its way through his stomach. What if Lowe was right? What if it really was too soon, and he couldn't handle the pressure?

For better or worse, he was about to find out.

'You OK, B?' DI Liam Craddock asked from the passenger seat.

'Aye, I'm fine,' Brian replied gruffly.

He turned to face Liam, who ran a slender, freckled hand through his ginger quiff as he studied his partner carefully, deep-set eyes boring into Brian like lasers. They'd met as fresh-faced constables on the beat in the heart of gangland and had been colleagues in East Strathburgh Ward's major investigation team for close to seven years. When you worked 12-hour shifts with somebody, day in, day out, for that long, you got a sixth sense for what was going through their head. But you didn't need to be an ace detective to guess what Liam wasn't saying, Brian thought. Was his trepidation that obvious?

'You sure?' Liam pushed. 'You look pale.'

'You're not exactly Jamie Dornan yourself, bud,' Brian clapped back.

The delivery was slightly too aggressive to be funny, but Liam chuckled good-humouredly.

'Point taken,' he replied. 'But, just in case. You know you've got this, right? You'll be fine.'

Brian nodded, but said nothing. To his relief, Liam didn't press the issue any further.

'So, tell me about our victim,' he said instead.

That, Brian could answer confidently.

'Raymond Higgins. Forty-one. IT consultant. Married, no weans,' he reeled off, his back straightening. 'Postie called it in. Heard the dog barking and got suspicious. So he went around the back through the vennel and spotted him on the living-room floor.'

'Don't all dogs bark at posties?' Liam asked. 'It's the oldest cliché in the world.'

Brian shrugged. 'Not this one apparently. Most cat-like dog you'll ever meet, the postie said. The barking was unusual enough to make him think something was wrong.'

Liam seemed to ponder this. Then said, 'Shall we get this show on the road?'

'After you,' Brian replied.

They walked up to the gate, where two officers stood at attention, guarding the scene so nobody could enter unless they had the right credentials. Brian flashed his warrant card, then headed to the staging area, suited up, and ducked under the crime scene tape before climbing up the three steps to the front door.

The hallway was deceptively spacious, with a view straight through to the downstairs living space and the garden beyond. Painted off-white, it was tastefully decorated with mid-century prints, a shaker-style bench with a distressed light-grey leather cushion, and notched wooden wall pegs on which hung a forest-green anorak, a black cotton tote bag, but, Brian noted, no dog leash.

'In there, sir,' a uniformed officer, who looked barely old enough to shave, said helpfully, pointing straight ahead with a pudgy, windburned hand.

'Aye, thanks,' Brian replied. 'Where's the postie, Constable ...?'

'Stebbings, sir,' the uniform replied. 'They took him to A&E. He's in shock.'

'Did you interview him?' Brian asked.

'Aye,' Stebbings said, patting his right trouser pocket, where, Brian guessed, he kept his police-issue notebook. 'And told him he'd need to come down to the station to make a formal statement when he got out of the hospital.'

'Good man,' Brian said. 'And the dog?'

'SOCO checked it for evidence, then a neighbour took it,' Stebbings replied. 'A Mr ...' – he pulled out his battered notebook and flipped through several dog-eared pages covered in a large, looping scrawl – 'Layton. Gerald Layton. He's the only neighbour we managed to talk to. Nobody else answered their doors. He's holding on to it while we get in touch with the victim's wife.'

'Did he see anything?' Brian asked.

'Said a panel van stopped here this morning. Assumed it was an Amazon delivery.'

Brian nodded. They'd need to speak to Layton again, try to extract as much detail out of him as they could. And then they'd need to find the delivery driver and interview them too.

'Give it some time, then canvas the neighbourhood again. Maybe somebody else saw something, too.' he said. 'And let's check for CCTV. There's a Ring doorbell outside – let's see what we can get from that, and some of the neighbours might have more footage that might help us, too.'

'Aye, sir.'

So far, so good. It was actually – dare he say it? – nice to be back. Focusing on the nitty gritty of an investigation. Trying to make order out of somebody else's chaos instead of his own. He looked behind Stebbings, taking in the hive of activity. The murmur of voices, clicking of cameras, and swishing of plastic as the SOCOs moved around the scene in their protective suits and booties filled his ears. He took a deep breath. Braced himself. Beckoned Liam with a nod. It was time to witness the main event.

They walked through the doorway and surveyed the scene. Even from ten feet away, there was no mistaking the two long streaks that snaked their way from the kitchen – located in a large alcove perpendicular to the lounge space – and ended in front of the white, *U*-shaped sectional sofa, even though they'd dried to a dark maroon. Raymond Higgins, dressed in grey tracksuit bottoms and a black Pierre Cardin T-shirt, must've been dragged all the way to the plush chevron-patterned rug that defined the seating area. He lay flat on his back with his arms by his sides, his head turned at an impossible angle. His eyes stared sightlessly at the sputnik light jutting down from the ceiling.

The injury to his neck, Brian surmised, would've probably been enough to end him. But the killer hadn't been satisfied with a quick, clean death. The poor sod's torso was covered in deep stab wounds. From a quick glance, Brian counted fifteen.

'Jesus,' Liam said, covering his mouth with the back of his hand. 'He must've really pissed someone off.'

Brian gulped. The sight of the body – *It's Ray Higgins's body. Not* that *body, silly. Don't you dare think about that. Don't. You. Dare* – had blindsided him.

The blood was rushing in his ears and his throat was as dry as the Sahara on an August afternoon. Good thing he'd skipped lunch.

'Looks like a frenzied attack, doesn't it?' Brian said, trying to keep his voice even.

He placed his hand discreetly inside his front trouser pocket, pinched the fleshy part of his thigh, and rode the wave of tender, burning pain. Embraced it with open arms. The memory of that other body—

Stop it. stop it. STOP IT.

—faded.

With a physical effort, he turned his mind to the task at hand. What could Raymond Higgins's body tell them about his killer?

He'd been on the scene for less than two minutes, so he needed to keep an open mind and make sure he didn't jump to conclusions. But the savagery suggested a crime of passion, not a random attack or burglary gone wrong. Most likely, Higgins had known his killer.

Brian squatted down in front of the body. Three deep lacerations – probably defensive wounds, given their location – snaked around the outside of Higgins's right forearm. Whatever happened, it must've happened fast. And Higgins was either taken by surprise or easily overpowered. He'd have expected a greater number of defensive wounds if there'd been a long struggle.

'DI Brandon.'

The greeting startled him from his reverie. He turned. Stood up. Fussed with the creases in his plastic overalls.

'Dr Grace.'

Pam Grace, who, having joined in September 2023, was the most recent addition to Strathburgh Police's team of forensic pathologists, looked at him over her mask, her blue eyes twinkling. Some DIs complained she was cold and aloof. But he suspected this had more to do with her clipped accent and the fact she'd come up from London, than with her actual personality. He enjoyed working with her. She was sharp, and he found her no-nonsense approach refreshing. He wouldn't have wished Harris Henderson, a painfully mediocre curmudgeon of a man who was too arrogant to realise he was way past his prime, on his worst enemy. Especially not on their first case back from a leave of absence.

'Some fucking end, eh?' Brian offered.

'You should see the kitchen,' she replied. 'It's a bloodbath.'

Peering over her PPE-clad head, Brian traced the maroon tracks to a large puddle that had pooled around the island. The edges of another pool peeked from behind it. They looked impossibly dark against the off-white tiles. A forensic technician was busying herself on the countertop, dusting the knife block for prints. Six slots and only five knives in the block.

That's where the attack must've started, he thought. *But why go to the trouble of dragging him from the kitchen to the living room, and then just leave him there?* Then, aloud to Pam: 'Have they found the knife?'

'Not yet,' Pam replied.

Brian turned back to Higgins's body.

'The broken neck looks like it might've happened post-mortem,' Pam said, anticipating his next question. 'Though, I'll have to confirm.'

'And the time of death?' he said. 'Can you tell?'

'Six to twelve hours, based on rigor mortis,' she replied. 'So sometime between two and eight a.m.'

Brian mulled this over. It was a fairly wide window, but it was *something*. And, at this stage of the investigation, he'd take all the *somethings* he could get. There's a reason why the first forty-eight hours of a murder investigation are critical. Leads are fragile things that go cold quicker than water in an Arctic storm. The sooner he could find them and see where they took him, the better.

'The post-mortem might help narrow things down,' Pam said, once again anticipating his thoughts.

She looked up at him, head cocked.

'How are *you* doing?' she asked. 'It's good to have you back.'

She reached out. Squeezed his upper arm briefly. Her hand felt pleasantly warm, even through the glove and the layer of PPE over his suit.

There was a faint stirring in his stomach and a tickle in his throat. 'Erm, I ...' he said, flustered. He coughed. 'I'm—'

'Ma'am!' Stebbings called from the hallway. 'Ma'am. Please just—'

Brian turned toward the commotion. A woman with

curly brown hair in a charcoal-grey trouser suit was trying to power her way into the living room. Stebbings stepped in front of her, arms wide, trying to use his bulk to block her way, but she walked deftly around him.

'Ma'am, please. You can't go in there,' Stebbings pleaded, in a voice that was about as authoritative as a fart in the wind.

'Get out of my way,' the woman hissed. 'I have to see him.'

Stebbings, his face pinched and a deer-in-the-headlights look on his face, made an ineffectual attempt to grab her by the arm.

'Get away from me,' she yelled, elbowing him. 'Ray? Ray! Where is he? Ra—'

The woman, who, given her state, Brian guessed to be Higgins's wife, froze midway between the doorway and her husband's supine form. Her throat worked. Her hand flew to her open mouth.

'Oh dear Jesus,' she whispered in a barely audible croak. 'Oh, good Lord.'

Her skin went clammy. Took on a greenish tinge. And, before anyone could stop her, she did the liquid scream on the bloodstained oak floor – to the outraged grunts of one of the forensic techs – spraying ropy, pinkish-orange chunks that must've gone down the other way as a smoothie.

Chapter Three

BRIAN SWERVED OUT OF THE WAY IN THE NICK OF time, the stream of sick missing him by a bawhair. Higgins's wife's skin went from lime green, to dirty grey, to deathly pale. The area under her nose took on a bluish, bruised look. She swayed. Doubled over and retched violently once, twice, three times, until her stomach was empty and she could only bring up foamy runnels of saliva.

'For fuck's sake!' Liam said to nobody in particular. 'A little help here?'

Her eyes rolled up in their sockets. Brian reached out and caught her before she could fall face first onto her late husband. She slumped into his arms, shaking uncontrollably, her teeth chattering.

'Anyone?' Liam repeated, his eyes searching the room.

Several forensic techs had stopped their work and were gaping openly. Brian, his mouth dry, numb, as if he'd just been beaten senseless with a stick—

It's Roystonmuir all over again. I almost mistook her for— Oh, for fuck's sake! ENOUGH!

—put an arm awkwardly around her and guided her to the dining area at the opposite end of the room. She sank into a deep-green vic chair. Slowly, the shaking subsided, but her eyes were glazed. She was going into shock. Pam, who'd left the room at some point between Higgins's wife's first heave and the moment she'd teetered on the edge of faintness, reappeared with a foil blanket and a bottle of water. She placed the water on the mahogany dining table and draped the foil blanket over Higgins's wife with hands that shook slightly. Brian couldn't say he blamed her for the uncharacteristic slip of composure.

'I must ...' Pam murmured, nodding toward Higgins's body.

'Aye. Go ahead,' Brian whispered.

He pulled out a chair and sat down next to Higgins's wife, who had sunk into the blanket and was sipping slowly, the water bottle cradled between her palms. Liam walked around to the other side of the dining table. Sat in a chair opposite Brian.

Brian wanted to speak to her as soon as possible, but, judging by her reaction, he wasn't going to get much out of her. Still, he looked on and waited. She sipped some more water, then placed the half-empty bottle carefully on the table. Her hands trembled.

'Mrs Higgins,' Brian said softly.

She cleared her throat and looked up at him. Her dark eyes were swimming. But Brian couldn't help noticing she hadn't cried.

It didn't mean anything, he told himself. People grieved in all sorts of different ways. And she'd clearly had a huge shock.

Still, it niggled at him. That and the lack of defensive wounds. Higgins seemed rather frail for a man his age. Would she have been able to overpower him?

'Mrs Higgins,' he tried again. 'I'm very sorry for your loss. I know this must be incredibly difficult for you, but it would really help if we could ask you some questions.'

Higgins's wife made a visible effort to collect herself. Brian swallowed. Wished somebody had brought him some water, too.

'Please,' she said in a hushed voice. 'Call me Alice.'

Brian leaned back in his chair, partly to give her space and partly so he could get a firmer grip on his own emotions.

Oh, God. Oh, God. Oh, God.

Stop whining and do your fucking job. Christ alive.

'Alice,' he repeated. 'Can we ask you a few questions? About Ray?'

'Please,' she whispered, her gaze fixed on a fleck of dust on the dining table. 'How can I help?' Her mouth had made the right sounds, but she seemed to have barely registered what Brian had just said to her.

Brian opened his mouth. Closed it. Counted to ten while he focused on his breathing. He'd interviewed dozens, if not hundreds of people in his time as a DI, and he'd got to a point where he rarely had to think too much about what to ask. He operated largely on muscle memory. Jitters or not, this was nothing he couldn't handle. He glanced at Liam, who raised an eyebrow, then gave a subtle nod of encouragement. Brian looked at Alice and tried again.

'I'm sorry to be blunt,' he prefaced, 'but is there anyone you can think of who'd have reason to hurt your husband?'

His mentor, DI Delia Campbell, a tough-as-nails Glaswegian with a three-pack-a-day Superkings habit, had told him when he was first starting out – God, it felt like an eternity ago – that it made no difference how diplomatically he worded his questions, interviewing a murder victim's family would always be awkward and unpleasant, so best get on with it. 'Stoap faffing aboot and get to the point,' she'd told him from around the cigarette clamped between her teeth. Brian reckoned she was probably right, but he still felt compelled to try and soften the blow.

Alice bit her lip.

'Alice?' Liam prodded gently.

She wrapped the foil blanket tighter around her, clutching it like her life depended on it as she looked down at her lap again.

'No,' she said, stretching out the syllable so it came out sounding like a wail. She cleared her throat. 'No.'

'A business rival, maybe?' Brian insisted. 'An unhappy client? Or ... a special friend?'

That last one was a shot in the dark. But only up to a point. Stabbing is personal. You have to get up close to do real damage. And the number of stab wounds suggested the killer had not only done that, but had done so while very angry indeed.

Alice winced. Let go of the foil blanket and folded

her hands in her lap. The blanket slid off her shoulders onto the back of the chair with a faint rustling.

'Are you asking me if Ray was having an affair?' she asked.

Liam knitted his eyebrows and swallowed.

'Aye.' Brian grimaced. 'I know this is tough. But we need to explore all possible avenues.'

'No,' she said, shaking her head for emphasis, as if she were trying to convince herself. 'No. Ray wouldn't do that. We—'

Her voice wavered, but Brian couldn't help noticing she hadn't maintained eye contact. What wasn't she telling them?

He changed tack.

'What was Ray's typical day like?'

'How do you mean?' she asked.

'His routine. What time did he start work? Where did he work from?'

This seemed like more solid ground for Alice. She looked up and, this time, held his gaze while she answered.

'He starts— *started* late and worked late most days,' she said. 'He was a penetration tester.'

'What's that?' Brian asked. He'd never heard the term before.

'That's— I mean, he's never told me much about his work, because most of it is confidential. But, as I understand it, it involves checking clients' IT systems' security.'

Brian nodded. 'So he never saw clients at home?'

'No. Not that I know of,' Alice said.

'And how was work going?' Brian asked. 'Was he

under stress? Was he working on a difficult project? Did he mention a client relationship going sour, perhaps?'

'I, er...' She faltered. 'It was fine.'

'So he wasn't worried over the past few weeks?' Brian persisted, sensing he was circling around something big. 'Out of sorts? Or maybe his demeanour changed some other way? We're just trying to establish if something unusual might have been going on in his life.'

Alice shook her head.

'Are you sure?' he said. 'Even something that seems insignificant to you might be important.'

Alice picked the water bottle up from the dining table. Sipped. Studied Brian.

'He is. *Was*. Very busy,' she said, placing the bottle back on the table with a soft clunk. 'But I wouldn't say that was unusual. He loved his job. Was good at it. And he was in high demand.'

Was that an edge of resentment in her tone?

'So you were happy?' Brian tried.

'Happy?' Alice repeated flatly, as if she hadn't understood.

'Aye,' Brian said. It was a simple enough question. 'Things were going well between you?'

'Aye,' Alice replied a tad too readily. Once again, she wasn't meeting his eye.

'What time did you leave home this morning, Alice?'

She flushed. 'You're not suggesting that I... I...?'

She didn't finish. Her right hand fidgeted with the left cuff of her blouse. Her behaviour, the strength of her reaction, and the fact she'd gone straight to thinking he was accusing her of having something to do with her husband's death made Brian's spidey senses tingle. Whatever had been going on, she wasn't telling them the whole story. He was almost certain of it.

'I'm not suggesting anything at all, Alice,' he said, striking a placatory tone. 'It's a routine question. To help us work out a possible timeline of events. Can you walk us through it, please?'

'Well, I-I-I left home at five-thirty this morning,' she said. 'Ray was in bed. Still asleep.'

'And is that usual for you?' Brian asked. 'Leaving home that early?'

She flushed again. 'Aye, I ...'

Her right index finger and thumb tugged at her left cuff and released. Tugged and released. The edge of a fresh, semicircular abrasion, the kind somebody might have made if they'd grabbed her wrist – somebody, say, who was trying to defend himself from a knife attack, or assaulting her so that *she* had to defend herself with the first weapon she could grab off the kitchen counter – peeked out from beneath her sleeve. Brian filed the information for later. He'd let her chatter on, then wrong-foot her with it. See how she reacted. Unless she was exceptionally skilled at thinking on her feet, he'd know if she was lying.

'I was at the gym,' she finished, her tone suddenly more confident. 'They'll be able to confirm that. I had to punch in with my PIN code and there'd be CCTV. It's Active Life, off St Kentigern's Square. Then I went to the office. Whitney and Grayson PR. They'll be able to confirm I was there until your two officers arrived to tell me about ...'

She shook her head. Swallowed. Her throat made an audible click.

Brian made a mental note. He recognised Whitney and Grayson. It was a fancy PR firm whose client list was a who's who of Strathburgh's rich and famous. They and the gym would have all the proof she needed. But that didn't put her out of the frame. Given the estimated time of death was 3 a.m. to 8 a.m., Alice could've easily done it and left for the gym with time to spare. The question was, did she seem cold-blooded and calculating enough to murder her husband, then go get a workout in before heading to the office? Brian wasn't so sure. And even if she were, the crime scene suggested that this wasn't the kind of person the killer was. No. This was somebody who had acted on impulse.

'What happens now?' Alice said, cutting off his train of thought.

'Well,' Brian said. 'We'll have to take Ray to the Royal. To conduct the post-mortem.'

She winced.

'We'll also need your fingerprints and a sample of DNA.' He forestalled her with his open palm. 'For elimination purposes. In case the killer left evidence behind. It would also help if we went through his things, to see what we can find.'

She nodded faintly. Technically, the whole house was a crime scene, so they didn't need a warrant or her permission to search it. But it would go down much easier if they brought her on board. He looked at Liam, and they both stood up.

'Thank you, Alice,' Brian said gently. 'Once again,

I'm very sorry for your loss. The family liaison officer will be in touch soon, and we might come back to ask you some further questions when we know more. In the meantime, please call us if you think of anything else.'

Brian handed her a card and began walking away, Liam in tow, then turned back with an innocent look.

'Och, sorry,' he said. 'May I ask how you got that abrasion on your wrist?'

Alice's right hand closed protectively over her left arm, just over the wrist, the knuckles white. Her cheeks coloured.

'Och. That?' she said. 'It's, it's silly, really. I-I-I was playing with Sindy – that's our dog – and she got overexcited and bit me.'

It was a rubbish excuse if he'd ever heard one. The wound looked nothing like a dog bite, even to his untrained eye. The dog's canines would've punctured the skin, giving it a distinctive pattern.

'Actually,' she ploughed on. 'Where's Sin—'

A SOCO cut her off.

'DI Brandon?' the tech said, breathless.

'Aye?'

'We found something,' she said.

'What is it?'

'You better come and see.'

Chapter Four

The bifold doors in the lounge area led to a decked patio with a beige rattan three-seater sofa, two armchairs, and a fire pit under a pergola. Climbing down the patio steps took you to an expanse of grass and strategically placed wooden planters from which sprouted a series of closely packed evergreen shrubs.

Relishing the chill air, which lightened the oppressive dread that had settled on him like an invisible cloak – noticeably there, but impossible to define or quantify – Brian stepped across the threshold and crossed the garden toward the entrance to the vennel that connected it to the front of the house. A SOCO was snapping photos of the ground with a Nikon digital camera. He moved closer, squinting at the patch of soil the tech was pointing the lens at, wondering what was going on.

And then he saw it.

In between the darkening sky and the object being still half buried in the soil and covered in blood that had dried to a shade of maroon, Brian's eyes hadn't registered what they were seeing. Then, the Nikon's flash glinted off a small patch of stainless steel, and Brian made out the triangular, smooth-edged blade of a carving knife.

The murder weapon. It had to be.

'Dr Grace will confirm whether the blade matches the wounds. Then we'll check for fingerprints and DNA,' the SOCO said. 'If we're lucky, we might get a match on the PNC.'

'If we're lucky' was doing a lot of heavy lifting. Violent acts rarely happen in isolation. People who kill tend to have a history of troubling behaviour leading up to the main event. But that didn't necessarily mean their killer had already been in trouble with the law. Maybe they'd managed to get away with it so far. Or maybe the solution was staring them right in the face and it was Alice Higgins. They'd have to wait and see.

When the photographer had finished taking snaps of the knife in situ, another SOCO picked it up carefully with gloved hands and placed it into a clear plastic evidence bag that would be sealed and sent over to the pathologist's office to be examined and then to the lab for analysis. The black handle with three equidistant stainless-steel handle fasteners was identical to the other five handles jutting out of the knife block on the kitchen counter. The missing knife.

'So the killer attacks Ray Higgins in the kitchen, with a knife from the island,' Brian told Liam, who nodded agreement. 'Then they drag him into the lounge area and leave the house through the garden, dumping the knife en route.'

'Aye. Makes sense,' Liam said.

But why? Brian pondered. Why move the body, only to abandon it a few feet away from where the murder had taken place? Had the killer been meaning to do something else – make the body disappear, perhaps – but got interrupted? Maybe by the delivery driver?

He needed to speak to Layton, the Higginses' neighbour, to get a clearer picture of what he'd seen. And they needed to find the delivery driver as soon as possible.

Brian scanned the garden. It would be full dark soon, and the SOCOs were hustling so they wouldn't have to get out the floodlights to carry on with their sweep. But he had a feeling the crime scene had already given them everything it had to give.

The answers to his questions would probably come from victimology – Ray Higgins's personal history, background, and what was going on in his life in the run-up to the murder. And from whatever the two witnesses, Layton and the van driver, had to say.

Feeling a surge of adrenaline at the prospect of beginning the chase, Brian walked back toward the patio door and into the lounge area beyond. It was time to go and speak to Layton to get a first-hand, blow-by-blow account of what he'd seen.

But, first, there was somewhere else he needed to go.

Chapter Five

RAY HIGGINS HAD BEEN A TIDY, METHODICAL MAN. That was evident. His home office, a nine-foot-by-ten-foot room just off the first-floor landing with a large window overlooking the garden, was meticulously organised and clutter-free. One wall was covered in shelves stacked with technical manuals and non-fiction books he'd sorted alphabetically, by name. The shelves also held an ageing Canon inkjet printer with a stack of printer paper next to it and several award trophies. Irrefutable proof of Higgins's on-the-job prowess. *Penetration Tester of the Year* 2020, one of them – a white-and-blue triangular chunk of glass with rounded edges – said in serif-style lettering. *Best Cybersecurity Business* 2021, proclaimed a rectangular faux-marble plaque.

Across the room, positioned to make the most of the view but remain shielded from the afternoon glare should the sun decide to make an appearance, was a desk with brushed steel hairpin legs and a pine surface. A large monitor hovered over the desk, hanging from a stand that had been bolted to the desk's underside. The rest of the ensemble consisted of a keyboard, a mouse, a black pen holder containing two Parker ballpoint pens and three black-and-yellow Staedtler pencils, and a banker's lamp. On the wall behind the desk hung a metal rack with a display of running medals. Brian moved in for a closer look. *Men's 10K 2019*, a star-shaped one with an orange ribbon said. *Strathburgh Half Marathon 2021*, said another, a chunk of bronze that had been shaped into a crude approximation of the gryphon on the city's coat of arms.

'Weird,' Brian muttered, his eyes fixed on the rack.

'What is?' Liam asked, moving next to him.

'See here?' he said, pointing at the medals with a stubby finger. 'There's two or three of them for every year, starting in 2015. But none from 2022 onward.'

'So?' Liam asked. 'Work got too busy and he no longer had time to train.'

'I don't know,' Brian said. 'When you're passionate about something, you make time for it.'

'What are you suggesting, then?' Liam asked.

'Nothing. At least, not yet,' Brian said carefully. 'But it's interesting, isn't it? Didn't he look a tad frail to you?'

'He was stabbed repeatedly to death,' Liam said. 'Of course he looked frail.'

Brian didn't reply, but the gears were turning. What had happened in 2022 for Higgins to go from running two to three long-distance races a year to none at all? And how did that fit into the wider picture he was trying to piece together?

There was also another thing that struck him as odd.

'Did you notice?' he asked Liam.

'Notice what?'

'The photos,' Brian said. 'Well, the lack of them.'

There wasn't a single photo frame anywhere in the office. No family photos. None of him and his wife together, or of his wife posing. Wouldn't he have wanted to decorate his workspace with memories of good times? Especially if he worked long hours? A picture was starting to form of a marriage that wasn't as idyllic as Alice Higgins had tried to imply.

'Look at this, B,' Liam said, cutting off Brian's train of thought.

'What?'

Brian pivoted around. Liam nodded at the desk.

'Monitor. Keyboard. Mouse ...' Liam said.

'But no laptop,' Brian finished. 'And that looks like a standalone monitor, not a desktop computer.'

'Spot on,' Liam said. 'So where'd the laptop go?'

Brian scanned the room from one end to the other. In front of the bookshelves, angled away from the window, were a black PU leather lounge chair and ottoman. Empty. Beneath the desk, next to one of the hairpin legs, a wastebasket made of steel mesh. Also empty. Attached to the door, three metal hooks, one with a leather messenger bag hanging from it. Brian crossed toward it in five steps. Rummaged inside. A laptop charger. An A4 Pukka Pad notebook. Brand new and unmarked. Another Parker ballpoint pen. No laptop. The desk didn't have any drawers where Higgins might have stored it when he wasn't using it.

Brian opened the door and walked back out onto the landing. It was a narrow, carpeted hallway—

Much like... No, stop it. It's not like it at all. It's clean. Spotless, for one. There's no shite smeared on the walls, and no... STOP!

—with four doors on the left. The one next to Higgins's office led to a family bathroom. This was followed by two double bedrooms, the last of which Brian guessed to be the master, given that the bed was unmade. Higgins's everyday clothes – blue jeans with a belt still looped around its waist, a black T-shirt, and a checked button-up shirt – lay in a neat pile on the back of a grey wing chair across from the bed.

Brian trod slowly into the room, which smelled faintly of body odour, expecting the floorboards to creak and—

Nothing. nothing's going to happen.

The side tables were both as clutter-free as Higgins's office, empty except for matching lampshades and a digital alarm clock with a big, deep-blue display. He opened each of the four side-table drawers, then checked the closet. Clothes. Underwear. A shaving kit. A bright blue box that held a set of dumbbells. But no laptop.

He looked at Liam, who just shrugged and shook his head. They crossed the landing and went back downstairs into the main living space, where the crowd of SOCOs had thinned out. Higgins had been bagged and taken away to the mortuary. All that was left of him were smears of dried blood mixed with chunks of his wife's vomit to make a gruesome stew. Alice sat slumped in the vic chair where they'd left her, staring in front of her with a glazed, faraway look.

'Constable Stebbings,' Brian said, moving into the hallway. 'Where's the evidence log?'

'Em, she has it, sir,' Stebbings said, pointing to a forensic tech with a clipboard in her hand.

'May I?' Brian asked her. She handed it over. 'And everything's been logged on here already?'

'Yes, sir,' she confirmed.

He ran his finger down the list, going through each item. No unopened packages or open packaging that would suggest a recent delivery, he observed. So their van driver either hadn't completed it, or they hadn't been a delivery driver at all.

More to the point, no laptop had been logged. And no phone, either.

Brian sighed. From an investigative perspective, it wasn't insurmountable. They could get Higgins's phone records from the network, track down his email provider, and ask social media networks for his account histories. But their disappearance from the scene could be – scratch that, probably *was* – significant.

Had the killer taken them?

And, if they had, what did Higgins have on them – or what did the killer think he had on them – that they'd murder him for it?

Chapter Six

With that last question ringing in his ears, Brian walked out of the crime scene and stripped off his plastic oversuit. His next stop was to head across the road to speak to Gerald Layton; hopefully the conversation would put them on the right track to start finding some answers.

'What did you make of Alice Higgins?' Brian asked Liam as he looked right, then left, then stepped off the pavement.

Liam considered. 'Everyone reacts to shock differently,' he said, fussily adjusting the knot of his tie, 'but there's something about her behaviour that didn't sit right with me.'

'Agreed,' Brian said.

The fidgeting. The hesitations. The lack of eye contact. Plus, she'd had the means and opportunity. And her explanation for the abrasions on her wrist didn't ring true.

But why drag her husband's body halfway to the garden, then stop? And why take his laptop and phone? That last part, especially, didn't fit with the theory of a domestic gone too far. Unless she was trying to muddy the waters to throw them off her scent ...

The Laytons' end-of-terrace had the same L-shape, anthracite UPVC window frames, wrought-iron gate, and neatly manicured lawn as the Higginses', but the front door was a bright shade of red and, in place of the water feature, there was a well-tended rose bush. To the left, a dark blue Renault Kadjar peeked out from the flag-stone driveway.

Brian swung the gate inward, climbed the three steps to the front door, and rang the bell. Seconds later, the door cracked open just a fraction, revealing a sliver of forest-green cable-knit sweater.

'Aye?' the voice attached to the sweater said.

'Gerald Layton?' Brian said.

'Who's asking?' the voice replied.

Brian flashed his warrant card to the small gap between the frame and the door. 'We understand you have some information about Raymond Higgins's murder?'

The red door opened wider, revealing a rotund man in his early fifties with a droopy moustache and a head that was completely bald except for the sides, where the remains of his salt-and-pepper hair stuck out in tufts, giving him the appearance of a mad scientist.

'Aye,' he said noncommittally, after carefully inspecting Brian's warrant card.

They sized each other up. Layton's brow furrowed. Was that mistrust? Hostility? Or just an unintentionally serious expression?

'May we come in?' Brian asked when Layton didn't say anything else.

'I already spoke to the polis,' Layton replied.

'Aye, I understand,' Brian said. 'But it would really help if we went over your statement.'

'We just have a few routine questions, and we'll be out of your hair,' Liam added.

Brian couldn't help stealing a glance at Layton's bonce and wincing. Trust Liam to put his foot in it.

'We'll only take a few minutes of your time,' Brian reassured him. He spread his lips in what he hoped was a disarming smile.

Layton sighed. Opened the door wider and stepped aside, motioning the way with his hand. 'Well, you better come in then, eh?'

Brian stepped inside the hallway, and he and Liam followed Layton to the main downstairs living area. Unlike the Higginses', the wall between the kitchen and the living-cum-dining room hadn't been knocked down to create a single open-plan space. There were no floor-to-ceiling bifolds here, either. Access to the garden was through a solid UPVC door with an opaque window panel. So where the Higginses' space was bright and airy, this felt cramped.

Layton pointed toward an overstuffed three-seater sofa where a British bulldog was curled up with its ginormous head cradled in its forepaws. It looked up laconically at Brian with one half-open eye, then promptly went back to sleep, snoring lightly.

'This must be Sindy?' Brian asked. 'The Higginses' dog?'

'Aye,' Layton said, easing himself into a well-worn black faux-leather armchair with a grunt. 'Poor thing. She was inconsolable.'

Of course, he'd only observed her for a few seconds, but, right then, Brian reflected, the dog didn't look particularly playful or excitable. Certainly not to the point where she'd bite. He took out a battered notebook and a Bic pen from the inside pocket of his suit jacket.

'I take it you were close, then?' he asked. 'You and the Higginses?'

Layton seemed to mull this over.

'I wouldn't say close,' he said slowly. 'But we were friendly. He took my Amazon deliveries a few times when I wasn't in. I did the same. And we said hello when he was out walking Sindy. Maybe borrowed tools or whatever from each other if we were in a pinch. We didn't go down the pub or anything like that if that's what you mean.'

'No, no. Right,' Brian said. 'But you liked him?'

'Och, aye,' Layton said. 'Lovely man.'

'So how did you come to ...' Brian paused, unsure how to put it. 'How did you take Sindy? What happened?'

'Ah. Aye,' Laytoo said. 'Well, my office window looks out on the street. I was working. You know, mulling things over and staring into space, and I saw the commotion outside, so I went to see what was going on. Spoke to

PC, em ... whatshisface ...' He snapped his fingers, like the name was on the tip of his tongue but his brain couldn't quite compute it.

'Stebbings?' Brian offered.

'Not sure,' Layton said. 'Young bloke with a face like he'd spent all morning smelling shite.'

Brian and Liam couldn't suppress a smile at Layton's blunt but fairly accurate description of the young constable.

'Aye, that's him,' Brian said. 'So what is it that you do, Mr Layton? Em, can I call you Gerald?'

'Suit yourself,' Layton said. He shrugged. The gesture was intended to convey nonchalance, but it came across as vaguely uncomfortable. Brian's interest was piqued. What was this bloke all about?

'I'm afraid I didn't catch that,' Brian prodded gently. 'What is it you said you do?'

'Och. I'm a consultant,' he replied. 'Logistics.'

Brian waited for him to elaborate. Layton didn't. Most witnesses were happy to help with a police investigation, especially if the victim of the crime was a neighbour they liked enough to take in their dog. So why wasn't he being forthcoming? Was it a personality quirk – natural reserve – or did he have something to hide?

Brian changed tack. 'So,' he said. 'Constable Stebbings said you saw a van stop by the Higginses' house this morning. Is that right?'

'Aye, that's right,' Layton said.

'Can you walk us through it?' Liam asked, with barely concealed frustration.

Brian shot him a warning look, but Liam's face

reflected his own feelings; extracting information from Layton was like getting blood out of a stone.

Layton said nothing.

'Can you walk us through it please, Gerald?' Brian repeated, unconsciously moving closer to the edge of the sofa.

'Aye, sure,' Layton said. His forehead creased. 'I was in the kitchen, making a mug of coffee, and the van parked in front of their gate.'

'What did the van look like?' Brian asked.

Layton's eyes narrowed in concentration. 'Not sure of the make. It was dark grey, with windows only in the front and all storage in the back.'

'Do you remember what time this was?' Brian asked, making a note.

'Seven-ish. I think?' He frowned in concentration. 'Aye. Give or take.'

So slap-bang within the time-of-death window, Brian thought. *Why were you there? What's your role in this?* To Layton: 'Did the van have any branding at all?'

'How do you mean?' Layton's brow furrowed.

'Like a logo? Company name? A phone number or email, perhaps? Something distinctive that might tell us who the van belonged to.'

'No. Plain dark grey.'

'And did Ray open his door for the driver?'

'No idea.' Layton shook his head.

Brian waited. The silence didn't seem to faze Layton, who looked expectantly at Brian, his hands folded in his lap. Brian made a beckoning gesture with his head, inviting Layton to continue with his account.

'Look,' Layton said finally. 'I don't stand by the kitchen window all day long, spying on my neighbours' business. I had stuff to do. All I know is the van parked, the driver got out, and when I was back in the kitchen maybe five minutes later, it was already gone. So I didn't think any of it until the polis arrived and started sticking crime scene tape everywhere.'

Five minutes or less. Would that have been enough to argue with Higgins, stab him repeatedly, drag him to the living room, hide the knife in the garden, and then leg it back out the front door? No. It sounded thin. The more likely explanation was that the delivery driver had interrupted the killer.

'And you didn't see anyone else come out of the Higginses' house?' Brian asked.

'As I said, I don't spend my day keeping track of my neighbours' goings-on.' Layton shrugged. 'But no. The only person I recall seeing is Babs. Johnston – that's the Higginses' next-door neighbour – leaving in a rush. This was around eight-ish. No idea what happened in between.'

So the killer had either left earlier, which meant the van driver didn't interrupt them after all, or they'd slipped out while Layton was in his office.

'Do you live alone?' Brian asked.

'Afraid so,' Layton answered. 'It used to be me and Andrew, my husband. But he passed away three years ago this month. Pancreatic cancer.'

Layton's demeanour changed. His eyes misted over. He nodded toward a large, silver-edged frame that had pride of place in the centre of the sideboard. A much trimmer version of him in a kilt, unrecognisable with thick jet-black hair in a side part and no moustache, was smiling widely, his arm around a plump man with similarly styled blonde hair also wearing a kilt.

He cleared his throat. 'Sorry.'

'Och, no. Please,' Brian said, reconsidering his opinion of Layton. 'I'm sorry for your loss.'

This explained his brusque manner. He was still grieving.

'Aye. I am, too,' Layton said.

'Did you get a good look at the van driver, Gerald?' Brian asked, powering through the awkwardness.

'Not really,' Layton said. 'It was dark.'

'Anything you could tell us would help,' Brian insisted. 'Clothes. Gender. Distinguishing marks... Moles, scars, tattoos.'

Layton shrugged. 'Jeans. Black jacket. Cap. That's about it. As I said. I didn't get a good look.'

Brian made a note, but his heart sank. The cap was unusual enough to grab his attention. It smacked of somebody trying to conceal their face. But thousands of people wore jeans and a black jacket at this time of year. They needed to see the Higginses' doorbell footage ASAP; it was starting to look like their only hope of getting at least a basic description of their van driver that they could release to the press.

'And I don't suppose you got the van's plate number?' Brian tried, but he could guess the answer to that.

'Not in the habit of taking down random vehicles' number plates,' Layton said. 'It didn't look to me like there was anything suspicious going on.'

'How did they seem to you as a couple?' Brian asked, suddenly struck by a thought. 'The Higginses?'

Layton gave another one of his shrugs. 'Didn't see them together much. And, to be honest, that was fine by me. Ray was a good bloke. But her...' A shadow flitted across his features. 'Didn't care for her much.'

Brian exchanged a look with Liam. His pulse kicked up a notch.

'How so?' Liam asked.

Layton said nothing.

'Why did you not care for her?' Brian elaborated.

'Walked around like she had a stick up her arse,' Layton paused. 'They got into it... this must've been, maybe a week ago?'

Brian and Liam both leaned forward.

'Who?' Brian asked.

'Ray and the missus. I was in my office. Couldn't catch what they were saying, but they were loud enough that they caught my attention. She was having a go at him right outside, on the kerb.'

Ah. So *that's* what Alice had been holding back. Was it a one-off, or were things not so rosy in the Higginses' marriage?

'Did they argue often?'

'Maybe,' Layton said noncommittally. 'I only heard them the once, but I wouldn't put it past her. She sniffed at me like I was a piece of gum that had got stuck to the bottom of her shoe.'

Brian sighed. This was all very interesting, but they were starting to stray away from facts and into prejudiced conjecture. Time to bring this interview to a close and explore other, hopefully more fruitful, lines of enquiry.

Wherever the evidence would lead them, though, Brian had a feeling their next conversation with Alice Higgins would be very different from the one they'd just had with her an hour earlier.

Chapter Seven

East Strathburgh Police Station stood out like a sore thumb: a three-floor steel-and-glass monstrosity in a sea of rundown, graffiti-riddled two-up-two-down pebble-dash terraces. Purpose-built during the mid-1990s in the heart of a gang hotspot, the station's idiosyncratic architecture was meant to be a statement of intent; a defiant monument to law and order in one of the roughest parts of Strathburgh. But, almost thirty years later, it hadn't proved to be much of a deterrent. Not that you needed to be a genius to realise that, by itself, building a large, aesthetically controversial building wouldn't stop those who plied their trade in the neighbourhood's dark, pish-stained alleyways from continuing to do so. Particularly when, all too often, that trade was the only way they could scrounge a half-decent living or bring some relief to their otherwise dismal existences. Had Brian not been too busy flitting about town on his fire-red BMX pretending to be Jim Taggart at the time, he would've told the powers that be himself and spared them the expense.

As it happened, now that he'd been working in the building for seventeen years, first as a uniformed officer, then rising up the ranks into CID, he didn't have much of an opinion about it one way or another. He barely ever gave a second glance to the expanse of shite-brown carpet and faux-pine laminate that adorned the building's interior. Most of the time, he was either too busy or too preoccupied to notice. Nor did the yellowing faux-marble vinyl floor in the lavvies – the butt of endless watercooler jokes, some good, many mediocre, some toe-curlingly bad ('Say, d'you hear the downstairs lavvy won an award? Most Ap-*peeling* Floor of the Year, ba, ha, ha, ha.') – bother him.

Now, a stop-start forty-minute drive in rush-hour traffic after leaving the crime scene later, standing in front of a sink in the third-floor lavvy for the second time since his return to active duty, Brian opened the tap, splashed his face with cold water, and swallowed dryly while he stared down his reflection, willing the tension that was bubbling up inside him to ease. He'd seriously underestimated the willpower required to keep it together when every single detail of the case he was working on – a man lying on the floor, viciously attacked, the grief-and-shock-loaded atmosphere, doorways behind which you weren't sure what you'd find – triggered bad memories. Reminded him of ...

Of blood-soaked carpet—

This isn't the same and you know it. It has nothing to do with anything.

Of runnels of blood radiating outward and pointing toward him like accusing fingers from one plate-sized puddle beneath—

Shut up. Don't say it. Don't even think it!

He closed his eyes. Exhaled shakily through his nostrils. Thought about the large whisky he'd pour himself when he got home that evening, already relishing the fiery warmth it would produce as it slid down his throat. *If* he got home, he corrected himself. There were so many threads to unravel. So much to do if they wanted to make the most of the evidence while the trail was still fresh.

'B?'

Brian pivoted, startled. Saw Liam standing in the doorway.

'B, are you OK?'

Liam's lightly freckled forehead crinkled with concern. He sidestepped a lump in the vinyl and walked to the sink next to Brian's, wet his fingertips and ran them through his hair.

'I'm fine, bud, honest,' Brian said. His heartbeat had gone from jackhammer to Dremel. Still deafeningly loud, but not as intense. And was his chest slightly less constricted than when he'd walked in?

'You don't have to do this if you're not up to it. You've nothing to prove to anyone. You know that, right?' Liam continued. 'Somebody else can—'

'I said, I'm fine.'

Liam turned to face him. 'Suit yourself,' he said, rolling the words around in his mouth before speaking them. 'But, at the end of the day, it's just a job.'

'Just a—'

Liam lifted his hand. Brian noticed a tiny scratch, barely visible, on the pad of his left pinkie finger.

'Aye, it's an important job,' Liam said. 'But no job's worth sacrificing your well-being for.' He smiled ruefully. 'Take it straight from the horse's mouth, eh?'

Something inside Brian – an itchy weight just below his breastbone – shifted. He sighed.

'I'm genuinely fine,' he said. He moved his head to one side, then to the other. Felt the joints crack. 'But I wish you'd run the meeting. You know I can't stand these things.'

Liam clapped him on the back. 'It's your show. You'll do fine. As always.'

In one of the station's three conference rooms, a drab rectangle on the second floor, furnished with cheap plastic chairs, an oval table, and more shite-brown carpet, two constables had set up a large whiteboard that, so far, was pristine except for three photos. Two of them were Blu-Tacked next to each other at the top of the board: a police photo of Ray Higgins, staring up at nothing, glassy-eyed and very dead, and a candid snap of him in a racing green polo shirt, staring into the distance. Beneath them, they'd blue-tacked a photo of the blood-encrusted knife in its sealed evidence bag. The table was laid out with glasses and a pitcher of water. The officers that formed part of the Major Investigations Team – a mix of detective inspectors, detective sergeants, and uniforms – were gathered around the table in various stages of getting situated, some chatting animatedly while others did so in hushed tones.

As Brian walked into the room with his hands in his pockets – a deliberate choice he'd made in order to portray an air of casualness and ease – the chatter quieted down to a low murmur pierced by a single, bark-like chuckle. The thread of nervousness worming its way around his stomach tightened into a knot. He turned. Caught Murray McGillivray – a squat detective sergeant in his mid-thirties with a fleshy mouth and a boxer's flat nose, who Brian had clashed with on several occasions over his propensity for cutting corners – eyeing him and gesturing at his temple with his index finger. A young uniform next to him was covering his mouth with a hand the size of a shovel, looking apologetic.

'Something you want to share with us, Murray?' Brian asked, clearing his throat and looking McGillivray in the eye.

'Private joke, sir,' McGillivray sneered. 'Bit hard to explain.'

'Try me,' Brian shot back, hardening his voice.

A hush descended over the room. Several sets of eyes stared at Brian. Waiting to see whether he'd snap, he guessed.

'Never mind,' McGillivray said, dropping his gaze to the floor. He was a brash, arrogant man. But not to the point where he'd mock a superior officer to his face in a room full of witnesses.

'Good,' Brian said.

Inwardly, he sagged with relief. The first test of his authority, of his fitness to lead a murder investigation, and he'd passed. Only just. And only because, at heart, McGillivray was a coward. All bluster, and no follow-through. But he'd passed. He'd cross the next bridge when he reached it. For now, he was just happy to have managed to put his best foot forward.

Brian looked up toward the back of the room, where Liam stood slouched against the doorjamb. Liam nodded approvingly. Smiled encouragement. Brian coughed lightly, covering his mouth with the back of his hand. Willed himself not to wipe his forehead or fidget with his tie. Instead, he stuck his clammy hands back inside his trouser pockets and pinched his thigh through the fabric. Rode the wave of delicious pain until it crashed, clearing his brain fog.

He walked to the whiteboard, which the officers had placed at the head of the conference table, and pointed at the photo of polo-shirt-clad Ray Higgins.

'This is Raymond Higgins. 41. Married. No weans. IT consultant. Does security audits for his clients,' Brian started. 'As you've probably heard by now, he was found dead this morning in his home. The post-mortem is tomorrow afternoon. But, given he had multiple stab wounds, it's safe to say the circumstances surrounding his death are suspicious.'

He looked at the room. They were all silent now – even McGillivray, though his face was creased into a faint scowl. Hanging on Brian's every word. Good. He was getting into the swing of it. And why not? He was in his element. Knew exactly what to do. The Dremel in his chest became the ticking of a wind-up clock.

'So,' he continued, standing up straighter and pulling his hands out of his pocket. 'Here's what we know so far. Preliminary time of death is between two and eight a.m. That's a big window, but his wife says he was asleep when she left for the gym at five thirty. Which narrows it down from six hours to two and a half, give or take.'

Assuming she isn't lying, Brian thought but didn't say. It was too soon to air these suspicions out loud. They had to look at the evidence first, then confront Alice Higgins with what they found. He cleared his throat.

'The neighbour across the street, Gerald Layton, says a grey panel van stopped in front of the Higginses' house at seven a.m.,' Brian continued. 'He didn't get a good look at the driver, but the Higginses have a video doorbell, and I'm guessing some of the other houses and shops in the area will have CCTV. Where are we with that?'

'Sir?' a young detective sergeant with light-brown hair tied into a tight ponytail raised her hand.

'Yes, DS Atwood. Fiona,' Brian said.

'We're working on it. Without the laptop and phone, we can't get the doorbell footage. We had to get in touch with Ring.'

Brian frowned. 'Couldn't his wife hand over the footage?'

'Says she doesn't have access to it,' Stebbings cut in.

Odd, Brian thought. But then again, if my spouse were an IT consultant, maybe I wouldn't bother with these things, either.

'Well, do we have an ETA?' he asked testily.

'ASAP, they said,' Fiona replied.

'Tell them we need it yesterday,' Brian said. 'Keep up the pressure.'

'Are they a suspect, sir?' Fiona asked. 'The van driver?'

Brian thought back to what Layton had told them. The van had been parked in front of the Higginses' house five minutes or less. It seemed improbable the driver would wreak that much damage in such a short time. If they'd even managed to go inside. Still, why were they there, and what did they see?

'Just a witness, for now.' he replied. 'But an important one. We need to speak with them. So keep chasing Ring. And, in the meantime, let's try and get our hands on any other footage from the area. We might be able to get a number plate or some other bit of information that enables us to track him down.'

'Already on it, sir,' Fiona said. 'I also managed to speak with Barbara Johnston on the phone. The Higginses' next-door neighbour.'

'Good work,' Brian said. 'What did she say?'

Fiona looked visibly pleased with the compliment. 'She's coming down tomorrow morning to make a formal statement. But says she left the house around eight fifteen – she was running late for work – but didn't hear or see anything.'

'Right,' Brian said.

This was disappointing. Layton had mentioned he'd seen her leave in a rush, so at least it did confirm that what little they'd got out of him was on the money.

'She did say she'd heard them arguing recently,' Fiona continued.

'Who?' Brian asked, his ears pricking up.

'The Higginses.'

So his instincts were right. First Layton, now Barbara Johnston. There *was* trouble in paradise. 'Did she say what about?' he asked.

'No,' Fiona said, shaking her head.

'We'll ask Alice Higgins directly, but let's try and find

out more first,' Brian said. 'Perhaps when Ms Johnston gives her statement tomorrow.'

'Aye,' Fiona said, before scribbling down a note.

Brian reached for the carafe, poured himself a glass of water, and took a long sip. His head was pounding. It was time to bring this briefing to a close.

'Over the coming days,' he said, 'I want you to get to know Ray Higgins inside out. Who was he? What made him tick? Who did he hang out with? Who had it in for him? And, most importantly, who benefits from his death?'

He looked at each officer in the eye briefly to impress these points. Drained his water.

'Let's dig deep, people. Go through his bank records. Social media accounts. Find out who his clients, collaborators, and subcontractors were. Speak to his accountant. Relatives. Friends. There's a reason somebody killed him, and that's where we'll find it. Clear?'

'Aye,' the room chorused.

'Let's catch the scum who did this.'

Chapter Eight

I'M NOT GOING TO LIE. AT FIRST, I WAS NERVOUS AND a bit scared. Partly because I was in uncharted territory. But mainly because of that goddamn doorbell footage.

I thought I'd done a fairly good job getting rid of the evidence, all things considered. There'd be suspicions, of course. Theories that might even come within brushing distance of the truth. But there was nothing specific that could point the finger of blame toward me. I was certain of that. No, not by a long shot.

But that footage.

That was a frustrating misstep. An inconvenient loose end. The one thing that could come back to bite me.

I worried about what would happen once it came out – which I was certain would be sooner rather than later, disappeared phone and laptop, or no disappeared phone and laptop. Oh, how I worried. How did I not think this through? What the hell was going on in my head?

That night, I barely slept. My brain just wouldn't shut down. I kept putting together all these terrible scenarios. Wargaming how this might end. And, every time I came up with an argument for why it was unlikely that such a scenario would play out in real life, my brain countered with something worse. The mind's funny like that when you're under so much stress you're not thinking clearly.

Then, morning came, and nobody was banging down the door to come and arrest me.

That calmed me down. Gave me confidence.

Sure, the problem hadn't gone away. I knew that. But if I hadn't been arrested already, that meant I'd handled things much better than I'd thought.

And then, once I stopped catastrophising, something odd happened.

I got angry.

Really angry.

Because this was all that selfish bastard's fault. If he hadn't screwed up my plan, I wouldn't be in this situation. And the more I thought about it, the more I realised that all this, all this risk, it would've been for nothing if I didn't carry on and finish what I'd started. I'd worked too hard for too long to get where I was. I'd suffered too much.

But, more than that, there'd never be a right time. The longer I waited, the easier it would become to just let it go. Shelve the whole thing for good.

And there was no way I was going to do that. No way in hell.

It was now or never.

Chapter Nine

Tuesday, 9 January 2024

'Sir?'

'Aye, Fiona,' Brian said, placing the water glass on his desk with a hand he was trying hard to keep from shaking, and beckoning her to come in.

It had just gone 10.30 a.m., but his fourth coffee and second dose of paracetamol with a Rennie chaser had barely made a dent in the fug of tiredness that stuck to him like an ill-fitting skinsuit. When Brian had got home the previous night, the emotions he'd worked so hard all day to suppress had erupted with the force of the Eyja-whatever-it-was-called – that Icelandic volcano that had released so much ash it had grounded flights for eight days. He'd knocked back half a bottle of Monkey Shoulder, then poured the rest down the sink so it wouldn't whisper sweet nothings to him while he lay in bed trying to sleep. But it was still a very long time before he'd managed to drift off into a restless slumber. And now his head ached like a rotten tooth and his stomach felt like he'd been force-fed a bowl of hot gravel in place of his morning porridge.

Fiona gave him the briefest of glances, and quickly looked away, staring down at her blue leather pumps. He supposed he looked like something the cat had dragged in. But, except for that furtive look, her face was neutral.

'What is it?' he asked. His voice broke on the last syllable and he cleared his throat. Poured himself more water from the carafe next to his laptop.

'I think I found it,' she said, a note of triumph in her voice. 'The panel van.'

Brian sat up straighter and slammed an open hand down on the desk. 'Did you?' he said, ignoring his smarting palm and the ice pick piercing his frontal lobe. 'So we have the doorbell footage?'

'Not yet,' she said. 'We should have it by this afternoon. But it occurred to me that, if our driver had anything to do with the murder, or interrupted the killer, they might've peeled off in a hurry. So I checked speed cameras in the area and – would you know it? – a dark grey Vivaro panel van got zapped doing thirty-five in a twenty-mile-per-hour zone, five streets away from the Higginses'. At just gone seven a.m.'

'That's absolutely smashing work, Fiona,' Brian enthused.

Fiona looked up at him, her eyes twinkling. 'Thank you,' she said briskly, her tone all business. 'So I've tracked the van down to Reid's Antiques, on Northeast Bank.'

'Good,' Brian said. 'And do we know who was driving the van yesterday morning?'

'Not yet,' Fiona said. 'But I'm about to go down there and find out.'

'Smashing,' Brian said. 'I'll tag along.'

This was just what he needed. A field trip. Real, honest-to-God police work. Not sitting in his office trying not to think about the thumping in his head while pushing around the massive amount of paperwork murder investigations always seemed to generate to fill the time until three in the afternoon, when the post-mortem was scheduled to take place. Feeling some of his energy return, he grabbed his coat from the stand in the corner and walked down the hallway toward the stairs, waving cursorily as he passed by Liam's office.

Reid's Antiques was a hole in the wall with a Georgian storefront that had been painted deep-sea blue, located in one of the narrow cobbled streets that snared Strathburgh's historic riverfront. Brian eased his car in an empty spot three streets away from the shop, paid for one hour's parking, muttering at the exorbitant £7.25 charge, then made the uphill trek to the main drag, where the small gaggle of tourists who had braved the dismal weather were milling about in overpriced plastic waterproofs and tartan wool hats they'd bought from the various gift shops that made up a growing chunk of the area's retail real estate.

He stopped at the entrance and looked at Fiona. 'It's

your lead, so you question him,' he told her. 'I'll be right behind you.'

She nodded and they went in.

The shop door opened with a tinkle of bells into a cave-like room that smelled faintly but not unpleasantly musty and was packed to the rafters with all manner of trinkets, knick-knacks, and curiosities. A trio of Bakelite rotary telephones on a dusty oak sideboard with rounded edges and elaborate gold-leaf detailing. Several enamel kettles – some like new, some lightly scuffed, one with a large black dent on the bottom – stacked on a pristine-looking Hotpoint range that must've dated back to the 1950s. Gilt-edged mirrors in various shapes and sizes. Clocks ticking, not all of them in sync. Standing behind the oak-panelled counter, on which sat an old-fashioned cash register and nothing else, was a florid man Brian judged to be in his late forties, sporting an old-fashioned handlebar moustache, curled at the edges. A gold chain – presumably linked to a pocket watch – trailed out of the pocket of his waistcoat. The vertical stripes on his trousers and the front of his waistcoat lengthened his gaunt features, giving him the appearance of a haunted pencil. His white shirt was so heavily starched, it creaked as the man moved.

'Stuart Reid?' Fiona asked, her voice punctuated by Brian's heavy breaths. That uphill climb had winded him, and his nose was dripping with rain. He produced a tissue from inside his coat pocket and mopped his forehead.

They both flashed their warrant cards. The man placed his index finger in the middle of the book he'd been reading – *The Winds of War* by Herman Wouk, a dog-eared door stopper. His glasses slid down his blade of a nose and he peered at the warrant cards over the round silver frames.

'How may I help?' he asked in a nasal voice.

'Do you own a dark grey Vivaro panel van, plate number, err ...' – Fiona checked her notes – 'SJ14 CJC?'

'Ye-es?' A note of wariness had crept into Reid's voice.

'We're looking for the person who was driving it yesterday morning,' Fiona said. 'Can you tell us where we can find them, please?'

Reid went pale.

'Good Lord,' he said. 'What's he done now?'

Chapter Ten

'Who's done what, Mr Reid?' Fiona asked. 'May I call you Stuart?'

Reid ignored the second question and sat heavily on his stool, his index finger still stuck inside the book. It creaked alarmingly, but held.

'Danny,' he said. 'My nephew.'

There it was. They had a name. Now, to find this Danny so he could tell them what he'd seen.

'So you can confirm the van's yours and your nephew – em, would he be Daniel Reid? – was driving it yesterday morning?' Fiona repeated.

Good, Brian thought. They needed to be definite. Make absolutely sure Reid couldn't later claim there'd been a misunderstanding.

'Em, Daniel Walton. He's my sister's son. And yes,' Reid said, pushing up his glasses with his free thumb. They slid back down his wafer-thin nose. He pushed them back up, and they slid again. He gave up and looked at them over the frame with his watery blue eyes. 'He helps with deliveries part-time. He, em ...'

'We just want to talk to him,' Fiona said in a reassuring tone. 'We think he saw something that might help us with an investigation. But he's not in any trouble.'

At least, not yet, Brian thought. *But good thinking, Fiona. He's more likely to cooperate if we don't scare him off.*

Reid looked up at them, his mouth slightly agape. 'I don't know where he is,' he said.

'When is he due at work, Mr Reid?' Fiona asked.

Reid flushed with indignation. 'Yesterday afternoon. He never showed up. I had to do the deliveries myself with the old Transit.'

'And he never got in touch to say why he wouldn't be coming?'

'No, I haven't heard from him.' He shook his head. Tutted. 'My sister asked me to hire him. *Insisted,*' he said, speaking mainly to himself. 'Said working here would keep him out of trouble. Instead, he's been nothing *but* trouble.'

Brian and Fiona moved closer to the counter. This was interesting. Could Walton be involved somehow, after all? That might explain how he'd got into Higgins's house – if he'd managed to enter. The sneaking worry that this might all be a waste of time entered Brian's head, and he pushed it away.

'How do you mean?' Fiona asked.

Reid opened his mouth to say something, then thought the better of it.

'Mr Reid, this is a *murder* investigation,' Brian cut in, his tone stern.

Reid looked thunderstruck. 'Ehm,' he fumbled. 'But surely Danny had nothing to do with that? He wouldn't.'

'As I said. We just want to ask him a few questions about what he saw at this stage,' Fiona said. 'So we'd be grateful if you could tell us where we could find him.'

'Well–' Reid said. He opened the book, folded the top-left corner of the page, then snapped it shut and placed it on the counter by his elbow.

A thought struck Brian. 'What was Danny doing at seven a.m. in Inchview Road? Did he have a delivery?'

'Delivery?'

'Aye. For a Mr Higgins,' Brian said. 'Raymond Higgins. Ring a bell?'

Reid shook his head slowly. 'No. We... we usually deliver in the afternoons. So if a client had requested a delivery out of those hours, I'd remember it. It would be unusual.'

'So you're saying you've never done business with Ray Higgins?' Fiona insisted. 'We're checking his bank records as we speak, so if there are any transactions with Reid's Antiques, we'll know.'

'I'm fairly sure I haven't, but I can check,' Reid said, getting up from his stool and making another unsuccessful attempt to push his glasses up the bridge of his nose.

He bent down, rummaged around under the counter, and produced an iPad with a bright green silicone cover that looked jarringly out of place among the stacks of antiques. He unlocked the screen, thumbed an app open, and scrolled down with an immaculately manicured finger.

'Just looking at the sales records,' he muttered. The light from the iPad's screen and the relative darkness of the shop gave his features a ghostly glow. 'No. No Higginses in the last three months. If there'd been, I'd have kept a record.'

He balanced the iPad on top of the book and gave them the look of an inexperienced poker player who'd bluffed with three twos and won the hand.

'Well,' Brian said, wondering what on earth Walton had been doing at the Higginses house at seven in the morning if he wasn't delivering any antiques, 'we'll still need to get a hold of him.'

Reid sighed. He bent over for another rummage beneath the counter, and produced a spiral-bound notebook and an old-fashioned, but cheap-looking fountain pen. He ripped out half a sheet of paper and wrote down a number and an address in a flamboyant hand.

'Here,' he said, handing over the note. 'His address and mobile number, and my sister's address. If he isn't there, he's probably at the gym. That's all I know.'

Fiona caught the piece of paper between her index and middle fingers, folded it neatly down the middle, and placed it in her notebook for safekeeping. They'd send some uniforms around Danny and his mother's house to track him down.

'What gym is this?' Fiona asked Reid.

'He's a personal trainer,' Reid replied. 'At Active Life on St Kentigern's Square.'

Alice Higgins's gym.

Chapter Eleven

Back at his desk, Brian opened his laptop and logged on to Facebook. Alice Higgins's profile was an open book. Public. And, until half noon the previous day, extremely active. With multiple posts every single day.

Her profile picture was a smiling selfie of her clad from head to toe in pastel yellow Lululemon activewear, with a rack of free weights in the background. Her posts were a mishmash of motivational quotes – '*Your attitude, not your aptitude, will determine your altitude*' one of them read, in bold white letters on a background of pastel flowers and deep-green foliage. *What the fuck does that even mean?* Brian wondered – and more gym selfies interspersed with posts about crushing it and hard work paying off.

Brian scrolled down her page, giving each of her posts a cursory glance. Seven posts down, he found the proof he needed. Proof that Alice Higgins and Danny Walton knew each other.

Nailed it, babe [bicep emoji].

Brian's fist clenched, and his heartbeat ticked faster. He clicked on the name. His laptop's browser redirected him to a Facebook profile that was the male version of Alice Higgins's. A catalogue of platitudes masquerading as cleverness – *'Tough times don't last, but tough people do'* one announced in yellow calligraphic script over a background of snow-capped mountains – interspersed with shirtless selfies that showed off his muscle definition to the best advantage in as many different settings as possible. At the gym. Outdoors, astride a mountain bike. Smiling next to three other blokes who could've been carbon copies of him: same clothes, same buzz cut, same bold, neo-traditional tattoos.

Other than the lone comment Brian had stumbled on, there were no interactions between Walton and Alice Higgins. But, according to his profile, he worked as a personal trainer at Danny Walton Fitness, and held classes at Active Life. Helpfully, his business page had a timetable, which Brian downloaded and printed out.

More interestingly, when he keyed in the name and date of birth into the Police National Computer, a nineteen-year-old Danny Walton, his right eye blackened and swollen half-shut, peered back at him defiantly. The notes said he'd been arrested for antisocial behaviour and breaching the peace outside The Green Lady – a gang-affiliated pub about a mile and a half away from the station that had been gutted during a gang-related attack which had turned into a full-scale riot the previous year— and fined £1,500.

Was it a coincidence that somebody known to Higgins's wife – the wife Higgins was apparently arguing with – would show up on the morning when Higgins was murdered? If Brian were a betting man, he'd put good money on it not being the case. He really, really, really wanted to speak with Walton. Needed to. And, after that, he was going to have a heart-to-heart with Alice. Let her know, as kindly as possible, that it was in her best interest to tell them everything.

'Sir?' Fiona popped her head inside the office. 'The doorbell footage is here.'

'Smashing!' Brian said, shutting his laptop and getting up.

They already knew the van driver was most likely Walton. So, from that perspective, Brian didn't expect any earth-shattering revelations. But video evidence placing him at the scene of the murder within the time of death was still good. If nothing else, it would encourage him to be forthcoming when they found him and sat him down for a chat.

They trooped to Fiona's cubicle, Brian gesturing Liam to join them as they passed by his office. The email app on her laptop was open. She sat down, selected the email at the top of her inbox, and clicked the encrypted download link in the body text while Brian stood behind her, his hands on the back of her chair.

It was a big file, and the station's broadband connection was painfully slow – a constant source of resentment. The status bar got stuck at 10 per cent. The minutes ticked by. Brian huffed. Drummed an irregular tattoo on the back of the chair with his fingers. Sucked the air between his teeth. Fiona looked impassively at the screen. Staring at the dialogue box. Liam, his usually impeccably styled hair slightly mussed, stepped next to Brian, who nodded a silent greeting and pointed at Fiona's laptop. Liam ran a hand through his quiff, managing to smooth down most of the strays, except for a stubborn tuft on the crown of his head.

Thirty per cent downloaded, according to the status bar. Five minutes left.

'Fuck's sake. This is ridiculous,' Brian scoffed. 'The dial-up at Ma's house was faster.'

'Only the best for Strathburgh's finest, eh?' Liam said.

In the chair in front of him, Brian felt Fiona stiffen. The anticipation was getting to her too. They looked on in silence, waiting.

The status bar leaped from 50 to 90 per cent. Then, as if on purpose, it slowed back to a crawl, inching forward 1 per cent at a time.

91.

92.

93.

94.

95.

And then it got stuck again. Four minutes left for the download to finish.

'How is it even possible, in 2024?' Liam breathed.

Brian shook his head in disgust.

The status bar leaped to 97 per cent. Then 99. Another two minutes of painful waiting later, the download finished.

'Halle-fucking-lujah,' Brian said.

Fiona double-clicked the zip file. It unzipped into a folder that had ten video files, each one time-stamped.

'Let's start at six fifty-five a.m.,' Brian said. 'Layton seemed certain it was seven when the van pulled up. But just in case.'

Fiona double-clicked on one of the videos. Moved the slider until the timestamp said 6:55 a.m. On the screen, they saw the flagstone pathway to the Higginses' wrought-iron gate and the street beyond, dotted with parked cars and deathly quiet.

6:55 a.m. became 6:56 a.m. The minutes ticked by. Still nothing. Seconds before the clock struck 7 a.m., a dark grey panel van stopped in front of the Higginses' gate.

The figure in the driver's seat got out, looked around, as if to check the coast was clear, and jogged through the gate up the pathway to the Higginses' front door. The way the baseball cap was tilted down meant it was impossible to make out their features at first. But their man made an amateur mistake. He looked straight at the camera, confirming he was, in fact, Danny Walton, dressed in jeans and a black jacket, just as Layton had told them.

'Well, no surprises so far,' Brian observed.

Walton wasn't carrying any packages in his arms, he noted. And, if Reid was correct and Higgins wasn't a customer, there was nothing for him in the back of the van, either. So what had brought Walton to his doorstep at that early hour?

They waited to see what he'd do next, Brian's right leg bouncing nervously up and down. Would Ray Higgins open the door? Would their killer? Or would

Walton knock, wait, and leave when nobody answered, making this a royal waste of time?

Brian moved closer, peering at the video playing on Fiona's laptop monitor. He realised he was holding his breath.

On the laptop screen, Walton rang the doorbell. Waited. And for around thirty seconds, nothing happened.

But, just as Brian began to fear he'd turn around and drive off, Walton picked the fourth option they hadn't thought of. He inserted his hand into the front pocket of his jeans, produced a key, and let himself in.

Chapter Twelve

THEY REWATCHED THE VIDEO FIVE MORE TIMES. Pausing. Rewinding. Fast-forwarding. Watching at normal speed, half speed, and twice the speed. Brian scoured every pixel, not wanting to miss a single detail.

Each time they played the recording, the exact same sequence of events unfolded. Walton got out of the van, walked up to the Higginses' front door, and looked straight at the camera. Rang the bell. Waited. Produced a key. Grimaced when the key got stuck in the lock, jiggled it around, then opened the door and disappeared out of view. Precisely three and a half minutes later, he raced out like someone had lit his arse on fire, slamming the door behind him, then jumped in and started the van, before peeling off. Because he had his back to the doorbell, they couldn't see his face as he left, or spot any telltale traces of blood. But the clothes left no doubt that the person legging it out of the house was the same person who'd gone in.

'Where did he get that bloody key?' Brian wondered

aloud. 'Is it a skeleton key? Did he steal Alice Higgins's key while she was working out and cut a copy? Did the Higginses – Alice or Ray – give him one? And, if so, why?'

Neither Fiona nor Liam answered.

He was unreasonably annoyed at himself for not having thought of this fourth option. But who the fuck would've seen *that* coming? Aye, given the type of injuries and the murder weapon, he'd been fairly confident Higgins had known his killer. But this changed everything.

'Would three and a half minutes be enough to do that much damage?' Brian asked.

The detectives considered the question in silence.

'These things can happen fast,' Liam mused. 'You know that.'

Brian winced at the implied reference.

Don't start with this, bud ...

Brian swallowed. Took a breath.

'I don't know,' Fiona replied. 'But, whatever happened, it doesn't look good for him, does it? He had a key.'

'It does raise lots of questions,' Brian said. 'The way I see it, this could've gone one of two ways. Walton is the killer, or he interrupted the killer.'

'Or he found Higgins dead,' Fiona said. She hesitated, then voiced Brian's unspoken suspicions. 'Do you like Alice for it? What if she did it and Walton found him?'

Brian grunted, not wanting to commit yet. It was too soon. 'None of the three scenarios explain how Walton came to have a key to the Higginses's front door,' he said. 'We need to learn what's going on with that.'

They went through the other videos, starting at 1 a.m. all the way to 9 a.m., but they learned nothing further. At 5:31 a.m., Alice Higgins, wearing a wool cap and a puffy coat over activewear, a handbag in her hand and a large gym bag slung across her shoulders, slipped out and locked the door behind her, looking for all intents and purposes as if she was headed to the gym, just like she'd told them. At 7 a.m., Walton arrived. At 7:04 a.m., he blazed out and drove off. Nobody else made an appearance until 11:30 a.m., when the postie turned up while doing his rounds. His hand, which was holding a stack of white envelopes interspersed with a few leaflets, paused midway to the letterbox. He cocked his head and stood still, listening to something, for several minutes, then disappeared from view, presumably going to the back of the house through the vennel, where he spotted Higgins's body and dialled 999.

'They didn't find any CCTV at the back, did they?' Brian asked. 'Maybe the killer entered and left from there?'

Fiona shook her head. 'It's odd, isn't it, though?'

'What is?' Brian asked. Then he saw it and nodded agreement. 'Aye, you're right. Bloke's a security professional. Invests in a video doorbell. But he has no CCTV aimed at the vennel or the patio doors, which are arguably more vulnerable entry points?'

'Unless the killer took the cameras, along with the laptop and the phone,' Liam said.

Brian thought this over. 'We need to find Walton.

Send uniforms to his home address, to his ma's, and to Active Life, where he works.'

'Already done that, sir,' Fiona said.

'Good. If they don't find him, release his name.'

'Aye, sir,' Fiona replied. 'Meanwhile, should we talk to Alice Higgins?'

Brian shook his head automatically. 'No. Not yet. We need more information. Where are we on the Higginses' finances?'

'We've been looking at their bank statements, but there's a lot to get through. Three personal accounts, two joint accounts, a savings account, and his business bank account. And I still haven't touched his business records.'

'So you managed to get those?' Brian asked.

'Aye. I looked Higgins up on Companies House and downloaded his latest accounts. His accountant's name was on them. I called them up and they handed over the login to Higgins's bookkeeping software.'

'That's great,' Brian said. 'Absolutely smashing. And the—' He glanced at his watch. 'Och. Shite!' he said, with feeling.

It was four thirty, and Dr Pam Grace had scheduled him for three. But even if he hadn't been one and a half hours late, it was a thirty-minute drive from the station. Probably longer in rush-hour traffic. He wouldn't be there until at least five. And, by that time, she'd be closing him up.

'I need to call the pathologist's office,' he said, taking out his phone and pressing the contacts app.

In all the excitement, Brian had completely forgotten about Higgins's post-mortem.

Chapter Thirteen

Brian waved to Pam, who was sitting in a corner booth, thumbing her phone screen, an untouched latte and a cinnamon swirl in front of her. They'd agreed to meet at seven in Bluebeard's, a café in Kingshill – a part of town halfway between the morgue and the station known for its wide, tree-lined avenues flanked on both sides by rows of sandstone tenements interspersed with independent shops.

Brian joined the short queue, ordered a coffee and a muffin, then waded through the gaggle of tables, deftly juggling his tray without spilling so much as a drop, and slid into the seat across from Pam. She looked up at him and gave him a wan smile. He lifted the muffin to his mouth, took a large bite, and looked at her.

'Henderson working you too hard?' he asked. 'You look knackered.'

'It's been a day,' she said, dropping her phone into her handbag. She tore off a small piece of cinnamon swirl with her thumb and forefinger and placed it daintily in her mouth. 'I had five post-mortems back-to-back.'

'Crime never sleeps,' Brian commented.

'No, it doesn't,' she said.

She sipped her latte and sat up straight, and Brian couldn't help feeling the same faint flutter in his stomach he'd experienced at the Higgins crime scene. She wasn't wearing any make-up and there were dark circles under her eyes. And yet, she looked absolutely stunning.

He pushed the thought away. This was neither the time nor the place. More importantly, she was a colleague. Even if she were interested in him, and that was a big if – what did *he* have to offer her? What did he have to offer anyone, really? He couldn't even...

I didn't see him. I didn't see him. I didn't see him!

No, never mind...

I refuse to think about Roystonmuir.

It would place them firmly in conflict-of-interest territory.

'I appreciate you meeting me this late,' he said, covering his mouth to chew. 'Sorry I missed the post-mortem.'

'Exciting day?' Pam asked.

'Aye,' Brian said. 'Got tied up chasing a lead and it slipped my mind.'

She looked at him with an inquisitive gaze, but didn't prod. He didn't elaborate.

'So, what do you have for me?' he said, holding the mug of coffee between his hands and relishing its heat. He'd parked only two streets away, but his fingers were numb with the cold. It was minus one outside.

'Cause of death is massive blood loss, likely from a severed aorta,' she said.

'Not the neck, then?' Brian said.

'No. There was no swelling, so it was probably broken post-mortem.'

Brian nodded. On the one hand, whether the injury to Higgins's neck had happened pre- or post-mortem didn't make that much of a difference. The number of stab wounds didn't leave any doubt that their suspect wanted to – if not kill him – hurt Higgins very badly. On the other hand, if their killer had dropped Higgins's body hard enough that his neck was twisted at that angle, it might reveal something about their identity. Maybe that their build meant they'd struggled with the body's dead weight. Walton was squat. On the short side, but broad-shouldered and well-muscled. Alice was tall and toned, but thin. Who would've had more trouble handling Higgins's body?

'Penny for your thoughts?' Pam said.

Brian looked up. 'Och, sorry. Just thinking about what the injured neck might mean.'

'Well, you're the inspector, but cause of death is still suspicious,' she said with a wry smile. 'I'd say what likely happened is the killer dropped the body while trying to move him.'

'Aye, agreed.' Brian said. 'Could you tell if the wounds were caused by the knife we found on the scene?'

Pam sipped her latte. 'Yes, I'd say so. The serrations on the edge of the wound were consistent with the serrations on the blade.'

Good. So they had a murder weapon. That would be very handy once they arrested the killer. It might even point them in the right direction. 'Did you send it to the lab?'

'Yes. It's in the hands of the DNA gods now,' she said.

'Here's hoping they favour us,' Brian said.

'Hear, hear,' Pam said.

They clinked their mugs briefly.

'Anything else I should know?' Brian asked. 'Did you manage to get a more specific time of death?'

She shook her head. 'Still sometime between two and eight a.m., I'm afraid,' she said. 'I couldn't narrow it down any more than that.'

'And no other surprises?' Not that he was expecting any. But he had to ask.

Pam's hand stopped midway to her mouth.

'Actually, yes,' she said. Her voice dropped to a hushed whisper. 'There was one. Stabbing or not, I think Mr Higgins might've died anyway.'

Chapter Fourteen

'CANCER?' BRIAN REPEATED, AFTER PAM HAD explained what she'd found when she'd opened up Higgins.

Pam pushed her cinnamon swirl away, half-eaten. Brian put the remains of his muffin down, too, releasing a light dusting of crumbs on the reclaimed pine table. Suddenly, he didn't feel very hungry, either.

'Yes. That's what it looks like,' she said.

'Advanced?'

'It's not my field, so I can't tell you definitively how serious it was. But his liver and spleen were measuring almost double the normal size, and there were several lesions in his lungs and stomach. So whatever kind of cancer he had, it had spread.'

Did this change anything? Well, murder was murder, whether the victim had cancer or not. But why hadn't Alice mentioned it? They'd asked her specifically if there'd been something unusual going on in her husband's life. You'd think being sick with cancer, especially cancer that had spread, would be pretty fucking unusual. They needed to look at his medical records. Speak to his oncologist to get the full lowdown. And then they'd bring Alice in for a formal interview.

Lying by omission was still lying. By that yardstick, if he was right about Sindy the dog – and based on what he'd seen, both of the wound on Alice's wrist and of the dog's temperament, he was pretty sure that it wasn't a dog bite – this was the second lie he'd caught her in. Why? How did lying about important details benefit her, if not because she'd had something to do with the murder and she didn't want them connecting the dots?

'I did notice he looked a bit frail,' Brian said. 'But it didn't occur to me he might be sick.'

'Yes. Probably why he'd quit running.'

Brian stared at his half-drunk coffee. *Shite.* The bloke was, what, three years older than him? And, in spite of the dark thoughts that had been nipping at his consciousness over the past few weeks, he couldn't help feeling a stab of fear. Life was so fragile. One second you were bursting with health, and the next you were—

Lying on a threadbare carpet, in a pool of blood

—sick with a life-threatening illness. Just like that.

'Forty-one's no age, is it?' he said.

'No,' Pam sighed. 'No, it isn't.'

Brian was shaking his head unconsciously.

Nor is...

He stopped himself.

Pam placed her hand over his. It was warm and welcoming. Comfortable. Even though the skin was incredibly dry, probably from all the scrubbing and from wearing rubber gloves for long stretches of time every day. He wondered briefly why pathologists scrubbed up. It wasn't like their patients needed to worry about germs. Debated asking... It was because of cross-contamination. Of course it was. That, and the risk the pathologist themselves might catch something. Why was he rambling? *Twat.*

'How are *you* holding up?' she said, her voice laced with concern.

'Fine,' he said. But it came out slightly shaky.

'I didn't think you'd come back to work so soon.' She withdrew her hand, and he wished she hadn't. 'I don't mean to pry. It's just...' She shrugged. 'You know. You look like you're dealing with a lot.'

Brian couldn't argue with that, but he wasn't about to admit he was struggling to somebody else.

'Have you talked to anyone?' she asked.

Brian chuckled. It was the exact same question Lowe had asked him on the morning he'd pleaded his case.

'Sorry,' she said. 'You're right. I—'

'No, no,' Brian cut in. 'I genuinely appreciate your concern. Thank you, I promise I'm OK.'

'Well,' Pam said, 'If you ever want to talk, I'm happy to listen.'

'That's... That's very kind of you,' Brian said.

She got up and shrugged on her coat. 'Anyway, I'm off.' She squeezed his hand briefly. 'Take care of yourself, Brian.'

He watched her walk out purposefully, head held high, shoulders squared. A picture of effortless sophistication. Something tightened in his groin.

What the hell had just happened? Was he imagining this, or had she ...?

No. He had imagined this. She was simply showing him kindness and compassion. Christ alive, what the fuck was he even thinking?

Chapter Fifteen

For a very long time, I thought the real trouble started when my father put my mother in the ICU.

They'd always had a volatile relationship, did Mum and Dad. But, when I was growing up, their rows were like flash fires, not full-on blazes. One second, they'd be at each other's throats, screaming the foulest, most deeply personal insults they could think up. And the next, they'd both be rolling on the floor, laughing, hugging, and kissing. Like nothing had just happened. The flick of a light switch.

But then again, while Dad had 'liked a drink' for as long as I can remember, he'd always been firmly in control of the bottle. It was once the tables turned and the bottle took control of him that everything changed.

And that wouldn't have happened were it not for...

Ugh.

There's no good age or good way to lose a parent. But if they die of an illness when they're eighty-five, you can at least take comfort in the fact that they had a long, full life, and cherish all the good memories you shared.

Losing a parent when they're relatively young – when *you* are young – is... is...

It's like turning the page midway through a book and finding out there's nothing else to read. The author didn't even bother to finish the sentence. So life becomes a series of what-ifs. What would they look like if they'd lived? How would've they aged? Where would they have ended up? What would they have made of this or that? What would our relationship have become like? How would they see me? Would they approve? Would they be proud?

And when the way you've lost a parent is...

Well, let's be real here. Brutally blunt. Let's take the gloves off. Peel away every last bit of sugar coating.

When your father beats your mother so badly that she dies of a brain haemorrhage before you can make it to her deathbed. And when he was so completely out of it, so utterly stinking drunk, that he couldn't remember doing it...

Well, there's no closure. You'll never see your lost parent again. You didn't get to say goodbye. And you're suddenly left to fend for yourself. Forced to deal with the fallout of events you had nothing whatsoever to do with when you don't yet have the mental equipment to process it in a healthy way.

I'm not really sure what the argument that kicked things off was about and how it escalated to the point where he bashed her head in with a dining chair. But it doesn't matter, does it? In the grand scheme of things?

All I know is that I didn't make it in time.

I rushed to her bedside as fast as I could. But, by the time I got there, she was already cooling in the morgue.

That lit a fire in me.

But, curiously, my rage wasn't directed at my father. At least, not entirely.

Don't get me wrong. He did this. He killed my mother all by himself. And there's no excuse. Life is 20 per cent what happens to you and 80 per cent how you react to it. And he chose to react to it by becoming a bitter, mean, violent drunk.

But he was also just as much a victim of circumstances as my mother was. Because he didn't ask for any of it. Fundamentally, he was a good man. A man who worked hard, and played hard, sure. But also a man who cared for his family and minded his own business. A man who just so happened to have also made a convenient scapegoat.

So, no. I was wrong.

The real trouble didn't start when my father put my mother in the ICU. Not really.

It started much earlier.

It started on that godforsaken day when we met for the first time.

Chapter Sixteen

Wednesday, 10 January 2024

Brian leaned back in one of the uncomfortable plastic chairs in the conference room and rolled up his shirt sleeves. It was a frigid day. The kind when it felt like you were breathing liquid nitrogen, not air. But, in here, it was tropical.

'Christ, can't somebody turn the heating down?' he huffed. Sweat from his armpits was trickling down his sides, and his head was pounding, which was worsening his already foul mood.

'Thermostat's broken,' Fiona said, shooting him a look that was part apologetic, part disconcerted.

Next to the whiteboard, Liam stood with his back to them, staring contemplatively out the window, as if the thick clouds, which were making it feel like dusk despite it being only half noon, might give him a brainwave.

Brian drank down half a glass of cold water. Mopped

his brow with a tissue. Promised himself he'd lay off the whisky, or at least make an effort to cut back. He was starting to rely on it way too much to quieten down the increasingly unsettling swirl of emotions that assaulted him every minute of every day. Pressure to perform. A constant sense of dread he couldn't pinpoint the reason for. Guilt for—

Why couldn't I stop it?

—what happened in Roystonmuir.

And now, as if that weren't enough to be dealing with, a confusing attraction to a colleague. He closed his eyes briefly and pinched the bridge of his nose. Counted to five.

'I'm sorry. Go on,' he told Fiona. 'What did Higgins's GP have to say about his cancer?'

Fiona had already managed to track down Higgins's GP surgery and speak to the doctor who'd seen him, even though Brian had only texted her about it yesterday evening after his meeting with Pam at Bluebeard's. She tugged at her ponytail. Leafed through the pile of notes she'd written in neat, legible script. She'd pressed down so hard the words looked like they'd been etched into the paper.

'Non-Hodgkin's lymphoma. Stage three,' she repeated. 'Dr Craig – Higgins's GP – said she saw him for the first time a year and a half ago. He was complaining of persistent fatigue and just generally not feeling well. She ordered some tests, but found nothing untoward. He was visibly anxious and looked despondent, which she took as confirmation it was his mental rather than physical health that was the issue. So she told him to try to take it easy and come back if his symptoms didn't resolve.'

'And then they didn't.' Brian finished. He stretched. Rubbed his aching neck. God, he could really use a good night's sleep.

'No, they didn't.' Fiona sipped some water and shuffled her notes. 'He went back to the GP surgery and insisted something was wrong. Said he was having night sweats, too. So Dr Craig ordered more tests, and this time the results came back abnormal. A CT scan confirmed the diagnosis, and she referred him to Oncology at the Royal.'

'This was when?' Brian asked.

'He got the official diagnosis in late 2022,' Fiona said.

So Alice couldn't reasonably claim she didn't know about it. Could she? How realistic was it that her husband would successfully hide that he had cancer for over a year? And why would he go to the trouble of doing that, particularly if they had a happy, supportive marriage? But then again, why kill him when he—

'Was he dying?' he asked Fiona.

'The oncologist said it was grade three A – one of the more aggressive types. He did two rounds of chemo but it wasn't responding as well as they'd hoped.'

'So he *was* dying,' Brian said.

'I couldn't pin the oncologist down on that,' Fiona said. 'She said there were still some things they could try. But get this. After the second round, Higgins decided to discontinue treatment.'

'This was when?' Brian asked.

'November 2023,' Fiona said. 'Right after he completed his second round of chemo.'

'Just like that?' Brian asked, sitting up. 'Did he say why?'

What had happened? Had Higgins given up? Or was it something else?

'The oncologist said he told her he was going to explore "alternative options", whatever that means. Her words, not mine,' Fiona said. 'She said she made it very clear stopping treatment at that stage was a bad idea. He said he wasn't stopping treatment. Just going a different route.'

'So he went private?' Brian asked.

'That's the impression he gave the oncologist.' Fiona hesitated. 'But I've looked through his bank statements and there's no record of him paying any private hospital bills. Or medical insurance premiums. And look at this.'

She set her notes aside and fired up the browser on her laptop. Brian dragged his chair closer. Liam walked silently behind them. She pulled up a screen with several bar charts. Some of the bars were green, but most of them were a bright shade of red.

'What am I looking at?' Brian asked.

'This is Higgins's bookkeeping software,' Fiona said.

'Christ,' Liam muttered under his breath.

Brian leaned forward. Peered at the screen through squinted eyes. 'Business wasn't going so well, was it?'

'That's one way to put it,' Liam said.

The bar chart at the top of the screen, which was named *Cashflow*, showed money going out of the business and barely anything going in. The bar chart below it,

Invoice Timeline, showed that, for the previous four months, Higgins hadn't billed any work at all.

'His last big project was in October 2023. For Mango Bank,' Fiona said. 'He billed a few bits and bobs after that, and then business went dead.'

Brian recognised the name. Who in Strathburgh wouldn't? It was one of the biggest companies to come out of the city's financial services start-up scene, constantly celebrated as an inspiring story of ambition, ingenuity, and fortitude – though Brian thought the company's success had more to do with the fact that its co-founders, Sir Russ Bidmead and Angela Shawcross, were the son of a minor noble and prominent government donor, and the daughter of an oil magnate, than with the 'pulling yourself by the bootstraps' narrative the company's marketing literature made such a big deal out of. A *disgraced* oil magnate, he corrected himself. But still.

'—odd.'

'Sorry, say again?' Brian said, shaking his head.

Fiona cleared her throat. 'Here's what's odd,' she repeated. 'She pointed the cursor at a list of invoices. Clicked on one of them. 'This invoice here says twenty-five per cent *Upfront Deposit*.' She pressed the back button and clicked on another invoice. 'This one here says *Milestone 1*. And then there are no further invoices. That's it.'

'So he didn't finish the project?' Brian said.

'Sure seems like it,' Fiona agreed. 'If he had, there'd be a final invoice, wouldn't there?'

'Too sick to carry on?' Liam wondered.

'Too sick to carry on... or something else happened?' Brian ventured.

But what?

'So Higgins learns he's sick,' Brian said, thinking aloud. 'So sick that the treatment he endured for several months isn't doing him much good. If anything, it's made him sicker. He puts a brave face on it. Carries on like normal for as long as he can. But he reaches a point where it's no longer sustainable. Money gets tight. And ...'

He stopped lamely. Sighed. It made no sense. None of it. Money was a pretty strong motive for murder, but he couldn't see it playing out in a scenario where the issue stemmed from being diagnosed with a serious illness. And why would he stop his treatment? Trying something not available on the NHS might be the logical step. But only if you had insurance or could afford to pay for the treatment out of pocket. And Higgins's bank records suggested neither was the case.

'Ah. Shite,' Brian sighed. 'Let's check with private clinics anyway, just in case. Even if he couldn't afford treatment, he might've gone for a second opinion.'

At the very least, they might be able to gain a deeper insight into Higgins's state of mind during the last few months of his life.

'I'm on it. It's odd that his wife didn't think to mention this, though,' Fiona said, once again voicing his unspoken thoughts.

'Aye. The more we learn about Higgins, the more the state of their marriage stinks,' Brian said. 'It's time we brought her in for a formal interview. Confront her with what we know.'

'Aye, sir,' Fiona said.

'Call her in and let me know when she's here,' Brian said, getting up. He turned to Liam. 'In the meantime, let's get to the bottom of the deal with the Mango Bank contract.'

Chapter Seventeen

Mango Bank's headquarters occupied three floors of a dildo-shaped high-rise in Strathburgh's financial district, a four-square mile agglomeration of steel and glass in the north-western part of the city, on a hill overlooking the bypass and green belt beyond. Officially, the building was called the Circa Tower, but the locals knew it as the Big Prick. Which, to be fair, wasn't far off the mark.

Brian and Liam walked into the spacious, marble-covered ground floor lobby at 2:15 p.m. on the dot. Brian flashed his warrant card to the mouse-haired, bespectacled receptionist. The receptionist gave him side-eye and kept tapping on her keyboard.

'Is Sir Russ in?' Brian asked impatiently, when a minute had passed and she still hadn't acknowledged them.

The receptionist kept typing for a few more seconds. 'I'm afraid not,' she said in a disconcertingly high-pitched voice, her eyes never leaving the computer monitor.

'Do you know when he'll be in?' Brian prodded.

The receptionist stopped typing and looked up at him with watery eyes that looked impossibly small behind her thick lenses. 'I'm afraid not. But Ms Shawcross might be available, if it's urgent?'

Brian nodded. 'Aye. Please. Can you check?' he said.

The receptionist's neutral expression came alive with interest. 'May I ask what this is regarding, please?' she said.

'We'd rather tell her directly,' Brian shot back.

The receptionist pursed her lips, like he'd just let rip an extraordinarily loud, noxious fart in her face. She lifted the receiver and dialled an extension, her lacquered nail gliding over the phone's keys with the acquired confidence of somebody who performed this particular action countless times a day.

'Hello, Diane. It's Mary downstairs,' she sing-songed in a tone that was so different to the one she'd deployed with them that, for a second, Brian thought she'd switched places with somebody else. 'Is Ms Shawcross available please? Em... it's...' Mary gave them more side-eye, then turned slightly away and stage-whispered. 'It's the police. They'd like to speak with her.' She listened. Nodded. 'Em, of course. No, I... of course. Of course. Thank you.'

She placed the receiver back in its cradle with a soft click. Looked up at Brian without making eye contact.

'Ms Shawcross is in a meeting just now, but she'll be available in fifteen minutes, if you'd like to wait for her?'

'Aye,' Brian said, making a momentous effort to keep his tone polite. 'Aye, that's absolutely fine.'

Mary fumbled beneath the reception desk. She produced a ledger with an orange-and-green cover – Mango Bank's corporate colours – and proffered it together with a branded click pen.

'Please sign in,' she said.

Brian groaned inwardly. It wasn't like he was planning to sneak around the building to steal corporate secrets. And even if he did, who would he share them with who'd care to use them for nefarious reasons? Grudgingly, he snatched the pen from Mary's hand, glanced at his wristwatch, and scrawled the time and his signature. A dour security guard who'd appeared out of nowhere guided them toward the lift and up to Shawcross's second-floor office.

'Good afternoon,' a rail-thin thirty-something woman who Brian assumed must be Diane said from behind a desk opposite the lifts. 'Ms Shawcross will be with you shortly. Please have a seat.'

They sank into two brown leather Chesterfield chairs that had been strategically placed in front of the floor-to-ceiling picture window, presumably so guests could take in the views. In the distance, snow-capped mountains stood in stark relief, looking impossibly white against the red-tinged sky. Beneath them, matchbox-sized traffic trundled along the bypass, which snaked its way through clusters of closely packed Douglas firs, then doubled back, encircling the city.

Diane's gaze returned to her monitor, her chin resting in her left palm and her right hand poised over the mouse. Brian cleared his throat and rifled through the magazines on the small coffee table between the two chairs: a stack of week-old *Financial Times* newspapers, three issues of *The Economist*, and one *Global Banking & Finance Review* with Angela Shawcross herself, dressed in a bespoke dark blue pinstripe power suit, her hair impeccably styled and her hands crossed, smiling knowingly from its cover.

Redrawing the lines: Mango Bank's blueprint for the digital age, the accompanying caption said. *Exclusive interview with Angela Shawcross, co-founder and* CEO.

Brian flipped lazily through the magazine's glossy pages, his right leg bouncing up and down soundlessly on the plush cream-coloured rug. Shawcross flashed him another one of her knowing smiles from a spread midway through the thin magazine, a puff piece littered with innovative solutions, accelerating progress, and something about the importance of cooperation over competition. He showed it to Liam, who was pretending to be engrossed in a *Financial Times* column about Americans and their attitudes toward EVs.

Liam scanned it and scoffed. 'Might as well be written in a foreign language.'

The oak double doors behind Diane opened. A broad-shouldered man with expensively barbered and heavily pomaded hair and a jaw that could split walnuts open just by being in the same room with them emerged, pulling a heavy grey coat over his checked blazer and red slacks. The dour security guard who'd escorted them up reappeared out of thin air and guided him toward the lift with a muttered, 'This way, please.'

Brian nodded to Liam and stood up. Diane cleared her throat and gave him a withering look. 'If you could just wait there, Ms Shawcross will be with you in a moment,' she said. 'I'll let you know.'

'Fuck's sake,' Brian said, sinking into the Chesterfield. His phone pinged. He peeled it out of his trouser pocket. Fiona.

AH here. Put her in interview room 2.

Brian replied with a thumbs-up emoji. Good. Let her stew. Maybe that would persuade her it would be best if she levelled with them.

'Excuse me?' Diane's voice interjected.

'Aye?' he snapped.

She drew her lips into a thin line, as if he were a piece of dirty bog roll that had stuck to her shoe. *Jesus wept, these people,* he thought. *All acting like they're dog's bollocks.*

'Ms Shawcross will see you now,' she said.

'Och, right,' Brian said, getting up and smoothing the creases from his trousers. 'Ta.'

He and Liam walked to Shawcross's imposing office door. Brian rapped it twice with his knuckles.

'Yes, come in,' Shawcross called, a queen summoning her courtiers.

Brian turned the brushed stainless-steel knob. The door opened soundlessly onto an office that was probably double the size of his flat.

'Good afternoon, Ms Shawcross,' Brian said, flashing his warrant card. 'Thank you for seeing us at short notice. We appreciate it.'

Shawcross gave Brian a bemused look from her spot

at the head of an enormous glass-topped conference table that took up one whole side of the office.

'Please, have a seat,' she said, making it sound like an order. 'I'm sorry to have kept you waiting. Can I offer you something to drink?'

'No, ta,' Brian replied.

Shawcross pressed the white button on a small black box that was attached to the table. Two thin, barely noticeable wires snaked out of the contraption's back, through a hole in the conference table's top, and disappeared from view.

'Ms Shawcross?' Diane's tinny voice said through the box.

'Can I have some water, please, Diane?' Shawcross said.

'Of course, Ms Shawcross. I'll be right there.'

Barely a split second later, there was a knock at the door.

'Come in,' Shawcross commanded.

Diane entered the room, nodded a greeting, and made her way to a gleaming art deco bar cart that stood midway between the conferencing area and Shawcross' enormous desk. She poured water from a crystal decanter into a cut-glass tumbler and brought it over, carefully placing it on top of a leather coaster.

'Are you sure you don't want anything?' Shawcross said. 'Coffee? Tea?'

'No, thank you,' Brian said, his impatience mounting. Was this show for their benefit, or was she always like this? 'This won't take long.'

'That will be all for now, Diane,' Shawcross said. Diane walked out.

'So,' Shawcross said once Diane had shut the door softly behind her. 'How can I help?'

Brian cut to the chase. 'We're investigating a murder, and were hoping you could shed some light on our victim.'

Shawcross remained impassive. But, now that he was sitting just a few feet away from her and could look at her up close, Brian noticed her eyes were slightly red-rimmed, as if she'd been crying and had hastily redone her make-up to cover up the evidence. He wondered briefly what she'd been discussing with the bloke who'd just left her office. Had it been personal? An unhappy boyfriend, perhaps? Unlike Bidmead, who had no qualms about using his platform to air his controversial – and, often, deliberately inflammatory – views, Shawcross was notoriously private, despite doing most of Mango Bank's PR.

'Murder?' Shawcross said, interrupting his train of thought. Like her expression, her voice didn't betray any emotion. Not even a hint of curiosity.

'Aye. The murder of one of your contractors, actually,' Brian said. 'Raymond Higgins?'

'Yes,' she said, in the same impassive tone. 'The name rings a bell. But I seem to remember we haven't worked with him for quite a while. We terminated his contract some time ago.'

'I see,' Brian said. Terminated. Not ended. Interesting choice of words. 'And was there any particular reason for that?'

Shawcross didn't reply immediately.

'At this stage, we're trying to build a picture of Mr Higgins's life. To find out who might've benefited from his death,' Brian explained.

A very brief shadow flitted across her brow. It was gone as quickly as it had appeared. She grasped her untouched water glass with both hands.

'We fired him,' she said slowly, as if saying what she was going to say out loud required physical effort. 'For breach of confidentiality.'

Chapter Eighteen

When Shawcross uttered that last sentence, the black dog that had been following Brian around all morning scurried into a corner at the back of his mind. His heart skipped a beat.

'What happened, Ms Shawcross?' he said with barely restrained excitement, leaning forward, his fingers drumming on the conference table.

'He got his hands on information he shouldn't have had access to,' she said, all in one breath. 'Proprietary information about our high-net-worth clients. Names. Addresses. Account details. You get the idea.'

'Oh?' Brian felt himself deflate. So that was it? 'This might sound like a stupid question,' he said. 'But isn't that what you hired him to do?'

'Yes, that's correct,' Shawcross said through pursed lips. 'But he did more than just test our systems. He copied the data.'

'How do you mean?' Brian asked.

'He literally copied it from one of our servers and pasted it somewhere else. A flash drive.'

For a minute, Brian was stunned into silence. This might be significant.

'And Mr Higgins admitted to this?' he said.

'No,' Shawcross replied. 'He strenuously denied it. There was no way we could prove it, so we let the matter drop.'

'I'm sorry, I'm struggling to understand,' Brian said. 'How do you know he copied the data if you had no evidence?'

'In a nutshell,' Shawcross said, 'he spoofed one of our staff members' logins. We picked it up during a routine system audit. We wouldn't have noticed anything improper, but the staff member had had to leave work unexpectedly because of a family emergency on the day the IT team recorded the activity. So it couldn't have been him.'

'And it was Mr Higgins because?'

'IT isn't really my area of expertise, Inspector,' Shawcross said in a tone that could slice through reinforced steel. 'But my CTO says he's the only one who could've had the means to do it, and I trust him implicitly. He's been with us from day one.'

Could Higgins have also stored the data on his laptop? Found out something about someone who didn't want to be found out? It would explain why the phone and laptop had vanished. But not necessarily how Higgins knew his attacker, or why they'd gone to his house on Monday morning and killed him. Unless ...

'What happened once you found out, Ms Shawcross?' Brian asked, faintly aware that his heart was thumping.

'As I said, we terminated the engagement,' Shawcross replied. 'And we agreed not to take the matter any further on condition he returned the data.'

'And he did?'

'He handed over a flash drive and agreed to his laptop being inspected.'

'So you're certain he didn't keep a copy?' Brian was unconvinced.

'Well, that's the thing, isn't it?' Shawcross said. 'It was always going to be our word against his.'

She caught herself fidgeting with the buttons on her suit jacket and stopped herself.

'I'll tell you what, though, Inspector.' She gave Brian a no-nonsense look that made him straighten to attention. Here was the much vaunted grit that had built Mango Bank into the force it had become. 'Banking is a small, closed industry. People talk.' She spread her hands and held Brian's gaze. 'He knew it wouldn't do him any favours if word got out he'd tried anything improper. Which I'm guessing is why he played ball.'

And yet, he hadn't worked since, Brian reflected. Was it because he'd been too sick to take on new projects, or because word of him getting caught red-handed had got out? And how would a man in need of money, fighting for his life, react to that?

He glanced at his wristwatch. Three thirty. Alice Higgins could afford to wait a bit longer. 'Is your CTO available?' he asked. 'We'd like to speak with him.'

Chapter Nineteen

Mango Bank's CTO was the last person Brian would've pegged as being the chief technology officer of a successful financial services start-up. Short, completely bald, and well into his fifties, his eagle's beak of a nose, vomit-green shirt, and chunky, ill-fitting gold signet ring on his right pinkie said 1970s cartoon baddie, not IT guru. Except, once he'd ushered them into an office that was about half the size of Angela Shawcross's but just as opulent, he didn't threaten them with a menacing growl, but launched into a ten-minute explanation of firewalls, MIB files, syslogs, and other enterprise network components Brian wasn't sure how to pronounce and the various ways in which they could be accessed by someone with the skills and wherewithal to do so.

Most of the technical detail went over Brian's head, but the delivery was so confident he could only conclude the CTO had no doubt in his mind Ray Higgins had copied Mango Bank's data without permission, and that he'd arrived at this conclusion because he knew exactly what he was talking about. But, walking toward the car with an email listing the clients whose information Higgins had copied burning a hole in his pocket, he couldn't shake the edge of frustration that was nipping at the base of his skull. While he was satisfied that the trek to the Big Prick had been productive, what they'd learned complicated matters. Alice was the obvious suspect. But, clearly, there were others – at least ten people, according to the list the CTO had emailed – who might have had reason to take umbrage at Ray Higgins. The question was, would they have taken enough umbrage to get their hands dirty? Or hire somebody who'd do it for them?

'We'll need to eliminate them all as suspects,' he told Liam as he eased himself into the car and started the engine. 'Listen to their stories. Check their alibis. The works.'

Liam was engrossed in a tiny maroon speck on the tip of his shirt collar. He produced a linen handkerchief from his trouser pocket, wet it with the tip of his tongue, and dabbed at the speck, muttering to himself.

'Bud?' Brian prodded.

'What? Sorry,' Liam said, turning toward him. He had dark circles under his eyes, and a thick tuft of hair stuck out of his quiff.

'I said we'll need to eliminate them all as suspects,' Brian repeated.

'And how do you feel about that?' Liam said, rearranging his hair in the side mirror.

Brian indicated right and negotiated the on-ramp onto the city bypass. The traffic wasn't stop-start yet, but it was getting heavier as rush hour loomed.

'Honestly? I don't know,' Brian said. 'I'm not sure whether it's a wild goose chase.'

'So you're confident it's Alice?'

'Well, she's guilty of *something*,' Brian said. 'I'm fairly sure of that. Why wouldn't she tell us about the cancer and the money troubles? Or that her husband got fired off a big job for misconduct?'

'But?'

Brian made a guttural sound of disgust in his throat. *Shite.* The whole point of returning to work was that it was supposed to keep him occupied. Make him feel better about himself. Help him move forward. Why was it turning out to be so difficult? Why was it making things worse?

They drove the next two miles in silence, except for the faint hum of traffic and the drone of the newsreader on Strath Radio, who was going on about the outrage somebody had sparked by tweeting – Brian refused to call it X – a debunked conspiracy theory. The lights at the large intersection into town turned green, and Brian indicated right, turning onto the two-lane street that would lead them east toward the station.

'This isn't the first time Sir Russ Bidmead has aired his controversial views online. He has a track-record ...'

At the mention of Mango Bank's co-founder, Brian's ears pricked up. Imagine hearing about him on the radio barely two hours after they'd turned up at his office. He cranked up the volume, taking his eyes off the road for a split second to find the knob. When he looked up, he realised he was approaching a zebra crossing with a pedestrian waiting to cross. Brian jammed his foot down on the brake. There was a faint squeal of tyres and a horn blared angrily behind him.

He waited for the bloke to cross, drumming his fingers on the steering wheel, willing the man to move it so they could get back to the station and interview Alice. The bloke took his sweet time, negotiating the crossing at a snail's pace, and fiddling with the bill of his cap with a colourfully tattooed hand as he did so.

Hang on a minute.

Where had he seen that cap? And that ink?

He shot up straight in his seat.

'Liam?' he said hoarsely. 'Bud?'

'Eh?'

'Holy shite. That's Danny Walton!'

Chapter Twenty

BRIAN SAT IN THE CAR, MOTIONLESS. A USELESS lump. Staring out the windscreen. Unable to compute what he was seeing.

Danny Walton edged his way across the street. Head down. Cap strategically placed so it would hide most of his features. Only a single pimple surrounded by the beginnings of a very scraggly looking goatee were visible from beneath the bill. The colourful ink on the back of his right hand stood in stark relief against the black of his frayed jacket sleeve.

He ambled toward the other side of the road, step by interminable step. One dirty Converse-clad foot after the other. A harried woman pushing a double-buggy overtook him. He was two feet away from the kerb. Then one. Then a few yards.

'B! Are we going to approach him or what?'

The urgency in Liam's voice broke Brian's paralysis. He jammed his index finger on the driver's side power window button and fumbled in his pocket for his warrant card.

'Call for backup,' he told Liam. 'Tell them we're... Where the fuck are we? Inchview Way.'

Brian pulled out his warrant card with a sweaty palm, and it slipped. He gripped it. Stepped out of the car in slow motion, blood rushing in his ears. Behind him, the sound of more horns.

'Danny Walton?' Brian said in a commanding voice, holding up his warrant card.

Walton walked on. Inches away from the kerb now. Hadn't he heard him? Or was he pretending not to?

'Danny Walton!' Brian called louder.

Walton's head jerked up. He looked straight at Brian and froze mid-stride. Brian had milliseconds to register Walton's eyes widening. He darted off and crashed into a bin with a clang of flesh on metal that cut through the buzz of car engines.

'Shite!' Brian screamed. 'Fuck!'

He took off in pursuit. The car behind him had tried to drive around his vehicle, which was still idling with the driver's side door open, and it hit him, the bumper digging into his shins. Brian barely felt the impact.

'What the FUCK do you think you're doing?' an angry voice yelled over the squeal of brakes.

Brian flashed his warrant card absently and kept running, the faint aroma of exhaust and tyre rubber lingering in his nostrils. Walton had already scrambled to his feet, seemingly none the worse for wear, and legged it.

From the corner of his eye, Brian saw Liam slaloming

between two nonplussed OAPs with effortless grace and going off in hot pursuit, his quiff bouncing up and down. Brian followed, scanning his surroundings and trying to get his bearings. Liam had crossed the road and was about ten yards up to his right, arms and legs pumping, his suit jacket flapping behind him. Walton hazarded a look back. Crossed to the other side, forcing a Vauxhall Mokka to brake suddenly, eliciting another chorus of horns. He was headed south toward the riverfront, no doubt because it was all downhill and the tailwind would give him an advantage.

Brian dashed forward. Crashed into a bloke who was going the opposite way with his head down.

'Hey, prick. Watch it!' the bloke growled, bending to retrieve the boxes of mince, loose carrots, and cantaloupe that had spilled out of his Aldi bag for life.

'Police!' Brian yelled without looking back, picking up the pace so he could catch up.

Liam veered into a side street. Brian kept going straight. If he could catch up and Liam managed the pincer movement, they'd corner him. But Brian had been sleeping too little, drinking too much whisky, and avoiding his daily three-mile run. His right side was on fire, and his windpipe felt like it had been lined with razor blades.

More cars sounded their horns. A thick-set older motorist with a gravelly voice opined loudly that Walton was a twat, a gormless bastard, and a grade-A eejit all rolled into one. Brian crossed, hot on Walton's heels, and almost got run over for the second time in under two minutes. The thick-set motorist, his lumpy face the colour of fired clay, shouted something Brian didn't quite get but was sure wasn't very complimentary.

As he reached the other side of the street, Liam reappeared and converged on Walton. He was almost within snatching distance. Walton hazarded another look back, his face a mask of fear. What was he running away from? Innocent people didn't leg it from the polis without even waiting to see what they wanted to talk to them about. *This makes him look guilty as sin.*

Walton barrelled through a crowd of pedestrians and made a beeline for the Starbucks at the end of the road.

'Get him!' Brian shouted in between laboured breaths. He could feel himself slowing down, his energy – not much to begin with – flagging, and Walton was widening his already considerable lead. Liam was their only chance of catching him.

Liam dived toward Walton, hands outstretched like a goalie attempting a last-ditch save. He missed by an inch. Walton sidestepped him with an unexpectedly deft and graceful movement and ducked into Starbucks, which was buzzing with people who'd got off work early or nipped out for a cheeky afternoon pastry. Brian darted in behind him. Stopped, chest heaving, breath whistling, and scanned the space. Walton was nowhere to be seen.

'Where the fuck has he gone?' he yelled at Liam, who'd added several streaks of road grime to his shirt and was looking exceedingly sheepish. 'Ach. Fuck. Why didn't you grab him?'

'Bud, are you fucking serious right now?' Liam fired back. 'I threw myself at him.'

'We need to find him,' Brian said louder, patting his

chest and trouser pockets. A wave of dizziness overcame him and he doubled over, breathing harshly. 'Where's the ...? Ach. Shite. Where's my fucking phone?! God!'

He slammed his fist into a plaster column. A lightning bolt of pain shot up his arm.

'Er, excuse me. Sir?' a timid voice said from behind him.

Brian pivoted violently around. A short, pimply teenager in a green Starbucks polo peered up at him from behind thick, black-framed glasses, his face scared but determined.

'What?' Brian snapped.

The barista visibly flinched, but held his ground.

'I'm sorry, sir. But I'm afraid I'm going to have to ask you to calm down or leave the premises. You're upsetting the customers.'

Brian swivelled around and saw a mother shooting daggers at him while cradling her two weans. Both looked beside themselves. Somebody tutted.

Brian closed his eyes. Sweat trickled from his temple down his cheek. He tried to breathe deeper. It elicited a coughing fit. His heart was jackhammering in his chest, and his shirt had stuck to his back. He made a visible effort to regain control. Turned back to the barista, who, to his credit, was still looking up at him, jaw set and shoulders squared, even though his face looked like he wished the floor would open beneath him and swallow him whole.

'I'm sorry,' Brian said, flashing his warrant card. 'We were pursuing a suspect and he ran in here. Did you see a bloke in a cap and black jacket? Colourful tattoos down the backs of his hands?'

The barista didn't have to think about it.

'Aye,' he said, pointing. 'He went toward the lavvies.'

Brian was about to make off.

'He went through the fire exit,' the barista continued. 'It set the alarm off.'

'Shite,' Brian muttered under his breath. 'Shite. Shite. Shite.'

'I'm sorry, sir,' the barista butted in. 'But I really must insist you behave appropriately.'

'Aye, right. Sorry,' Brian said, not meaning a word. The adrenaline rush was dissipating, replaced by a deep weariness. 'Let's get the fuck out of here and regroup,' he told Liam.

They walked out, stopping under the green awning to scan the street. But it was packed with pedestrians, and pinpointing Walton, in his nondescript clothes, was next to impossible. He was one more black jacket in the multitude.

'Now what, B?' Liam said.

'What, what?' Brian said.

He laughed hysterically. Ran his hands through his hair.

'Let's go get some answers from Alice Higgins.'

Chapter Twenty-One

Half an hour later, they made it to the station. Brian's mood, bad to begin with and made worse by the unsuccessful chase, had been dipped in venom and blowtorched to a crisp by a traffic jam that had added ten minutes to their journey. Ten minutes of complete motionlessness while a swarm of ants jacked up on methamphetamines crawled over every inch of his skin.

'B, take a breather,' Liam said as Brian tried to parallel park, got the angle completely wrong, and began slamming his palm on the steering wheel so hard the whole car vibrated.

He stopped. Placed his face on the steering wheel. Hyperventilated. He wanted to utter a throat-shredding scream and willed himself not to do it. He'd noticed Fiona, McGillivray, and a few others giving him weird looks and avoiding his gaze since he'd returned to work. Imagine if one of them passed by the car right now and heard him doing his best banshee impression? They'd cart him off and throw away the key.

Brian had to bring himself back to the moment. Sitting in his discomfort. Embracing it. There. That wasn't so bad, was it?

What was it that had set him off like this?

It was partly the frustration of not having made much headway in the investigation. Of there still not being a clear path through to the killer that he could see. And time was running out. Day three was already almost over. But it was also the emotions he was hiding. And the longer he hid them, especially from himself, the harder dealing with them was becoming.

He shut his eyes tighter. The white spots in front of his eyes resolved into an arm. A young, impossibly thin arm, with ivory skin marred by several circular bruises and irregularly shaped haematomas. A black line snaked down the crook of the elbow, stopping in the middle of the forearm. The syringe, its plastic yellowed from reuse, was still stuck in the vein the blackness originated from. Just above the elbow, a piece of rubber tubing tied in a tight half-knot. But the worst thing was—

The eyes. The eyes.

So empty I couldn't tear my gaze away. That's why I didn't realise—

'B!' Liam said. 'Are you OK?'

Brian swallowed. His breathing had evened out, but his hands were clammy and his shirt was drenched.

'Aye,' he said weakly.

'You're not thinking about ...?'

'No,' Brian said emphatically. 'No. I'm not.'

He spotted a parking space that was wide enough for him to drive forward into. Revved the car angrily. When he'd managed to park more or less parallel to the kerb, he wiped his forehead with a tissue and got out. The blast of chill early-evening air made him feel hot and cold at once.

'I'll be right there,' he told Liam and raced up the station's steps two at a time, making a beeline for his office.

He slammed the door shut. Sank into his chair. His breathing quickened as he bent over and fished out the quarter bottle of whisky he'd hidden in his desk's bottom drawer beneath several as yet unused notebooks with a trembling hand. He fought it off. Forced himself to breathe slowly. Not now. He had a suspect to interview – because, let's face it, she was a suspect. He unscrewed the cap and took a long gulp. Grimaced as the whisky hit his stomach and exploded with burning heat.

Aye, that was better. Much, much better.

The liquid fire numbed him right down.

Another gulp, and it was all infinitely more bearable.

Another, and, suddenly, the whole episode – the failed chase, the traffic jam, his meltdown – it all seemed like a bad dream.

How stupid. Why the fuck had he reacted like that? It was just a traffic jam.

Just a traffic jam. That's all it was. Nothing to see here. No. Nothing at all.

He screwed the bottle tight and shut it back in the drawer, burying it deep beneath his pile of fresh notebooks. Then he got up and made his way to the lavvy.

Best rinse out his mouth before going into the interview room.

He wouldn't want to give anyone the wrong idea.

Chapter Twenty-Two

The Alice Higgins in Interview Room Three was a shadow of the woman who'd elbowed her way past Constable Stebbings and spewed all over her husband's crime scene three days earlier. Her formerly lustrous hair hung listlessly against her shoulders. A dead squirrel pelt. Her emerald-green eyes were flat and glazed, staring unnervingly into the middle distance at a grey smear on the whitewashed wall across from the interview-room table.

Brian entered the room with slow, deliberate movements and sank into a chair in front of Alice, where Liam, now wearing a streak-free shirt, was already waiting. Brian's phone pinged. He made a show of extracting it from his trouser pocket to check it. But the smile that touched his lips when he pressed the notification alert and read the email it pertained to – the report from the lab – was genuine. He bit it back, setting his features into a poker face.

'Good afternoon, Alice,' Brian began, clearing his throat. 'Sorry to have kept you waiting. We got... held up.'

Alice muttered a barely audible grunt of assent. She was wearing black Lululemon leggings and an oversized salmon hoodie. The hoodie had a large, irregularly shaped brown stain on the chest that could've been coffee or HP sauce.

'So, just to reiterate,' Brian said. 'You're being interviewed under caution. You don't have to say anything, but it may harm your defence if you don't mention something when questioned that you later rely on in court. Anything you do say may be given in evidence. You have the right to have a solicitor present during this interview. And you're not under arrest. You may leave at any time. Do you understand?'

Alice nodded faintly and toyed with the frayed edge of her hoodie's left cuff. Her nails were jagged, the ones on her left thumb and pinkie chewed down to the quick. She looked shell-shocked. Numb. And Brian had to wonder. In spite of the circumstances surrounding the murder giving her ample opportunity to do it. In spite of the omissions and half-truths. In spite of the new information that had just hit his email inbox. Did she have it in her to kill her husband? Because, if she was guilty, this was the performance of a lifetime.

'Can you say that out loud, for the recording?' Brian repeated. 'Do you understand your rights?'

'Aye,' she said in a cracked voice.

'And do you want us to call your solicitor?'

A pause. A faint light flickered behind her pupils.

'I've nothing to hide,' she said more firmly.

Brian nodded. This was good. A solicitor would cramp his style. Break his flow. Maybe even suspect—

Suspect what? I'm not drunk. not even close. It was just a wee nip to take the edge off.

'Can you walk us through what happened on the morning of Monday the eighth January once more, please?' Brian opened, pouring himself a glass of water and offering the jug to Alice, who shook her head.

On the surface, it was an innocuous question. Something they'd already asked and which she'd already replied to. If she was guilty, it would lull her into a false sense of security. Lower her guard. And if the universe decided to do them a solid, she'd contradict what she'd told them previously. Give them just the opening they needed to corner her into telling them the whole truth.

Alice answered straight away, in a low but strong whisper. 'I left home for the gym at five thirty, then went to work,' she said. 'As I said the first time we spoke.'

So she was sticking to her story. Which, to be fair, the recording from the video doorbell backed up. It was the other aspects of what she'd told them – or, well, not told them – that they needed to get to. All in good time.

'And what happened next?' Brian persisted. 'Walk us through it.'

'How do you mean?' Alice asked, her gaze never leaving her hands, which were lying on the desk, still busy fidgeting with the cuffs of her hoodie.

'You went to work, and?' Brian elaborated.

'Well, there was an emergency, and I was tied up in crisis-management meetings all morning.'

'What was the emergency?' Brian said.

Alice scoffed.

'Just trying to get a clearer picture of what happened,' Brian said.

'Well, if you must know, the co-founder of one of our biggest retainer clients put his foot in it... Except, no. Sorry, that's not accurate. This was deliberate rage-baiting. And we had to clean up his mess.'

Brian raised an eyebrow. It couldn't be. Or could it? Strathburgh's elite ran in a pretty tight circle.

'Would this client, by any chance, be Mango Bank?' he ventured.

'Aye,' Alice said. Her gaze never left her fingers, which kept busying themselves with her cuffs, but Brian still didn't miss the faint curl of her upper lip.

'What happened?' Brian asked, thinking back to the snippet he'd caught on the radio before Walton had dropped unexpectedly in his lap, only to slip through his fingers.

'Shit-stirring,' Alice said. 'As per.'

'Can you explain?' Brian asked, growing impatient. Why was she speaking in riddles?

'Well, I suppose it's out there in the open, so I won't break confidentiality if I tell you. One of the co-founders, Sir Russ Bidmead, posted a conspiracy theory on X,' Alice said. 'That's—'

'Twitter. Aye, I know,' Brian said. Most of the time, when he logged on to social media, it was for work – he'd never seen the point of spending your free time with your eyes glued to your phone, scrolling endlessly for no reason, when you could—

Drink? Ruminate? Revel in what a useless waste of space you are?

But he'd heard of the buyout and the ensuing drama, including an overnight change in name he hadn't managed to get on board with because it just didn't roll off the tongue. 'What'd he say?'

'That gender dysphoria was made up by big pharma to sell more meds and boost their profits,' Alice said.

Brian's toes curled. This was another reason he didn't like social media. It gave anyone a platform to say anything. And no matter how outrageous or divorced from reality that person was, there'd be people who'd accept what they'd said. Believe it. Amplify it without question.

'That must've gone down like a lead balloon,' he commented.

'By the time I got to work, *#BoycottMangoBank* was trending,' Alice said. 'So no. It wasn't ideal.'

'What time was this?' Brian asked.

'Around seven thirty.'

'Was it usual for you to go to work this early?' Brian asked.

'Aye. I—' Her mouth shut abruptly, with an audible snap of teeth on teeth. 'Can I have some water, please?'

'Aye, of course.'

Brian poured her a glass. She accepted it with a hand that was shaking slightly and drained half of it. Some of the water dribbled on her chin, and she wiped it away absently with the sleeve of her hoodie, a gesture which managed to seem delicate and oddly helpless at the same time. Brian waited. She'd been about to tell them something but caught herself. What was it? He was dying to know, but they needed to be patient. If they pushed her now, she'd clam up and the interview would be over.

Alice placed the glass on the table, and her fingers automatically went back to the cuff of her left sleeve. The seam had unravelled. She inserted her right thumb into it and began tugging at it lightly, widening the opening. The silence weighed down on them, oppressive. Brian sipped water. Waited. Next to him, Liam sat impassively, studying Alice.

'It's quiet,' Alice offered, at last.

'I'm sorry?'

'The office,' Alice clarified. 'I like going in early to get a head start on the day. Once people start coming in, the phone starts ringing, and my email inbox begins pinging – it gets harder to block time for deep work.'

Brian nodded. 'So you went in at seven thirty, and then?'

'Stella – that's my assistant,' Alice said. 'She called me en route. Told me what happened, and Willy... err William Grayson, my boss, he... he wanted an all-hands meeting to discuss a game plan. What we'd do to respond to the backlash.'

'Right. So you brought in Sir Russ? How does it work?' Brian asked.

It could be nothing. But it seemed to him like a pretty astonishing coincidence that, on the morning of her husband's murder, Alice was working for the very client who had fired him for misconduct. Could there be something there? And what might that connection be?

Alice scoffed. 'Who? Russ Bidmead?' She wasn't

making any effort to conceal her contempt. 'That's not his style. He messes the bed and moves on while his underlings handle it. Because that's who we are to him. Underlings, not partners.'

Brian felt himself tense with anticipation. This was their opening.

'So you don't like him much, then?' he asked.

Alice shook her head and didn't hold back. 'Not really. Nightmare client. He thinks fawning adoration is the only acceptable reaction to anything he says.'

'So it's personal, then? You have a personal dislike for him?'

Her brow furrowed. 'I'm not sure where you're going with this, Inspector.'

'Just answer the question.'

'I don't think he's a very nice man, no.'

'Because he's a bad client, or because of what Mango Bank did to your husband?'

At his question, her face rearranged itself into... Aye, that was confusion. The reaction took Brian aback. Not a single flicker of understanding about what he was talking about. Had Higgins hidden the dire situation his business was in? He wouldn't have been the first spouse to do so. But how did the pieces all fit?

'I'm sorry?' she asked. Her fingers stopped fidgeting, and she looked up at them, suddenly alert.

'Well, Mango Bank fired Ray, and he'd been struggling to get work in,' Brian elaborated. 'That must've stung. Especially with things being how they were. With his health.'

Alice's face went from confused to completely befuddled. 'Excuse me?'

'The cancer. We know about that, Alice. And – I'm going to be honest with you here – we're wondering why you didn't tell us. It seems like a pretty significant thing to leave out.'

Alice dropped her gaze. Began shaking her head in slow motion. The frizzed-up clumps of her hair didn't move. 'I've no idea what you're on about, Inspector,' she said, her tone measured. 'What cancer?'

Brian exchanged a look with Liam, who shrugged. Brian turned back and studied her. Shoulders slumped. Eyes downcast. Head still moving slowly from one side to another, a mechanical manifestation of denial. For all intents and purposes, she seemed utterly clueless about what he'd just told her. But how could that be possible? Hiding that you're going through a rough patch at work is one thing. Hiding cancer from the person you were married to, shared a bed with, was completely different. Even if Higgins hadn't told her, how could she not have realised he was struggling? That he was ill?

'You didn't know?' Brian asked. His tone was dubious, but he'd been thrown for a loop. Just when he thought he had it worked out, this case kept moving the goalposts.

'I didn't know what?' Alice said.

No. There was no way somebody could feign ignorance so well. Either she genuinely didn't know, or she was a psychopath who had them wrapped around her little finger. And that didn't fit with her behaviour at all. None of it seemed rehearsed or superficial.

'We spoke to Dr Craig, your GP, and to Ray's oncologist,' Brian said. 'He had stage three lymphoma. He'd been undergoing chemotherapy.'

Alice doubled over. Shuddered. 'But that, can't—How? When was this diagnosed? Was it recent? When did he see a specialist and start treatment?' The barrage of questions stopped abruptly as her voice broke. She sobbed quietly.

Brian shifted in his seat – which was more accurately described as an instrument of torture than a chair. His arse was numb. But, more than that, Alice's raw emotion was making him extremely uncomfortable. It was—

—how I feel inside.

He cleared his throat. Took a breath. Leaned forward and softened his tone.

'Do you need a break, Alice?'

Alice looked up at them, making no effort to wipe the tears that were flowing freely down her cheeks.

'Look. I didn't know. I didn't know any of it. You have to believe me, OK? We were—' She convulsed. Emitted a strangled laugh. 'I was leaving him.'

Chapter Twenty-Three

ALICE'S WORDS HUNG BETWEEN THEM, CRACKLING with intensity. Brian held his breath, as if even the barely audible sound of air filling his lungs would break the spell.

'He—'

Her voice wavered. She put her face in her hands and sat still, sobbing softly, shoulders shuddering. When she lifted her head, she looked more composed, but her eyes were red-rimmed and there were dark circles beneath them.

'He changed. He—' She clutched at her water glass, drained what was left in it. Wordlessly, Brian refilled it. She gave him a grateful look.

'He was always a driven man,' she said, after drinking down most of the fresh glass. Her gaze was fixed firmly in front of her as she spoke. Her voice flat. Toneless. 'But... I don't know. I guess he got to a point where his work took over and nothing else mattered anymore. He was preoccupied all the time. He started coming to bed later and later. And then he took to sleeping in the spare room.'

'When was this?' Brian interrupted.

Her eyes looked upward at the interview room's grimy ceiling. 'This was about a year ago,' she said. 'Give or take.'

So right around the time he'd received his diagnosis. 'And he didn't tell you whether anything was wrong?' Brian asked.

'No,' Alice said emphatically. 'I tried to get to the bottom of it. I really did. But I just couldn't get through to him. It was like trying to have a conversation with a brick wall. He'd ignore me completely. Or he'd say he was fine and storm off. Or get… aggressive.'

Brian's ears perked up. Was she about to give them motive?

'How do you mean, aggressive?' he asked.

'How do you think I mean, Inspector?' She gave him a stern look. And, for a brief moment, Brian saw the ghost of the woman Layton had described to them as snobbish, but which Brian thought would be more accurate to call *assertive*. A woman who didn't suffer fools.

Brian leaned forward. Spoke softly. Confidentially. 'Look, Alice,' he said. 'Nobody would blame you if—'

'I. Didn't. Kill. Him,' she snapped, enunciating every word. She held his eyes for the entire time while she said it, her gaze never wavering. It was incredibly convincing, and, once again, he wondered if he was mistaken. Except …

No. The content of the email he'd received was his trump card. He wasn't going to play it just yet.

He changed tack. 'How do you know Danny Walton?' he asked her.

'Danny who?' she said. Her voice cracked on the last syllable. She was back on shaky ground.

'There's no use denying it, Alice,' Brian said, pressing his advantage. 'We know he's a trainer at your gym, and you're Facebook friends.'

'I'm Facebook friends with lots of people,' she fired back. 'Many of them people I haven't seen or talked to in years.' But she was still avoiding his gaze.

Brian folded his hands in front of him on the table. Looked at her intently. 'That's a fair point,' he said. 'But I doubt any of those friends have a key to your house, do they? So how do you know Danny Walton?'

She recoiled as if he'd slapped her.

'What are you insinuating, Inspector?'

Brian straightened up and puffed his chest. He'd got under her skin. He could see that. Her face was flushed, and she'd ripped the seam of her cuff all the way round. Was now busy worrying at a loose thread. Some more careful prodding, and she'd unload everything.

'I'm insinuating nothing,' he said calmly. 'It's a fact that Danny Walton had a key to your home. And it's also a fact that he showed up on your doorstep on Monday at seven in the morning. We have it on video.'

He stood up on legs that felt shaky, partly from sitting in the uncomfortable chair, partly from his unplanned dash after Walton down Inchview Way, and partly from the whisky. He laid his hands on the table, palms down, and bored into her with a steely gaze.

'So,' he said. 'I'm sure you'll understand if I'm a bit

thrown. Why, if you don't know Danny Walton, did he show up at your house on the morning your husband was murdered and let himself in with a key?'

'You'll have to ask him that,' Alice said, her eyes fixed on her restless fingers.

'Och. We've tried. Believe me,' Brian said, standing straight and taking two steps back. 'Except the minute he saw my warrant card, he legged it. It's why we were held up, you see?'

Alice said nothing, but her lip trembled.

It was time to dial up the heat to eleven.

'How do you explain your DNA under Ray's fingernails and on the knife?' he spat.

Her mouth made an O of surprise. She looked up at him, slack-jawed. Lost for words. The voice at the back of his head, which kept nagging him that something wasn't right, that he was barking up the wrong tree while the real killer walked away into the sunset, grew louder.

'My what?' she said.

'Your DNA,' Brian repeated. 'We took a sample, remember? For elimination purposes. Except we found it under Ray's fingernails and on the knife.'

He paused.

'The knife he was murdered with,' he said, punctuating every word with a stab of his index finger on the desktop.

Alice's throat worked.

'That's how you got the wound on your wrist, isn't it?' Brian pressed. 'He grabbed you during the attack.'

'No. No, I didn't kill him,' she insisted. 'You have this all wrong.' But her right hand moved protectively over her left wrist. It was all the confirmation he needed. That wound was no dog bite. She'd lied outright. Higgins had hurt her.

'He attacked you. So you defended yourself, and it all got a bit out of hand,' Brian continued, implacable. 'And once you realised what you'd done, you went to the gym to alibi yourself and asked your friend Danny Walton for help. Except he couldn't handle the scene and ran off. Let you down. Is that about the long and short of it?'

She sat there, in stony silence, shaking her head in negation and gripping her left wrist so hard her knuckles were white and the blue veins on the back of her hand stuck out, pushing through the thin skin.

She squeezed, tightening her grip. Then released.

Squeezed. Released.

Squeezed. Released.

'Alice?' Brian said, more gently. 'Help us help you. Nobody'd blame you if you were defending yourself. If you did it because Ray made you feel unsafe.'

She stopped shaking her head and gave him a defiant look.

'I think I'll speak to my solicitor now.'

Chapter Twenty-Four

Brian flipped through the umpteenth photo from Danny Walton's packed Facebook feed – a snap of him brandishing barbeque tongs while wearing a novelty kitchen apron with Michelangelo's *David* printed across the front – and pushed his laptop away in disgust. Once Alice had played the solicitor card, they'd been forced to pause the interview. That had been an hour ago. An hour Brian had spent pretending to trawl through Walton's social media accounts and the Police National Computer in the hope he might figure out where to look for Walton if not at home, at the gym, or at Reid's Antiques. In the meantime, Alice's solicitor – a bloke who still had faint traces of acne on his cheeks, but whose shock of silver hair jarred with his unlined skin – had arrived, and they were conferring in the interview room.

He leaned back in his office chair and ran a hand through hair, which, if possible, felt thinner than it had been that morning. He sighed wearily and rubbed his stinging eyes. Considered another cheeky nip from his stashed whisky bottle, but thought the better of it. Not now. Not if he was going to interview Alice with her solicitor present. He'd make it up once he got back home. If he did get home. The way things were shaping up, it was going to be a late one.

He blew a raspberry and closed his eyes. The truth was that, instead of giving him the clarity he craved, what he'd learned from Alice during the interview had confused him further. On the one hand, DNA was damning evidence. And asking for her solicitor when she'd started out by saying she had nothing to hide wasn't a good look. On the other, the murder weapon was a knife from the block on her own kitchen counter. Any solicitor worth his fee could plausibly explain the DNA away. She'd cut her finger while chopping veggies for tea. Or shed skin cells. Sweated into the handle. Just three perfectly reasonable explanations he'd thought up off the top of his head. Similarly, Ray grabbing her wrist hard enough to hurt during an argument didn't necessarily mean said argument had escalated into a stabbing.

More than that, though, something just wasn't adding up. She seemed too sincere. News of the cancer seemed to have genuinely blindsided her. And, if not in the heat of an argument, why would she kill him? What would her motive be? She had a good job that made her financially independent. There were no weans to think of. And, so far, they hadn't found any substantial savings, investments, or life insurance policies that might have tempted her. Plus, if money were the motive, you'd think she'd choose a less conspicuous way to murder him than making him bleed out all over their kitchen floor.

Ach, Christ. What a fucking shiteshow.

He glanced at his wristwatch. Seven p.m. There was a knock at his office door.

'Fiona,' Brian said. 'You're still here?'

'I was about to leave for the day, sir.' Fiona entered his office. She looked as tired as he felt. 'Just came by to say Alice is done conferring with her solicitor.'

Brian rapped his knuckles twice on his desk and got up. 'Great, thanks.' He walked to the door. 'Not that we're going to get much out of her now that her solicitor's involved. But we'll see. Stranger things have happened.'

In the interview room, Alice was looking much more together than when they'd left her, even though her eyes were raw and still had the faraway look of somebody who couldn't believe what they were going through was real life and not just a bad dream. Next to her, the solicitor was leaning back in his chair with one leg crossed over the other, his leather briefcase balanced precariously on his knee.

When Brian entered, the solicitor swept the briefcase beneath his chair, stood up, gave him a peremptory handshake, and sat back down.

'At this time, Mrs Higgins wishes to make a brief statement,' the solicitor said, getting right down to business. 'Then I must ask that you either charge her or let her go.'

Brian pressed play on the ageing recorder and sat down. He wasn't holding his breath for a breakthrough, but he was still interested in seeing how she'd play this. Whatever happened now, it would give him an insight into what she was thinking. He folded his hands in front of him. Waited.

Alice looked up, avoiding his gaze, then cleared her throat.

'Ray and I,' she began, 'had been de facto separated for several months before his murder.'

Brian raised an eyebrow at the legalese, but said nothing. It was obvious she'd worked out what she was going to say with her solicitor. But that was to be expected.

'Around the time of his murder,' she continued, 'we were, for all intents and purposes, living as roommates, not as a married couple. On the few occasions we did speak to each other, things got heated. And, on the seventh of January, when I told him I intended to file for divorce and asked him to move out of our home, he—'

She choked up. Sniffed. Wiped her nose savagely with her hoodie sleeve, which had taken an even worse battering in the time she'd been speaking with her solicitor.

'He refused flat out. Grabbed me by the wrist,' she repeated. 'Injuring me. It didn't go any further than that, but I was afraid, so I decided I'd be the one to move out of the house.'

Another pause. She stared at the desk, her throat working.

'As I've already stated to the police, on the eighth of January, I left home for the gym at five thirty a.m., after which I went to the office. Two police constables arrived at my workplace and asked for me at around twelve thirty p.m. They informed me Ray had been stabbed, so I went home as quickly as I could. I did not hurt or kill my husband. I'd never do that. Ever.'

Brian blew air through his teeth. His nerves tingled.

'And what about Walton?' he pressed. 'Where does he fit into all this?'

'No comment,' Alice said, her face a rigid mask.

'Why did he have a key to your house?' Brian insisted.

'No comment.'

'Why was he there on the morning of the murder?'

'No comment.'

'Do you know his current whereabouts?'

'No comment.'

'Al—'

'You heard Mrs Higgins,' the solicitor cut in. 'She has nothing further to say at this time. So what's it going to be? Is she under arrest, or can she leave?'

Brian's fist clenched. He bit back a scream of frustration.

'So?' the solicitor prodded.

Brian lowered his eyes. 'No. At this stage she's not under arrest,' he said reluctantly. 'But I must advise her to stay local for the next twenty-eight days.'

He'd take what they learned to the Procurator Fiscal, and it would be up to them to decide whether there was enough to charge her. Personally, he didn't think the PF would go for it. Not yet. Her story had holes big enough to drive a lorry through, and her refusal to comment on Walton was suspect as hell. But that didn't change the fact that what they had was a theory backed up with mostly circumstantial evidence.

If they were going to prove she killed her husband, they needed more. Something definite, that left no doubt she was guilty.

The question was, where were they going to find it?

Or, more accurately, was this all just a waste of time?

Chapter Twenty-Five

During the first ten or so years of our acquaintance, I don't think we spoke more than six or seven times. And, mostly it was 'Hiya, how are you?' and 'Hiya, how are you?' back. You know how it is. The kind of meaningless, mechanical exchange you have with people you don't really know that well to stop and chit-chat with, but know well enough that it would be awkward not to acknowledge each other when you crossed paths.

I never did have a strong opinion about our relationship. Well, about the lack thereof. It was neither here nor there. We lived close, but moved in different circles. Our lives were poles apart.

And then, out of the blue, we became friends.

Except, were we ever friends? Really? Hindsight is twenty-twenty and all that. But I honestly don't think so. I think it was a matter of convenience – of 'what use might you be to me in the future?' – all along.

I remember the night when we first talked – really

talked – not because of what happened with us, but because of the test I was studying for. Statistics. The bane of my existence.

It was unseasonably hot, which didn't help. I kept banging my head against the metaphorical wall, trying to work out the differences between means, medians, and modes to no avail. It all kept blending together into complete nonsense, making my head feel like it was fit to explode. So I stared out the window at the trees in the distance, barely registering what I was seeing, pen poised over a blank page in my notebook, until the voices brought me back.

My mother and father argued about two things above all else. Money (specifically, my mother's inability to stick to a budget) and alcohol (namely, my father's inability not to finish a bottle once he'd opened it). That night, it was a heady mix of both.

'And you spent it on that?!' my father bellowed, banishing all thought of mathematics from my head. 'Are you mad? It's ghastly.'

'Better than literally pissing it away,' my mother shot back, her voice so cutting I winced, even though there was a closed door, a corridor, and a flight of stairs between me and the person her barb was directed toward.

If she'd meant to push my father's temper to the brink, she'd succeeded. The shouting became louder and more incoherent. And then it was followed by the sounds of smashing crockery and several howls of protest.

As far as my parents' fighting went, this wasn't the worst I'd seen up to that point. Not even close. That had probably been when my father tipped the dining table over, food and all, then went into the kitchen and ripped out the stove. But that night, with my skin flushed and clammy from the heat and concepts I couldn't seem to make head or tail of swirling around in my head like a thin soup, I couldn't take it. The walls of my room closed in on me. My chest constricted. I felt trapped. Suffocated. It was all too much. I had to go out. Get some air. Step away from the constantly ticking time bomb that was my home life, if only for a brief respite.

One of the trees outside my room was close enough to the window that I could reach out, grab on to a thick branch, and shimmy down into the bushes. I'd done it many times before, usually on those nights when sleep wouldn't come – either because my bottom hurt too much from the beating I'd been given for some perceived affront to my parents' authority, or because it felt like I was locked in a cage, with no means of escape.

Beyond the bushes, there was a narrow gravel path that cut through the trees for three miles before doubling back and circling around the other side of the estate. When I slipped out after dark, I'd walk and walk. Sometimes for an hour or more. I'd think about how much I hated the constant drama. How the atmosphere in the house always felt dangerous, like both my mother and father were seconds away from making a permanent mistake. Crossing the point of no return. What would happen then? Where would I go? Who would I live with? But, other times, I thought, so what? It might not be so bad if the worst happened. I could even see the appeal. Perhaps I'd get adopted by a nice family. A boring, predictable family. A family where the parents weren't at each other's throats all the time, and I was given the space I needed to just ... be.

I'm not sure what I was thinking about on this particular night. But, anyway, it's beside the point. What matters is, whatever thoughts were going through my head, I was so engrossed in them that I didn't see the lamplights in the clearing. I just kept going and stumbled right into a large plastic cooler.

I looked up, startled, and saw ten pairs of eyes studying me, first crinkled with fear, and then, as soon as they realised I wasn't an adult who'd come to lay down the law, with surprise and curiosity. The smell of barbecue hung in the air, making my mouth water and reminding me I'd skipped dinner. A bottle of vodka, half empty, was going around the circle they'd formed on the ground.

My initial reaction was to back away. They were a few years older than me, and we were chalk and cheese. So I was afraid they'd make fun. Pick on me. Or threaten me in case I told on them. But then, somebody – I don't remember who – held out the bottle to me. I took a small sip. Grimaced. Spat it out.

They laughed. But it wasn't malicious. Or, at least, it didn't seem so. It was good-natured. Conspiratorial, even. Like they'd decided they were going to let me in on their little secret.

And then they made room for me in the circle so I could join them.

It was that easy. Can you believe it?

When I returned home, I wasn't dizzy with vodka,

but with excitement. Because, for the first time ever in my little life, I'd felt like I could be somebody else. Somebody different. Better. Perhaps even somebody who deserved their parents' unconditional acceptance.

God, I really misjudged what was going on, didn't I?

But there's no shying away from the truth. That's how it felt in the moment.

And, yes, I'll admit it. I revelled in it.

Especially after Lucy almost died.

Chapter Twenty-Six

Thursday, 11 January 2024

Below the two photos of Ray Higgins on the whiteboard in the conference room, someone had hung a photo of Alice – a gym selfie they'd lifted from her Facebook profile – with *MOTIVE?* printed in black marker beneath it, alongside nineteen-year-old Danny Walton's mugshot, captioned, *WITNESS?/ACCOMPLICE?*

Despite having issued a public appeal, Walton had proved stubbornly elusive. Other than a handful of false alarms, there'd been no reported sightings of him after he'd lost them in Starbucks the previous afternoon. So, having endured another night of tossing and turning and just about two hours of a whisky-induced stupor, Brian was back at it, hip-deep in the haystack he hoped would produce the needle he needed to stitch the case closed.

He sipped from a mug of weak coffee. He'd diluted it heavily with milk to blunt the bitter, burnt-plastic taste, but to no avail. He grimaced. Wished he had a nip of

Monkey Shoulder he could fortify it with. He surveyed the five officers sitting around the table. Fiona, McGillivray, Liam, and two detective constables.

'What do you have for me?' he asked.

McGillivray muttered something that sounded dangerously like it ended in *distillery*. One of the DCs sniggered. Brian stole a glance at Liam, who gave his head an imperceptible shake. He was right. Whatever McGillivray had said, the words were too indistinct for Brian to challenge him openly without risking being told he'd misunderstood. So he said nothing and shot them both a look that said, '*I'm in no mood this morning, so try me. I dare you.*' instead. The DC's facial muscles rearranged themselves into a stricken expression. McGillivray raised his palms in surrender and looked blankly in front of him. Brian nodded approval, his point made, and turned away.

'Sir,' Fiona said.

'Aye?'

'So I've finished going through the Higginses' bank statements, and there are definitely no payments to private healthcare providers or medical insurance premiums that I could find,' she said.

'But?' Brian asked.

'Well, I've gone through the list of private clinics in Strathburgh that offer cancer care,' she said, shuffling through a thin sheaf of papers. 'There's three of them. Spire, Northwestern, and St Ninian's.' She paused. Took a sip of water. Spilled a tiny drop on one of the papers and brushed it away with the tips of her fingers. 'He was registered at St Ninian's,' she finished.

'St Ninian's?' Brian whistled. Out of the three clinics, it was the most exclusive. 'That's like—'

'Three hundred and fifty pounds for a half-hour consultation,' McGillivray finished. 'My mother-in-law looked into getting a hip replacement there. Ended up waiting for her turn on the NHS – they quoted twenty thousand or something ridiculous like that.'

'And do we know what treatment he was getting and how he was paying for it?' Brian asked.

'Not yet,' Fiona said. 'But I have an appointment with the head of oncology in' – she glanced at her watch – 'forty-five minutes.'

St Ninian's had none of the squat boxiness or medicinal smells you'd associate with a hospital. Its long, meticulously landscaped gravel driveway and the traditional sandstone façade, with its evenly spaced sash windows and Ionian columns framing the doorway, gave off boutique-hotel vibes. Whereas, inside, Brian picked up the pleasant scent of vanilla and coconut. The marble tiles sparkled and the stone-grey walls were adorned with framed print reproductions of modernist paintings, including two with the uniquely angular execution that marked them out as Picassos, even to Brian's untrained and inexpert eye.

A smartly dressed receptionist with high cheekbones and lustrous blonde hair styled in a pixie cut pointed them toward a spacious waiting area lined with squishy leather chairs and fresh flowers in crystal vases. Brian and

Fiona had barely sat down when a man with round, wire-rimmed glasses and brown curly hair down to his shoulders walked up to them.

'DS Atwood?' he asked in a pleasant baritone.

'Aye,' Fiona said. 'And this is DI Brandon, my boss.'

'Pleasure to meet you both,' he said, shaking their hands with practised warmth. 'I'm Doctor Bernard Smyth, the head of oncology here at St Ninian's. Please follow me.'

He led them down a wide corridor, his rubber-soled, highly polished Oxfords squeaking faintly, until they turned left and stopped in front of a gleaming oak door marked with his name on a brushed silver tag. He turned the knob, walked in, and sank into a white mesh-backed office chair behind a large, cluttered desk.

'Please have a seat,' he said, his tone courteous and quietly confident. The tone he probably used with all his patients to set them at ease.

Brian and Fiona sat in the two chairs in front of the desk. Smyth leaned forward and grasped his hands together, resting his elbows on the desk.

'So,' he said. 'How can I help Strathburgh's finest?'

Brian nodded to Fiona.

'We're here to ask about one of your patients,' Fiona began. 'Raymond Higgins.'

Smyth's brow creased briefly, then smoothed itself out, his expression returning to neutral. 'Ah, yes,' he said. 'I read about his murder in the paper. Terrible.' He shook his head and tutted his disapproval, as if to say, '*What's the world coming to?*'

Brian studied him. Behind his desk, Smyth seemed

relaxed and at ease. Fully in charge of his domain. And that made his concern come across as being only skin deep. A veneer. An emotion he'd expressed because it was the done thing, not because he really cared one way or another. Then again, Brian supposed taking every case personally was the path to—

Despair.

—needless stress.

'Can you tell us how long you'd been seeing Mr Higgins?' Fiona asked.

Smyth turned to his MacBook, which was resting on a stand. He moved a wireless mouse around. Double-clicked. Studied the screen, humming tunelessly under his breath.

'Mr Higgins had his first appointment in October last year,' he said. 'The thirty-first, to be exact. He'd been diagnosed with lymphoma that wasn't responding well to treatment, and he wanted a second opinion. So we ran some tests.'

'And what was the outcome of those tests?' Fiona asked.

Smyth cleared his throat. 'They weren't promising, DS Atwood,' he said. 'The cancer had spread, despite two rounds of chemotherapy.'

So far, nothing they didn't already know. But Fiona was doing the right thing letting Smyth relate the facts at his own pace. It gave him the space to reveal details he might gloss over if they rushed him.

'How did he take the news?' Fiona asked. 'How did he seem to you?'

Smyth sighed. Brushed a stray curl away from his eyes.

'May I speak frankly, DS Atwood?' he said.

'Please do,' Fiona replied.

Brian was intrigued. Why had Smyth felt the need to preface his answer like that?

'Telling a patient their cancer isn't responding to treatment is always difficult,' Smyth said carefully. 'It's not a conversation any doctor looks forward to. Obviously. Nobody takes it well. But different people handle it, you know ... differently.'

He spread his hands in a preacher-like gesture and smiled faintly. The smile didn't touch his eyes.

'How do you mean, Dr Smyth?' Fiona asked.

'Well,' Smyth continued without missing a beat. 'You know. Some are tearful. Some take it with a stiff upper lip. Some come right out and ask how long they have left, saying they want the brutal truth.'

'And Mr Higgins?' Fiona asked. 'What did he do?'

Smyth bit his lip. Gave them a brief sad-puppy look.

'Mr Higgins, how shall I put it?' He ummed. 'He didn't take it well. He flew off the handle.'

Brian felt a rush of adrenaline. If Smyth was about to say what Brian thought he was about to say, it would confirm that he had a penchant for violence. Which might buttress their theory about Alice killing him in self-defence.

'How did he "fly off the handle"?' Brian asked.

'Tell you what, DS Brandon—' Smyth said.

'D*I* Brandon,' Brian corrected him.

'DI Brandon. My apologies,' Smyth said. 'It was

unpleasant. He stood up. Raised his voice. It was quite scary, actually. Of course, I told him I understood the news was distressing. But I warned him I'd have to call security if he didn't calm down.'

'And did he?' Brian asked. 'Calm down?'

'Ye-es ... Up to a point,' he said.

Brian let this last statement hang.

'He seemed to be having a very hard time accepting his illness and how it had progressed. And he'd clearly done his research,' Smyth continued, when neither Brian nor Fiona said anything. 'He asked me all sorts of questions about treatments that aren't available on the NHS and whether we'd be able to offer them.'

'And, do you?' Fiona asked.

This was very interesting. Higgins obviously had a temper. And it also looked like he was ready to do whatever it took to save his life. The question was, where did he plan to get the money to pay for it all, when his business had nosedived and he hadn't told his wife about any of it?

'Well,' Smyth continued, 'some of the treatments he asked about aren't offered on the NHS because they've been proven not to be worth it. They're costly, and have significant side effects for little benefit. But I did suggest an alternative therapy, yes – with the caveat that it was still experimental and there were no guarantees, you understand.'

'Of course. And did he agree to try?' Fiona asked.

They'd both leaned forward in their chairs. Brian's head was spinning, trying to connect several dots he still couldn't see clearly.

'He'd just finished his second round of chemotherapy, so we couldn't get started straight away. We recommend a break from treatment so the body can recover, you see,' Smyth said. 'But yes. He agreed. He was very keen to get started as soon as possible. And once we were happy he'd had an adequate break and his body was up to it, we began.'

This was it.

'And had you billed him for any of it, before his murder?' Brian asked, itching to hear the answer. 'Or did you at least talk about how he planned to pay?'

'Oh, he paid his bills bang on time. No questions asked,' Smyth said approvingly. 'In cash.'

Chapter Twenty-Seven

With no SOCOs or uniforms bustling around the place, no dead body stiffening on the living-room floor, and no spewing widow to handle, an eerie calm had descended over the Higginses' house.

As it was technically still a crime scene, it was unoccupied. Alice Higgins had moved temporarily to an Ibis off the Strathburgh city bypass. But the quiet, punctuated by the faint hum of the American-style fridge-freezer and the ticking of the radiators as they cooled, was pregnant with unvoiced violence. Only the pools of Ray Higgins's blood – now dried to a shade of maroon that, had not Brian known better, could've been mistaken for spilled wine – spoke of the horror that had taken place here just four days prior.

'But why here?' Liam, who'd joined them after their chat at St Ninian's, asked for the third time, as he, Brian, and Fiona ducked under the police tape and let themselves in. 'SOCO already searched the place from top to bottom. They didn't find anything.'

'The cash had to have come from somewhere,' Brian insisted. 'If it's not in the bank, it stands to reason he hid it. SOCO might've missed it.'

'It could be in self-storage,' Liam countered.

'Aye, it could be in self-storage,' Brian agreed. 'We should check whether Higgins had a unit. But this is as good a place as any to start looking for it.'

Liam and Fiona both scanned the living room dubiously.

'Tell you what,' Brian said. 'Let's approach this logically. Let's start with the office. Maybe there's a hidden compartment or a safe we didn't find because we weren't looking for it. Then we'll try the bedrooms, the attic, and move on to the rest of the house.'

'I could do downstairs while you do upstairs,' Fiona suggested. 'It might save us some time.'

'Aye, OK. Give us a shout if you find anything.'

Brian and Liam took the stairs to Higgins' office. The systematically organised workspace Brian remembered from his previous visit had been torn down and rearranged by someone who didn't have one iota of Higgins's attention to detail. Books had been put back on the shelves haphazardly, several of them with their spines turned inward so you couldn't read their titles. The pen holder was lying empty on its side, the pens fanned out on the desk and the keyboard and mouse stacked carelessly next to them. The running medals had been taken off the display and left in a pile on the carpet.

The state of the room made a compelling case for the thoroughness of the crime scene team's search. But Brian wasn't going to let this dishearten him. Cash wasn't like bank accounts or cards – numbers on a screen. It was tangible. Took up space. It needed to be stored in a physical location. If Higgins had had enough of it lying around to pay St Ninian's astronomical fees, they'd find it. They *had to* find it, he corrected himself. There was no way he could've magicked it into existence.

Brian got to work taking the books and assorted knick-knacks off the shelves so he could check whether there was some secret compartment behind the wall. In all his years of policing, he'd never stumbled on a hidden safe, but you never knew. A picture was starting to emerge of a man who'd been in full-on fight mode, desperately hanging on to dear life and willing to do whatever it took to conquer his illness. Who knew what went through the mind of somebody like that?

Extreme pressure—

You mean despair. *Say it. Say it. Say it.*

—made people—

You. You. You.

—do things they wouldn't even fathom under normal circumstances. Had Higgins attempted to steal the data on Mango Bank clients so he could use his skills as a penetration tester to dig up dirt and blackmail them for cash? Was that how he'd been raising the funds to pay for his private treatment?

He edged the bookshelf out of the way and squeezed himself in. Ran his palms methodically over every inch of the eggshell-smooth wall. Searching. For what, he didn't know. An invisible panel that sprang open if you pushed it? A notch he could insert his finger into to prise out part of the wall?

'Find anything?' he asked Liam while his palms kept moving.

'Zero. Nada. Zilch,' Liam said from behind him, sounding out of breath. 'Told you there'd be nothing here. They already looked.'

When he'd finished checking all four walls to no avail, Brian walked every inch of the room, putting one foot carefully in front of the other, concentrating on the feel of the subfloor under his feet in case a section of it felt loose. When that didn't turn up anything, he checked the carpet's edges to see if any of it came off. But it had been glued down firmly and wouldn't budge.

'Well, strike one,' Brian said, feeling the faint stirrings of frustration but putting a brave face on it. 'Let's check the bedrooms, and try the attic if that doesn't work.'

The bedrooms had received the same treatment as Higgins's office. In both rooms, the built-in closets' sliding doors were open, coat hangers pushed haphazardly to one side, some of them in a pile on the floor. The drawers were open, socks, underwear, and assorted accessories – scarves, gloves, hats – spilling out of them like woollen guts.

'Where the fuck could he have hidden it?' Brian grunted.

They'd moved back to the landing, and he was pulling down the Ramsay ladder so he could climb up into the attic.

'We're barking up the wrong tree,' Liam said, a lugubrious edge to his voice.

'Jesus, bud,' Brian snapped. 'Aren't you a ray of fucking sunshine.'

Brian placed his foot on the first rung of the ladder and began climbing up into the attic. The ladder had a thin, rickety frame, and it shook ominously as he moved. He gripped the rails tighter.

'I'm just saying,' Liam continued. 'How likely is it he'd leave a pile of cash just lying around the hou—'

'Come and see this!' Fiona's voice, laced with excitement, cut in.

Chapter Twenty-Eight

Brian clambered down the Ramsay ladder and sped to the ground floor, taking the stairs two at a time.

'I'm in the garden,' Fiona called out.

He power-walked through the living area, Liam hot on his heels, stepping over the bloody tracks the killer had made when dragging Higgins from the kitchen, and exited through the bifold doors. Fiona was squatting next to the shed – a large, slate-grey structure that looked much too elegant just to be used for storage – staring at a jumble of grimy, bunched-up kitchen roll, aluminium drinks cans, and assorted plastic and cardboard packaging that was spilling out of the Higginses' green wheelie bin, which was lying on its side in the grass.

'Did you find the cash?' Brian asked breathlessly.

'No,' Fiona said. 'No sign of it so far. But look at this.' She pointed to a can of Monster Energy drink that was peeking out of a large wad of grease-soaked kitchen roll.

'What am I supposed to be seeing?' Brian asked.

He moved closer, his brow furrowing. The thick

runnels of yellow-orange fat on the kitchen roll, which had coagulated into jelly and crusted over, made his stomach lurch. The wad of kitchen roll was lying on top of a half-torn cardboard egg carton stained with what he hoped was dried yolk and fuck knew what else. Coffee grounds? Seasoning? Bits of raw fat and vegetable peel? All of the above? He looked away, wincing at the ripe smell wafting into his nostrils.

'Here,' Fiona said. 'Can't you see it peeking out of the can?'

She produced a pair of nitrile gloves from the back pocket of her trousers and snapped them on. Picked up the Monster Energy can, the lurid green *M* on the black background glinting in the weak early-afternoon sun.

'Still no clue what you're on about, sorry,' Brian said.

Fiona tipped the drinks can. A faint clattering noise came from inside it. A few drops of caramel-coloured liquid spilled out onto the kitchen roll, wetting a patch of grease. Fiona grunted. Shook the can, which made more clattering noises.

'I think this is why they missed it,' she said. 'Looks like it's stuck in there.'

Brian kept his eyes studiously on the grass, well away from the nauseating ocean of rubbish stretching out in front of him.

Fiona inserted her gloved index finger into the can's opening and fished around. With her finger still inside, she tipped the can upside down.

'Careful,' Brian said, 'You don't want to cut your finger on the edge.' Christ knew what bacteria had colonised the can during its residence in the wheelie bin.

'It's fine,' Fiona grunted. 'I. Have it...'

In a flash, Fiona discarded the can and picked up what had fallen out of it: a rectangular piece of white plastic with a pink cap.

Brian recognised what it was immediately. How could he not? For fourteen long months, before his marriage imploded with the most underwhelming of whimpers, he and his ex-wife had spent a ridiculous chunk of their grocery budget on those blasted things. And, with every negative result, his sense that he was letting her down, that he was failing at the one thing every single living organism, no matter how rudimentary, was supposed to be able to do, had raised the unspoken tension between them just a little bit higher. From guitar string, to ukulele string, to violin string. Until it was stretched so tight it had snapped clean off, taking a chunk of his heart with it.

Fiona passed him the pregnancy test so he could see for himself.

Pregnant and a circle with two vertical lines and, beneath it, *Not Pregnant* and a circle with one vertical line were printed in grey on the test's side. In the oval window next to the instructions, there was a thick pink vertical line and a faint but visible second pink vertical line.

'It's positive,' she said.

Chapter Twenty-Nine

'You need to level with us,' Brian said, pacing around the interview room. 'And the sooner you do it, the better.'

At the table, Alice Higgins sat impassively, her hands folded in her lap, lips pressed in an invisible line. Her solicitor was sitting next to her, legs crossed loosely, head resting in his palm, doodling on a notepad with his free hand. Across from them, Liam looked on, his hands across his rumpled shirt, his hair looking like he'd inserted his index finger into a socket.

All the excitement – plus the fact Brian had only managed one mug of ghastly station coffee and skipped lunch – had turned what, that morning, were just faint tendrils of discomfort licking at the edges of his temples into a pounding headache. He loosened his tie and unbuttoned his collar. It didn't help him breathe easier. The air in the windowless room was stifling.

'Did Ray know you're pregnant?' Brian repeated. 'Is that why you argued?'

He stopped pacing. Closed his eyes and pinched the bridge of his nose. Bright white spots flashed in front of his field of vision. God, if he didn't eat something soon, he was going to pass out right here. But he needed to get to the bottom of this. And he wasn't going to make any headway unless he softened his approach. The bad cop routine wasn't working.

He walked to the interview table. Dropped into the chair next to Liam's like a sack of potatoes. Sighed. Unbuttoned his left shirt cuff and rolled the sleeve midway up his forearm, slowly, precisely, then did the same with his right sleeve. He tried to make eye contact with Alice, but she was looking fixedly in front of her.

'Look, Alice,' he said, his voice barely above a whisper. 'We're not trying to fit you up. All we want – all *I* want – is to get to the truth. To find out who killed your husband. Don't you want that, too?'

'I don't know how many times I have to tell you,' she said tonelessly. 'I had nothing to do with Ray's murder. Nothing at all.'

Brian took a deep breath. Counted to ten. 'And I want to believe you, Alice,' he said. 'I really do. But I have to go where the evidence leads me, and it keeps leading me straight to you. See my problem?'

He let this sink in. Waited a beat. But Alice said nothing further.

'It's not just yourself you have to think about now, is it?' Brian gambled. For all he knew, she intended to terminate the pregnancy and his appeal would fall flat. But he had to try. He was running out of ways to get through to her.

'I ...' she began, then slumped in her chair. 'Look.'

Her hands kept fidgeting with the bottom button of her navy blazer. Her nails looked even more ragged than they did the last time they'd interviewed her, the skin beneath them chewed red and raw.

'You're not going to believe me,' she said matter-of-factly.

Brian waited another beat. 'Try me.'

'You don't have to say anything,' the solicitor reminded her. But his protest was weak. Bored. The tone of somebody who could think of a million and one other places he'd rather be. Where Alice's reticence had set Brian's teeth on edge, it looked like the endless back-and-forth had made the solicitor mentally check out.

Alice's mouth opened. Then shut. Her jaw worked. She looked intently in front of her, the battle between the part of her brain that wanted her to unburden herself and the part that was telling her it was better to keep mum playing out on her face. In the creases on her brow and around her eyes. Brian waited, his head pounding in time with his heart, his chest stuck mid-inhale.

'He wasn't always a bastard, you know?' she began. 'Ray. When we met, he was funny. Carefree. Always up to dropping everything at a moment's notice and hopping on a plane or going for a road trip. He made me laugh. He bought me flowers for no reason.'

She looked up at Brian.

'And then he just...' She sighed.

Brian said nothing. He realised his fists were clenched and he was on the edge of his seat. Was she about to confess, in a roundabout way? Or was she going to upend all his certainties?

'I didn't mean it to happen,' she continued.

With a huge effort of will, Brian restrained himself from shooting to his feet.

'The affair, I mean,' she clarified. Her eyes took on a flinty look. She curled her lip into a half-amused smile. 'No, I didn't kill him. Banish the thought, Inspector.'

Brian was getting whiplash. What the hell was she driving at? But he didn't dare prod her, in case it put her off.

'But Danny was so nice. So considerate.' She gave him a defiant look. 'When I was around Ray, I felt like a ghost. Like I was two inches tall. Danny made me feel good about myself again. He made me feel appreciated. Important. Loved.'

Brian couldn't believe his ears. Was she saying what he thought she was? That she and Danny Walton had had an affair and she was pregnant as a result?

'What really happened on Monday, Alice?' he ventured. 'Why was Danny at your house? Are you covering for him? Is that it?'

'No!' she protested. 'No. Danny had nothing to do with this!'

She placed both hands palms down on the table. Leaned forward. Looked Brian straight in the eye.

'Look. This is the whole truth, OK? I swear.' She exhaled. 'Ray knew, somehow. About me and Danny. About the pregnancy. He. Knew.'

She punctuated the last two words with her index finger.

'I think he had access to my phone, and he'd had it for quite some time, because he brought up stuff he couldn't have possibly found out about unless he'd been going through my emails and texts.' She swallowed. Her eyes glistened with unshed tears. 'He... he said if I left him he'd ruin me. He was... he was like a wild animal, foaming at the mouth.'

'So what did you do?' Brian asked in a barely audible whisper, unable to contain himself any longer.

'So I slipped him two sleeping pills to make sure he'd still be out for the count when I left the house,' she blurted. 'And then I packed a bag.'

Holy. Shite. She'd drugged him. So that was why his killer had had such an easy time overpowering him.

'This was Monday?' Brian asked.

His voice was almost inaudible over the hiss of the recorder.

'Sunday night,' Alice said. 'I crushed them and mixed them into a mug of tea. Except, in the rush to leave the house, I forgot my Apple Watch. I'd taken it off to charge, and I didn't put it back on.' She barked out a laugh. It was a humourless sound. Wretched. 'I should've just left it. But I was scared he could hack into it somehow. And Danny offered to get it for me, and here we are.'

'What are you saying, Alice?' Brian asked. 'Did Danny see something?'

'He ...' She hesitated. 'I think he barged in on the killer. But he won't tell me what he saw.'

Now, Brian did jump to his feet. The plastic chair's legs squeaked on the sticky vinyl.

'Where is Danny now?' he demanded.

Alice just stared at him dumbly, spent.

'Alice, where is he?' Brian repeated. 'We need to speak to him as soon as possible. He has critical information that could lead us to Ray's killer.'

Alice bowed her head. She was a statue. Deathly still. Deathly quiet. Tears streamed silently down her cheeks.

'Alice, I know Ray didn't do right by you,' Brian said, wincing as the words came out. 'Not doing right by you' was probably the understatement of the century. But he couldn't openly say that the man was a bastard. He had to keep this professional. 'Perhaps you might even think he deserved it. But nobody has the right to go around stabbing people to death in their own homes. If they did it to Ray, they might do it to somebody else. And where do you draw the line?'

The words hung in the air between them. Even the solicitor, who'd faded into the background, looked transfixed. Had he botched it? Or had his words managed to get through to her?

'I'll ...' she hesitated. Sighed. 'All right. But let me speak to him first, OK? I'll persuade him to come in.'

Chapter Thirty

I DON'T KNOW ABOUT YOU, BUT I'VE NEVER BEEN particularly fond of dogs. They're messy. Slobbery. Needy. And just way too happy. How can you trust anything that has so much boundless enthusiasm for life all the time, for no apparent reason?

But Lucy... Well, Lucy converted me. It was hard not to love her. She drew you in and stole your heart.

I met her about a week after I'd stumbled into that barbeque. School was out, and I'd pushed any thoughts of studying to the back of my mind. I was fairly sure I'd failed statistics, but I told myself I'd worry about that in September. In the meantime, the lazy summer months were stretching out before me. And, other than my part-time job, I had nothing much to do except read and roam around the countryside, hoping I'd bump into my new friends again.

Lucy was a Yorkie with gorgeous, silky brown fur you could never tire of sinking your hands into. Feisty, but affectionate. She could spend hours playing fetch or just chasing her tail while we watched her and passed a bottle of wine around. But she could also be unbelievably calm. Happy to just lay around, basking in the sun, or snuggling.

Our first encounter wasn't very promising. The minute she saw me, she unleashed a volley of barks, then reared up on her hind legs and pawed at me. You might think it's stupid. And I know how it sounds. It's not like she was a Great Dane or a St Bernard. But despite her small size, she was thrumming with energy, and it made me nervous. There was an air of unpredictability about her that set me on edge. Like being locked in a room with a bomb you know is there but aren't quite sure if or when it will go off.

When they saw me flush, they laughed at me. And, for a minute, I thought I'd made a terrible mistake. Maybe the night of the barbecue they'd just wanted to keep me sweet so I wouldn't tell on them. How could I have had the audacity to think they'd want to be friends? With me?

But then that voice set me at ease. 'She's just excited to see you. It's how she is with everyone.'

I peered at Lucy down my nose. Her bubblegum pink tongue was lolling out of her mouth, and she was panting and wagging her tail at a mile a minute. She wasn't baring her teeth or anything like that. So I extended my hand. Tentatively, fearing she'd snap and bite it off. Then more decisively. She licked it. Wagged her tail even harder. So hard I half expected it to fall off.

And that was that. I was in her good books. Part of the pack.

I'll always remember those summer months as some

of the best of my life. We had more sunshine than I'd ever experienced in the ten years since we'd moved. But, more than that, the air felt electric. Ripe with possibilities. I'm not sure how else to explain it. The future was ahead of me and I felt good about it. Even my parents' arguments weren't bothering me that much. And it was all because I'd found people I felt comfortable around who I could spend my free time with, so I never was home long enough for the toxic atmosphere to get to me. Or to get caught in the crossfire.

Lucy was our constant companion throughout. She kind of became our mascot. Showering us with attention. Entertaining us. Even giving us excuses to meet up, because she needed lots of exercise. I know. I know. The person who prefaces their story by saying they never liked dogs turns out to have become a dog person. Even if just a one-very-specific-dog person. Sort of like the atheist who becomes a born-again Christian. Or the three-pack-a-day smoker who quits and starts ranting about lung cancer to every Dick and Jane they meet, right? But ... I suppose you'd have had to meet her to understand.

The day Lucy almost drowned started out like any other. It was a Sunday in August. Hot and muggy. The kind of day when you feel sticky even after you've showered. When everything feels like it requires far too much energy for you to bother trying. We'd all headed to Alkmund Park Pool, which was surprisingly quiet given the weather. Everyone had made an effort, and we'd managed to pull together quite the spread. Fresh butter-and-ham baguettes from Waitrose. Six-packs of Walkers salt-and-vinegar crisps. I'd even pinched a bottle of wine from my father's stash.

With the place mostly to ourselves, we'd settled down in a flat patch of grass, half under the shade and half in the sun so everyone could get their vitamin D and cool off when the heat got too much to bear without moving so far they couldn't be part of the conversation. The water was a panel of clear blue glass. And there wasn't a single cloud marring the sky. You could see for miles.

I'm not sure what we were talking about when it happened, but it wasn't anything particularly heavy. Probably small talk about our plans for later. Or who was better – Britney or Christina. All in good fun, of course. It never got heated. And, all the while, we were sharing crisps out of a pack, passing a bottle of wine around, and lobbing a stick for Lucy to fetch.

Then somebody – I don't remember who – threw the stick into the water. But nobody thought anything of it. Lucy bounded off like a miniature rocket. A dog on a mission. Laser-focused on retrieving it. And we kept arguing good-naturedly, not realising how far out into the lake she'd gone.

When Lucy started barking, the others didn't give it much thought. Yorkies bark almost as much as they breathe. It's what they do. But, I don't know. There was something in her barking that raised my internal alarm. It had a frantic quality. It's hard to explain how I knew. I suppose years of tiptoeing around my parents, of trying to guess their moods and how they might impact the way they'd react even to innocuous things, had made me hypersensitive to nuances other people might miss. So I looked up to see what was going on. What had got her into that state? And there she was, out in the middle of the lake.

'Oh no!' I said.

Even from that distance – at least fifty feet away – it was clear she was struggling. Her head was barely above water, but she'd stubbornly held on to the stick and it was messing with her balance, making it harder for her to swim back to safety. Ripples were spreading out in concentric circles around her. But despite the energetic paddling, she wasn't making any headway. It was like something was holding her back. Dragging her down.

Our chatter slowed, then stopped. But nobody moved or said a thing. There was no question she'd drown if somebody didn't dive in and get her. But it was like everyone was frozen in the moment. Rooted to the spot. Unable to compute the tragedy that was unfolding right in front of their eyes.

People like to talk a good game about the heroics they'd get up to when the scenario's just a hypothetical. Or they'll embellish their contributions after the fact. But the truth is, until you're thrust into the situation, until you're living and breathing it, you can't possibly know what you'll do. It's all instinct. Something takes over.

In the moment, there wasn't any conscious or coherent thought process. I didn't say to myself: *I must go get her, or she'll drown.* I simply did. I stripped to my underwear, my hands moving of their own accord, and dived into the lake.

The water was pleasantly cool on my sun-scorched skin, and I front-crawled halfway toward Lucy in what felt like an instant. Arms cutting rhythmically through the water. Body sliding powerfully forward. Breathing even and regular – left arm forward, breathe in, right arm forward, breathe out. The cold pocket was the last thing I expected. A blast of Arctic chill in the middle of the desert.

The gasp that wracked me was so sharp I thought my lungs would collapse in on themselves. It was impossible to breathe. I was hyperventilating, but somehow incapable of drawing any oxygen into my body. I stopped and tried to stand, so I could ride the wave of panic my breathlessness was bringing on, but found no purchase. The bottom of the lake had dropped out of my reach without warning.

I went under and inhaled freezing water through my nostrils. I flailed about, fighting to get my head back out. Coughing and spluttering in between gasping breaths. I turned in a half circle, trying to get my bearings, but I could only see an endless expanse of blue. Alkmund Park Pool had somehow tripled in size, leaving me stranded in no-man's land. How would I return to the shore? There was just no way. It had been really stupid of me to go into the lake like that, with no plan. Stupid and reckless.

Then, the outside of my hand brushed against something rough. Just a glancing touch. But it was enough to reorient me. It was the stick, still protruding from the sides of Lucy's mouth while Lucy's paws struggled to keep her tiny body afloat. Her jet-black eyes seemed human. Childlike. Wide with fear. Her fur sodden, making it harder for her to stay buoyant. I wasn't sure how much time had passed, but it couldn't have been more than three or four minutes. And yet, she was already slowing down, physically and mentally exhausted by the ordeal. Soon, she'd go under and not come back up.

I closed my eyes. Tried to regain control of my faculties and motor skills. The worst of the cold shock had passed and some feeling was returning to my extremities. I cradled Lucy in one arm, and pushed forward with both my legs as hard as I could. We moved a few inches, and something pulled us back. Pulled Lucy back. She'd got one of her paws tangled in the weeds. That's why she'd been unable to swim back to us with the stick.

I felt Lucy's paws with my free arm, afraid to duck underwater and look because I still couldn't trust my breathing. There it was. Stringy, slimy, slippery leaves, bunched together and knotted around Lucy's back legs. I gripped fistful after fistful. Ripping. Tearing. Scrambling to untrap her. Running purely on adrenaline. Desperately pushing for survival.

Something gave and the tugging loosened. I pushed forward once more. No, not quite there. A wayward tendril of weed was holding on, not willing to let go of its prey. I screamed in frustration. The skin of my fingers had pruned over, and its tightness was making me shudder. The cold was settling into my bones, and tiredness was taking hold. I ripped. Bunches and bunches of weeds that stuck to my hands, my arms, my face, with more floating lazily around us. At last, we broke free, and I half swam, half dragged us both to shore. By the time we landed on the grass, we were both shaking uncontrollably, and it was a long while before we got ourselves back under control. And, in the meantime, they were all just there, sitting down, legs crossed, staring. Mute. Dumfounded.

Who was it that said that when people show you who they are, you should believe them?

This was the perfect example.

Oh, don't get me wrong. In the immediate aftermath, I was showered with praise. Feted. Declared the best friend in the world.

But what did it matter? Words are cheap. It's how you act under duress that counts.

You know what? Maybe I should've let Lucy drown. Maybe that would've been for the best. Because when push came to shove—

Ugh.

I saved the bloody dog. Almost drowned doing it. And I still got thrown under the bus.

Chapter Thirty-One

Friday, 12 January 2024

Approaching the steps that led inside the dilapidated building in Stringbell – a graffiti-riddled scheme on the fringes of west Strathburgh – where Danny Walton was lying low, Brian was overwhelmed by an ominous sense of déjà vu. This was Roystonmuir all over again. The signs were everywhere. Same poor-quality chipboard front door that somebody had stomped a trainer-shaped hole into. Same unreadable black scrawls sprayed across every available square inch of cracked pebble-dash façade. Same chicken-wire-fenced, rubbish-riddled verges. The uncanny familiarity of the surroundings made his heart trip-hammer irregularly and his palms sweat. Even though the situation was completely different. Or so he'd told himself, a hundred million times, during the forty-five-minute drive from the station.

In the interest of putting the extremely antsy Walton at ease enough for him to open up, Brian had agreed to interview him here, in his hideout. But that didn't mean they were taking any chances. The area had been put under surveillance the minute Alice had reluctantly given them the address, and an armed-response unit had set up a perimeter. Walton wasn't going to leg it this time round. No fucking way. Not if Brian had anything to do with it. By hook or by crook, he was going to tell them what he knew. Whether he'd do so in the comfort of this flat or in an interview room back at the station was up to him.

So, no. This was nothing like Roystonmuir. And yet—

The eyes. The eyes. Those glassy, dead eyes.

—the dread stuck to Brian like a bad smell as he stepped inside the building with Liam by his side.

The communal area wasn't much of an improvement over the exterior. There were long, deep gashes in the plasterwork, as if a freakishly large tiger had clawed its way inside. The stairwell was littered with assorted detritus – torn bin bags overflowing with empty crisps packets, chocolate wrappers, soft-drink cans, greasy take-away boxes, construction material, and even the odd syringe caked with brownish residue. The whole place reeked so badly of cigarette smoke you could feel your lungs shrivel as you breathed. The dulcet tones of Boy George bemoaning the Karma Chameleon assaulted Brian and Liam's eardrums at mega-decibel volume, adding to the atmosphere of deranged hopelessness.

'Christ alive, who listens to this shite at eleven in the

morning?' he told Liam. He'd barely finished the sentence when the song ended and the opening bars of 'The Final Countdown' filtered down toward them as clearly as if the speakers were blasting the music from two feet in front of them.

'It's like we've travelled back to 1986,' Liam muttered. 'Shame we're not sporting mullets and moustaches.'

Brian snorted, but it sounded fake, even to his ears. It was an exercise in deflection. An attempt at putting a brave face on the situation. In reality, with every step, his heart was beating faster, and his head was getting swimmy. The images of the scene that had unfolded in Roystonmuir – God, was that a month ago already? – flashing in front of him. The track-marked arms. The ragged can bottom that had been used in place of a spoon.

The hockey stick. The hockey stick. The hockey stick.

'He's got a fucking hockey stick. Where did he get that from?! WATCH OUT!'

He stopped, hand resting lightly on the grime-encrusted plastic railing, and mopped away the sweat that was beading at his temples with the sleeve of his suit jacket. He was itching to run away. To hide in some deserted corner where he could let go and hyperventilate in peace, without anyone asking him if he was OK. But he ignored it.

Not now.

Not yet.

Later.

When—

The battle's lost and won.

—they'd done the job they were here to do. Find out what Walton knew. What he'd run away from on Monday morning, and why he'd chosen not to come forward.

'All good, B?' Liam asked, forming an *O* with his thumb and forefinger.

'Aye,' Brian wheezed. 'Aye, I'm fine.'

'You sound like you've just run ten miles,' Liam said.

Liam didn't look too hot either. His eyes were blood-shot and weary. His shirt was rumpled, its tail peeking from under his charcoal-grey suit jacket, which had a streak of—

Blood. So much blood. Oh God.

—some greasy-looking substance running down its front. On the shirt collar, there were two faint maroon drops.

Not in the mood to argue – too preoccupied with how he was feeling and how it might impact this potentially crucial interview to do so – Brian said nothing. They stepped onto the top floor's dusty concrete landing and made their way to the door marked G. It was a faux-pine number that had yellowed with age and nicotine residue. Strips of the thin vinyl covering were peeling away at the edges, revealing dirty chipboard beneath. A spiderweb of cracks adorned the opaque Perspex window that made up the door's top half.

Brian closed his eyes. Took a breath.

'Are you sure you're OK, B?' Liam asked.

'I said I'm fine,' Brian snapped. 'Shall we?'

Without waiting for an answer, he raised his index

finger, but found a hole with a piece of copper wire protruding from it in the spot where the doorbell was supposed to be. Knocked instead.

'Danny Walton? It's the pol—' Brian began over the hollow thunking sound his knuckles produced when they rapped on the cheap material.

The door cracked soundlessly open, stopping him mid-sentence. It was a development that dialled up the dread. Shouldn't it have been locked shut if Walton was in hiding? Why would he be so careless as to leave it open? This building wasn't exactly the Ritz. But, under the circumstances, he'd have expected Walton to be alert enough to at least replace the lock if it was broken. Or hide some place that, at a bare minimum, had a lock that actually... locked.

Across the landing, 'The Final Countdown' had faded out and Boy George was back, once more telling anyone in a hundred-mile radius about the Karma Chameleon's flakiness.

'Danny?' Brian repeated, sounding unsure.

His heart was no longer a trip hammer in his chest. It was a chunk of rotten apple in his throat. He looked sideways at Liam, and they exchanged an uneasy look. Liam shrugged noncommittally.

'It's open. We can go in,' Brian said.

'Call for backup,' Liam replied.

'We already have backup. There's a whole army outside, remember?' Brian said. 'No way he could've legged it.'

But was that what had happened here? And if what he suspected had happened had, in fact, happened, how did they manage to— Ah, shite. They were going to have to work through this.

He pushed the door wider with the tips of his fingers. It opened onto a narrow hallway covered in zany seventies wallpaper and threadbare, cigarette-burn-riddled grey carpet. Christ, how had Walton stuck it out here for five days? Rents were getting ridiculous in Strathburgh. Had been getting ridiculous since Covid. He knew a thing or two about that. But even for someone on the run, this was appalling.

'Danny?' Brian called, stepping into the hallway.

Something creaked.

Brian flinched, then cursed himself. It was a loose floorboard.

He was an experienced DI with a squad of armed police waiting downstairs, ready to come up at his say-so, for God's sake, not the first casualty in a slasher film walking toward his inevitable demise. And yet, he suddenly felt hot despite the chill. Oh, so very hot. His armpits were drenched. His mouth bone dry. He was trying to look everywhere at once. Looking for—

The jakey with the hockey stick.

—some sign of what might've possibly transpired. Why was Walton not answering them? Why was his front door unlocked?

'Danny?' Brian repeated. 'Danny, it's the police. We're coming in.'

Still no reply.

Boy George finished his song and started over. Second time back-to-back. Did whoever was playing the blasted thing get a cut of the royalties? *Nobody can possibly like Culture Club that much.* Brian fought down a bray of hysterical laughter. Christ, the wheels were coming off. He was inches away from losing it completely.

He edged forward, with Liam behind him. Inch by suffocating inch. The hallway was too narrow for them to walk side by side. A piece of wallpaper, liberally peppered with furry green mould, brushed against Brian's ear, sending a cold shiver down his baking spine. The squeaking of the subfloor sounded impossibly loud, cutting through the music even though the latter should've drowned it out. Three feet ahead, the hallway opened into what Brian assumed was the studio room. From his vantage point, he spied bits of ratty furniture. A torn armrest that belonged either to a sofa or an armchair. A splintered wooden chair on which rested a white lamp base with a CFL energy-saving bulb attached to it. A plastic vase, dented in several places and covered in a thick film of dust.

'Danny?' Brian called.

Still no answer.

Something was wrong. Something was terribly, terribly wrong. Brian knew it. Could feel it in his bones. The rotten apple core in his throat throbbed in time with his breathing. His stomach dropped.

'Dan—'

Brian reached the threshold where the carpet ended and became scuffed faux-marble vinyl.

Froze.

His vision doubled. Fuck, his *brain* doubled on itself.

The music, deafening up to this point, suddenly

sounded tinny and far away. Like it was being filtered into his ears down a long piece of string and through a cup. The hallway's walls came down and disappeared, replaced by bare brick. He was in—

Roystonmuir.

—two places at once. Trying to make sense of what he was seeing in front of him, and why his brain was superimposing it on another—

Completely different. Totally unrelated. It has nothing to do with it whatsoever.

—scene.

Of how it could possibly have happened right under their noses.

Brian stared at Walton's lifeless form. Taking in every detail. The black bib of blood around his mouth and pooled under him like a macabre aura. The glazed eyes, fixed on the crumbling popcorn ceiling. The right leg, ending in a foot that was twisted at an unnaturally acute angle.

Walton was still dressed in the clothes he'd been wearing the day he'd managed to slip away from them through the fire exit at Starbucks, minus the cap. Swathes of pink scalp peeked through hair that looked fragile and wispy, even though Walton had cut it brutally short in an effort to conceal his losing battle with genetics.

On his torso, there were two deep stab wounds. One to the stomach, and one just beneath the solar plexus. Through the whirling brain fog, Brian thought absently that the latter wound would've likely been enough to kill Walton on its own, because it was very close to the heart.

Brian's mouth opened. His throat worked. No sound came out.

And then he made a sort of gurgling, gagging sound in his chest, and enough air managed to pass through his voice box that the sounds formed barely audible words.

'Oh shite,' he squeaked. 'Oh. Fuck!'

Chapter Thirty-Two

It took thirty minutes for the SOCOs to arrive after Brian called in Walton's death. Thirty long minutes that, in his dazed mind, stretched out like days.

After they got over the initial shock of their discovery, Brian and Liam backed out of the flat, carefully, so they wouldn't contaminate the scene any more than they'd already had. Then, having placed the call and started the process of securing the scene – and battling the sensation that he was watching himself from outside his own body – Brian sat on the top step of the landing, oblivious to the grime that would penetrate the fabric of his suit trousers and ruin them.

His throat was constricted and his body was in flames, his armpits, palms, and the backs of his knees sticky with sweat. He fixed his gaze on a brown stain on the wall opposite that looked suspiciously like shite that had been smeared in a wide arc, and willed himself to ignore the roiling in his guts.

Liam sat down next to him and said nothing. Brian's

heavy breathing was drowned out first by George Michael – who'd replaced Culture Club at some indeterminate point after they'd made their gruesome discovery – followed by Starship, followed by Alphaville. Brian lost track after that. His senses, too alert to focus on one single stimulus for any length of time, were tuning in and out like a phone with spotty reception.

'You can't keep pretending like nothing's happened, B, you know?' Liam said, finally, as the opening saxophone bars of 'Careless Whisper' reverberated around the building. 'Because it did. Something *did* happen. Don't you remember?'

Brian stared at the floor. Shook his head mechanically. Muttered under his breath.

'Look at me, B,' Liam said.

'No,' Brian said.

'Come on,' Liam cajoled. 'Look at me.'

Another shake of the head. Goddamn Liam. He had a talent for picking his moments, didn't he?

'What is it that makes Roystonmuir so hard to stomach?' Liam insisted when Brian said nothing.

Brian took a deep, shuddering breath. It was a good question. What was it? Was it the initial shock, or the aftermath? The sense that he could've prevented everything ... if only—

'We're not having this conversation,' he snapped, mainly to stop his thoughts from—

Going there.

—spiralling.

'Not on the stairs of an absolute shitehole, to a soundtrack of cheesy eighties pop.'

The joke didn't land. Liam sucked his teeth.

'B, listen,' he said. 'This isn't sustainable. You're getting worse. You know that. It's only—'

A beefy SOCO hauling a large moulded plastic case cut Liam off. Brian got up to his feet, only too happy with the interruption. Liam might broach the subject again. Hell, the subject was going to come up again, whether Liam brought it up or not. Because Liam was right. He *was* getting worse, with every minute that passed. This case was a mental minefield, and there were tripwires everywhere. But, for now, he'd enjoy the reprieve. Try to distract himself with the nitty-gritty of the crime scene. He'd deal with his emotions later. Douse them with liquid fire until they left him the fuck alone.

More SOCOs trooped up the stairs, suited up, and entered the flat. They got to work, placing numbered markers around the scene and snapping photos like deranged paparazzi. The clicking of the cameras and the coppery smell of blood set Brian's teeth on edge. The tiny studio room, crowded and stuffy, and the plastic oversuit he'd put on, made things worse. It took a huge effort of will not to jump every time somebody snapped a photo.

He walked the scene with Liam, but it told them nothing aside from the obvious: that Walton was dead and whoever had done this had taken him by surprise. The flat, aside from being barely habitable, was sparsely furnished. The sofa – an overstuffed three-seater with frayed seams that were vomiting chunks of mould-spotted foam – doubled as a bed and dining area, and the splintery wood chair served as a nightstand, table, and desk. The kitchenette – if you could call it that – consisted of a two-burner hob crusted with burnt tomato sauce, an under-counter fridge-freezer, a sink piled with dirty plates and cutlery, and two cupboards with their doors hanging askew. A large gym bag held all of the belongings Walton had brought with him: a stack of underwear, one pair of jeans, two sweater vests, and two gym outfits. Clearly, he'd packed in a hurry and opted to travel light. Maybe because Alice could fetch him whatever he needed. Speaking of which ...

'Where's his phone?' he asked a SOCO who was busy dusting the chair for prints.

'Didn't find one,' the officer mumbled without looking up.

'Shite. Just like the Higgins scene,' he told Liam.

Could they be dealing with the same killer? Or was it possible that the two murders were unconnected and the timing just a coincidence?

If Walton was a witness to Higgins's murder, it made perfect sense that the killer would want to silence him before he talked to the polis. It also made sense the killer would take his phone. They might still be able to read his conversations with Alice through her phone and retrieve the rest of his messaging history from his network carrier. But, as with Higgins, this would slow them down.

The problem was that Alice hadn't left their sight since they'd brought her in. She'd called Walton from the station. So had she finally told them the truth? Was she really innocent of her husband's murder? Or was Walton already dead when she'd placed the call? No, that was too much of a stretch. Given her behaviour during the interview, he didn't think she'd have the stomach to keep up a one-sided conversation with somebody she knew to be dead – somebody she'd *murdered* – in front of the polis, would she? And then there was the MO. On the face of it, similar, in that they were both stabbings. But where Higgins had been killed in a frenzy, the attack on Walton was controlled. Calculated. The killer had stabbed him strategically, directing the knife where it would inflict maximum damage.

'DI Brandon.' A deep, sonorous voice interrupted his train of thought.

Brian turned. His stomach dropped when he saw the stiff, wrinkled man the voice belonged to. He couldn't help it.

'Dr Henderson,' he greeted the forensic pathologist with barely concealed dismay. 'I wasn't expecting you.'

It came out before he could stop himself. He winced. And he could feel Liam do the same, even though Brian didn't dare hazard a glance at him. Not after the conversation they'd just had.

'Aye, it's been a busy morning,' Henderson replied, seemingly oblivious to the implied slight. Or too self-absorbed to notice, Brian guessed. 'But I happened to be available.'

I wonder why, Brian thought. His mind flitted briefly to Pam Grace's warm hand on his arm. The concern in her eyes. Her invitation to lend him her ear so he could unburden himself if he wanted to. He resented being seen as somebody to be pitied. But he'd be lying if he said her attention hadn't awoken something inside him he'd started to believe wasn't there anymore. God, he was all over the place. Why did everything have to be so complicated?

Henderson peered at the body over his glasses, muttered to himself in a way that sounded more like an affectation than genuine bemusement, then squatted down. His knees popped, and he grimaced. He rummaged inside his equipment bag with one horny, liver-spotted hand and produced a rectangular device with a white stick attached to it via a coiled cord. A rectal probe.

Brian's gorge rose and he swallowed down sour bile. It burned his throat. Murder scenes were always difficult – even though he liked to think he'd done a reasonably good job of learning how to detach himself emotionally and approach them objectively—

That was before. Before. Before.

Before the shite hit the fan. Well, before the hockey stick hit the head. Tee-hee-hee.

—over the years.

But this scene was pushing him to the limit. It was bad enough that Walton had felt compelled to hide in this utter shitehole and ended up being murdered for his troubles. Now, he'd also have to suffer the indignity of being poked, prodded, and cut open; his most intimate secrets pored over by a team of strangers.

Anger coursed through Brian's body like poison, and he clenched his fists. If this was the same person's work – and even though logic made a plausible case for Higgins and Walton's murders being unrelated, his gut said this was no coincidence – their killer was laughing at them. And he wasn't having that. There was no way he'd—

Feel so helpless. So completely out of control.

—let them get away with this. Not if he could help it.

'Time of death is eleven to fourteen hours, I'd say,' Henderson cut in.

'So between eight and eleven last night?' Brian asked.

That definitively put Alice out of the frame; she'd been sitting in the custody suite at that time. Still was, waiting for the outcome of their chat with Walton. But they'd also had Walton under surveillance. So how had the killer managed to do it right under their noses? Unless …

'How sure are you?' Brian asked.

His thoughts flitted briefly to a case six months prior, which Henderson had declared a murder-suicide. Except he'd failed to account for the petechial haemorrhaging in the eyes, which suggested the suicide had been already strangled to death when he supposedly slit his wrists.

'As sure as I can be,' Henderson said with a tone of finality. He straightened up and gave Brian a scornful look. 'Rectal temperature is twenty-two degrees Celsius. If his temperature has been dropping at the standard rate – two degrees in the first hour and one degree thereafter – that's fourteen hours. Accounting for the poor insulation in this flat and the cold temperature, it's reasonable to assume body temperature might decrease by one and a half degrees an hour after the initial drop, which brings us to eleven.'

Brian nodded. He wasn't about to argue. Not here, in front of a crowd of SOCOs. Henderson might be well past his prime, but he still had clout, and Brian couldn't afford making an enemy of him on top of everything else.

But if Henderson was right, this threw a giant spanner in the works. Brian had either got it horribly wrong, in which case Walton had died because of him. Or he now had two murder investigations on his hands.

Either way, Brian could feel the weight on his shoulders growing heavier and heavier.

He needed to get to the bottom of this, fast. Before the ground crumbled under him and he was thrust into the void.

Chapter Thirty-Three

Back at the station, Brian gathered the team in the incident room for an impromptu briefing. Everyone was there except Liam, who'd had to beg off early to help his wife with the preparations for their son's fifth birthday the next day.

He turned to the whiteboard. Wiped off *WITNESS/ACCOMPLICE?* from under Walton's mugshot and replaced the photo with one from the crime scene: a close-up of his face, his expression frozen in a permanent rictus of pain and fear. Beneath the photo, he wrote *CONNECTED?* in black marker, then turned to face the people gathered around the conference table.

'What have we managed to find out?' he asked.

'This is the extent of the text chain between Alice and Danny from the time he left the Higginses' house on Monday morning to Thursday evening,' Fiona said.

She passed Brian a printout.

Monday 08:23

Alice: All PK?
A: *OK
Monday 09:32
A: Did you find it?
Monday 10:45
A: Dan?
A: Everything all right??
Monday 10:48
Danny: Aye
A: Are you sure you're OK? Something happen?
Monday 11:03
D: We should talk

Brian sank into the chair at the head of the conference table and set the printout aside. On the face of it, the text chain confirmed what Alice had told them: that Walton had stopped by her house to pick something up for him, only to walk in unexpectedly on something he shouldn't have seen. But, in reality, it was a terse, generic exchange that didn't give much away. It could mean anything. There could be so much more hidden between the lines that they didn't yet know.

'Did you find anything else in their messaging history?' Brian asked. The question was perfunctory. He had a feeling he knew the answer already.

'Not really,' Fiona said. She leaned back in her chair and rubbed her eyes.

Brian scanned the room. With the exception of McGillivray. who looked as fresh as if he'd just woken up from a long siesta, the team looked tired and weary, and it made him flush with guilt and shame. He didn't have the monopoly on feeling rough. The case was taking a toll on everyone. Well, almost everyone.

'—it confirms Alice's story,' Fiona finished.

'Sorry, say again,' Brian said. 'Didn't get that.'

'I said their chats are either flirty exchanges, gym talk, or rendezvous plans. Nothing that jumps out as being suspicious.'

'And what about Ray Higgins's messages? Any luck with that?' Brian asked.

'Nothing,' Fiona said. 'His emails were all work-related. Well, those he did receive. His inbox was quiet over the past few months.'

'Which confirms what we found out from his accounts – that business had slowed to a trickle,' Brian continued.

'Aye,' Fiona agreed. 'And he barely ever texted anyone. So either he was a recluse ...'

'Or he was texting and emailing using apps we don't know about,' Brian finished. The killer had really managed to get one over them by taking Higgins's phone and laptop.

He slid the chair backward and got up. Paced in front of the whiteboard. 'Any luck with the scene?'

'Not much,' Fiona replied. 'The flat belongs to the council, but it's been unoccupied for three years because it was declared unfit for human habitation.'

'Shocker of the century,' McGillivray commented. Nobody laughed.

'There are two CCTV cameras in the whole area,' Fiona continued, ignoring him. 'Neither works. Vandalised and never replaced.'

Brian stopped pacing. Exhaled through his teeth. Shite. Stringbell wasn't as rough as it used to be since the Company – the organised-crime gang that had ruled west Strathburgh with an iron fist for two decades – was brought down in 2023. But crime and poverty went together like smoke and fire. Desperate people did desperate things. It was as inevitable as it was tragic. And those with the means to bring about lasting change were too comfortable living in their own private bubbles to care.

'When did the surveillance team arrive?' Brian asked.

'We got there around nine p.m.,' McGillivray said.

Alice had called Walton at six thirty and they'd spoken for around twenty minutes. So, if Henderson had the time of death right, that left about an hour unaccounted for. An hour in which their killer could've slipped into Walton's flat, done the deed, and slipped out unobserved.

Brian suppressed a flash of annoyance. 'What took you so long?'

'Traffic,' McGillivray said. His nonchalance was making Brian's blood boil.

'A two-hour delay?' Brian snapped, glaring at him. Alice had given them the address at around seven-ish, as soon as she'd ended the call. 'You do realise somebody *died*, Murray? Right?'

McGillivray had the good grace to look embarrassed. But he didn't back down. 'There was some sort of media event at the community centre and they diverted traffic. It was chock-a-block.'

'What media event?' Brian asked.

McGillivray shrugged. Brian placed his hands in his trouser pockets and clenched them into fists.

'Well, find out!' he said, his voice just a few decibels shy of being a full-blown roar.

McGillivray flushed crimson and his jaw tightened. 'It's not like it's the middle of nowhere,' he complained. 'Police are constantly getting called out there for domestics and antisocial behaviour and what not.'

'Find out about that too,' Brian said, holding his gaze until McGillivray dropped his. 'The residents might not want to talk, but somebody from the event or the local polis might've seen something. I shouldn't have to tell you this, should I?'

McGillivray scowled and said nothing. Brian rolled his eyes. There was a limit, and he was way past it. Thousands of miles past it.

'Have next of kin been informed?' he asked, turning away from McGillivray, disgusted.

'Aye. We spoke to Danny's mother,' a young detective constable fresh out of uniform said. The death knock never got easier, but the DC's eyes had the shell-shocked look of somebody who had next to no experience of it. They'd all been there. 'She took the news very badly ... as you'd expect. We didn't get much out of her, except that she couldn't think of anyone who'd want to harm him.'

Spoken like a mother.

'What about Reid?' Fiona cut in.

'Reid?' Brian said. 'Ach. Aye. Walton's uncle.'

The bloke hadn't seemed particularly impressed with Walton's character, Brian reflected. He'd all but told them he disapproved of his nephew. Could that have had something to do with why he'd wound up dead?

He glanced at his watch. Quarter to five. Assuming rush-hour traffic wasn't too bad, they might just about make it to Reid's shop before closing time.

'That's a good shout,' he told Fiona. 'Let's go have another chat with him.'

Chapter Thirty-Four

If Stuart Reid had seemed haunted when Brian and Fiona had spoken to him on Tuesday, he looked positively funereal today. Dressed in a midnight black, double-breasted three-piece suit and matching tie over a shirt so white Brian had to shade his eyes despite the early-evening gloom, he looked more like an undertaker from 1871 than an antiques dealer from 2024.

When Brian and Fiona reached the shop, damp from having had to walk from the car in the drizzling rain, Reid was in the process of locking up and pulling down the shutters. He greeted them with a mumble that was barely audible over the whirr of the shutter mechanism and carried on with his work. If he was surprised to see them, he didn't show it. Brian surmised that, if he was close enough with Walton's mother that she'd persuaded him to give her son a job despite his obvious misgivings, news of the murder would've likely reached him already. He didn't seem particularly grief-stricken at the news of his nephew's untimely death, though. Then again, a bloke who embraced Victoriana this wholeheartedly probably lived and breathed the stiff-upper-lip philosophy.

'Can we talk, Stuart?' Brian said gently.

'DI Brandon,' Reid replied. 'Yes, of course.'

He turned the shutter key anticlockwise, reversing the mechanism. When the shutters had retreated back up, he walked inside the shop and gestured for them to follow him.

'I assume this is about Danny,' he said, when he'd settled himself on the stool behind the counter. A statement, not a question. So the news *had* reached him. 'It's a waste. But I can't say I didn't warn him about the company he kept.'

Brian's ears pricked up.

'Why do you say that, Stuart?' he asked.

Reid looked at them with his watery eyes, his mouth moving uncertainly.

'Anything you can tell us could help us catch who did this,' Brian pressed.

Reid nibbled the inside of his cheek. Then he dropped his eyes and his shoulders sagged.

'Well, I suppose it's not like he could get into trouble at this point now, is it?' he said. 'My sister's completely devastated, you know? She tried very hard to do right by him after that' – his lips curled in distaste – 'wastrel of a man who got her pregnant ran off.'

Brian waited. He felt Fiona tense next to him and realised he'd been drumming his fingers on his thigh. Stopped.

'He was hanging about with people I didn't much care for,' Reid continued.

'Why not?' Brian asked.

'Well, for one, they came around the shop at all hours,' Reid said. 'They distracted him from his work. Wasted his time... and mine.'

His face was impassive, but his Home Counties accent slipped. *Hours* came out *uhrs* and his speech took on a more lilting cadence.

'And then there was the way they dressed. Track-suits. Heavy chains around their necks,' he continued. His face was a mask of contempt. 'He'd slink off with them, then come back looking guilty. I'm a fairly good judge of character. You learn to read people after twenty years in my line of work, you know? But you didn't need to be an expert to know he and his friends were up to no good. It was written all over his face.'

'Did this happen often?' Brian asked.

'Often enough that I told him to watch it,' Reid replied. 'I told him straight and plain. I'd kept him on out of respect for my sister, because his work ethic was ... not great, let's put it that way. But at the end of the day, I have a business to run and I can't have shady people hanging about my premises, scaring customers off.'

The cogs were turning in Brian's brain. The blokes Reid was describing sounded suspiciously like organised-crime gang members. Had there been some kind of wheeling and dealing going on? Drugs? Could that be possible? It didn't really fit with Walton's personal-training fitness-nut persona. But not all drug dealers are addicts. The savvy ones – those who get rich off it – don't touch the stuff. They know getting addicted to their product is bad for business.

'Would you recognise—'

The tinkle of bells interrupted Brian's question.

'All right. Danny in?'

Brian and Fiona pivoted around in tandem, a movement so perfectly synchronised they couldn't have pulled it off so well if they'd planned it. When the man the voice belonged to saw them, he stopped mid-stride, recognition wiping the smile off his face.

Brian took in the cable-knit sweater – today it was a deep yellow-brown. The colour of wholegrain mustard if you were being generous, or of especially nasty diarrhoea if you weren't – peeking out from under the heavy winter coat that couldn't quite hide the bulging belly. His bald pate was peppered with raindrops, but the hair at the sides wasn't sticking out in tufts like the last time Brian had seen him. Today, it was slicked back and neatly combed. Together with the moustache, it gave him the air of a benevolent grandfather.

His mind whirred. How did this make any sense? How could they know each other?

Gerald Layton, the Higginses' neighbour, had been the one to tell them about the van at the scene.

So why would he, of all people, come looking for Danny Walton?

Chapter Thirty-Five

'You've got a lot of explaining to do,' Brian said, pacing around the interview room back at the station, where they'd taken Layton for questioning under caution. 'If I were you, I'd start talking.'

The reservoir of adrenaline and nervous energy that had kept Brian going from the time he and Liam had discovered Walton's body up to now was almost entirely depleted, and the cracks were starting to show. He was sweating profusely. A pig in a sauna. And every heartbeat sounded like a bass drum rumbling in his ears. He willed himself to stop pacing and stuck his hands deep into his trousers pockets while staring Layton down. Pinched both his thighs and barely felt anything. He might as well have pinched a mannequin. Layton returned the stare impassively, his hands folded neatly in his lap. Layton's solicitor, a forty-something bloke with expensively barbered hair and a suit which, Brian guessed, probably cost more than two months' rent on his flat, scribbled something in a notebook.

'How did you know Danny Walton?' Brian asked.

'No comment,' Layton responded.

'What was the nature of your relationship with him?'

'No comment.'

'Why didn't you tell us you knew him the first time we spoke?'

'No comment.'

Brian groaned. They'd been at this for fifteen minutes and Layton was yet to concede an inch. If anything, he looked like he could keep it up for hours. It was time Brian couldn't afford to waste. First, because the longer it took to establish possible lines of inquiry, the colder the trail that would lead to Walton's killer would become. But more importantly, though, because he was closer than ever to losing it completely and doing something he'd regret. The tips of his fingers were trembling, he could feel them through his trouser pockets. And he wanted a drink. Needed one. More than anything in the world.

With a huge effort of will, he pulled out the chair next to Fiona's and sat down heavily. He leaned forward, his forearms resting on the edge of the table, gripping his hands together so they wouldn't shake, and stared Layton down.

'Where were you yesterday evening between eight and ten?' he asked.

It was an abrupt change of subject. Layton's brow furrowed. His solicitor looked up from his notebook.

'Where are you going with this, Inspector?' the solicitor sneered. 'What are you suggesting?'

'*I* ask the questions in here,' Brian said, spittle flying.

He turned back to Layton and fixed him with a death stare. 'We know the van driver you told us you saw at the Higgins scene was Danny Walton, the same bloke you were asking after at Reid's Antiques this evening. We tracked him down.'

He paused for effect. Layton didn't flinch.

'Except we couldn't speak with him, because he was dead,' Brian continued. 'Murdered.'

If Layton was disturbed at the turn the interview had just taken, he didn't show it. He barked a laugh. A sharp sound that hurt Brian's ears.

'And, what?' he scoffed. 'You think I did him? Because if you do, you're barking up the wrong tree, bud.'

'Well, in that case, you won't have a problem telling us your whereabouts yesterday evening. Or explaining why you weren't upfront with us about knowing Walton.'

Layton considered, his eyes darting around the room as he did so.

'I walked Sindy. She's still with me. Ray's wife doesn't want her. Not into dogs, apparently. And then I watched *Grand Designs* reruns on the telly.'

'Anyone can vouch for that?' Brian asked.

'Sindy,' Layton deadpanned.

Brian suppressed the urge to grab the table and smash it against the wall. Despite his best efforts, Layton was getting under his skin. And he could tell the bloke knew it. The bastard was enjoying himself. He could see it in the way his eyes glinted when he spoke. He pinched the bridge of his nose with his thumb and forefinger. Christ, what an absolute fucker of a day. When was it going to end?

'I ordered takeaway,' Layton volunteered unexpectedly. 'From Shalimar. Lamb bhuna. You can check.'

Fiona made a note.

'Do you remember what time it was when you made the order?' Brian asked.

Layton shook his head. 'Nine-ish? Something like that.'

It wasn't watertight. Henderson could've underestimated or overestimated the time of death. Layton could've placed the order on his way home from the murder. Both could've happened. Could've. Could've. Could've. They were grasping at straws. Tying themselves in knots. And for what? Alibis were rarely perfect. Nobody went around ensuring they could account for every second of their day in case they got questioned about a murder – unless they were expecting to be questioned about said murder. Plus, why would Layton have gone looking for Walton at his uncle's shop if he knew he was dead? It made no sense.

Brian sighed. 'Look, Gerald,' he said. 'You obviously knew Walton—'

The solicitor was about to speak. Brian raised a hand to stop him.

'Let me finish,' he said. 'We both know you knew Walton. So here's what I don't understand. Why tell us about the van at all? Wouldn't it have been safer to say you saw nothing?'

Layton emitted a sigh of his own.

'OK. I'll bite,' he said. 'But this is all I have to say on the matter. I told you about the van because you'd have worked it out eventually, and I wanted to get in front of it. But I've no idea what he was doing there or why. And, frankly, I don't care. It's none of my business.'

'How did you know him?' Brian tried again, hoping Layton's willingness to answer the last two questions signalled a change of heart.

Layton dashed his hopes straight away. 'No comment,' he said, defaulting to his standard reply.

Chapter Thirty-Six

Fine, I'll admit it. I panicked, OK?

Happy?

And, honestly. Can you blame me?

I can't tell you how many times I've replayed the scene in my head. Hundreds, thousands, tens of thousands of times.

He'd just about reached the doorway into the downstairs living space when he spotted the bloody tracks. And the second he realised what was going on – that the bastard Higgins was dead and I was still there, in the house – he screamed his head off and headed back out of the front door at two hundred miles an hour. The big baby. All those airs, all that testosterone flying about, and he bailed the second he was within sniffing distance of needing to show his mettle.

If there's one type of person I can't abide, it's a coward and a hypocrite. But, anyway. Never mind. The point isn't his spinelessness. It's that, no, he couldn't have possibly managed to get a good look at me. How could he? I'd barely let go of that bastard's arms when I heard the van's engine rumble into life and the squeal of tyres as he peeled away from the kerb. There was no time. Not even for a fleeting glance. At least, that's what I convinced myself had happened once I realised I'd forgotten about that damn doorbell.

And then he legged it. And that conviction came crashing down with the strength of a knockout punch. Why would he have done that, if not because he feared what would happen if he talked?

Except, I got that wrong, didn't I?

Because the stupid, stupid, cowardly excuse for a man did agree to talk.

So he'd seen. He knew. He had to... he was going to spill the beans, wasn't he?

And, once he did that, it would be game, set, and match for me. He'd ruin everything.

So, there you have it. It wasn't my fault. How was I supposed to know that conniving harridan would send her fuckboy on an errand to her house the same day the proverbial excrement hit the fan? He was at the wrong place at the wrong time, and there was no room to be sentimental. This was self-defence. Me or him. I'd made one mistake, and there was no way in hell I was going to make another one.

Lucky for me, he wasn't – how can I put this generously? – the sharpest tool in the shed.

Oh, I'm sure he thought he was smart, stashing himself away in that disgusting pigsty. Who'd think to look for him there? They'd be put off just by its reputation, right? But, if anything, that worked in my favour.

People who live in schemes look out for each other. But, first and foremost, they look out for themselves. And that means knowing when to keep their mouths shut. Besides, I reasoned, he wasn't exactly Strathburgh's answer to James Bond, international man of mystery. His options were limited. All I needed to do was be patient.

And, you know what?

I overestimated him. I kept tabs on Alice in the hope she'd lead me to him – even though I wasn't holding my breath. I didn't believe either of them could be so stupid as to meet in public.

Except they did. At a Costa, of all places. Sipping skinny lattes and holding hands the whole time like two teenagers on their first date.

It was sickening.

But I stuck around, observing them from behind a magazine until they kissed goodbye. I decided I'd follow him to where he was staying and, this time, do things properly. Recce the area. Make sure that, when I did face up to him, I wouldn't be going in half-cocked like I'd done with that bastard Higgins.

That first bit was way easier than I expected. The idiot's idea of going unnoticed involved pulling his cap down over his eyes and ambling forward in a sort of half-strut. He might as well have worn a sandwich board saying 'I'm hiding from the police, but my dick's still making the decisions' for all the good that did him.

I was careful to stay far enough away that I could keep an eye on him but he wouldn't spot me if he turned. But I needn't have worried. He didn't check if anyone was following him. Not once. And the streets were busy enough that I could blend into the crowd.

I followed him right up until he went into the building, and then I saw the light go on in his living room. A quick duck in and out of the common area confirmed he was in flat G.

I knew I didn't have much time to plan it out. But I didn't think he'd be so easily persuaded. That forced my hand.

Tell you what. I almost called it off. Well, I did call it off. I wasn't completely sure I could get away with it undetected. And, after all, I kept telling myself, he didn't have anything of value to say.

But saying things to yourself is one thing. Knowing is very different. The uncertainty ate at me.

And then, like a bolt out of the blue, after all the messes... after all the needless palaver, the universe smiled at me. Gave me a reason to be in the area without arousing suspicion.

When he opened the front door to his flat and saw me, his eyes immediately widened with recognition. I knew right then that I'd made the right choice going through with it, even though the way I'd decided to go about it – because I didn't have time to wait for the ideal opportunity to present itself – was risky. Well, OK. Downright reckless. But it got the job done, didn't it? And, turns out, I hadn't been paranoid. He really did get a good look at me. Now I had proof.

I kicked the door inward and barged in. Already stunned at finding me on his doorstep, this caught him off-guard. His eyes, which were the size of saucers, grew into dinner plates. He staggered backward. The hallway was too narrow for him to stretch his arms and pinwheel for balance. His foot hit the floor at an awkward angle and he twisted his ankle. His legs folded under him and he fell, banging the back of his head in the process with a dull thud.

The tightness of the space, the pain in his ankle, and the blow to his head made him powerless as I loomed over him. But I was taking no chances. I landed a swift kick to his groin. There was no way he could dodge it. I got him good. Hit him square in the balls. The air whooshed out of him in a keening wail. He tried doubling over and whacked his temple against the skirting board.

I squatted, careful to keep my centre of gravity so I wouldn't overbalance if he tried anything funny – not that he was in any condition to do so at this point. I pulled his injured leg out from under him, which elicited a weak groan, then lifted him like a wheelbarrow, pulling him into the living room, his head lolling bonelessly.

I grabbed the first thing I found on that sorry excuse for a kitchenette: a steak knife. The blade looked flat and dull in my hand, but I needn't have worried. It ripped through his clothes and entered his stomach as if they were a pool of melted butter.

I have to admit, now that I'd done it once, I felt a certain sense of exhilaration watching the life ebbing out of him. A sense of power. Of control. Like I'd previously been seeing in black and white and now everything was in technicolour.

And I will say this for the bastard. He didn't beg. He didn't plead. But maybe that had more to do with him being unable to talk with his mouth full of blood than with bravery or acceptance of the inevitable. His hands reached for his stomach. He tried to look as he felt his own warm, sticky blood wash over them, but couldn't summon the strength to raise himself up. He gave me a plaintive, puppy-eyed look that almost made me feel guilty.

Almost.

Until it reminded me of Lucy, and that set me off all over again, sending an eruption of anger through me that I had to work very hard to control. I was determined that this would be quick and clean, you see? Restrained. Unlike Higgins. Because that would throw everyone off. Make them second-guess themselves and, hopefully, back themselves into a blind alley.

Oh, sure. There'd be misgivings. I knew that. How could there not be, given Walton's established link with the other victim?

But, tough. Once the techs went through the scene, not much could be done. If the evidence says 'This is how it happened', then that's the conclusion you have to reach, whether you like it or not. Right?

What I didn't bank on is that dogged persistence, even after everything.

Damn it.

Damn it to hell and back.

Why couldn't you leave well enough alone?

Chapter Thirty-Seven

Saturday, 13 January 2024

When Brian got home from the station, it was past midnight. Food was the last thing on his mind, but he made himself a cheese sandwich and a chicken-and-mushroom-flavoured Pot Noodle anyway, just to get some sustenance, even though their nutritional content was questionable at best. He ate half-heartedly, sitting on his well-worn Ikea sofa with only the sound of the fridge's motor for company, and swigging Monkey Shoulder straight from the bottle in between mouthfuls that tasted like wet cardboard. The alcohol didn't produce its intended effect. Instead of bringing blessed oblivion, it conspired with the wheat, dairy, and sodium in his food to concoct an epic case of heartburn. So he spent the night tossing and turning, grimacing every time he swallowed, his mind a jumble of disconnected thoughts.

Walton's murder had rattled him more than he cared to admit, because it—

Hit too close to home.

—complicated matters.

He now had two murders on his hands, which felt – but might not be – connected. And he wasn't sure how to proceed. He wasn't sold on Layton as Walton's killer, and the evidence so far backed him up. The restaurant had confirmed they'd delivered takeaway to Layton's house at 9:27 p.m. And there was no sign of Layton's Renault Kadjar anywhere near an ANPR camera on Thursday evening. But, then again, Layton had lied to them about knowing Walton. And his stubborn refusal to talk about their relationship was a huge red flag. When people replied 'No comment' when questioned by the polis, it was usually because they didn't want to incriminate themselves. So what was Layton mixed up in? What was he afraid he'd incriminate himself in if he talked?

Exhaustion finally caught up with Brian at 6 a.m. He slipped into a light slumber, only to jerk violently awake two hours later, drenched in sweat, his duvet tangled and cast to one side and the image of rotting teeth, a swinging hockey stick, and blood splattering against bare brick imprinted on his retinas. He raced to the bathroom. Retched violently. Pulled up a jet of foamy amber sick that hit the edge of the toilet seat and dribbled onto the floor. He grabbed the toilet with both hands to steady himself. Slipped on a puddle of sick and banged his forehead against the ceramic, biting his tongue in the process.

'Urgh. Shite. FUCK!' he mumbled, as the room spun and his skull exploded.

He retched again. This time, the sick went where it was supposed to: into the bowl. When he was done, he rinsed his mouth so he'd rid himself of the worst of the sickly sweet-and-sour aftertaste and the fragments of half-digested food stuck to his teeth, mopped the tiles, then padded to the kitchen for a mug of coffee.

His stomach was still pickling in its own juices. But, faced with the choice of worsening his heartburn or exacerbating his headache with caffeine withdrawal, he opted for the former. He switched on the coffee maker – a DeLonghi he'd paid way too much for but didn't begrudge a single penny – added ground Colombian roast to the filter, and swallowed two paracetamol with water he drank straight from the tap while he waited for the coffee to brew. When it was ready, he poured some into a mug, but stopped when he'd filled the mug about halfway and debated. But briefly. Oh so very briefly. Just long enough to maintain the increasingly tenuous illusion that he still had a choice in the matter. Then he fished the whisky bottle from the cupboard under the sink and filled the mug the rest of the way.

He padded into the living room without turning on the light. The curtains were drawn and it was still dark outside, but he made his way around the furniture with the practised ease of the chronic insomniac. His phone buzzed. Who could it be this early on Saturday morning? A new development in the case? He took a long gulp of whisky-laced coffee – it was probably more accurate to call it coffee-laced whisky – and padded to the bedroom to retrieve his phone.

Matty's birthday party is today at noon. Our house. We hope you can make it.

Brian sank onto the bed and sighed.

Shite.

He and Liam went back. Way back. Still. After everything that had happened, Brian had secretly hoped he wouldn't be invited to his son's birthday party. That Amelia, Liam's wife, wouldn't want him there. Not after …

But here it was. Right on cue.

So what now? Should he go or should he just ignore the text?

If he went, it would be unbelievably awkward. And if he didn't, it would also be unbelievably awkward, with the difference that, in the latter case, he'd feel like he'd let Matty down. Could he do that to him? Could he bear another heaped helping of guilt on top of the pile he was already buried in?

When his ex-wife had floated the idea of them having a wean, he'd been on the fence about it, but he'd agreed to try for her sake. And then, when it hadn't happened for them, when the tests had revealed they had issues, he'd rebelled against the notion that nature had taken the decision out of his hands. That he'd need the help of science to do what seemed to come—

Now there's an unfortunate way to put it. Tee-hee-hee.

—effortlessly to blokes – well, let's face it, weans – barely old enough to shave. That, even with the help of science, there were no guarantees.

In those dark days, when the baby-shaped wedge between him and his ex-wife had grown and grown until it was a chasm that was just too wide to cross, Matty had filled the void. The void which had become the third wheel in his marriage. He loved the wean. Enjoyed his boundless enthusiasm and curiosity. Enjoyed spending time with him. Being, in some small way, part of Liam's family.

But the prospect of showing up there, after everything, of spending the afternoon like—

Nothing had happened.

—old times was too much.

His fingers hovered over the screen.

I'm afraid I'm busy

He pressed the delete button. Vehemently. Too formal.

I can't

Ugh.

His mind flashed back to a sweltering Sunday afternoon in August. Brian, his ex-wife Laura, Liam, and Amelia sitting in Liam and Amelia's garden, sipping homemade Long Island iced teas while two-year-old Matty squealed for attention and spun round and round and round, delighting in the dizziness the movements produced. How they'd laughed. How he'd imagined a future where, perhaps, his own wean would be doing the same. Or chasing Matty around the garden as the grown-ups whiled away the time.

But that was then. Before ovulation calendars, schedules, GP appointments, tests, follow-ups, more tests, referrals, injections, and procedures that culminated in negative pregnancy test after negative pregnancy test after negative pregnancy test took over their lives, dragging them down an increasingly narrow rabbit hole that would eventually turn him and Laura into complete strangers. Before—

The sickeningly dull thud of the hockey stick, a watermelon being cracked open.

—Roystonmuir.

His throat clenched. His eyes stung. His face crumpled.

He doubled over. But nothing came out. He didn't wail. Didn't shudder. The tears didn't flow. It was over as quickly as it started. Over the past month, it was like he'd lost the ability to cry. To feel anything except varying degrees of anger, dread, or numbness. He was starting to believe the well had run well and truly dry, never to fill up again. Then again, maybe that wasn't all bad.

He shook his head.

Fuck it.

Of course I'll be there.

He closed his eyes and sent the text, pressing the screen blindly with his thumb before he could change his mind.

Chapter Thirty-Eight

Liam and Amelia's house was a 1970s two-up two-down mid-terrace in an estate that had been designed by somebody who should've been executed for crimes against architecture. But, monstrous design aside, the area was quiet and leafy, and all the neighbours had somehow managed to not only get along, but become friends. So when Brian walked through the vennel that connected the drive at the front of the house to the long and narrow garden at the back, Matty's last-minute birthday present – a Hot Wheels extension track he'd snagged from a Toytown on the way – in a gift bag that kept banging uncomfortably against his thigh, he was greeted by a swarm of people nursing drinks and buzzing with good-natured chatter.

They'd lucked out on the weather. It was biting cold, but sunny and cloudless. So the party had spread out into the garden. There were even a few people in T-shirts and shorts – leave it to the Scots to strip off the second a square inch of sun made an appearance, never mind that the high was five degrees Celsius. A gaudily coloured bouncy castle shaped like a crocodile, its opening a bright red maw lined with pearly white plastic canines, took up most of the small expanse of grass. Several five- and six-year-olds were jumping about inside, their excited shrieks making Brian wince. On the decked patio area, beneath a tent Liam had probably erected for the occasion – sun or no sun, this was still January in Scotland – there was a fold-out table with two jugs of squash, a large bowl of crisps, rainbow-coloured paper plates and cups, and a *Paw Patrol* birthday cake.

In the thick of the bedlam around the bouncy castle, Liam, his quiff impeccably styled but his shirt visibly rumpled, even from twelve feet away, was sipping a Corona and holding court with a short, stubby man Brian seemed to remember was called Jonny, and a forty-something he'd have mistaken for Liam's garden rake were it not for the humongous beer belly jutting out of the waistband of a pair of jeans that looked too shiny to be anything but pack-fresh.

Brian waved hesitantly, gripping the gift bag as if his life depended on it. Christ, this was a terrible mistake. He shouldn't have come. There were too many people. Too many memories. And he felt – and probably looked, despite his best efforts – like shite. He took a tentative step backward. But then Liam waved back and pointed at the patio door in a gesture meant to convey, 'Go inside and help yourself.' He'd been spotted. No turning back.

Reluctantly, feeling his stomach clench and a cold tingle at the base of his skull, he waded through the crowd and climbed up the three steps that lead into the kitchen-diner.

'B! There you are,' a warm voice greeted him as soon as he'd crossed the threshold. 'Thank you for coming.'

Amelia went over and hugged him. Tight. Tighter than he expected. He returned the hug as best he could, wrapping his free hand around her. Then she held him at arm's length and studied him.

'How are you, Amelia?' Brian said gruffly.

A cocktail of sadness and pain—

And guilt... Oh, so much guilt. I caused this. Aye, I did. Aye, I did.

—ambushed him. He swallowed.

'I'm well, thank you,' Amelia replied. 'As well as ... well, you know.' Her eyes glistened, but she held his gaze. 'How are you?'

How was he? What a question. Ghastly. That's how he was. Like the ground was crumbling beneath him and he was too tired to keep up the pace required to stay ahead of the cave-in for much longer.

'Good,' he lied. 'Aye. Doing OK. Chugging along.' It didn't sound convincing.

'You know you can't blame yourself, right, B?' Amelia said. 'And I'm sure he'd tell you the same if he could—' Her voice caught, and she didn't finish.

As ever, her seemingly uncanny ability to voice what others were feeling took him by surprise. He used to admire this quality in her. Sometimes, he even joked she'd make a better DI than Liam. But, today, he resented it. It made him feel like he was naked in front of a crowd of strangers. He took a breath. The tightness in his throat eased just enough for him to trust himself to talk.

'You're looking well,' he said.

And she did. Her strawberry-blonde hair was tied back in a careless ponytail, and the black jumper and blue jeans she was wearing accentuated her slim figure in all the right places. It was only her eyes that betrayed tiredness and, perhaps, some deeper emotion she was fighting hard to keep hidden. But you'd have to be looking for it to notice.

'Matty asks after you, you know,' she said.

'It's been a busy time,' Brian said. 'I just got back to work and I have two investigations on my hands. But I promise I'll do my very best to visit soon.'

'Well, I'll hold you to that, OK?' Amelia said.

She smiled warmly as she said this. It crinkled the corners of her eyes and made her irises twinkle. Whatever shadow had been hiding behind them disappeared, at least for the time being.

'Speaking of Matty,' Brian said. 'Where's the birthday boy?'

'Jumping around on the bouncy castle,' Amelia said.

'Aye, right. Of course he is.'

He swallowed, the awkwardness of this first meeting not completely shaken off.

'Och, I got him this,' he said, brandishing the gift bag. 'Where shall I put it?'

'On that table there,' she said, pointing to a fold-out next to the dining table that was overflowing with assorted gifts in various shapes and sizes, wrapped in brightly coloured paper. 'Sorry, B, I need to go play host. But please help yourself to the food and there's beer in the fridge. We'll catch up later, OK?'

'Aye, of course,' Brian said. 'Got to be the lady of the house, right?'

She laughed at that. 'I know. It's not my scene at all. But needs must, eh?'

She gave Brian a friendly pat on the shoulder, squeezed lightly, and walked toward two men who were standing by themselves in a quiet corner of the kitchen, looking so out of place they might have been teleported there from another dimension. Amelia greeted them and shook their hands. They both visibly relaxed.

Brian walked to the gifts table, which was stacked high like a giant Jenga tower. He perched Matty's gift on the flattest surface he could find. It teetered ominously, then stilled. Satisfied the pile wasn't going to tip over and tumble to the floor, he headed to the dining table and helped himself to a morning roll, which he stuffed with cheese and a thick slice of ham. Then he grabbed a Corona from the fridge, opened it, and walked outside under the tent.

'Oi, leave some food for the other guests,' Liam said.

Brian chewed carefully and swallowed. This was good. Much better than the sorry excuse for dinner he'd forced down and then brought back up.

'Hey,' Brian said. 'You pulled out all the stops.'

'Only the best,' Liam said with a wink.

'Aye?' Brian replied. 'So where's the caviar, you cheap bastard?'

'Up yer arse,' Liam said.

They both laughed, then fell into a companionable silence.

It was good to banter like this, Brian reflected.

You'd think nothing happened. But it did. It did.

ENOUGH!

Maybe it hadn't been such a bad idea, coming here, after all.

He scanned the garden. A girl who couldn't have been older than four, dressed in a frock covered in pink-and-grey unicorns over a dark blue background and a pink hair band topped with cat ears, was dragging her da toward the bouncy castle. The bloke was making a show of resisting, but Brian could tell from his laugh that he was welcoming the excuse to let loose and act like a wean, if only for an afternoon.

'The Layton thing looks like it's not going anywhere,' Brian said, more to make conversation than anything else. The case was on his mind. Active cases always were. It was how he worked. But he was trying to let it simmer in the background, hoping his unconscious would make a connection that would lead to a lightbulb moment.

'Let's not talk about work, come on,' Liam pouted. 'It's Saturday afternoon. It's my wean's birthday. And the sun's out for a change. Take two hours off, will you?'

'Fine,' Brian said mildly. 'Never mind.'

He sipped his beer, relishing the bitterness on his tongue.

'You know what your problem is, B?' Liam said.

'Eh?' Brian replied.

'You need a life outside of work, bud. Something to take your mind off things,' Liam said.

Brian opened his mouth to protest. To say that work was all he had. That it enabled him to maintain his grasp on his increasingly slippery sanity. That it gave him an outlet. A way to channel the turmoil inside him and put it to good use. But, standing on the patio with the sun's weak rays on his face and the roll and the beer settling his stomach, he was starting to think that, perhaps, Liam was on to something. Away from it all – from work, from his empty flat, from being alone with his thoughts – there was even an inkling he might find a way through.

'Maybe you're right,' he conceded, around a sip of beer.

'Our work,' Liam continued. 'The shite we deal with. Especially ... you know. You can't be focused on that twenty-four seven. It's not good for you.'

Liam's words put an end to Brian's brief respite. There he was again, in the middle of a room that had been stripped back to brick. Unable to tear his gaze away from the girl. From her dead eyes, and the black track marks snaking down both her arms. The hockey stick, coming out of nowhere. The crunch of wood on splintering bone. He felt a catch in his throat.

'How long has it been?' Liam said.

'Eh? I didn't catch that, sorry. My mind drifted for a second.' Brian said.

'I said you should start dating again. How long has it been since Laura?'

And there it was. The topic of life after his divorce

coming up like a bad penny, with no forewarning. Give Liam an inch, and his unhealthy interest in Brian's love life would come out at some point.

'Ah, aye. Thank you for reminding me I'm a cliché,' Brian snapped.

It was meant as a joke, but it fell flat. If Liam weren't such a nosey prick, he'd have even apologised.

'Sorry I didn't mean it that way. You're not a cliché, bud. You did your best. Sometimes people drift apart and it's nobody's fault.'

Liam sucked his teeth in, bounced on the balls of his feet. Sipped his beer.

'Aye, too right,' Brian sighed.

The atmosphere was getting oppressive. He looked at the half-eaten morning roll in his hand, and wondered how the hell he'd been enjoying it. The sight of it was turning his stomach.

'Whew, what a downer,' Liam laughed. 'Let's talk about something fun. It's a party after all. Weans' party. But still.'

'It's fine, I—'

'Hey, have you met Lisa?' Liam asked, pointing to an olive-skinned woman who was helping herself to a handful of crisps from the snacks table a few yards away.

At the mention of her name, Lisa's head snapped toward them, her mouth frozen mid-chew. Matty chose that exact moment to collide head on with another boy. They fell off the bouncy castle onto the rubber mat below, grasping at each other like two discombobulated drunks sliding down a hill. Both let out ear-splitting, high-pitched wails and simultaneously burst into tears.

'Uh-oh. Got to go, bud. Duty calls,' Liam said. 'I'll catch you in a bit, but you guys get to know each other in the meantime, eh.'

He dropped Brian an exaggerated wink, which Lisa couldn't possibly have missed unless she was half-blind, and jogged gracefully through the crowd. Lisa and Brian's eyes locked. She looked like she'd just suffered a bad case of whiplash. She swallowed her mouthful of crisps, then scanned the garden, looking for somebody who might extricate her.

Och, Liam, you fucking prick, Brian thought. 'Er, hello,' he said to Lisa, as smoothly as he could, which wasn't especially smooth.

'Hi?' she said, her tone unsure. She wiped her free hand on the seat of her jeans and offered it to Brian. They shook. 'Lisa.'

'Aye, I figured. And I'm B. Brian,' he said, returning her firm grip. 'So how do you know the family?'

'Och, my daughter's at school with Matty,' she said. 'That's her there.'

She pointed at a tall girl in blue jeans, a green Gap T-shirt, and a purple cape tied around her neck.

'She's been obsessed with that cape lately. Even wears it to bed.' She laughed – a nervous titter. 'But I'm sure you know how weans are.'

'Och, er, I don't have any of my own, I'm afraid, so my knowledge is all second-hand,' Brian said.

'Ah, right, sorry. I shouldn't have assumed. So how do you ...?' She made an expansive gesture with her hand.

'Och, I ... I'm polis. I work with Liam,' he said.

He glanced in the bouncy castle's direction. The

crisis seemed to have been averted. Both Matty and the other boy were back inside the crocodile's mouth, jumping as high as they could go as if nothing had happened, their shrieks mingling with those of the other weans to create an impressive racket. You had to give it to them, Brian reflected. Weans were resilient.

Lisa stepped away from him. 'Och,' she stammered. 'Och. Right. You're... Right!'

Brian watched her, nonplussed. Why was she so taken aback? What the hell was going on?

'I'm sorry,' he said. 'Have I said something wrong?'

'Mummy! Mummy!' the girl shouted, going in between them, grabbing Lisa by the hand and pulling. 'Come! Come with me on the bouncy castle!'

'Er. No. No, you're fine. Em—' Lisa said, unable to disguise the relief flooding her face at having received this unexpected get-out-of-jail-free card. 'Sorry, I... I've got to go.'

Brian watched them make their way to the bouncy castle – the girl striding resolutely forward while pulling Lisa behind her – unsure what to think about what had just happened. In general, he found people tended to react to his job in one of two ways: morbid fascination, or embarrassment. The former usually started firing questions and spouting off absolute garbage they'd learned off *CSI* and *Law and Order*. The latter squirmed, usually because they'd had bad experiences with the polis in the past. But if Lisa was the second kind, why had she come to the party? Surely, she knew Liam was a DI?

Speaking of which, where was Liam? Where'd he disappeared to?

Brian lifted his beer to his lips. It was empty. At some point, he'd drained the bottle. He stared at it for a long second, as if doing so would fill it back up. Shrugged.

People could be odd sometimes, he reflected, as he made his way to the kitchen for a refill. Really fucking odd.

Chapter Thirty-Nine

Despite the rollercoaster of emotions, Brian thought he was handling being at Matty's birthday party reasonably well. Until they cut the cake.

He wasn't sure what it was about watching Matty blow out the five blue-and-red candles on his *Paw Patrol* cake while the guests belted out a tuneless rendition of 'Happy Birthday' that set him off. Maybe it was Amelia, fighting to keep her composure as she took photos of the cake-cutting with her phone. Or Matty's ear-to-ear smile and chocolate-streaked cheeks. How he seemed blissfully unaware that anything out of the ordinary was going on in his life.

Whatever it was, it stole over Brian then gripped him in its steel claws. One second, he was mumbling the words to the song under his breath, another hopelessly off-key voice in the multitude. The next, he was wondering what Matty had been told. Which led to visions of jakies bashing in skulls with bats and a crushing weight on his chest that made it almost impossible to breathe.

Even though they were out in the garden, his body flushed as if he'd been bundled in quilts and locked in a sauna with the heat turned up to maximum. White spots flashed in front of his eyes. The chatter of the guests rose to an impossibly loud level. So loud it hurt his ears, which were ringing faintly – a high-pitched whine like a dentist's drill.

What happened next was a blur. He vaguely remembered saying his goodbyes, promising he'd visit again sometime soon, perhaps for Sunday lunch. Starting his car, his breathing and the tinnitus so loud they drowned out the engine's sewing-machine whirr. Taking a roundabout too aggressively and slamming his right rear wheel against it. Skidding briefly and crossing lanes, eliciting a chorus of horns. Reversing into the car parked behind him and setting off its alarm – an urgent blare that couldn't mask the sound of his wheezing lungs.

By the time he'd raced up two flights of stairs and reached his flat's front door, his hands were shaking so badly he missed the lock by an inch. The key dug into the soft pine, leaving a deep scratch like a toddler's squiggle, then fell out of his hands and clattered to the floor.

'Fuck. Shite!' he muttered, his breath quickening, the ringing in his ears blotting out everything else, a black curtain framing his field of vision.

He bent down to pick up the key and banged his forehead against the door. Saw stars. Shut his eyes and tried, unsuccessfully, to control his breathing. His sweat-slicked hand closed on his key ring. It slipped, and he caught it just in time before it took another dive to the floor. He stood up with a grunt. Tried again to slide the key in the lock and missed. Grabbed it with both hands, so hard the tendons bulged, and guided it into the slot. The door squeaked open, and he crossed the threshold, slamming it shut. Leaned back against it and closed his eyes. As soon as he did so, the images that lived rent-free in his head – black, syringe-scarred skin, dead eyes, blood, dish-sized pools of the stuff, running toward him, over him, threatening to drown him – shot back up into his consciousness, like puppets on springs. Eating at the last shards of self-control. Corroding his soul.

His stomach back-flipped. The room spun. He crossed the hallway in three shambling strides and popped his head in the kitchen sink, turning the tap. Ice-cold water drenched his hair, slid under his shirt collar and down his back.

He stood like that for a full minute, his eyes closed, water washing over him. His temperature dropped. He began shivering, big shuddering shakes that racked his whole body from head to toe.

'What a state you're in, B,' the voice behind him said, cutting through the silence. Liam's voice. 'God, what a fucking sorry state you're in.'

Chapter Forty

Brian froze. Pivoted around toward the living area, water dripping from his soaked hair onto the kitchen's worn vinyl floor.

'It's sad, seeing you reduced to this, bud,' Liam said. 'A fucking tragedy. Shame nobody has the guts to tell you to your face.' He made a disgusted sound in his throat. 'Some friends.'

He was on the sofa, legs crossed, looking more dishevelled than ever. The seams of his black slacks were frayed, and there were bright green splotches on his socks. Slime? Mould? Something else? Brian couldn't bear to think about it. His shirt, once cream, was so filthy it had turned an indeterminate shade of beige-grey. Maroon streaks snaked their way down from his collar, ending in brown flowers on his chest.

'Liam,' Brian said, between gasping breaths. 'What the fuck are you doing here?'

He took a step back, and another, and another, until

the edge of the chipboard countertop dug into the small of his back. The room spun.

'You tell me, B,' Liam said quietly, looking at him with red-rimmed eyes. 'You're the one who keeps bringing me back.'

Brian scrunched his eyes shut. Took three deep, shuddering breaths.

'Look at me, B,' Liam said.

'No,' Brian replied. He repeated the word under his breath and shook his head mechanically. It was as if the muscles in his neck had developed a mind of their own. 'No. No. No.'

'I said look at me, B,' Liam said.

Reluctantly, Brian stopped shaking his head. Hazarded a brief glance. Looked away. Liam's head had a strange, caved-in look. His quiff, the left side of his face, and his neck were crusted with black blood.

'Oh God, Liam,' Brian said. 'I'm sorry. I'm so fucking sorry.'

'It's not your fault, B,' Liam said. 'It happened too fast. There was nothing you could do.'

'But there was,' Brian said. 'I let my guard down. I was ... I could've ... I-I-I ...' The lump lodged in his throat was making it hard for him to form the words. They came out in a strangled croak. 'I should've paid more attention,' he repeated. 'Why didn't I pay more attention?'

'It's. Not. Your. Fault,' Liam repeated. His voice had taken on a gurgling quality, like water that's heated up to a rolling boil. 'I don't hold it against you,' he continued.

'You're just saying that,' Brian said.

He squatted down, then let himself fall into a sitting

position with his back against the kitchen cupboards. A square stainless-steel handle dug into his back, between the shoulder blades. Cold tap water ran down his face and onto the floor, soaking his jeans. He ignored it.

'I'm not, B,' Liam said. 'I'm not just saying it.'

'You... you aren't?'

His face contorted. The pain was unbearable. Overwhelming. Oh, God. What had he done?

'You need help, B,' Liam said.

Brian buried his head in his hands. The dam broke. Hot tears spilled down his cheeks, mixing with the tap water. His shoulders shuddered. What had he been thinking a few hours earlier? That he'd be unable to cry ever again? Well, look at him now. The last time he'd cried like this was after they'd taken Liam to the hospital to operate.

He cried and cried. Pitiful animal whines.

'I'm sorry. I'm sorry. I'm sorry. I'm so sorry.' He kept repeating the words, over and over, like a mantra. Until they became garbled and lost all meaning.

Eventually, the tears ran out, and the rhythmic shudders that racked his shoulders and twisted his gut became intermittent, until they stopped completely. When he regained control of himself, Liam was no longer there, but his words still rang in Brian's ears.

Because he was right, Liam was. Absolutely spot on.

Brian needed help. He was in desperate need of it.

And if he didn't seek it out, it wasn't going to end well for him.

Chapter Forty-One

Brian sat on the kitchen floor, with his back against the cupboards, for a long time. But reflecting on what had just happened, how he'd been punched in the face by what he'd spent the last month working so hard to suppress, didn't bring a sense of closure. If anything, things felt even more unresolved, like a film that had ended on a cliffhanger but had no sequel in the works. All the confrontation with the version of Liam that lived in his head had achieved was to lay bare the extent of what he'd locked away inside him and the damage it was doing. A rotten mass eating at his very core.

The more he tried to avoid facing up to what had happened at Roystonmuir – to the toll it was taking on him, physically, mentally, and emotionally – the worse things would get. He knew that now, beyond a shadow of a doubt. He could run, but he wouldn't be able to hide. Not forever. Not even for the short-to-medium term. But that made the bottomless pit of emotion buried within him no less terrifying. What if he toppled into it and couldn't pull himself back out? What if he lost himself in its depths for good? Then what? It was a question he was scared to even attempt to answer.

He ran his hands through his hair. They came away wet with freezing water, and he realised his feet, arse, and fingers were numb, even though the heating was on. He stood up on legs that felt like rubber. Peeled off his clothes, which had stuck to his skin, and jumped into the shower, turning the heat all the way up.

He stood beneath the water until it scalded him. When he could no longer bear the burning pain, he turned the mixer all the way to freezing. He gasped, the cold taking his breath away, the water like needles pricking the angry red patches that covered his skin. When his lungs felt like they were about to burst, he turned the water off and stepped out of the shower, shivering. Towelled himself dry and put on fresh underwear, a clean pair of jeans, and an argyle-patterned jumper.

Scrubbing away the afternoon had faded some of the numbness, but he was still in a zombie-like trance when he walked back to the kitchen and took out the Monkey Shoulder from the cabinet under the sink. He'd cracked the seal open the night before, but there was only about a finger and a half of the amber liquid left in the bottle. How had he guzzled it all down? Fuck. It hadn't felt like he'd drunk that much. But, obviously, he'd been mistaken. He stared at it, hands resting on the counter, unsure what to do. Removed the cap and took a long inhale. The sharp, sweet, slightly medicinal aroma made his eyes water and his stomach lurch.

He was going to have to do something about this too,

wasn't he? Cut down drastically, or lay off the sauce completely. Brian was one of those rare people who didn't drink for the sake of it, but because he genuinely enjoyed the taste. Or, at least, that's what he used to tell himself. But since Roystonmuir, it was no longer an indulgence. It was—

A support structure.

—much more than that.

God, even the thought of having to control his drinking made him panic. How would he be able to face day after day after day? See the case through? Shite, how would he get through another night in this flat, with only the ticking of the living-room clock's second hand for company, marking time?

No. He couldn't do it. Not today. Today had been too taxing.

Scratch that. Today had been completely draining. His spirit was broken and it needed its crutch to get about.

He took a tentative swig of whisky. Grimaced. The alcohol burned his lips. Lit his stomach on fire. But the warmth that spread across his chest was like being greeted with a warm hug after a long journey. His lips curled upward involuntarily in a half-smile.

He put the bottle down with a clink. Savoured the whisky's faintly spicy aftertaste. Rolled it around his mouth. Aye, this hit the spot. It was just what the doctor ordered. The medicine of the gods.

So he wouldn't take charge of the issue today. But that was fine. That's what tomorrow was for. And the day after, if it came to that.

He drained what was left of the bottle in one swallow, then headed out for a refill.

Chapter Forty-Two

WHILE BRIAN HAD RATIONALISED – AYE, HE STILL had enough self-awareness to recognise it for what it was – his need for a fresh bottle of Monkey Shoulder, that didn't mean he was fine with buying it from the Tesco Metro down the road from his flat, where one of the cashiers was bound to remember that he'd only just bought his last bottle on Thursday evening.

Instead, he headed to the Sainsbury's two miles over. Close enough for him to walk it – he was too shaky to drive – but big enough and far enough from his flat that it would give him a reasonable level of anonymity. Whatever he told himself, he was under no illusions. Especially not after what happened earlier in the afternoon. But that didn't mean he was ready for the surreptitious murmuring and sneaky glances the cashiers at his local convenience shop would start throwing in his direction if they realised how much of his pay cheque he was contributing to William Grant & Sons's bottom line.

It was 5 p.m., and Sainsbury's was teeming with

customers. Families doing their weekly shops. Young couples and groups of friends buying last-minute bits and bobs for their Saturday night revels. OAPs selecting which microwave teas they'd consume in front of their tellies before they'd drift off into carb-induced slumbers.

At the till closest to the door, a six-foot woman and her average-sized partner were busy stacking six-packs of beer, bottles of wine, and assorted snacks – crisps, popcorn, and Bombay mix – into their trolley while the cashier ran their purchases through at warp speed. Across from him, in the vegetable aisle, a bald man in a black coat was pushing a trolley with two toddlers sitting in it, stopping occasionally to pick up items from the chiller.

'Daddy! Daddy! Fast!' one of the weans shouted. 'Go fast!'

Daddy scoured every inch of the Romaine lettuce he was holding, placed it in the trolley, then grabbed the trolley handle with both hands and sprinted down the aisle. Both weans squealed with delight.

Brian took a shopping basket from the stack next to the supermarket's double doors, and headed down the snacks aisle. He wasn't hungry. But, now that he was here, he reckoned he might as well stock up. His fridge and his dry-goods cupboard were starting to look neglected. And, once he'd got some more whisky into his system, he'd feel peckish. He selected a 'sharing' pack of Taylor's ready-salted crisps, then headed to the instant meals aisle for Pot Noodle and Cup-A-Soup. The sodium content would do his blood pressure no favours – another thing he'd need to look at now that he was approaching forty, and, with it, heart-attack territory – but he pushed the thought away with promises he'd revisit it once he felt better.

With his shopping basket full enough to give the impression whisky wasn't the only thing on his mind, he made his way to the drinks aisle for the main event. The thought of the smooth liquid sliding down his throat and lighting up his guts made him salivate and his heart beat faster. He quickened his pace, power-walking across the corridor that separated the aisles toward the back of the shop with his head down. He saw the parked trolley, jam-packed with groceries, almost too late and dodged it in the nick of time. It was an abrupt, ill-considered movement and he crashed into the person behind him, sending their iPhone clattering onto the floor.

'Och. Sorry. Sorry,' he said, flustered, placing the shopping basket on the floor haphazardly and kneeling down to pick up the phone.

The phone had taken a beating, but the screen, he was relieved to see, hadn't cracked. He placed it in its owner's freshly manicured hand. The woman, a fifty-something in a camel Barbour trench coat sporting an inch-thick layer of foundation and blood-red lipstick, her eyes two daggers, nodded imperceptibly, snatched the phone away, and walked off, tutting.

Brian turned around, toward his shopping basket, and locked eyes with the woman in the aisle to his left. He flushed. Of all the people he wouldn't have wanted to run into on his whisky run. And, like this. While he was on his knees like a supplicant because he'd been too busy thinking about drinking to watch where he was fucking going.

To her credit, Dr Pam Grace seemed as embarrassed as he was at the circumstances of their encounter. She'd frozen in her tracks, eyes narrowed, shopping basket slung carelessly in the crook of her left arm, phone attached to her right ear. But they'd made eye contact for several seconds. There was no pretending they hadn't seen or recognised each other. She said something inaudible into her phone, ended the call, and slid it into her coat pocket. Brian got up, dusted off the front of his jeans, a slight tremble in his hands, and picked up his shopping basket. He gave her a sheepish smile and shrugged, as if to say, 'Whoops.' Then he walked toward her, hoping against hope he didn't look as uncomfortable as he felt and cursing himself. Why was he acting like a fucking schoolboy?

'Dr Grace,' he said.

'DI Brandon,' she greeted him back. 'I didn't know you lived in the area.'

'Och, no, I ...'

What the fuck was he going to say? That he'd made the two-mile trek so the cashier of the place where he usually shopped wouldn't put two and two together and conclude he was a walking cliché? Another divorced, lonely detective with incipient alcoholism, brought down by the stresses of the job?

'I was passing through and stopped for provisions,' he finished lamely, patting his shopping basket.

'Oh. Right. Why else would you be in a Sainsbury's?'

She smiled. It lit up her face and warmed Brian's stomach. She switched the shopping basket from her left arm to her right. It was filled with much fancier – and healthier – fare than his. Dry-aged rib-eye steak, a bag of baby potatoes, mushrooms, and a bottle of Argentinian Merlot.

'I had a birthday party,' he said. 'Matty. Liam— DI Craddock's son.'

'Oh, I ...' she said. 'I didn't know you were close.'

Brian nodded, not trusting himself to speak.

'I suppose that must... It must've made it all much harder,' she said, her voice hushed. 'The assault, I mean.'

You have no idea, Brian said to himself. For a moment, he was back in his flat, having a conversation with a ghost. Hell, he'd spent all week having conversations with a ghost. What must've everyone thought? Stebbings. Pam. Fiona. That good-for-nothing bastard McGillivray ...

Pam must've seen something in his expression, because she leaned in and touched his hand. 'Do you ... do you want to grab a coffee? Have a natter?' she said.

He thought of his plans for the night. How it would most likely end as his nights always did these days: sweat-drenched nightmares followed by his head buried deep inside the toilet bowl, acid burning his throat and snot, sick, and saliva caking his face. He considered telling her he had somewhere else to be. But she was eyeing the assortment of bachelor staples in his shopping basket, and he decided that, seeing as he had to work with her, a pity coffee was better than letting her go home and think what a pathetic excuse for a human he was.

'Sure, but I don't want to spoil your plans,' he said, nodding at her shopping basket.

'Oh, you're fine,' she said. 'Nothing that can't wait. A coffee would be nice.'

'OK, great,' Brian said as they headed for the tills, aiming for nonchalance but unsure whether he'd succeeded.

It would probably be good for him not to go back home just yet. And, perhaps Pam was right. A coffee would be nice.

So nice that he temporarily forgot what he'd gone to Sainsbury's for.

Chapter Forty-Three

'No way!' Brian said. He wiped the tears that were streaming down his cheeks with the back of his hand. His stomach ached. 'God, I'd heard rumours. And, of course, I've had to deal with his fuck-ups a few times. But this is ...'

'A whole other level,' Pam finished. 'You can't make this stuff up.'

She'd been regaling him with tales of Dr Henderson's shenanigans for the past half an hour. Each story more outlandish than the previous. The latest one – which had made Brian laugh so hard the septuagenarian with a liver-spot-encrusted pate and inch-thick lenses in tortoiseshell glasses at the next table had given them a startled look over his copy of the *Daily Record* – involved her boss releasing an arson victim to the funeral home, only to realise, four hours after the body had been collected, that he'd accidentally left his wristwatch inside the chest cavity.

'I suppose that's one way to try to work out the time

of death,' Pam said, dropping her voice in a weirdly accurate approximation of Henderson's bass.

Brian doubled over as his stomach muscles cramped with laughter and accidentally hit the table with his elbow, spilling coffee everywhere.

'Ah. Shite. Sorry,' he said, mopping the puddle of liquid with a napkin.

'It's fine,' Pam said. Her cheeks were flushed, as if she'd been drinking cocktails, not an almond-milk latte, and her eyes twinkled.

'I hope he hasn't made you regret moving here,' Brian said, balling the coffee-soaked napkin and placing it on his saucer. 'He does my head in – and I don't have to share office space with him.'

'He's not that bad once you get used to him,' she said. 'It's like a fridge's motor. You learn to filter it out.'

Brian barked another laugh. 'That's one way to look at it.'

From the few interactions they'd had, Pam had always struck him as having an irreverent side, but she'd surprised him with just how droll she was. In a very good way. Sitting across from her at a corner table in the Sainsbury's café, it was like he'd pressed pause on his life, or slowed down the playback speed. He was in the moment, enjoying every instant to the fullest. For once, nothing else mattered. Not Ray Higgins and the tangled web he'd weaved. Not Danny Walton. Not Alice Higgins or Gerald Layton.

Not Liam or his family.

Was this how people who—

Hadn't watched a colleague and friend get their head bashed in on the job.

—had their head screwed on straight felt all the time? One could get used to it.

'What brought you here, anyway?' he asked, partly to keep the conversation going and partly because he was genuinely curious.

'To Strathburgh, you mean?' she said, shifting in her seat.

'Och. Sorry, I didn't mean to pry,' Brian said, hoping he hadn't put her off by being too nosey.

'No, no. It's fine. I ...' she hesitated. 'Well, I moved here for university, and quite liked the place.'

She took a sip of coffee, then slid an errant strand of golden hair behind her right ear. A careless gesture which, disconcertingly, made Brian's heart flutter.

'But you know how it is,' she continued, choosing her words carefully. 'When you're young, you have an idealised view of how your life should go. And at the time I thought that meant living in London.'

'Ah,' Brian said. 'Personally, I've never seen the attraction.'

'So you've always lived here?' Pam asked.

'Aye. Born and bred.'

They held each other's gaze. Time stretched. Malleable. Elastic. Pam broke eye contact first.

'You're not missing much, to be honest,' she said, rolling a sugar sachet between her thumb and forefinger. 'I think many people who move to London do it because they like the idea of living there. And then when they get there, they discover there's a big gap between their dreams and reality.'

'What's it actually like then?' Brian asked. And then, on the heels of that, 'Sorry, I didn't mean to turn this into an interrogation.'

Pam snorted. 'It's fine. I don't feel interrogated.' She glanced at Brian, then placed the sugar sachet on the table, moved it around in a small circle. Brian felt a not entirely unwelcome heat creep up his neck and settle in his stomach.

'It's ... hard,' Pam continued. 'Everything's difficult. And expensive. At a certain point, you start wondering what you're getting out of it and whether you need to live there at all to be successful. I don't know if that makes sense, but it did to me at the time.'

'So you thought you'd come back to the devil you knew?' Brian asked.

She flashed him a wry smile. 'Something like that. But it's good to see you laughing. I don't know exactly what happened, but I'm sure it must've been difficult for you.'

Brian sobered. 'You don't know?'

'Well, I ...' She hesitated. 'I've heard stories, of course. But you always have to divide second-hand knowledge by two, don't you?'

Even though he'd suspected that people talked behind his back – how could they not? Police work was dangerous, but it still wasn't every day that a DI got seriously hurt on the job; Pam's confirmation that they had, in fact, done so – might still be doing so even as they spoke – annoyed him.

His irritation must've shown on his face, because Pam touched his hand. 'It's not personal, you know?' she said. 'As terrible as it sounds, it's probably the most exciting thing that has happened in ages.'

Brian sighed. Lifted his coffee cup to his lips. It was almost empty, and what was left was cold.

'You know what the worst thing is?' he said slowly.

She gave him a quizzical look.

'What I remember most about that day is the rain.'

He held the cup between his palms, as if for comfort, and stared at the balled, coffee-soaked napkin in the saucer, not daring to look at Pam while he was so close to revisiting the events—

That had thrown him for such a devastating loop.

—in Roystonmuir.

'I got caught in a downpour and he wanted me to change my clothes before I got in the car.'

He blew air through his lips. Pushed away the coffee cup in disgust, as if it contained the most rancid bits of his emotional gunk.

'My mate got put in a coma, and the first thing that comes to mind about that day is that he gave me grief about dirtying the car. A car from the fucking pool,' he said, the bitterness in his voice curdling his features. 'How ridiculous is that?'

Chapter Forty-Four

Thursday, 14 December 2023

I WAS AT THE CO-OP DOWN THE WAY WHEN LIAM called me. I was supposed to be getting lunch. But, instead I was wrestling with my bloody umbrella, trying and failing to lock the runner in place.

'*Why not make it picnic season all year round?*' an enthusiastic radio voice proclaimed, loud enough for me to pick up the slight sibilance, even though I was standing almost eight feet away from the store's entrance.

As if on cue, the cast-iron sky split open, and frigid raindrops the size of pebbles pelted down like they were coming out of the world's biggest shower head. By the time I reached for the umbrella, I was soaked. And the wind was blustering with such force I couldn't open the bloody thing. The shaft juddered, straining the tendons in my wrist, and the panel turned inside out.

'I'll give you picnic season, you fucking prick,' I

muttered to myself as I fought my losing battle with the runner.

Then my phone vibrated.

In the aftermath, when it was all said and done, I'd ruminate about this moment for days. Telling myself that if I'd ignored the call, walked into the Co-op and bought a BLT sandwich and a Fanta, as I'd planned to do, maybe none of it would've happened.

But these thoughts came later. With the benefit of hindsight. In the moment, I didn't think. I felt my phone vibrate in my chest pocket, looked down, and saw that it was perilously close to slipping out and taking a dive into the puddle of grey water in front of me. So I dropped the umbrella, reached for it, and swiped right.

The screen was covered in raindrops almost straight away. It was so wet it took me three tries before it responded to my thumb's pressure. Was this another omen? One last warning before I answered the call and could no longer take it back? It's easy to say the signs were everywhere. But, in truth, if I make the effort to distance myself, to be objective, I have to concede that, whatever I'd done at this point, it wouldn't have changed the fact that it was too late. The chain of events that would end with Liam unconscious in a dilapidated flat in Roystonmuir, suffering from an intracranial haematoma, had already started. Things were in motion, with or without my involvement, and there was no way I could stop them.

'Brandon,' I said, gripping the phone and reaching down for the umbrella.

'B, it's Liam,' Liam said, sounding flustered. 'We … I … I … She …'

It all came out in a garbled torrent, and I could barely make out a single word.

'Liam, bud,' I said. 'Slow down. What's wrong?'

I heard a deep honking sound. Liam blowing his nose. What the hell?

He tried again, his voice thick but clear.

'It's Lizzie. She's … she's dead.'

The first emotion I felt when he said this was relief.

Is that bad? God, it's ghastly, isn't it? But, in my defence, for a second there I thought something bad had happened to Amelia. Or, worse, to Matty.

Lizzie was a confidential informant who Liam had made the terrible mistake of taking a personal interest in. (Probably – even though he'd never admit this, not even with a gun to his head – because she reminded him of the younger sister he lost to neuroblastoma.) Lizzie was a bright fifteen year-old. But, despite his best efforts, she kept slipping back into old habits. And now, not only had his efforts gone to waste, but so had her life. Lost to skag's deadly embrace.

'Och, shite,' I said. 'I'm so sorry, bud.'

I knew it was cold comfort. But what the fuck are you supposed to say in situations like these?

'It was bound to happen,' Liam said, though the gravel in his voice made it clear that he wasn't any less torn up about it. 'I kept hoping it wouldn't. That I could help her turn her life around. This fucking job, eh?'

We said nothing. I gazed fixedly at the cars trundling down the street. The rumble of engines and the patter of rain punctuated the silence. A bag – one of those green compostable ones – billowed southward in fits and starts until a gutter permanently stopped its progress.

'Where are you?' Liam said.

'At the Co-op. Trying to buy lunch and getting soaked to my skin,' I replied.

I'd moved under the Co-op's awning, but it hadn't been much use. My clothes were plastered to my tubby frame, as if I'd jumped head first into the deep end of the loch.

'I'm going to the scene,' Liam said.

I switched the phone from my left ear to my right. 'Why?'

'I have to,' he replied.

'Don't do this to yourself,' I said. 'Let somebody else take the case.'

Liam sighed. 'I have to see it through. For her.'

I closed my eyes. Squeezed them tight. 'Are you still at the station?'

'Aye.'

'Wait for me. We'll go together,' I said. 'I'm five minutes away.'

With a longing look at the Co-op, I turned around and trudged back uphill. My stomach grumbled faintly.

When he spotted me, Liam peeked out of the driver's side window of the silver Insignia he'd signed out of the pool. 'Fucking hell, bud,' he said. 'Forgot your umbrella?'

I shook it uselessly. The runner had broken, proving it was no match for Strathburgh's fine weather.

'Well, what are you waiting for?' Liam said, a tad impatiently. He was doing a good job of holding it together, but I could tell he was upset. He was never edgy like this. 'Go on then.'

I walked to the passenger side door. Grabbed the handle.

'What are you doing?' Liam said.

I frowned in confusion. 'Getting into the car? So we can go?'

'Change first,' Liam snapped.

'Eh?' I genuinely had no idea what he was on about.

'The water will seep into the seats and the car will stink,' he said.

'Fuck do you care?' I snapped.

'I do,' Liam said.

God. The hunger must've been messing with my blood sugar, because he was irritating me beyond words. But I said nothing, because I didn't want to make this already shitty situation worse. His mood was understandable, given the circumstances.

'I've a spare shirt and trousers in my locker,' Liam insisted. 'Take them. You'll thank me when you're not bed-bound with man flu.'

'Or maybe I won't,' I shot back as I walked into the station.

Ten minutes later, wearing my still-damp winter coat over black trousers half an inch too short and a striped shirt whose two sides barely met across my chest, I slunk into the passenger seat.

'Do you know who found her?' I asked.

'Anonymous tip,' Liam said.

He turned his eyes to the road and pretended to focus

on navigating the post-lunch rush. But his hands gripped the wheel too tight, and his jaw worked.

Shite, I thought. It's Policing 101. You never, under any circumstances, get emotionally involved. Especially not with people who won't help themselves. It only ever ends in heartache.

Little did I know ...

Liam crossed the Brompton roundabout, famous for its pigeon-shite-infested brass statue of a Westie called Patches which, legend has it, still faithfully roams the grounds of the crematorium nearby, pining for his mistress, a laird's wife who died in the late 1800s.

Six hundred yards later, Liam made a left, entered Roystonmuir – a collection of towers covered in gang tags – and eased the car face forward into an empty parking spot next to a litter-strewn patch of listless grass. From across the street, a group of youngers in identical charcoal-grey Lonsdale trackies looked on with interest, their mouths pulled into practised sneers.

Liam and I got out of the car, giving the youngers the death stare as we walked toward a tower, the entrance of which was marked with blue-and-white police tape. One by one, the youngers dropped their gazes. All except one, a pimply teen so fair it looked as if he didn't have eyebrows, who spat his gum on the ground without breaking eye contact. A challenge.

We both let it pass. Liam seemed caught up in a bubble of despondency, walking with his head down and his hands buried deep in his trouser pockets. As for me, I'd seen the likes of him before and knew exactly how his story would end. The wean – because he wasn't much more than a wean – could have his moment. He could play at being tough as much as he liked. But he wouldn't be so cocky when he inevitably found himself in the custody suite, looking at a long stretch in one of His Majesty's finest facilities for those who like playing fast and loose with the law, his higher-ups having decided he was low enough down the food chain to be acceptable collateral damage.

The uniform at the door, looking sombre, nodded at our warrant cards and wordlessly pointed up the filthy stairs. We climbed to the fourth floor. My nose burned from the stench of dry pish and stale cigarettes. I produced a packet of tissues and used one to cover my mouth and nose. Offered the packet to Liam, who took one and did the same. In the corner of the landing, dry greenish-brown diarrhoea was splattered against the walls and heaped over a nest of used syringes.

The front door of the flat Lizzie's body was in had been lifted off its hinges and left across the narrow hallway, blocking the way. We had to step over it. SOCO were yet to arrive, and the place was eerily quiet. Pulling on rubber gloves and plastic booties, we entered the lounge. It was empty, except for a sofa in an indeterminate shade, with stuffing coming out of it in several places and dark patches on the seats and back cushions.

On the floor, across from the sofa, slumped against the wall that had been stripped back to brick, was Lizzie, looking heartbreakingly young and helpless in a torn pink tank top with *SMILE* in bright rainbow lettering across the chest. Her straight black hair, which in life had been silky and lustrous despite her hard-living ways, lied dry and listless against her neck and shoulders, like straw that had been left out in the summer sun for several days. Foamy drool and chunky yellow vomit had dribbled down her sore-covered chin and dried on her neck. Her arms, so thin they were practically bone, were a map of raised, blue-black track marks. She'd tied off her right arm with a piece of rubber tubing. A needle, still stuck in her forearm, just below the crook of her elbow, told us everything we needed to know about what had happened. She was another statistic. Another casualty of the war we'd been losing since the eighties.

But it's her eyes that would haunt my dreams. Half-closed, the formerly sparkling and now dull green irises peeking out from the wee gap between her hooded lids. For reasons I'll never be able to explain, they disturbed me more than everything else.

Liam squatted down in front of the body. Bowed his head.

'Oh, Lizzie,' he whispered, defeated.

I stood back, my eyes locked on Lizzie's. My throat so dry it was painful to swallow. I was appalled. Who wouldn't be? What a waste of a life. Thrown away like a piece of garbage. And, for what? Because her parents couldn't handle her? Because they were equally troubled? Whatever the reasons, it just wasn't right. No fifteen-year-old's life should end like this. No fifteen-year-old's life should end, period. Not before they got a real chance to do something meaningful with it.

I tore my gaze away from Lizzie's just long enough to give the room the most cursory of glances. It would've looked like an open-and-shut case even if I were a casual observer. The flat had been vacant for a while. The piles of syringes, fire-blackened spoons, and exhausted lighters marked it as a place to fix and ride your high undisturbed. Unless it all went wrong and somebody had enough of their wits about them – or enough of a conscience – to call 999. Coupled with how we'd found her, it had 'accidental drug overdose' written all over it.

SOCO started trickling in. Setting up their equipment. Taking photos. Dusting for prints. But I knew this was a waste of time. Nothing was going to come of it. The place was too messed up to turn up any usable evidence. Besides, all the evidence we needed was right in front of us. In the needle stuck in Lizzie's arm.

'Are you OK, bud?' I hazarded.

What a stupid question. Of course he wasn't bloody OK. In the few minutes we'd been here, he'd shrunk. He looked smaller than his five foot ten, and several years older.

'Maybe I should've tried harder,' he whispered.

I shook my head vehemently. Gripped his upper arm and gave it a comforting squeeze.

'Don't you dare say that,' I growled. 'Not now, not ever. You went above and beyond.'

I wasn't just saying this. I really meant it. Because it was true. He'd gone to great lengths on her behalf. Pulling strings and calling in favours to get her a place in rehab. Driving her there himself. Checking in on her to see how she was doing. But the damage she'd suffered ran too deep. Only drug-induced oblivion could give her the peace she craved.

My gaze wandered back to Lizzie's face. To her half-lidded stare, once alive with mischief and intelligence, and now blank. Empty. Forever and ever and ever. I was transfixed. I couldn't tear my eyes away, even though the sight of them – of her – churned my guts. The sounds of SOCO doing their work were barely audible. A faint buzz at the very back of my consciousness.

And so was the horror-movie creak of the door just off the kitchen.

The door to the closet I hadn't even noticed, let alone checked. Because I let myself get caught up in the moment, like a fresh-faced fucking rookie.

Because I let my guard down.

The jakie – another wean, three weeks away from his eighteenth birthday – peered out, unsure what to do. Later, while I was trying and failing miserably to get to grips with what had happened, I'd learn he hadn't given the body a second thought when he'd arrived at the flat. He'd been dying for a fix. Craving it so badly he hadn't stopped to think the girl slumped against the wall might be dead. Let alone that maybe, just maybe, somebody had called the polis. By the time he woke up from his drug-induced daze, the uniformed officers who'd come to investigate were climbing up the stairs, and there was no way he could escape. So he hid where he could, behind a stack of mildewed boxes in the closet. Waiting them out. Except the uniforms didn't leave. They stood guard outside. And then, more people, more polis turned up. And his urge to flee overwhelmed him.

I caught him from the corner of my eye, but dismissed him at first. Lizzie's eyes were too magnetic. They pulled me in like a deadly siren song, snaring me. Taking up every ounce of my attention. It was only when the room went deathly quiet that I looked properly, toward the direction everyone else was staring in.

The jakie's pigeon chest rose and fell in rapid bursts under his ripped black T-shirt. His eyes darted from one corner of the room to the other. They were the eyes of an animal that had lost all capacity for critical thinking. An animal incapable of assessing its situation. Of realising it was cornered and there was no way to escape. So, instead of doing the rational thing – surrendering – he doubled down. Stepped out of the closet. The door slammed violently against the brick wall with a deafening whip crack, startling me. Distracting me long enough that I didn't see the weathered hockey stick he was gripping in his right hand until he'd raised it above his head.

Liam and I both took an unconscious step forward. Liam raised his hands, palms out. Another moment I'd keep fixating on. What the fuck was he thinking? Was he trying to show the bloke he was non-threatening? Because, if so, it was his undoing. This jakie was beyond reasoning. His eyes were wide, the pupils so big I couldn't tell what colour his irises were. His nostrils flared. He screamed, the whoop of an ancient warrior going into battle. Charged forward.

Later – there's that word again. That lazy, hateful, cop-out of a word – I'd tell myself it happened too fast. That there was no time.

But let's be honest here. I was maybe four feet away from him, with Liam close by. I should've known what was coming, because it was written all over the jakie's face. I should've pushed Liam away and blocked the jakie with my body.

Should've. Should've. Should've.

Instead, I stood frozen in place.

I did ... nothing.

Liam raised his arms to protect his head. Stepped sideways. But the move didn't have the intended effect. If anything, it made him an easier target. The hockey stick connected with the crown of his head with a sound I'll never forget. Like walnuts being cracked open. Blood flew. Liam crumpled. Fell to the floor.

The blood spatter, impossibly warm on my face, shocked me into action. I ran toward the jakie. Tackled him. He tumbled backward, with me on him, banging his head on the threadbare carpet. The hockey stick clattered hollowly to the floor, covered in splinters and gobbets of blood. The jakie screamed. Writhed beneath me, surprisingly strong despite his waif-like build. His decaying breath, cloying in my nostrils, made my gorge rise. Two uniforms and a burly tech stepped in to help me. It took our combined efforts to subdue him. Meanwhile, Liam was lying on the floor. Bleeding. The pressure on his brain mounting from where the hockey stick had cracked his skull.

I handcuffed the jakie and turned around. Ran to Liam. Felt frantically for his carotid artery to check for a pulse. It was irregular. Faint.

'Call an ambulance, for fuck's sake!' I screamed.

The blood was everywhere. I knew head wounds tend to bleed a lot, even when they're not serious. But this was definitely serious. Deadly serious. And there was so much blood. God. So, so much. My hands were covered in a glistening red film. The floor was puddled with crimson. Liam's breathing was ragged. Rattling. I didn't care for the sounds coming from his chest one bit.

'Call a fucking ambulance!' I screamed, tearing my throat to shreds. 'Hold on, bud. Help's coming.'

But Liam didn't move. He was already in the depths of the coma. The healthy parts of his brain trying to preserve themselves. To protect him from the shock he'd suffered.

He'd—

Chapter Forty-Five

Saturday, 13 January 2024

'BRIAN?'

Brian jerked his head up, startled out of his trance. For a second, he couldn't get his bearings or work out his surroundings. Travelling back to that abandoned flat in Roystonmuir, where the only sounds were the clicking of digital cameras and the swish of brushes dusting for prints—

And the crunch of wood on bone. And screams ... Oh, so much screaming.

—had taken him away. Shut reality out. The clinking of mugs and the buzz of good-natured chatter were jarring. Out of time and out of place.

Then he saw Pam squatting next to him. Her hand squeezing his. The concern etched on her face. His brain caught up.

'Sorry, I ...' he whispered. 'I don't know where all of that came from.'

It was true. What had come over him? Why had he unburdened himself like this, to a colleague he might be attracted to but didn't know that well? And in a Sainsbury's café, of all places?

He reached for his coffee cup. It was empty. The only thing left of his Americano was a small ring that had dried to black on the white ceramic interior.

'Do you want another one?' Pam asked, nodding toward the mug. 'Or some water, maybe?'

He waved a hand. Shook his head.

'I'm sorry,' he repeated weakly. 'I shouldn't have offloaded on you like that. It's not your burden.'

'It's all right. I—'

'It's just... Seeing Liam's wife struggle to act normal at the birthday party. His son...' He scoffed. 'It's been a day, I can tell you that.'

Plus, he mused, sitting here, chatting with her about this and that, had lowered his guard. Disarmed him.

Then again, maybe it wasn't Pam. Perhaps it was just that everything had come to a head. The events of the day making him reach the end of his tolerance for keeping things bottled up. Perhaps it didn't matter to whom the ears that had heard his tale belonged; he'd have unburdened himself to anyone in his current state.

Or would he?

'It sounds horrible,' Pam offered, with feeling. 'Just horrendous. I mean ... I knew more or less what happened. But hearing the whole story ...'

'It was. And I just ...' He bowed his head. 'I keep going over it. I keep asking myself. "What if? What if?

What if?" But I can't think of ... I ... maybe I should've checked the closet. Or maybe if I—'

She placed a finger on his lips to silence him. Her skin felt cool.

'You can't torture yourself like this,' she said. 'Things always seem simpler with hindsight. But you couldn't have possibly known.'

Hearing her reflect back to him what he repeatedly told himself every night at 3 a.m., when he'd been tossing and turning for hours and had finally given up on the prospect of getting any sleep, should have made him feel better. Given him a sense of validation. But if it did, it was hollow.

'I suppose you're right,' he said. 'But that doesn't make it any ...'

Any what? Any easier? Make him feel any less guilty?

He looked up at Pam. She held his gaze. Her eyes were the deep blue of the ocean on a clear summer day. He could get lost in those depths, and he wouldn't mind it. No, not one bit. She wrapped her arms around his neck, and hugged him tight. He buried his face in her neck.

She smelled of lavender soap and coconut shampoo.

Of comfort. Of—

Home.

—safety.

For the first time in weeks, he felt like...

Almost like—

It will all be all right.

—like he used to before.

Before...

Pam returned to her chair, and they sat for a while, saying nothing. But the silence between them wasn't the awkward emptiness of two people who had exhausted every possible topic of conversation and had no idea what else they could possibly say to each other. It was the silence of two people who didn't need to use words to communicate.

When she finished her coffee and they got up to leave, it felt like the most natural thing in the world to walk with her toward her house, which was an easy one-mile stroll through a quaint warren of tree-lined cycle paths. And she didn't even invite him in out loud, simply opened the front door, looked at him, and stepped aside so he could climb up.

Next thing he knew, they were in her bedroom. On the bed. Kneeling in front of each other. Drinking each other in.

Their mouths joined, and her tongue slid into his. Probing. Exploring. Their fingers flying frantically over buttons, then ripping. Tearing. Too impatient to do the undressing properly or worry about making the clothes unwearable.

Seconds after he entered her, Pam arched her back, moaning softly. Shuddered. Brian thrust. Hard. Fast. Faster and faster. His face flushed. His forehead beaded with sweat. The veins on his temples bulging.

But he wasn't sprinting toward a climax. Though when that did come, it produced an explosion in his stomach and a light-headedness that made his muscles tremble helplessly in ecstasy.

No, what he was really doing was running away.

Running away from himself.

Chapter Forty-Six

Sunday, 14 January 2024

When Brian woke up after a deep, dreamless sleep at eight the next morning – a lie-in, by recent standards – he felt refreshed. Probably because, for the first time in a month, he didn't have the pounding headache, burning throat, or dragon-shite-tasting breath a whisky hangover brought with it. He was actually – dare he say it? – hungry.

He stepped into the shower, standing beneath the hot water for as long as he could bear it, his mind completely blank, then changed into jeans and a plaid shirt and headed into the kitchen, feeling better than he had in ages. There was even a subtle but unmistakable spring in his step. Who'd have thought?

But, as he moved from one side of the kitchen to the other, brewing coffee, making toast with what he could salvage from the loaf of sliced white he'd found mouldering in a dark recess of his dried-goods cupboard, and reviewing the events of the previous evening, his elation slowly but surely dissipated. Eroded by apprehension and then replaced by the dread that had become a permanent fixture in his life.

One question kept bouncing around the four corners of his skull. What the fuck had he been thinking? What had come over him? Why, oh why, oh why had he bared his fucking soul and then gone to bed with her?

He liked Pam, aye. He was sure of it. She was smart. Funny. And the sex had been ... Well ... His sex life had fizzled out well before his divorce, and he'd never been what you'd call a ladies' man, so he didn't have much to compare with. But there was no arguing with how good it had been. For him *and* for her. And yet, he couldn't shake the feeling that this wouldn't end well. There was no way it could. He'd fuck it up. Poison it like he always did. One way or another—

Laura. Liam. Amelia. Matty ...

—those around him always got hurt.

'Bud, enough of this,' Liam whispered.

The voice was so close it made Brian jump. He could swear he'd felt warm breath on his ear on the final S in *this*. But when he turned around, clutching the butter knife and trying to look everywhere at once, the kitchen was empty. The only sound was the hot coffee bubbling out of the machine and into the mug.

He laughed. It had a high-pitched, hysterical edge he didn't care for. Christ alive. He was going round the bend, and the day hadn't even begun yet. He'd had half a notion he might work from home. Maybe even go for a run later. But there was no way he could do that now. It was too quiet. He didn't want to be around people, but he didn't want to be alone, either.

He poured his coffee into a travel mug and headed to the station, a breezy fifteen-minute drive on empty roads. Ensconced in his office, door shut against the chatter beyond, he went through the Higgins and Walton files, taking stock of where the investigations were at.

Walton's post-mortem was scheduled for tomorrow morning. Classic Henderson – God forbid he missed out on his eighteen holes at the weekend. But Brian had an inkling there wouldn't be any surprises there. Aye, there was the matter of Layton. But he wasn't convinced of his involvement. The timing of Walton's death, less than a week after he'd run out of Higgins's murder scene, and right after he'd agreed to talk to the polis, was too coincidental. It had to be the same killer, didn't it? The question was, how had the killer found out Walton was going to talk? Had they—

'Sir?'

He looked up. Fiona had cracked the door open and ducked her head inside.

'Fiona, come in,' he said. 'I thought you weren't in today?'

'I wasn't supposed to be.' She looked away, and Brian felt a flash of familiarity in the set of her jaw.

'Couldn't stay away?' he said.

She chuckled ruefully, as if to say, 'Busted!'

'No,' she said. 'No, I couldn't.'

She walked in and stood in front of his desk. He looked at her, absently tapping the pen he was using to take notes with against the edge of the desk. Outside, the traffic – both vehicular and pedestrian – was still sparse. Though, Brian reflected, it would likely get busier soon, seeing as the sun was peering tentatively from behind the pale-grey clouds. People would want to make the most of it. For now, the only activity was two gaunt men with sunken eyes and sallow faces walking northward, bent forward, their thin, ragged hoodies and filthy woollen caps no match for the chill.

Brian tore his gaze away from the window and looked at Fiona. 'So what is it?'

'I think I know what Layton isn't letting on,' she said.

There was no triumph in her voice, just grim certainty. Brian raised an eyebrow. Nodded for her to go on.

'The visitors Reid told us Walton was getting at the shop,' Fiona said. 'They sounded suspiciously like OCG members, right?'

'Aye,' Brian agreed. 'That's what I thought, too.'

'That got me thinking,' Fiona said. 'I asked around at Active Life. And, turns out, there are rumours you could get anabolic steroids from one of the PTs. If you're into that kind of thing.'

'Walton?' Brian asked.

'Nobody could – or was willing to – say,' Fiona said. 'But it made me wonder. What if that's the Layton connection?'

'You think Layton deals drugs?' Brian asked.

She took a step forward, pointed at one of the chairs in front of Brian's desk. 'May I?'

'Aye,' Brian said. 'Please.'

She sat down and leaned forward, folding her hands in her lap.

'That's right,' she confirmed. 'So I called up the OCG task force. Spoke to a DI Hendrie. She told me they've been looking at Layton. He was involved with the Red Hand, but he wasn't on their radar until Boaby Kiernan got killed. They think he's running a scaled back operation with what's left of the gang.'

The Red Hand was one of the two organised criminal gangs that operated north of the River Strath, the other one being the Company. They had occupied most of east Strathburgh's schemes until 2023, when the Chairman, the Company's leader, was arrested. After the Chairman's arrest, the tensions between the two gangs boiled over. In the ensuing war, Boaby Kiernan, who ran the Red Hand, was lured to a meeting with the Company's new boss, who went by the CEO, and poisoned to death. It got worse from there. The CEO was killed, and what remained of the Company and the Red Hand eventually cancelled each other out. Those on both sides who managed to survive had scattered. Gone independent or formed new gangs.

Brian took the information in, then shook his head.

'That's good work, Fiona,' he said. 'But, to be honest, I don't see it.'

'You think Walton's death is connected to Higgins?'

'I'm not dismissing it out of hand,' Brian said. 'But aye. I think Walton saw Higgins's killer and got silenced. Given the timing, it makes a lot more sense than him being killed over a drug dispute. Besides, why would

Layton go looking for him at the shop if he knew he was dead?'

'Plausible deniability?' Fiona offered. 'If the evidence points to him, he can say he has proof he didn't know because he was out asking after him."

Brian ummed. 'Maybe. Let's put a pin in it for now. Dig deeper into Higgins's life. If that doesn't get us anywhere we can look at this again. Where are we with the list of wealthy customers Mango Bank's CTO gave us? Have you managed to speak to any of them?'

'Just two so far,' Fiona said. 'It's hard going. I'm having a difficult time getting hold of most of them, and those I have managed to reach aren't very keen to talk.'

'Keep at it,' Brian said. 'Get someone to help you if needs be.'

Fiona nodded.

'How about Higgins's cash?' he asked. 'Has anyone checked out self-storage facilities yet?'

'I, em,' she stammered, colouring slightly.

'Don't worry about it,' Brian cut in. 'I'll look into that.'

Chapter Forty-Seven

According to Google, there were fifteen self-storage facilities in Strathburgh. Further googling confirmed two of them had permanently closed, while three others were outside the city proper, in commuter towns. Brian decided to exclude the latter for the time being, which left ten places to check out.

He started with Wildcat Self-Storage, the one closest to the Higginses' house, reasoning it would be the obvious choice for ease of access. But he was still going out on a limb. On the one hand, the cash Ray had used to pay his medical bills had to have come from somewhere. And if there were no withdrawals from his bank accounts for corresponding amounts and no cash at the house, a self-storage locker was the logical alternative. On the other hand, this logic, no matter how faultless – at least, in his mind – was the only thing he had to go on. There was no physical evidence that suggested Higgins had had a stash of hidden banknotes. Brian might be mistaken, and this would be a complete waste of time.

Wildcat Self-Storage was a small, squat building set back from the street that, for some reason Brian couldn't begin to fathom, had been painted canary yellow from roof to foundation stone. The bloke at reception, a spotty teenager sporting the first, tentative shoots of what might one day, given enough optimism, blossom into a full moustache, barely glanced at him – too busy keeping his eyes glued to his phone and, most probably, too underpaid to care about inconveniences like customer service.

Brian cleared his throat. Flashed his warrant card.

'Help you?' the receptionist said, glancing briefly at the warrant card before returning his attention to his phone. If he was bothered about the polis turning up at his workplace on a Sunday morning, he didn't let on.

'I'm looking to see if somebody has an account here,' Brian said. 'Ray Higgins.'

'Can't tell you, bud. GDBL,' the receptionist snapped, his eyes never leaving the phone, his thumb moving methodically over the screen.

Brian didn't bother to tell him it was GDPR, not GDBL. Instead, he stepped forward toward the desk and slapped it, palm open. The receptionist's head shot up at the whip-crack sound. He sneered.

'Look,' Brian said, not unreasonably, even though the coffee in his system had intensified the dread that had upended that morning's plans, driving him out of his flat and to the office and, now, here. 'This guy, Ray Higgins, is dead. *Murdered.*'

The last word wiped the sneer off the receptionist's face. He was all ears, his face set in an expression that said he realised it was very likely this would be the most excitement he'd ever get out of this job.

'Bottom line,' Brian continued, 'I need to know if he had an account here, because it might be important for the investigation. So you'll either tell me now, or I'll go get a warrant. And, in the meantime, I'll arrest you on suspicion of obstructing justice. How does that sound?'

The receptionist's head jerked back at that, as if looking for some means of escape. Then he composed himself. Did the maths and decided he'd rather take the easy way out.

'Ray Higgins, you said?' he asked, reluctantly letting go of his phone and typing something on the ageing desktop computer.

'Aye,' Brian said. 'Or Raymond. Try both.'

The receptionist pressed the *Enter* key with a flourish. 'Nope. Nothing.'

Shite. So this wasn't the place. But getting it on the first try would've been way too easy, wouldn't it? Lucky breaks like that just never happened.

'Are you sure?' Brian insisted.

'Listen, bud, I can only see what's on here,' the receptionist said, affronted, pointing at the grime-encrusted CRT monitor. 'There's no Ray or Raymond Higgins on file.'

Brian made a last-ditch attempt. He slipped out his phone, launched his photos app, and scrolled up until Ray Higgins smiled back at him from the screen. He turned it around so the receptionist could see it.

'Do you recognise this man?' Brian asked. 'Maybe you know him by another name?'

'No,' the receptionist said.

Brian sighed. Most self-storage facilities required photo ID and proof of address to open an account, so it would've been very difficult – though not impossible for somebody with Higgins's skills, he reasoned – to use an alias. But it had still been worth a shot.

'That wasn't so hard, was it?' he told the receptionist. 'Thank you for your time.' But the receptionist's eyes had already returned to his phone and whatever was on it that held his attention.

The three other visits Brian managed that morning were variations on the same theme. Some receptionists were more cooperative than others, but all of them were in agreement that Ray Higgins, or somebody who looked like him, had never been anywhere in the vicinity of their buildings.

At 12.30 p.m., his growling stomach reminded him he'd been subsisting on a single piece of buttered toast for over four hours. He stopped at Costa for a breakfast wrap and a coffee, and took them out to a bench overlooking the road, where he ate slowly in a weak patch of sunlight while he mindlessly scrolled the news app on his phone. The headlines were a depressing assortment of doom and gloom, ranging from the low-key panic-attack-inducing to positively apocalyptic. War in Yemen. Possible war in Sudan. Humanitarian disaster in Gaza. A volcanic eruption in Indonesia. A deadly mudslide in Colombia. Government corruption. Topping them off, a headline that, in comparison, was positively light-hearted, about how January was terrible for your bank account.

OVER HALF OF SCOTS AGREE: JANUARY MOST FINANCIALLY STRESSFUL TIME OF YEAR

Do they? Brian thought, chewing mechanically, barely tasting his food. *I don't recall being asked for my views.* Then again, what did he know? As far as he was concerned, every month of the year was financially stressful. A career in policing wasn't exactly a winning Euromillions ticket.

He balanced his phone on his thigh and reached for his coffee, which he'd placed on the ground, next to the bench's front leg. As he bent down, he must've hit the phone's screen somehow, because it scrolled up of its own accord. One of the headlines – sandwiched between a piece on what could derail the shadow chancellor's policies should she be elected into government and a piece on personalisation in medicine – caught his eye.

NEW MANGO BANK HUB BRINGS FINANCIAL EDUCATION AND WELLNESS TO STRINGBELL RESIDENTS

Brian picked up his coffee, cursing as some of the liquid spilled over the lid and scalded the back of his hand, took a tentative sip, and decided it was still way too hot to drink. He put it back down on the ground, scalding his hand again, and pressed his thumb on the headline.

On the next screen, he was greeted by Angela Shawcross, bundled up in a dark blue coat and pink patterned cashmere scarf, cutting a ribbon and smiling widely while a small gaggle of people he assumed were council functionaries looked on.

Residents of Stringbell can now access high-quality financial advice and literacy resources, free of charge, thanks to a brand-new, state-of-the-art Financial Wellness Hub.

Located in the heart of one of the most deprived areas of Strathburgh, this first-of-its-kind initiative aims to equip young people with the tools and knowledge they need to manage their money more confidently and achieve financial independence.

Angela Shawcross, CEO and co-founder of Mango Bank, the tech start-up that spearheaded this initiative in collaboration with charity Debt Advice Strathburgh, inaugurated the hub, called 'Pathways' last Thursday, 11 January in a small ceremony. Following the opening, residents of Stringbell were invited to attend an initial ten-minute financial MOT and get help opening a bank account.

'Today, in 2024, there are still around 66,000 adults in Scotland who don't have access to a bank account,' Ms Shawcross said. 'And most of them are on low incomes or from deprived areas. At a time when cashless payments are increasingly commonplace, this means there's a growing risk of financial exclusion. More and more, you can't be part of the economy if you

don't have a bank account. So people who are already in deep financial difficulties are stuck in a vicious cycle.'

Ms Shawcross, who founded Mango—

Brian looked away from the screen. He'd read enough. Could this be the cause of the traffic jam McGillivray had alluded to? The traffic he was supposed to look into the cause of but never got back to Brian about? The lazy, feckless bastard. He made Brian's blood boil. He'd have to have a word with him. He shook his head. Sipped coffee. It burned his throat.

No, he wasn't going to get sidetracked and lose his train of thought. What was it?

Ah. Aye. Mango Bank, coming up yet again.

He didn't doubt that McGillivray had exaggerated the extent of the traffic to suit his purposes because he'd taken a detour on the way – probably to Greggs or Krispy Kreme, like the cardboard-cut-out stereotype of a totally useless officer he was. But it was interesting that Ray Higgins' last big client – the one that had fired him because he'd tried to steal proprietary information – featured in Walton's murder too, albeit more indirectly. Another coincidence? They were stacking up, weren't they?

Brian's phone vibrated in his hand, startling him. He glanced at the screen and the notification made his heart leap in spite of himself.

Don't tell me you're still asleep? That was fun, but I didn't think I'd tired you out that much :P

He chuckled hoarsely. The edges of his mouth had curved upward ever so slightly of their own accord. He brought up the messaging app. Began typing. Stopped. Deleted. Stared in the distance, his mind blank.

Och. Fuck it.

He was a thirty-eight-year-old man, not a pre-teen in the throes of puppy love.

I really enjoyed myself, too.
We should do it again.

And, with that, he put his phone away, devoured the remains of his breakfast wrap, and headed onward to the next self-storage place on his list.

Chapter Forty-Eight

At 2:15 p.m., Brian crossed self-storage place number ten off his list and decided that, since he was already neck-deep into what was looking more and more like a wild goose chase, he had nothing to lose by checking out the three places outside of Strathburgh that he'd initially excluded.

He headed first to Premier Self-Storage in Laird's Manor, the town furthest away, reasoning that, if Higgins hadn't opted for the place that was closest to where he lived, maybe he'd taken the opposite approach and picked the remotest one out of an abundance of caution.

That reasoning proved to be wrong, too.

By the time he was back on the city bypass, headed north-east toward Bogtoun, his second stop, it was 3:30 p.m. The traffic was starting to pile up, thanks to all the people returning from their weekend getaways, and he wasn't holding his breath. At this point, it was purely an exercise in crossing the task off his list, so he could say he'd exhausted this particular line of inquiry.

Storage City was located in a desolate industrial park a few miles outside of town – 'town' really being just a two-mile stretch of high street lined with sandstone cottages, a ScotMid, a pub, and a tourist information office. Most of the warehouses in the three-square-mile complex were closed for the weekend, so it was deathly quiet. In the distance, a church spire oversaw the proceedings, looking down on the expanse of wood and aluminium siding from amid a small sprawl of houses that, from Brian's vantage point, looked like flecks of pepper on a giant's portion of green salad.

Brian blew air through his teeth and got out of the car. His arse was numb and his knees ached from driving all day. And even though a handful of good-natured text exchanges with Pam had kept his mood from souring completely, he still felt like there were ants trundling around in his shoes and tickling the soles of his feet.

He swung the aluminium door that led into Storage City inward, and crossed the threshold into a narrow, windowless corridor lit with fluorescent bulbs. At the other end, there was an old-fashioned metal desk that looked like it had been pillaged from an office building in the late 1960s. The air had the musty odour of places with poor circulation. Perched on an office chair that was far too small for her frame was a smartly dressed older woman with blue-grey hair, who looked up as soon as he entered. Judging by her expression, nothing much happened around these parts on a busy day, let alone on a Sunday afternoon in January.

'Good afternoon,' she said heartily.

At least, she seemed like she'd be pleasant to deal

with for the few minutes until she confirmed he'd driven all this way for nothing. The desk was crowded with paperwork and an inch-thick Toshiba laptop. Behind the receptionist, the small expanse of wall was lined with filing cabinets, each of them labelled in neat, printed handwriting: *AA–AF*, *AG–AM*, *AN–AT*, and so on and so on until they reached ZZ.

'Hiya,' Brian said, flashing his warrant card. 'I'm looking to see if somebody had an account here. It's to do with an investigation.'

The woman perked up even more when she heard this. Brian fished his phone out of his pocket and pulled up Ray Higgins's photo. He might as well get it done in one go so he could move on to the last place and get back to the station.

'Och,' the woman grunted. 'Oh dear.'

There was no mistaking the recognition in her voice. Her eyes widened briefly, then returned to normal. Brian's pulse quickened, his tiredness and irritation dissipating. It was moments like this that made the drudgery of investigative work worthwhile. Had he been right, after all? Had Higgins stashed cash away? And if so, where had that cash come from? Had he really been blackmailing somebody? Somebody who'd had enough and killed him, and then killed Walton because he'd walked in unexpectedly and caught them red-handed?

'Do you recognise him?' Brian prodded.

'Em,' the receptionist said, her hand pressed to her breast. 'Em, aye. Ray. Ray Higgins. But what's he done? Such a nice man.'

'I'm afraid he's dead,' Brian said. 'Murdered.'

The receptionist gasped. Her hand flew to her mouth.

'So if he had a locker here, I'm going to need to check it out, please,' Brian finished.

'Em. Em, aye, of course,' the woman said. Then she paused, as if checking herself. 'But, em ... Don't you need a warrant to—'

Brian flashed her a look that made her freeze and involuntarily push her chair back, almost bumping into the filing cabinets behind her. The desk clanged.

'I could go get a warrant,' he said, keeping his voice even. Her tone and the frown lines around her eyes and mouth gave Brian the sense that she wasn't trying to be unhelpful for the sake of it, like the receptionist at Wildcat Self-Storage. She was just cautious. Fearful of doing the wrong thing and getting in trouble with her higher-ups. So he didn't want to antagonise her. 'But what would be the point of that except to make me lose time? By the time I go back to the station, put the paperwork together, and the warrant's granted, it's going to be late, and whoever killed Ray will have managed to get away with it for another day. Does that seem fair?' He stepped forward, gave her an earnest look. 'Besides, I don't think Ray will mind, will he?'

The receptionist relented. 'No, I suppose he won't.'

'In fact,' Brian continued, 'I'd think he'd very much like us to find out who killed him. Don't you?'

He wasn't sure if this was laying it on too thick, but it seemed to work, because the receptionist unlocked the top desk drawer and fished out a padlocked strongbox, which she opened. She took out a black fob with a single key attached to it.

'Here,' she said. 'I'll have to come with you if that's all right. Just to make sure you—'

'Aye, aye. Of course,' Brian said. 'Thank you.'

She nodded. 'Follow me.'

She led him through a door, which he hadn't noticed coming in because it was sandwiched between the desk and the expanse of metal cabinets. Beyond it was another dark, musty-smelling corridor, which led into a surprisingly large, rectangular space lined wall to wall and floor to ceiling with gunmetal grey lockers. It looked like the world's largest gym changing room, except there were no showers or middle-aged men who thought highly enough of themselves to strut around with their gravity-hugging bollocks out on display. In the middle of the room, there was a metal table and several chairs, presumably so customers could comfortably peruse the contents of their lockers.

The receptionist crossed the room and scanned the wall of lockers, then inserted the key into number 79.

She turned the key.

Brian's pulse, which had been ticking away in an up-tempo rhythm, kicked up a further notch, hitting race pace. What was he going to find here? And what would it mean for the investigation?

What was stored in the locker was ... not what he'd expected.

But what *had* he expected? A gym bag full of cash and a ledger meticulously documenting where every penny came from, with dates, times, names, addresses, and the reason for the payment? The identity of the killer, with incontrovertible proof, wrapped and bow-tied, ready to be delivered to the Procurator Fiscal?

No. Maybe not.

But he was starting to gain a better understanding of the way Ray Higgins's mind worked. So, while the debit card was self-explanatory, he suspected it would take some doing to get to what was inside the flash drive and the external hard drive he'd gone to so much trouble to keep safe.

Chapter Forty-Nine

'It's a private key,' the officer from the digital forensics unit, who'd introduced himself as Frank Adams, said.

'A private key to what?' Brian asked, pouring water from the carafe on the conference table.

As soon as he'd seen what was inside Higgins's storage locker, Brian had called it in so the SOCOs could bag and tag it and look for fingerprints, fibres, and any other evidence that might be lying around. They'd followed up on the card with the issuer, while the flash drive and the external hard drive had gone straight to the digital forensics unit for analysis, with instructions to make them a priority. That had been two hours ago. Now, he and the three other detectives on shift had gathered in the incident room for an update.

Adams – a bloke in his early thirties who, with his sculpted frame, dark crew cut, and stylish herringbone shirt and perfectly pressed trousers, couldn't have looked more different from the stereotype of the IT nerd if he'd tried – clasped his hands and leaned forward. 'A cryptocurrency wallet,' he said. 'That's a—'

'Aye, I know what a cryptocurrency wallet is,' Brian cut him off. He was excited about the discovery, but waiting around for the techs to uncover its significance so they could develop lines of inquiry was making him testy. He hated being slowed down. 'So you're saying he owned Bitcoin?'

Adams seemed unperturbed. 'We're not sure yet if it's Bitcoin or some other cryptocurrency,' he said. 'We're looking into it. But the card is the kind that lets you convert cryptocurrency into pounds and withdraw cash, so it'll almost certainly be linked to his wallet. Once we have the details, we can find the transactions on the blockchain.'

'You mean you can find out who paid him and how much?' Brian asked.

'We can certainly find out how much and when,' Adams said. 'As for who the sender was ... that's going to be more challenging. In Mr Higgins's case, we can link the public key to him because we have his private key and can obtain his crypto wallet's details from the card issuer. The public keys of the users he transacted with won't necessarily be linked to their real-world identities.'

Brian sighed. When it came to the finer workings of blockchain technology, Adams might as well be speaking in Esperanto. But he'd got the gist, and the bottom line seemed to be that they weren't any closer to finding out who might have tired of Higgins's extracurricular activities.

'That's not fair,' Liam said from the corner of the room. 'You've made progress. Cut yourself some slack.'

Brian resisted looking in the direction of the voice with a huge effort of will. But Liam – well, the ghost of Liam – was right. They *were* one step closer than they'd been that morning. They now knew Higgins had a source of money that they hadn't been previously aware of. And the fact he'd held that money in cryptocurrency – the fact he'd gone to the trouble of renting a storage locker outside the city to stash away the things he needed to access that money – suggested what he'd been doing wasn't exactly above board. Had it been what had got him killed?

'How soon can you track down the transactions?' Brian asked.

'We're waiting on the card issuer to send us the paperwork,' Adams said. 'Then we'll use Blockchair to—'

'What's that?' Brian said, massaging his temples. All this talk about the fucking blockchain was making his head hurt. And that made him think of the bottle stashed in his desk drawer.

'It's a blockchain explorer,' Adams said. His face had rearranged itself into the expression of somebody who relished the opportunity to explain complex technicalities to somebody who didn't understand them – or had any inclination whatsoever to understand them – in unnecessarily minute detail. 'We'll enter the public key, and that will let us explore the information in the individual blocks on—'

'So you'll be able to get the basic information about the transactions? Sender, amount, and date? Is that it?' Brian finished.

'That's about the long and short of it, aye.'

'Good. What about the hard drive?' Brian asked.

Adams's expression changed to one of mild concern. 'Ach,' he said. 'That's going to take a bit more doing. It's password-protected. We're trying to crack it but haven't had any luck so far.'

Brian nodded and leaned back in his chair, still turning the almost empty water glass around and around in his hands. Why was it that the flash drive hadn't been password-protected or encrypted, but the hard drive had? Was it because the crypto wallet had been Higgins's primary source of money once business dried up, and having to constantly enter a complicated password and decrypt the key would be an annoyance? If that was the case, whatever was on the hard drive was likely on it for safekeeping. Backups of the information he'd collected on whoever he was blackmailing? It seemed likely. Unless Higgins had opted not to password-protect the crypto wallet for some other reason he couldn't think of and he was completely off base.

'Keep at it,' Brian said. 'We need to find out what's on that hard drive that Ray wasn't comfortable keeping it in his home office.'

'Aye, sir.'

Brian's phone vibrated. 'DI Brandon,' he answered.

'Sir? It's DS Atwood. Fiona.' Her voice was breathless with excitement at the other end of the line.

'What is it?' Brian asked.

'I've just had a chat with Paul Hamilton-Baynes. And he's ... Well, he's had some very interesting things to say about—'

'Woah. Slow down,' Brian said, though Fiona's excitement was infectious. 'Who's Paul Hamilton-Baynes?'

'He was on the list Mango Bank's CTO gave us,' Fiona replied. 'The list of high-net-worth individuals whose information Ray Higgins supposedly tried to copy and take off site?'

Brian sat up straighter. 'And?'

'And he had some very interesting things to say,' Fiona repeated.

'Such as?' Brian replied. Why was she being so cagey?

'If I may, I think it would be best if you heard the story from him directly, sir,' Fiona said.

Chapter Fifty

THE ONLY CHILD OF A VENTURE CAPITALIST WHOSE firm, Brian found out through a quick Google search, was one of Mango Bank's first financial backers, Paul Hamilton-Baynes lived in a Georgian townhouse in Merchant Quarters, a gridiron of wide, tree-lined avenues and leafy squares across the river from Strathburgh's old town, which, as the name suggested, had been built by members of the merchant class keen to show off their newfound affluence. Brian and Fiona were greeted at the gleaming, double-wide black door by a lugubrious butler who, after scouring every inch of their warrant cards with his doleful eyes, escorted them into a large front room with high ceilings and ornate cornicing, stuffed to the brim with lavish period furniture.

'Master Hamilton-Baynes will be with you presently,' the butler said with the enthusiasm of a funeral director leading mourners toward their deceased loved one's open coffin. He bowed minutely and stepped out of the room, leaving Brian and Fiona to stand awkwardly in a corner, waiting for Hamilton-Baynes to grace them with his presence.

The room was so jam-packed that, despite its cavernous size, there was barely anywhere to move, and the heating had been jacked up to an uncomfortable temperature. Brian's hands shot automatically to his coat. He stopped himself just in time, before he began taking it off. Every available surface – and there were a lot of surfaces: coffee tables, end tables, console tables, nesting tables, sideboards, whatnots, you name it – was stacked with knick-knacks that were polished to within an inch of their lives and looked far too ostentatious to be anything but genuine antiques. The last thing he wanted to do was accidentally knock over one of them and spend the rest of his life paying it off.

'Inspectors,' a deep, oily voice greeted them.

The voice belonged to a bloke in a checked shirt, dark blue, double-breasted sport coat, and beige slacks. The shirt was open at the throat, and a tuft of thick, black chest hair was peeking out. His carefully coiffed hair was working hard, but not quite managing, to conceal the thinning at the temples.

'Paul Hamilton-Baynes,' he said, crossing the room without a second glance at the furniture blocking the way, holding his hand out.

Brian and Fiona both shook it, grip disconcertingly weak. The deadest of dead fish. Brian took it to mean Hamilton-Baynes wasn't especially keen to see them.

'Please, have a seat,' Hamilton-Baynes said, pointing to one of two very uncomfortable-looking Brentwood sofas that were facing each other across the room.

Between them was a Victorian coffee table with a leather top, on which rested two large Ming vases with intricate detailing in a shade of blue just a few touches lighter than that of Hamilton-Baynes's sport coat. Hamilton-Baynes sat in the middle of the sofa opposite without waiting for them to take him up on his invitation, spreading his arms wide on either side and crossing his legs loosely, a gesture that managed to convey both possessiveness and defensiveness at the same time.

Brian and Fiona both sat. The sofa was even more uncomfortable than Brian had imagined it would be, the wooden frame's sharp edges digging into the flesh of his arse. All in all, the room felt more like a museum than a home. And that made him wonder about the bloke who sat before him. The bloke who was looking expectantly at them with a mildly interested expression, but who hadn't offered them anything to drink. A subtle hint to ask what they were here to ask and make themselves scarce? It certainly seemed that way. Hamilton-Baynes either thought they were beneath him, or he wanted to help out but didn't think his da – the bloke who probably still bankrolled his lifestyle – would approve of it. Based on previous experiences of dealing with his ilk, Brian leaned toward this being a heady mix of both.

'So, what did you want to see me about?' Hamilton-Baynes pressed.

Brian cleared his throat. It would be best to cut to the chase, he decided. 'I understand you spoke to my colleague DS Atwood about your relationship with Mango Bank?'

The fake smile plastered on Hamilton-Baynes' face

briefly curled into a sneer, then rearranged itself more neutrally.

'I wouldn't call it much of a relationship,' he said, carefully. 'My father was friends with Sir Robert, Angela's dad, before ... well ... you know all about that, I'm sure.'

Brian nodded acknowledgement, although he knew nothing 'about that', and remained silent, not wanting to interrupt Hamilton-Baynes before he'd even begun.

'So, anyway. When Angela and that popinjay Bidmead started the company, he felt obligated to help. He invested a couple million, and we all opened accounts to help kick-start the venture.'

'I gather you weren't keen on the idea?' Brian asked.

'I've never met Bidmead in person, so I can't really speak to him. But I know Angela. Her family and mine holidayed together at St Barts a few times. And I assure you, the woman-of-the-people persona she puts on for the media is purely that. A persona.'

'How so?' Brian raised an eyebrow. From the one encounter he'd had with Shawcross, Hamilton-Baynes's assessment didn't strike him as being far off the mark. She had the imperious air of somebody who wasn't used to being contradicted or challenged. But he wondered where Hamilton-Baynes was going with this. What had got Fiona all excited?

'I buy getting into business with someone who doesn't turn out the way you thought they were,' Hamilton-Baynes elaborated, 'but when that somebody shows their true colours and you remain in business with them, it means that, if not condoning them, at the very least you're tolerating them. Doesn't it?'

'I'm afraid I'm not understanding what you mean,' Brian said.

'Well, then, let me put it this way,' Hamilton-Baynes said, recrossing his legs. 'The difference between Russ Bidmead and Angela Shawcross is that Bidmead says the quiet part out loud. Do you know what I mean?'

So Angela Shawcross shared Bidmead's views? And so, probably, did others up and down the country, though, possibly, not to the extent that they believed gender dysphoria to be a marketing ploy cooked up by big pharma. But how was this knowledge relevant to their investigation?

'Mr Hamilton-Baynes,' Brian said, as tactfully as he could. 'This is all very interesting. But would you mind telling us more about your relationship with Mango Bank? How long have you held an account with them?'

'Oh, I don't have an account with them anymore,' Hamilton-Baynes said, no longer trying to hide his sneer. 'I cancelled that tout de suite. Angela called me personally. Tried to spin the data breach as a minor issue—'

'Data breach?' Brian asked. Shawcross had given him the impression they'd nipped the issue in the bud, forced Higgins to delete the data he'd copied from their servers and inspected his laptop to make sure he'd done so. Was there more to it than she'd let on? Had Higgins managed to take the data off site? Brian ran a finger along the collar of the T-shirt he'd worn under his plaid shirt. It came back damp. His arse had gone numb and, when he moved, pins and needles raced across it, making him wince.

Hamilton-Baynes didn't seem to notice Brian's discomfort. Or, if he did, he ignored it. 'Data breach. Confidentiality breach. Whatever. Same difference,' he said, waving his hand in a dismissive gesture. 'So some contractor tried to copy my file and they caught him. So what? It's like she forgot she can't fool me. I know how she operates.'

Brian and Fiona exchanged a look. She nodded to him, as if to say, 'Here it comes.' Brian said nothing, hoping Hamilton-Baynes would feel compelled to fill the silence and come out with whatever it was he wanted to say in his frustratingly roundabout manner.

'The incident,' Hamilton-Baynes said finally, as if he expected Brian to know all about it already. 'At uni. When she got expelled for blackmailing the Singh woman.'

Brian's brow furrowed, still not quite understanding what Hamilton-Baynes was getting at. 'You'll have to spell it out for me, please, Mr Hamilton-Baynes,' he said.

Hamilton-Baynes scoffed. 'I thought your girl had filled you in?' he said, nodding at Fiona.

'*DS Atwood* did indeed fill me in,' Brian said, barely managing to conceal his irritation. He was getting tired of the bloke's oblique way of speaking and the patronising undertone. He just wanted to learn what it was he knew and get the fuck out of this poor excuse for a steam room. 'But I wanted to hear it from you. To make sure nothing gets lost in translation, you understand.'

'All right,' Hamilton-Baynes said, leaning forward

conspiratorially. 'So, back when Angela started at King James, she was doing medicine, right? And then she got expelled because of a prank gone wrong. Except, knowing her, I doubt it was a prank.'

'What prank, Mr Hamilton-Baynes?' Brian asked. He'd known Shawcross had studied in Strathburgh. Both she and Bidmead had, and Mango Bank's marketing team milked the local connection whenever it suited them. But her medical background was news to him.

'Well, I was at Oxford at the time, so I got this second-hand,' Hamilton-Baynes said. 'But the person who told me is a mutual friend and I trust him implicitly.'

Brian nodded for him to go on.

'As he said it, this Singh woman drank too much, and Angela took compromising photos of her.'

'Did she?' Brian asked, his voice trembling faintly.

'Yes,' Hamilton-Baynes said. 'Then she threatened to send them to the whole year if Singh didn't do as she asked.'

Brian felt a rush of adrenaline that straightened his back. Could it be that the person Higgins had gathered dirt on was actually Angela Shawcross? If what Hamilton-Baynes was telling them was true, and Higgins had managed to uncover it, she'd have a pretty strong motive to kill him. Leaving aside the legal implications, blackmail was reputation-destroying stuff. She'd have a hard time rebuilding her image if the story got out. Would she want to risk it, especially after her father's scandal?

Chapter Fifty-One

I NEVER REALLY CONSIDERED MY CHILDHOOD TO BE difficult. At least, not until I saw my father in the dock.

If anything, up to that point, I had an issue with people who complained about how terrible their upbringings were, and how badly their parents' behaviour had screwed them up. I'm not sure why. It just ... It just seemed to me like a convenient excuse for poor life choices. The worst form of hindsight. Because, let's face it. As a child, you don't really have a frame of reference, do you?

Sure, you might have some faint inkling that your lived experience is different to that of your peers. Not entirely 'normal'. I know I did. I mean, it's not like you needed superior observational skills or above-average empathy to reach that conclusion. We lived in a comfortable house that stayed warm in winter, had no mould, and a roof that didn't leak. We didn't want for anything. Most other children in the area lived in hovels that weren't fit to be pigsties, let alone human dwellings. And their parents could barely afford the rent, despite working themselves to the bone on the estate.

But, here's the thing. Regardless of your background, regardless of how harrowing the experiences you've been through are, when you're a child, you're in a bubble. If the house you've lived in for the entirety of your short life has always had the same wallpaper – when that wallpaper, in that position, in that pattern and colour, is all you've ever known – you don't question it. You've no concept of whether it's nice, average, ugly ... or whether it should even have been hung on the wall in the first place.

How can you? It just is.

So you accept it. That's how it was for me growing up. I thought everybody's parents threw punches or whatever household items they could get their hands on at each other when they argued and things got heated. Or threatened to hang you from the rafters by your eyelashes when you misbehaved. I thought consuming several bottles of wine a week – sometimes several in a single extended sitting – was par for the course. And I certainly didn't understand our position. The way others viewed us. Our place in the wider bubble of our community.

And then, my father walked into that dock, looking frail. Weak. Vulnerable. A helpless, disoriented shell of the man I'd known. His face so drawn that the lines on his forehead, in the corners of his eyes, and at the sides of his mouth looked like they'd been sculpted into his face with a hammer and chisel. When he entered the courtroom, shuffling his feet and grimacing with every step, because he'd got into an altercation in the prison canteen and cracked his ribs, something in me just ... broke. Shattered.

Suddenly, everything I'd ever known, everything I'd ever believed about myself, my background, my place in the world, the things that shaped me into who I am today ...

Nothing made sense anymore.

Who was I? And, more to the point, who were the people I'd grown up with? What had they done to me? What were their real intentions?

They'd never been sincere, had they?

No, none of them had.

I'd been used and then discarded. Just like my father. And it was time to put all that right.

To exact my pound of flesh.

Chapter Fifty-Two

Monday, 15 January 2024

The Magnus Colbert building, which housed King James University's Student Conduct Team's offices, was a sprawling neo-gothic structure that encircled Union Square, a slab of urban green just off Merchant Quarters. When Brian and Fiona climbed up the front steps at 11:30 a.m., the sun's weak rays were refracting on the rain-flecked leaded windows, creating a kaleidoscope of light that gave the building and expanse of gardens in its centre it an ethereal glow.

'Who are we speaking with, again?' Brian asked as they walked into the vestibule and opened the glass door that led into the large, rectangular reception area. He stepped aside so Fiona could pass through first.

'David McCabe,' Fiona said. 'He was the case manager when Shawcross was at uni. He heads the department now.'

'Good,' Brian said.

You didn't have to be Sherlock Holmes to conclude there was no love lost between Hamilton-Baynes and Shawcross. Which meant there was a risk he'd exaggerated the story out of spite. Hearing it from someone who'd actually been involved and had no skin in the game would help clarify matters. Tell them whether this was a line of inquiry worth pursuing or whether they should keep digging in other aspects of Higgins's past.

They walked up to an empty reception desk. Brian looked around. Spotted an imposingly tall man in a dated argyle sweater and shite-brown trousers standing across the room. The man signalled for them to wait, then turned back to an ageing printer, which he was unsuccessfully trying to coax into life.

Brian huffed. Drummed a rhythm on the scuffed teak of the reception desk. The man pressed a button and muttered something, loud enough that they could hear but not understand the words. The printer emitted a series of ominous beeps, froze, then began spitting out papers with such speed they flew several yards before seesawing back down onto the black-and-white checked tiles.

Unfazed, the man bent down and collected the papers into an untidy pile. Then he walked toward Brian and Fiona with his right hand outstretched.

'DI Brandon? DS Atwood?' he asked, shaking their hands.

'Aye,' Brian said, flashing his warrant card.

The man looked at Brian's and Fiona's warrant cards intently, as if he were a barman trying to decide whether they were old enough to be served. Then he nodded to himself and looked up at them with watery-grey eyes.

'David McCabe,' he said. 'Please, follow me.'

He led them through a warren of corridors, walking with the hunched posture many overly tall men seem to adopt once they hit their mid-fifties and the aches and pains of middle age settle into their joints for the long haul. Several turns and a flight of steps later, he ushered them into a cramped, windowless office dominated by a melamine desk that seemed to be caving under the weight of the paperwork it held. What little space there was next to the desk was packed with cardboard boxes stacked on top of each other. Across the top one, somebody had taped a printout that read, *May be destroyed on 27/09/2026.*

McCabe sidestepped the leaning tower of King James University with fluid elegance and sank into the wooden chair behind the desk with a contented sigh. Then he leaned forward, hands folded in front of him, and looked at them expectantly.

'So, how can I help you today, Inspectors?' he asked.

'As my colleague mentioned over the phone, we'd like to discuss a student incident,' Brian said.

There was barely any room to stand, so he and Fiona were in the doorway. Fiona's shoulder dug painfully into his upper arm.

'Right,' McCabe said, taking off his thick glasses and polishing the lenses with the edge of his sweater. 'What's the student's name?'

'Angela Shawcross,' Brian replied.

McCabe looked at him quizzically. He was still

working on the left lens. Devoid of his glasses, his face looked narrow and pointy. Ferret-like.

'*The* Angela Shawcross,' Brian clarified when McCabe didn't reply. 'This would've been ... er ...' He made a quick calculation. '1999 or 2000, we think. We understand there was an incident that led to her being expelled.'

McCabe popped his glasses back on and stared at them, his eyes blinking stupidly. Then he snapped out of it and sat up straight, steepling his fingers under his chin.

'Och, aye.' His face curdled, like he'd just sipped his tea and discovered somebody had steeped the teabag in pish. 'Aye, I remember the incident you're talking about.'

Brian and Fiona waited for him to continue.

'Terrible business,' he said, after a few beats. 'If it had been up to me, we would've booted her out permanently and involved the polis. Funding be damned.'

'Excuse me?' Brian said.

'The dean intervened and my hands were tied,' he said. 'I wouldn't have stood for it, but I was still twenty years away from retirement and couldn't afford to lose my job. So I said nothing. You know how it is, Inspector. Sometimes you have to hold your nose and get on with it.'

'Would you care to share the details, Mr McCabe?' Brian said, ignoring the last bit of the statement, shifting his weight from one leg to the other.

McCabe opened his mouth to continue, then stopped.

'What is this regarding, if I may ask?' he said.

'A murder investigation,' Brian said.

McCabe blanched.

'It might or might not have a bearing on our case,' Brian clarified, 'but whatever you can tell us would be extremely helpful.'

McCabe was about to speak again, then coughed. Cleared his throat.

'It's been a very long time, so my memory is a bit hazy on the details,' he said. 'As I'm sure you can understand. But, as I remember it, she and another student broke into the dissection room, very drunk, and took some extremely disrespectful photos.'

'What kind of photos?' Brian said.

'Ehm. Sexual,' McCabe replied, his pasty face flushing dark red. He looked at Brian as if his question had been a personal affront. 'I'd rather leave it at that. It's incredibly generous of people to donate their bodies to science, and the least students can do is treat them with basic respect. And that's all I have to say about the matter.'

He leaned back in his chair, crossed his arms, and placed one leg over the other. The position forced him to turn slightly to the left, making him look as if he were warding off an attacker.

'How did the university learn about the incident, Mr McCabe?'

'The victim reported it.'

'The victim?' Fiona asked.

'Aye,' McCabe said, spitting the word out like it was a piece of rotting meat. 'That's where this gets all the more distasteful. Let's just say some of the photos put Ms Shawcross's friend in a less than flattering light, and Ms

Shawcross attempted to use them to obtain certain accommodations.'

'Accommodations?' Brian asked, feeling his heart lodge itself in his throat.

'OK, I'll be more blunt. It was a case of "Do my coursework or else",' he said.

Brian could barely suppress his triumph. And, judging by the way she'd tensed beside him, neither could Fiona. So Hamilton-Baynes hadn't been exaggerating. It really had been blackmail. On its own, it meant nothing. But if somebody was sufficiently motivated to track down proof of what Shawcross had done – somebody, say, who had a rapidly progressing, life-threatening illness and a pile of private medical bills to pay, and who wasn't averse to using underhand methods to raise the funds he needed to pay said bills – then it would blow the case wide open.

'Blackmail?' Brian said, wanting McCabe to confirm his thinking 'This could be material to an ongoing investigation, Mr McCabe,' Brian prodded when he didn't answer.

McCabe chose his next words carefully.

'That's correct,' he said at last. 'Ms Shawcross threatened to share the photos on the university intranet if she didn't get what she asked for.'

McCabe uncrossed his arms, raised his palms to his chest in a gesture that said, 'I don't want anything to do with this,' and recrossed them.

'And what happened next?' Brian asked.

'As I said, Inspector, I recommended that Ms Shawcross be expelled, but the dean intervened. Something about not letting a silly indiscretion ruin a promising student's future. At least, common sense prevailed and she wasn't allowed to continue medical school. She transferred to business studies. A poor compromise, if you ask me.'

'So this was more than a "silly indiscretion", wasn't it?' Brian asked.

'I reckon there was more to it, aye,' McCabe said, without hesitation. 'I think Ms Shawcross purposely got the other student into the room.'

'Why do you say that?' Brian asked, his body pounding with adrenaline.

'The victim mentioned they'd felt really out of it and couldn't remember taking the photos. Or how they'd ended up in the dissection room in the first place.'

'So Shawcross drugged them? Is that what you're implying?'

'I'm not implying anything. I'm saying the victim was adamant she'd been taken advantage of during a vulnerable moment.'

'And the victim was Ms Singh?'

'Aye. Priya Singh,' he said.

Brian nodded.

'Thank you,' he said. 'Did you believe Ms Singh?'

'Ms Shawcross and Ms Singh couldn't have been more different,' McCabe said slowly. 'Ms Shawcross strutted around campus like she owned the place, and her grades were middling at best.' Another shadow crossed his face. 'Whereas Ms Singh was a scholarship student. She had a lot to lose, and she wasn't the type to get up to these kinds of shenanigans. So, to answer your question, aye, I was inclined to believe that she'd been taken advantage of.'

'She wasn't the kind of student who'd get into trouble?'

'Priya Singh kept herself to herself. Quiet. Not the kind you'd peg for a troublemaker, no.'

'Would you know how we could get in touch with Ms Singh?' Brian asked.

'We most likely have an address and phone number for her, but I wouldn't be able to tell you for certain whether they're up to date.'

'That's fine,' Brian said, his mind reeling with the possibilities.

This was no longer feeling like a shot in the dark. The more he learned about this business, the more he thought Angela Shawcross warranted a closer look.

Chapter Fifty-Three

'DI BRANDON,' DCI LOWE BOOMED.

Brian, who'd been in the process of leaving a voicemail asking Priya Singh to get in touch with him as soon as she could, repeated back his mobile number, then ended the call, put away his phone, and looked up. Lowe was looming in his office doorway, his face cloudy beneath his toothbrush-thick eyebrows.

'Sir?' Brian said, wondering what could've possibly happened to warrant his boss's mood. To his knowledge, he hadn't messed up too badly. Yet. Or, at least, not in ways Lowe might've possibly found out about. Or had he?

He knows I'm talking to Liam like he's still around, doesn't he?

Or that I've been drinking on the job?

No. Somebody saw me and Pam together and told him.

God. He knows everything.

He knows. He knows. He knows—

'We got a call,' Lowe said. 'From The Fairways.'

'Right?'

Unease gave way to intrigue. The Fairways was an exclusive development within walking distance of Strathburgh's financial district. But, other than it being where many of the nation's elite chose to sit on their gold-plated lavvies and produce the same sounds and smells as everybody else, it meant nothing to Brian.

'It's Sir Russ Bidmead,' Lowe clarified, his voice dropping to a whisper. 'The maid found him dead. Called it in.'

Brian's body temperature dropped.

'Seriously?' he said. 'Is it natural causes, or does it look like he finally pushed somebody over the edge?'

'Too soon to tell. The maid was bordering on incoherent,' Lowe continued. 'Go and have a look. Take charge.' He looked Brian up and down appraisingly. 'Before it turns into a media shitestorm,' he added darkly. 'I need an experienced officer on this, and you have the lightest caseload.'

'Where do I—?'

Lowe raised a hand to stop him.

'Take DS Atwood with you, will you?' he said. 'And DI Brandon, I know you don't need me to tell you this, but I'm going to do it anyway. Do not, under any circumstances, speak to the media. See me first. We'll decide next steps once you've examined the evidence.'

His interest well and truly piqued, Brian fetched Fiona from her desk and they bustled out of the station.

'Where are we off to?' Fiona asked breathlessly, working hard to keep up with Brian's purposeful stride.

'The Fairways,' he said. 'It's Sir Russ Bidmead.'

'Och,' Fiona said. 'That's—'

'A pretty big coincidence?' Brian said. 'The universe sending us a sign we'd be idiots to ignore? Both of the above? Take your pick.'

He slid into the driver's seat and turned the ignition.

'What happened?' Fiona asked.

She looked more excited than she had any right to be. Which might be a problem, Brian reflected, given the amount of attention Bidmead's death was likely to attract.

'I'm not sure. Lowe said the maid who found him was too shocked to make much sense,' Brian said. 'Let's go and find out.'

They headed north-west toward Pentland Heights, two square miles of sterile steel and glass that loomed over the city bypass like an oversize vulture circling around a cow in its death throes. A news van was already parked outside The Fairways, slotted behind a police cruiser and a forensics van. A middle-aged journalist in a charcoal-grey suit who looked vaguely familiar was attacking his aggressively pomaded hair with a wide-toothed comb. The hair refused to do as it was told. His forelock stubbornly bounced forward over the bloke's forehead, snaking down over his right eyebrow.

'Ignore them,' Brian told Fiona unnecessarily. 'Lowe wants to handle this personally.'

'Sure. Understood,' Fiona replied.

They hurried up the steps, flashed their warrant cards at the uniformed officer standing guard outside the building, then caught the lift to the fifth floor and entered Bidmead's flat.

It was a flat only in name. Brian reckoned the hallway alone was three times the size of his bathroom. One side of the open-plan kitchen-living-diner was entirely taken up by an enormous, triple-glazed, floor-to-ceiling picture window with open views of the tall, modernist buildings and snow-capped mountains beyond. The rest of the room was as lavishly and tastefully furnished as you'd expect. Marble countertops. Brushed steel appliances. Solid pine chevron flooring. Designer furniture. Abstract artwork. The overall effect was luxurious, if impersonal. More hotel suite than home.

The ceiling was adorned with stepped cornices and exposed wooden beams that had been varnished in a dark stain. Around two feet of nylon rope had been tied to one of the beams and shaped into a noose. From inside the noose, the infamous Sir Russ Bidmead, clad in dark blue jeans, a herringbone shirt, and a salmon pink cardigan, stared sightlessly at the anthracite-coloured wall across from him.

Brian looked away. Buried his hands deep into his pockets, fingers ready to shake him out of the fog of anxiety with well-placed pinches to his thighs the second it thickened too much for him to see clearly. When it came to death scenes, Bidmead's body and this rarefied environment were as sanitised as it got. A far cry from—

Lizzie's discarded, drug-ravaged body.

—some of the scenes he'd attended. But his pulse, his lungs, and his sweat glands disagreed. All three had jumped into action. A concerted effort that gave him tunnel vision and made the room spin. Maybe because Bidmead's body was the third one he'd been confronted with in a week. Or maybe because the scene wasn't simply echoing Roystonmuir, but offering up a stark reminder of its aftermath. Of how, in those first few days after Liam had endured his marathon operation and been placed in intensive care, before Lowe had strong-armed him into a leave of absence, Brian had walked around feeling like he was sliding down a dark, bottomless well while covered in a thick layer of cotton wool.

He turned around, forcing himself to ignore the sweat beading his forehead, and surveyed the scene. Reminding himself he was a professional and this was just a job. A job he'd been doing for most of his adult life. The forensic pathologist hadn't arrived yet, he noted. That gave him an odd pang, like somebody'd pinched the inside of his chest, which added to the dissonance in his head. There'd been countless flirty texts with Pam since the first one yesterday afternoon. But, if she attended the scene, it would be the first time he'd speak to her in person after they'd—

Had sex? Fucked?

—unexpectedly got together, and it added an extra layer of nervousness. How would he feel if he saw her? More importantly, would those around them catch on? Seeing as most of his colleagues had been so discreet about his leave of absence – at least, given what Pam had told him, they'd been discreet in his presence – it seemed likely none of them would say anything to him about this, either. But he hated the idea of people talking behind his back. It made him feel—

Helpless.

—under scrutiny. Like he was some interesting specimen laid out flat on his back for others' scientific edification.

He shook his head. Took a deep breath. Forced himself to look at Bidmead. At his arms and legs, pointing downward, dangling listlessly. At his bulging eyes. At his darkening face as livor mortis – the blood settling at the lowest point it could reach now that there was no working heart to pump it around the body – set in. Below him, a few yards away, a stepladder lay on the floor on its side, slightly askew.

At first glance, Brian reflected, it seemed open and shut. Bidmead had climbed up the stepladder, put the noose around his neck, and then kicked the stepladder away so gravity could do its lethal work. But why? Why would somebody like Bidmead top himself?

Brian spotted a uniform and walked toward her.

'Anyone in the building see anything?' he asked.

The uniform turned away and coughed violently into the crook of her arm. A ripe, chesty smoker's hack. 'Excuse me,' she said, red-faced, clearing her throat. 'No. Nobody. The maid said she comes in every other day and he's not usually home, so she was expecting to be alone.'

'Any other visitors?' Brian asked.

'No. There's CCTV and 24-hour security. Other than the maid, nobody's been in or out of here. The security guard on duty said he saw Bidmead come in at eight this morning, just as he was starting his shift. He looked like he always did. Nodded hello and came up. Nothing unusual.'

'Right.'

It was now past 1:30 p.m., so that narrowed the time

of death considerably. But unless the maid had killed him herself and staged the suicide – which seemed unlikely given the state of the body and the fact that carrying his dead weight up the rickety stepladder would've taken some doing for a single person – knowing this didn't make much difference.

'Find anything else?' he asked.

'Nothing unexpected. His laptop, wallet, keys, and phone,' the uniform said.

Brian weighed up his options. Bidmead was a VIP. His death would feed the perpetually starving news cycle for days, if not weeks. And if journalists were already lining up outside the building, spouting Christ knew what sort of idle speculation to keep the clicks and views coming, this would soon turn into a circus. They—

I.

—would be under the microscope. So they needed to be thorough. Cross every last *T*, and dot all the *I*s.

'Send the laptop and phone to Digital Forensics,' he said. 'Best have a look at them. Maybe they can tell us something about why he did—'

A loud thump and a chorus of consternation made Brian pivot around. For a split second, he couldn't understand what had happened, and he scoured the room, looking for the source of the commotion. Then he looked up, saw the blue hunk of rope dangling from the beam, sans Bidmead, and several SOCOs crowded around the area, looking at the floor.

He walked into the fray and peered over a SOCO staring blankly at the scene in front of her over her blue disposable mask. Bidmead lay in a heap on the floor, the noose around his neck loosened. The rope had frayed and split where Bidmead had tied the knot, dropping him the ten feet from the ceiling.

The sight of Bidmead in a pile, dark, viscous blood oozing from where his head had split open as a result of its violent meeting with the floor, the livid, indented ligature marks on his neck a ring of bloody exclamation points, made Brian's gorge rise. He turned around, searching for Fiona. Saw Liam in the kitchen, his hands resting nonchalantly on the island. Liam smiled. Brian's throat constricted. His breath whistled in his ears, drowning out the SOCOs' voices. He had to get the fuck out of here. Now.

He staggered back toward the uniform, fighting to keep down the acid that was threatening to spill out of his mouth. 'Have next of kin been notified yet?' he asked weakly.

'There's only his ex, sir,' the uniform replied, her tone mildly surprised.

Bidmead's whirlwind affair with Amy Stevens, a dancer in the Scottish Ballet fifteen years his junior, and the implosion of their marriage, had played out in the most public way imaginable. Everyone had heard about it. Even those who consumed tabloid gossip sparingly or not at all. Over the years, Bidmead had also made much of the fact he'd grown up an orphan and was 'self-made', conveniently ignoring the fact that, while technically true – his parents had died in a plane crash when he was twelve, and that must've been terrible – they'd hardly left him destitute. He'd had a multimillion-pound trust fund, a considerable estate, and powerful connections to fall back on.

In the moment, this information hadn't even occurred to Brian. All he could think of was that he needed an excuse. Any excuse. A legitimate pretext to leave the scene so that, when he fell apart, it would happen in private. Next of kin was simply the first thing that had popped into his mouth.

'I'll do the death knock,' he said, his voice a croak.

He shambled toward the hallway and almost crashed head first into Fiona.

'Can you take charge of the scene?' he said without looking at her, his breathing barely under control. 'Something's come up.'

Fiona said something, but he didn't catch it. He'd already reached Bidmead's front door and was making a beeline for the stairs.

Chapter Fifty-Four

The mob outside Bidmead's building engulfed Brian as soon as he stepped out the front door. A pack of rabid St Bernards, baying for blood. The questions came thick and fast. An onslaught. Constant. Unrelenting. A rising, unintelligible cacophony of disembodied voices from every direction that made his head spin.

'Inspector! Does the police presence mean you suspect foul play?'

'Inspector! What can you tell us?'

'Inspector! Has foul play been ruled out?'

'Inspector! Any leads?'

'Inspector, Danielle James from the *Strathburgh Evening News* ...'

The smell of several different men's and women's perfumes coalescing with the bitter tang of coffee and cigarette breath assaulted his nostrils. His cramping stomach roiled, the reverse peristalsis harder and harder to suppress. A sea of microphones, portable recorders, and iPhones were thrust into his face. One of them connected with his lips, sending a bolt of pain up an incisor tooth. He felt something wet trickle into his mouth. Sticky wetness with a metallic aftertaste. He'd split the inside of his lip.

The panic inside him was swelling. Making his chest hurt. Filling him with impotent rage. He bent forward and tried to use his body weight to push his way through the scrum. But it was like trying to wade through quicksand. The more he struggled, the tighter the circle of journalists closed around him.

'Excuse me,' he muttered, in between increasingly raspy, ragged breaths. 'No comment. We have no comment at this time. Excuse me.'

His winter coat lay too heavy on his shoulders. His face was ice cold but his armpits were slick with sweat. The contrast of the chill air and his bubbling internal temperature made him shiver. A hockey stick, splintered at the edges, flashed before him, coming down in a swift arc.

'Excuse me,' he said more forcefully, pushing forward. 'We won't be making any comment just now.'

'Inspector. How do you—?'

'EXCUSE ME!' he roared. 'I said NO COMMENT!'

Blindly, he barrelled through the sea of bodies, waving his hands in front of him like a shield, muttering, 'No comment,' and swallowing down the sourness that was coming up and lighting his throat on fire. Somebody stepped on his pinky toe. Pushed a recorder in his face.

'No comment,' he said mechanically. 'No comment. Move out of the way. Please.'

Somehow, he made it to the car in one piece, turned the ignition, and backed out of the parking spot. The reporters converged on him, blocking the way, their questions bombarding him like word grenades. This was as bad as talking to them, he thought hysterically. It made no difference. They'd make up whatever shite they thought would sell most. He could already see the headlines.

POLICE REFUSE TO RULE OUT FOUL PLAY IN FINANCIAL WHIZ'S DEATH
MURDER IN THE FAIRWAYS
WHO KILLED RUSS BIDMEAD?

Jesus. Fuck.

He grunted in frustration. A guttural noise that worsened the burning in his throat. Somebody thumped on the window. A black curtain descended along Brian's peripheral vision. He had to go. Or he was going to lose it on national television, and then there'd really be hell to pay.

He put the car in gear. He hadn't pressed the clutch pedal all the way down and the car groaned loudly in protest. He tried again, his hand shaking. This time round the gearshift slotted in like a knife through butter. He pressed the accelerator pedal. The car lurched forward, the journalists still knocking at his window. Running alongside him. Until they realised he wasn't stopping, but accelerating. Going from first gear to second to third.

The car revved.

At the sound, the gaggle of journalists opened in front of him to let him pass, like the Red Sea before Moses.

He made it to an underground parking garage on the outskirts of the financial district. Barely. He'd run a red light and almost crashed twice on the way, to the other drivers' very vocal chagrin. He parked haphazardly across two parking bays, then killed the engine. Laid his face down on the steering wheel and closed his eyes. Breathing hard. His lungs unable to keep up. Bright white spots flashing in front of his field of vision. His mind racing.

Maybe he should escape. Just drive northward. Keep going until he reached John O'Groats, then grab a ferry to some uninhabited island with no phone signal or broadband. Somewhere nobody could ever find him. This was all too much. Everything was convoluted. Complicated. And if he carried on like this, he was going to—

Fail, again.

—let the killer slip through his fingers.

The heaving in his stomach was too strong to suppress. He fumbled with the door catch. Almost didn't make it. A stream of bitter, foamy yellow-brown liquid splattered onto the tarmac, looking lurid against the white paint that demarcated the parking bays.

'B,' Liam said, from the passenger seat. 'B, are you OK?'

'Christ alive. Not now, Liam. Please,' Brian moaned. 'Leave me alone.'

He dry-heaved violently. It was like his stomach had shrivelled up and was trying to come out.

'Breathe, B,' Liam said, ignoring his plea.

Brian fumbled with the glove compartment. Produced a packet of tissues and dabbed his mouth. The tissue came away flecked with brown. He lay back against the headrest, eyes closed, his chest juddering. Slowly, it became a more regular chug as his heart stopped pounding in his ears, neck, and wrists. And as his sense of control returned, the urge to disappear abated.

Jesus Christ. What the fuck had that been?

The ghost of Liam was right about one thing. If he didn't do something, this was going to end very badly. He needed help, didn't he? And not the kind Pam had offered him on Saturday; the dopamine hit of human connection and all-too-brief out-of-body experience of losing yourself in bodily sensations. No. Proper help. From a *professional*.

Briefly, he considered making an appointment with the counsellor. Then he shook his head, dismissing the idea just as quickly. He was fine. He'd be OK. He was just under pressure. Everyone got anxious sometimes, right? It wouldn't be right to waste the counsellor's time with his petty concerns.

He opened his eyes. Stared at the car's roof.

What had he been about to do, before he'd had this—

Freak out.

—episode?

Ah, yes. Next of kin.

Except Bidmead didn't have any next of kin, did he?

The closest was probably his ex-wife. And, given what Brian knew about divorce from personal experience – and about Bidmead's divorce specifically, after it appeared to be the only topic anyone had talked about for several months – he doubted whether she'd be too torn up. Still, who knew? Maybe she'd have something to tell them that might shed light on what had tipped Bidmead over the edge.

Where would she be now? At home? At the theatre, rehearsing?

He called up the station and spoke to the desk sergeant, who said he'd try to get in touch with her to find her whereabouts. Ten minutes later, Brian had a phone number and an address.

He paid for parking and drove out. But not in Stevens' direction.

First, he was going to make a quick detour to the nearest off-licence. He'd earned it.

If not on a day like today, then when?

Chapter Fifty-Five

THE ONLY OFF-LICENCE BRIAN MANAGED TO FIND IN the area didn't have any Monkey Shoulder, so a quarter bottle of Famous Grouse had had to do. He took several greedy gulps straight from the bottle, then rinsed the smell out of his mouth with takeaway coffee from the Costa machine.

Thirty minutes later, cocooned in numbness and with his hands no longer shaking, Brian was back in the financial district, headed toward another exclusive development, but this time to where the luxury flat Amy Stevens had won in her divorce settlement was located. Several journalists had had the same idea and were already camped out in front of the building. *Christ alive, what a pack of fucking vultures*, he thought, as he drove into a parking bay that was concealed behind a lush hedge, so the journalists would be unlikely to spot him. If she'd checked her news feed during the past hour, she most likely knew what had happened already. What a terrible way to find out.

He pulled out his phone. Checked his news feed. Just as he'd thought. The internet was abuzz.

BREAKING NEWS: Sir Russ Bidmead dead at 45.

Controversial tech whiz Sir Russ Bidmead found dead at his exclusive Strathburgh flat.

But then:

No evidence of foul play in fintech trailblazer's death, police confirm.

Brian's stomach dropped.

'Shite,' he muttered. 'Mother of fuck!'

Had Fiona said something? He shouldn't have left her on her own. She was too inexperienced. The mob had got to *him*, and he'd dealt with them many times before, though on nothing as high-profile as this. They'd have sensed she was green and gobbled her up for breakfast. God.

He took a deep breath, helped himself to more coffee, which he'd laced liberally with Famous Grouse. It was done. He'd deal with the fallout when it kicked him in the teeth. Which, he was sure, would be very soon. In the next hour, if Brian knew Lowe half as well as he thought he did. It seemed like all the bloke did all day, when he wasn't playing politics or pretending to be a father figure, was scour the news looking for negative coverage of the polis.

Brian dialled the number the desk sergeant had given him. His call was picked up on the third ring.

'Hello?' The voice was cracked. Its owner had obviously been crying.

'Ms Stevens?' Brian said, taken aback. He hadn't expected her to be this emotional. Then again, if she'd married the bloke, there must've been something, somewhere, at some point. You couldn't just turn that off like a switch.

'Aye?'

She sounded resigned.

'This is DI Brandon. From East Strathburgh Police,' he said. 'Sergeant Wilcock spoke to you on the phone? I understand this must be a difficult time, but I wanted to speak with you about Sir Russ, if possible.'

'Oh. Oh. Aye. Aye, sorry, I—' She sniffed. 'I thought you were another journalist. They've been calling non-stop since ...'

She couldn't finish.

Heat rose in Brian's chest. The absolute fucking brass neck. Parasites.

'Och. Aye, that's why I'm calling,' he said. 'I'm wondering if there's a back entrance I can use to come up? There's a group of them outside and I'd prefer to be discreet. Not give them more fodder, you understand.'

'A back? ... Och. Aye, of course,' she said. 'If you take the long way around across the gardens, there's a passageway between my block and the next that leads to a service entrance. You need a key card for it, but I'll come down and let you in.'

Brian had only been to the ballet twice – on his ex-wife Laura's insistence – and seen her picture in the news perhaps half a dozen times, but the woman who let him into the building looked nothing like the image of Amy Stevens he'd had in his head. Perhaps it was the hair. Usually done up in a tight bun, it was now coming down to her shoulders in thick curls that squared her heart-shaped face. Or maybe it was her lips, pressed into a thin line that made their fullness disappear. Or her eyes, dry but red from crying, with the wide, darting look of a cornered animal. It was the face of somebody who'd just suffered a terrible blow and had been hounded instead of being given the space to process it.

'I'm really sorry to intrude at this time,' Brian began, seating himself on the cleanest white sofa he'd ever seen.

'Can I get you something? Water? Coffee?' she said mechanically, slumping into the sofa across from him without waiting for an answer.

Brian pointed to his takeaway cup and shook his head. 'I'm fine, thank you. I'll make this brief.'

Stevens looked him up and down. 'You're surprised, aren't you?' she said. 'That I'm torn up.'

'I'm sorry?' Brian asked, his brow furrowed. He sipped his makeshift Irish coffee. It warmed his stomach and made his head buzz pleasantly. 'I wouldn't presume. I'd—'

'Please,' she said wanly. 'Spare me the platitudes. I'm going to get enough of those as it is.'

She looked him in the eye. Her expression had hardened. She looked formidable. Not in spite of, but because of how she was carrying herself in this moment of vulnerability.

'I know perfectly well what the tabloids say about me. But I'm neither blind nor stupid. Russ is his own worst enemy. But that's because he's surrounded by people who are too afraid to contradict him. I know he's said some disgraceful things ... But he wasn't all bad.'

Still speaking in the present tense, Brian observed. And she'd been right about him too. He had expected her, at best, not to give a shite and, at worst, to rejoice at the news of her former husband's death. Instead, she was defending him? Wonders never ceased.

'Were you still close?' he ventured. 'After, you know—'

'After the divorce? After the tabloids stripped us both naked and paraded us in front of everyone for their enrichment?' She barked a laugh. 'You can speak plainly. I might be petite, but I'm not made of porcelain. Just in case you're wondering.'

Her voice had taken on an aggressive edge, and her eyes glinted. Brian decided he liked this woman. She didn't mince words or fuck around. It was an attitude he could get behind.

'And, aye,' she continued. 'We still speak— *Spoke* ... on occasion.'

'When was the last time you spoke?' Brian asked.

Stevens considered. 'Three weeks? A month, maybe? We grab a coffee sometimes.'

'So you were friends, then?'

'I disagreed, vehemently, with his views and we didn't work as a couple. But we have ... *had* ... a connection. That doesn't go away just because you're not married anymore,' she said.

She'd gone on the attack, but she'd crossed her hands and her feet tightly in a protective gesture. It was as if he'd implied her continuing relationship with Bidmead reflected badly on her character. Brian supposed some people might think so. Tell me who you hang out with and I'll tell you who you are and all that.

'How did he seem to you, lately?' he asked her.

'How do you mean?'

'Well, did he seem despondent? Like he'd been thinking about, you know ...'

'Killing himself?' she finished. 'So it *was* a suicide then?'

Brian sipped more coffee. 'That's for the forensic pathologist to confirm. But the circumstances seem to suggest so. Aye.'

Stevens ran her hands through her hair. 'No,' she said, shaking her head as she did so. 'No, nothing like that. At least, not that I could tell.'

Nothing like that? Brian thought. *Then what?*

'Well, did he seem ... stressed?'

'He was,' she replied straight away. 'But that was par for the course. He doesn't see eye to eye with Angela. Hasn't for some time.'

Brian reached for the coffee cup, which he'd placed on the marble coffee table. Changed his mind. This sounded like it could be significant, so he needed his wits about him. Well, what was left of them – while he'd been interviewing Stevens, his head had gone from buzzy to floaty.

'What were they not seeing eye to eye about? Did he say?'

Stevens laughed wryly. 'Everything. He said it was

hot, she put on an extra jumper. She offered him coffee, he boiled a pot of herbal tea.'

'So it was personal?' Brian asked. His heart was hammering again. But, this time, it was a good hammering; the excitement of a brand new theory beginning to take shape.

'Personal *and* professional,' Stevens said. 'I didn't understand much of it, but there was this deal in the pipeline that was causing a lot of friction. It was all he wanted to talk about, lately.'

'A deal? What kind of deal?' Brian asked.

'Most of it went over my head,' Stevens said. 'But the gist is that she was pushing, but he was adamant he didn't want the deal to go ahead.'

Chapter Fifty-Six

Mango Bank and Settl announce Europe-first partnership that could revolutionise open-banking payments

Leading UK challengers Mango Bank and German open-banking trailblazers Settl have entered a strategic partnership that will make online payments safer, swifter, and more transparent for thousands of British consumers.

The first of its kind in Europe, this partnership will enable Mango Bank to embed Settl's leading open-banking payments infrastructure into its app, putting seamless real-time account-to-account payments at its customers' fingertips.

The technology, known as variable recurring payments, has been available in the UK since 2022, but only for transfers between accounts owned by the same person – a use case known as 'sweeping VRP'. The implementation of commercial VRPs, which make account-to-account payments to merchants possible, has so far been fraught with legal and technical issues.

'Our partnership with Settl couldn't have come at a better time,' Mango Bank CEO Angela Shawcross said. 'Now more than ever, customers expect secure, frictionless payment experiences that put them in control. And Settl's technology will enable us to hit the mark on all three fronts. Not to put too fine a point on it, but it's a paradigm shift.'

'It's an exciting time in payments,' said Settl CEO Walter Birkenmeyer, 'and we couldn't be prouder to be at the forefront of the revolution. Make no mistake, this is a big-bang moment. Customers can ditch outdated technologies and shop with more confidence than ever before.'

Sitting in the car, which he'd parked in an empty bay across the station, Brian reread the press release for the eighth time. And that still didn't do the trick. He had no clue what the hell any of it meant. All he knew was that the article was one of a dozen on the same topic that had come up when he'd googled *Mango Bank deal*. So, this had to be what Bidmead and Shawcross had been butting heads about. Bidmead wouldn't have been losing sleep over it if it hadn't been important. And nor would the trade press have spilled so many gigabytes of digital ink.

But was it important enough for Shawcross to try to get her way by doing to Bidmead what she'd done to Priya Singh all those years ago, at uni? Important enough, perhaps, to engage a professional to dig up dirt she could use against him? A plan that had somehow backfired spectacularly and ended with Higgins murdered and Bidmead dead by his own hand?

The more he thought about it, the more it made sense. It—

Bzzz. Bzzz. Bzzz.

The vibrations startled him, and he almost dropped his phone.

Ah. There he was. Lowe, probably foaming at the mouth. So he'd read the news headlines. Jesus wept.

Brian peered out the car window at the station's windswept entrance. Then back at the phone. The whisky-induced euphoria was wearing off, replaced by the first stirrings of what, judging by the sickly sweetness at the back of his throat and the screws tightening at his temples, was going to be a hangover for the books. Day drinking always had this effect on him. God. He couldn't face Lowe. Not like this. Not yet. He was in the middle of chasing down a lead, anyway. Wasn't he? The bollocking could wait.

He rejected the call. Took another stab at reading the press release. It didn't help further his comprehension by much. Above the fold, just below the headline, was a shot of a smiling Shawcross shaking hands with a blonde man in a pinstripe suit. Birkenmeyer? Aye, had to be, given the way he was soaking up the attention and – judging by the toothpaste-ad grin plastered on his face and the firm grip swallowing Shawcross's hand – relishing every second of it. In the background, two women looked on, all smiles, their hands frozen mid-applause. Next to them, Bidmead, ramrod straight with his hands folded behind his back. His expression unreadable.

The press release was dated Thursday, 11 January. Four days ago. Clearly, Bidmead had caved, or they wouldn't have signed the deal and made the news public, would they? So, what had persuaded him? If he'd been as adamant as his ex-wife said he'd been, this would've been quite the turnaround. Had he and Shawcross reached a quid pro quo of some sort? Was Bidmead, despite his tough alpha male persona, a bloke who'd be easily persuaded or manipulated? Or had he been given an ultimatum? An ultimatum so powerful it not only made him comply, but also put his neck inside a noose and pushed away the stepladder?

They needed to have another chat with Shawcross. A formal one. But, first, he needed cold, hard evidence. He wouldn't bring anyone in and start hurling accusations around without anything concrete to back him up. But Shawcross' high profile and the media attention around her business partner's death made this particular situation even more delicate. Lowe would have an aneurysm when he told him.

Speaking of which. While he'd been ruminating, Lowe had texted him.

Where the hell are you?? Get to my office as soon as you're here!!!

Brian winced. Shite. What a mess.

He glanced at the station's entrance. He needed to speak to Digital Forensics. See if they'd turned up anything on Bidmead's laptop or Higgins's hard drive. That would buy him some more time. But he wouldn't be able to postpone speaking with Lowe indefinitely.

Fuck it. He ran his hands through his hair. Had it thinned even further over the past week? There were several strands of short, silver-tinged hair curled around his fingers. He dusted them off on his suit jacket, zipped and buttoned up his coat, and headed toward the station, taking the stairs down to the suite of offices in the basement where Digital Forensics held court.

The faint sounds of the radio were punctuated by good-natured chatter.

'Admit it, it's because Aberdeen are absolute shite,' Frank Adams was telling somebody. 'Can't hold the ball for more than three passes.'

'The team is solid. It's the bloody VAR that's the problem. Ruined the game, it has. And it's not like it—'

When Brian walked in, McGillivray stopped mid-sentence.

'Sir,' he said, reddening slightly.

The fact McGillivray knew he'd been caught red-handed, chatting shite about the fitba instead of working, gratified Brian more than he cared to admit. So he decided to scowl and not say anything. Sometimes, the anticipation, knowing a bollocking was coming but not when, was worse punishment than the actual bollocking.

A bit like Lowe's call and exclamation mark-riddled text.

Brian turned to Adams, who was on his feet, leaning over his desk, while McGillivray sat in the office chair across from him.

'Any luck with the hard drive?'

Adams pointed at his desktop computer, which had a wire snaking out of it and into a black, rectangular box he recognised as the external hard drive he'd retrieved from Higgins's self-storage locker. On the monitor, there was a dialogue box open, with sequences of letters and numbers flashing rapidly. Underneath them, a status bar indicated the process Adams was running was 37 per cent complete.

'Still trying to brute force attack the password,' he clarified. 'No luck yet.'

'And Bidmead's laptop?'

'Haven't got to it,' Adams said.

'Could you try?' Brian asked, trying not to sound exasperated. He'd have thought, given the high-profile victim and the likelihood it was a suicide, Adams would've prioritised it, so he could get it off his plate. But, apparently, logic ran on a different set of rules down here.

Adams looked at his computer screen. The software was still going through possible password permutations. There'd be billions of them, Brian reflected. And they hadn't even touched the encryption yet.

'Sure, aye,' Adams said. 'Let's take it there.' He nodded to a free desk. 'Breaking the laptop password should be fairly straightforward. Then it depends what kind of security he had on it.'

He picked up the laptop, which was still in the evidence bag, and all three walked toward the desk.

Brian turned to McGillivray. 'Did you ever find out why there was so much traffic it took you two hours to reach Stringbell?'

'Em,' McGillivray stalled.

'*I* have,' Brian said, taking a step forward. 'And I wasn't even trying to. It was all over Google. So what's your excuse?'

McGillivray gritted his teeth.

'So?' Brian prodded. The lazy bastard. He was sick and tired of his attitude. How could he—

Pathways. Inaugurated in a small ceremony by...

It dawned on him. Shawcross was there, in Stringbell, around the time Walton was murdered. His anger fizzled out, replaced by tendrils of excitement at seeing the theory he'd only just come up with grow legs.

Except... how would she have known Walton was hiding out in Stringbell? And, more importantly, would she have been able to slip away to do the deed, with the press watching her every move?

'Call the Community Policing Team,' Brian said. 'Check if there were any call-outs to Stringbell on the eleventh, between seven and eleven in the evening.'

Somebody might've seen something.

McGilliray didn't move.

'Now, Murray!' Brian said, his voice not quite a yell but loud enough to make several people look up from their laptops.

'Aye. Sir.' The *sir* had an ironic undertone Brian chose to ignore. Instead, he turned toward Adams.

Adams had switched on the laptop and was typing something into it. 'I should be able to reset the password from the terminal,' he said.

Brian grunted. He didn't give two shites what Adams was doing as long as it got them into Bidmead's laptop.

Now that he'd placed Shawcross in Stringbell at the same time as Walton, he was keener than ever to see what was on it. Could it contain evidence that Shawcross had been blackmailing Bidmead? They'd still be far from proving Shawcross had committed murder. But it would be a step in the right direction.

'Ah,' Adams said, a note of triumph in his voice. 'Got you, you bastard! Just need to reset the password.'

Adams's index and middle fingers flew over the laptop's trackpad while he hummed tunelessly under his breath. 'There. It's prompting me to set a new password.'

Brian moved closer so he could look over Adams's shoulder. Adams was on his feet, hunched over the laptop. The screen went blank, then the Apple logo appeared, followed by a spinning globe. The screen went blank once more. This time round, when it reappeared, the Apple logo had been replaced by a photo of Bidmead over an orange-and-green background. Beneath Bidmead's expressionless puss was a dialog box for entering the laptop's password. Adams typed and pressed enter with a flourish.

'OK. We're in,' Adams said. 'What do you want to check first?'

Chapter Fifty-Seven

For a supposed tech whiz – somebody who had co-founded one of Europe's most valuable start-ups – Bidmead worked in a surprisingly old-fashioned way. There wasn't any evidence that he regularly accessed cloud-based apps in his browser history, though that probably meant nothing because most organisations used some form of online product suite for remote collaboration these days: even the polis had a Microsoft 365 subscription. Instead, it looked like he saved his documents on his laptop's hard drive, in a meticulously organised library of folders.

The vast majority of the files were work-related: spreadsheets, draft reports in various stages of revision, and several contracts, including one for the Settl deal that was covered in copious comments and tracked changes.

Reputationally problematic! one of the comments – made against a clause dealing with data-sharing – read cryptically, without explaining what was problematic about the text.

From a compliance perspective, this is a non-starter. WE own the data, another comment, just beneath *Reputationally problematic!* elaborated.

Completely unacceptable! a third comment screamed.

Most of the other comments on the five-odd pages Brian went through – the whole document was 200 pages long, though it would probably be a fair bit shorter if they accepted all the tracked changes – went on in the same vein. Of course, there'd likely have been intensive negotiations before the contract reached a point where the terms were agreeable to both sides. But, given how much stuff Bidmead seemed to have found objectionable – there were multiple comments next to almost every single line Brian had gone through – Settl would've had to make some pretty significant concessions to get anywhere close to appeasing him.

'What's that?' Brian asked Adams, pointing at a file titled 'A tiny experiment'.

Adams double-clicked on it.

'Charlie, I...' The words are struggling to come out, but I force myself to look her in the eye and carry on. I need to say it. If not now, when?

'Holy God. Bidmead was writing a book?' Brian scoffed.

He scanned the rest of the page. Not just any book. A *romance* book. The bloke had hidden depths, albeit not much talent. The prose was a collection of cheesy clichés that read like an abandoned episode of *Coronation Street*.

So I had another life. I'm not proud of it. But please believe me when I say this was the best thing that ever happened to me. You *are the best thing that ever happened to me. Not many people in my position get a second chance. But I did. And I struck very lucky.*

Brian shook his head. What was he expecting to find, anyway? A note that said 'Angela Shawcross was blackmailing me, so I decided to end it'? Suicide notes are a staple of film and television. But, in the real world, only around 30 per cent of victims leave a note, which makes the situation even more heartbreaking and tragic for the usually unsuspecting loved ones that are left behind.

If you have any loved ones to leave behind.

Brian shook his head automatically, as if to scare off that unbidden thought.

'Let's check his emails,' he told Adams.

They launched the Outlook app. The inbox screamed accusingly at them – 1,332 unread emails.

'Fucking hell, this will take days to sift through,' Brian grumbled.

'What are we looking for, exactly?' Adams asked, scrolling down the inbox. 'If you have something specific in mind – like a sender, or a topic – we can run a search for it, see what comes up.'

'That's the thing. I've no idea,' Brian said. 'Something that speaks to his state of mind over the past few weeks. Or points to the reason why he might've chosen to do what he did.'

And, ideally, point to Angela Shawcross as the cause of it, he thought to himself. Otherwise, he was wasting precious time and scarce resources investigating an open-and-shut case where no crime had been committed, instead of trying to catch actual killers.

'Och. Hello,' Adams said.

'What's that?' Brian asked, jerking his head up.

'I just ran a search for Settl, since that seems to be the main thing you're interested in,' Adams said. 'It's the deal you want to know more about, right?'

'Right.'

Brian squinted at the laptop screen. Was that subject line, sandwiched in between various exchanges about the Settl deal, saying what he thought it was saying? What the hell?

'Weird, right?' Adams said. 'It got caught in the search, even though it seems to have nothing to do with Settl.'

Brian scoffed. If dictionaries used voice notes to illustrate words' meanings, they'd have Adam's last comment beside the entry for *understatement*.

The sender field wasn't a person's name, but a jumble of letters and numbers. By contrast, the subject line was pithy and high impact.

Nice cock, Russ!

Chapter Fifty-Eight

The body of the email was just as short and to-the-point as the subject line. *We should talk.* But the attachments – all twenty-five of them – told their own compelling story.

'Holy shite,' Brian whispered, staring at one of the open attachments.

'Holy shite, indeed,' Adams agreed. If his mouth opened any further, his jaw would brush the floor.

'Am I seeing what I think I'm seeing?' Brian said.

'I'm fairly certain you are, because I'm seeing the same thing,' Adams said.

The image in front of them had been taken in a poorly lit room, and the background was blurry. But there was no mistaking what they were looking at. It was a screenshot of a bloke standing in full view of his laptop's webcam. There was a black ball-gag in his mouth, its thick leather straps winding themselves around his cheeks and meeting at the back of his head. But the rest of his face was completely visible. The expensively barbered hair. The intense eyes. The patrician nose. Every feature in stark relief. Contorted into a grimace Brian had to assume was pleasure. Because, except for the ball-gag and a watch with a heavy gold chain on his left wrist, he was completely naked. His bare chest glistened with sweat despite the poor lighting. His right hand gripped his erect cock so hard the knuckles were white.

At the bottom right of the screen, a woman was pouting her lips suggestively, egging the man on. One hand was teasing her nipple, and the other was touching her own cock.

The rest of the files continued the story. The woman – obviously a professional cam model, judging by her high-end set-up and the backdrop behind her – was leaning forward to display her breasts to full advantage, an index finger brushing her lips. Waving a leather whip, slapping it on her arse.

And, front and centre, clear as day, Sir Russ Bidmead. His face instantly recognisable. Going through increasingly intense stages of pleasure until he tipped over into orgasmic ecstasy.

'Holy. Fucking. Shite,' Brian repeated. So much for spreading misinformation about gender dysphoria being a marketing ploy. It hadn't stopped him from enjoying a wank with a trans cam model.

'Talk about overcompensating,' Adams said.

'The most vocal ones are always vocal for a reason,' Brian reflected. 'And it's usually to hide their own issues.'

His mind was reeling. The whisky-induced headache that had been coming on with a vengeance a mere half-hour earlier fading into the background. He leaned forward and pulled the laptop toward him so he could take a closer look. Bidmead had received the email on Tuesday, 9 January at 4:02 p.m. and replied at 11 p.m., seven hours later, with a terse, *What do you want?*

The blackmailer's reply had come fifteen minutes after that.

Let's meet by Riverfront Gate. Tomorrow, 7 p.m.

At that point, Higgins had been cooling in the morgue for more than twenty-four hours. So either he'd had absolutely nothing to do with this, or he'd been acting on somebody's behest. Somebody who'd carried on with their plan to blackmail Bidmead even after Higgins had wound up dead.

Was that somebody the same person who'd killed Higgins and, perhaps, Walton too? Or was he dealing with three different crimes: two unrelated murders and a case of sextortion that had ended with the victim taking his own life? It would be useful to see the final Settl contract, so they could check whether any of Bidmead's concerns had been addressed. If they hadn't, it would make his theory that he'd been blackmailed into signing it even more compelling. But that kind of document would be highly confidential. Even if they could come up with reasonable grounds to get a warrant – and, at the moment, there was no real link except what Brian's gut was telling him – Mango Bank's solicitors would fight them tooth and nail.

'Can we find out who sent the email?' Brian asked.

'Probably,' Adams said. 'They used a disposable email address. We could—'

'What's that?' Brian snapped.

'It's the email equivalent of a burner phone,' Adams said, warming to his subject despite the tension of the moment. 'I use one to sign up for online accounts and newsletters, so my personal email doesn't get spammed. But the service will be linked to an account. So we should be able to track it down. Then it depends on whether—'

'You do that. See if you can find who it belongs to,' Brian said. 'And email me those pictures, right away.'

He raced out of the basement and climbed the steps two at a time. The riverfront was two miles of pier dotted with craft beer pubs, restaurants, shops, art installations, and other attractions. It was always busy, which was probably why the blackmailer had chosen the spot. Bidmead was fairly recognisable, but they'd still be two other people in a crowd. The flipside was that at least one of the establishments was bound to have CCTV. And if they saw who Bidmead had met with at the rendezvous, that might be the huge break in the case they needed.

These thoughts swirled around Brian's head as he stepped onto the second-floor landing. First, he'd update the team. Then, they'd get to work. Find out who was behind the email account. And, more importantly, track down CCTV footage from riverfront establishments.

But he didn't make it to the bullpen.

'DI BRANDON!' Lowe bellowed, stopping him in his tracks. 'My office. Now!'

Chapter Fifty-Nine

Brian's heart sank like a punctured lifeboat. In his excitement about the break in the case, he'd completely forgotten he'd been dodging Lowe. *Fuck*.

Brian followed his boss wordlessly into his office, where Fiona was already waiting, head down, arms clasped protectively in front of her; a school girl who knew she was in deep trouble with the head teacher.

Lowe dropped into his office chair like a twenty-five pound sack of potatoes. The chair's steel tubing squeaked in protest under Lowe's weight. For a minute, it was touch-and-go whether it would hold, or whether Lowe would crash to the floor. A development which, while hilarious, would probably make the situation even worse for both him and Fiona. And then nothing happened. The chair held. Lowe closed his eyes and sighed, pinching the bridge of his nose with his thumb and forefinger; a gesture equal parts weariness and exasperation.

'DI Brandon, what did I tell you before you left for

the Bidmead scene?' Lowe asked, his eyes still closed. 'What did I specifically say I did *not* want to happen?'

Brian gave Fiona a reassuring nod. Neither of them said anything.

'So? Who spoke to the fucking media against my express orders?' he spat.

Fiona's jaw worked. Her lips trembled. She lowered her gaze and wiped her sweaty palms on her slacks. 'I -I-I —' she stammered.

'Nobody said anything to anyone except "No comment",' Brian said firmly, cutting her off. He'd be damned if a good DS ended in Lowe's bad books because some prick hack with no conscience had taken advantage of her inexperience. 'He chose to interpret that the way it suited him.'

'Is that so, DI Brandon?' Lowe said.

He'd raised his right eyebrow, but the puce in his complexion had faded to maroon. They weren't out of the woods yet. Not by a long shot. But, now that Brian had floated the idea of plausible deniability, Lowe just might grasp it. And that would postpone the eruption, at least temporarily.

'It's not like we haven't been here before. They're lying sacks of shite,' Brian continued. 'All of them. Remember that thing with ...'

Lowe's formidable right eyebrow dropped back in line with his other one, and they knitted together. Brian didn't need to elaborate further. Lowe knew exactly what he was talking about, because it was a recent and still extremely sore spot. Some stupid prick had jumped the gun and published the name of the suspect in a hit-and-run that had left a single mother and two of her weans dead, alongside his Facebook profile pic. Except it had been the right name but the wrong photograph. And while they were busy containing the fallout, the right one had legged it. Vanished off the face of the Earth. The DCC had given Lowe a thorough bollocking in the bullpen, in front of everyone.

Normally, nobody would dare bring this up. But Brian's gamble paid off. The memory seemed to have made Lowe more sensitive to their predicament. He let the silence stretch out, but he unclenched his hands and shifted in his chair, which protested loudly.

'Well, we still have a shitestorm on our hands,' he said, at last. 'We're going to need to call a press conference. Say we haven't ruled out anything yet. Who's the pathologist?'

'Dr Henderson,' Fiona said.

Brian felt a faint twinge of disappointment. If Lowe was in agreement with Brian's assessment of Henderson's talents, or lack thereof – and, skilled politician that he was, he went to great lengths to keep his true thoughts to himself – he didn't show it. 'When's the post-mortem?'

'He said he'd need to confirm. But probably tomorrow afternoon. He's yet to do Walton's, and it was scheduled for this morning. Said they're snowed under.'

Lowe leaned forward. Looked at Brian.

'What do *you* think?' he said.

'Honestly?' Brian said. 'Officially, we'll need to go through the building's CCTV and wait for the post-mortem results to make sure everything checks out. Unofficially, I think it's more likely than not to be suicide.'

Brian stopped there. Should he tell Lowe about his theory? The politics of this would be insanely complicated, and that would scare Lowe. Here was a high-profile suicide – one in which his team had already misstepped by speaking to the journos out of turn – and he was going to float the theory that the victim's co-founder had pushed him to it, was guilty of sextortion, sending threatening or menacing communications, and, quite possibly, two murders? Brian opted for a half-truth instead. Enough for him to be able to say he'd been forthcoming and, so, cover his arse later, but not enough to have his wings clipped.

'I think somebody pushed him to it,' he said carefully. 'We found ... compromising photos on his laptop. I was just about to speak to the team about it before—'

He was going to say 'we were rudely interrupted' but stopped himself just in time.

Lowe didn't seem to notice. At the mention of 'compromising photos' thunderclouds had reappeared on his brow.

Brian decided to rip the plaster off. Lowe would demand to see the photos anyway, in case his higher-ups came knocking. Which, once they heard about everything that had happened – who the victim was, and the ensuing media shitestorm – they'd do, as sure as night follows day. 'Photos of him on webcam, having a wank. With a trans cam model.'

Lowe looked at him, stunned. 'Jesus fucking Christ,' he said breathlessly.

'That's what I said,' Brian agreed, pressing his advantage. 'The question is who's the blackmailer. And whether there's a connection with Higgins and Walton.'

'You think they're connected?' Lowe asked.

'I'm not sure,' Brian said. This was, if not an outright lie, a gross misrepresentation of the truth. While the evidence was mostly circumstantial, Brian was 90 per cent certain they were connected. There was no way it was a coincidence that three people who were linked to each other – albeit, when it came to Walton, his gut said it was a case of wrong place wrong time – would all wind up dead within seven days of each other. But Lowe's knowledge didn't need to stretch that far. 'We're working on a few leads.'

Lowe's throat rumbled like a high-powered engine as he mulled this over.

'All right,' he said. 'Let's revisit this in a few days' time. Meanwhile, I'll make some calls. See they issue a correction and that the prick who wrote the article gets his ear pulled.'

Taking this as a dismissal, the officers moved to leave. Fiona shot Brian a grateful look as the stood and mouthed, 'Thank you.'

'Not you, DI Brandon,' Lowe said as Brian made to follow Fiona out the door. 'I need to speak with you.'

Brian's lungs, which had just about started working more freely, constricted again. *Now what?*

'Sir?' he said, when Fiona had shut the door behind them.

'Grab a pew, Brian,' Lowe said conversationally, nodding toward one of the chairs.

This was ominous, and not just because of his boss's

sudden change in demeanour. When Lowe called him by his first name, it meant he was going to be fatherly. And he much preferred a bollocking to a man-to-man. It took up less time and he didn't have to pretend to appreciate the concern. He stifled a sigh and sat down.

Lowe sized him up. Straightened his tie.

'So, how are things?' he said, his voice amiable but with an unmistakable edge. 'You settling back in OK?'

When it came to the memories Brian's mind could latch on to in response to this question, it was spoiled for choice. It chose the low-hanging fruit. That is to say, his episode a few hours earlier. Hyperventilating in the car after managing to extricate himself from the sea of journos clamouring for his attention. And then he remembered Pam's warm breath on his neck. Her crisp perfume. The softness of—

'Brian?' Lowe said. 'All OK?'

'Aye. It's all fine, I promise,' Brian said forcefully.

'You're sure?' Lowe said.

He didn't seem convinced. Had somebody said something? What would they say anyway? The increasing amounts of energy required to keep it together were draining him. But he was performing, wasn't he? Working the case. Doing a lot of the legwork himself even though he could delegate if he wanted to. And Brian could feel he was close. The solution was tantalisingly within reach. What else did the bloke want from him?

'I've heard ...' Lowe seemed to consider how he was going to phrase what came next. 'Rumours,' he finished.

'What rumours?' Brian asked. His voice had almost dropped to a whisper, and he could feel his face redden.

'That you're snappy. That you seem distracted,' Lowe said. 'And that you—'

'That I what?' he snapped. He couldn't help it.

'That you talk to yourself,' Lowe finished.

'I most certainly don't talk to myself,' Brian replied. But, if the heat he was feeling was anything to go by, he was pretty sure he hadn't done a convincing job of denying it.

He sat up straighter. Looked Lowe in the eye. To hell with this shite.

'Says who?' he challenged.

Lowe eyed Brian from behind his desk, his expression giving away nothing. Had Brian overcooked the air of self-righteous indignation?

'Why do you assume somebody said something?' he said, skirting the issue. 'I've got eyes. And to be frank, Brian, you don't look too good.'

But Brian was sure somebody had talked. He could see it in the way Lowe had avoided his question and his gaze. His mind went briefly blank. Then several pieces clicked into place. The snide comments. The irony. The bluster, bordering on insubordination. This had that useless prick McGillivray's name written all over it. It was his way of getting back at him for—

For what? He was tough, but fair. At least, that's what he liked to think. He appreciated that this was a job, and that people had lives outside of the station. But when they were here, he expected them to give 100 per cent. If there was one thing he wouldn't tolerate, it was laziness and unprofessional behaviour.

'Look, Brian,' Lowe said. The voice was even, the

posture relaxed, but Brian had a feeling he wasn't going to like what was coming. 'You're leading two murder investigations, and now, with this whole Bidmead thing, we're under even more pressure. With DI Craddock –'

In limbo? No-man's-land? For all intents and purposes, might as well be dead? Brian had to fight very hard to suppress the bray of hysterical laughter that was threatening to spill out of him.

' –I can't afford to lose you too,' Lowe continued. 'But I *will* bench you if I have to. You know I've done it before, and I'll do it again if things spiral. Understood?'

Brian counted to ten. Slowly. His hand crept into his trouser pocket, and his thumb and forefinger grabbed the fleshy part of his thigh.

'Understood?' Lowe repeated.

'Aye,' Brian replied.

'Good,' Lowe said. 'Glad we've cleared that up.'

Lowe placed his hand on the computer mouse and shook it to wake up his monitor. It bathed his plump face in white light. Brian waited to be dismissed.

'You have two days to get it together,' Lowe said. 'Then we'll reassess.'

Brian felt as if he'd been slapped.

'You wha–?'

'You heard me,' Lowe said. 'Och. And, to start with, I want you to see the counsellor–'

'Why should I ...?' Brian stammered. 'I don't–'

'Call it a gesture of good will,' Lowe said finally. 'Your way of showing me you're taking my concern for your welfare seriously.'

He looked Brian up and down with eyes like radars.

'It's for your own good, Brian,' he said. 'You might not feel like it now, but these things catch up with you eventually, and it won't be pretty. I've seen it happen before.'

The comment cut Brian to the quick, partly because Lowe had hit the nail on the head, and partly because Lowe probably had no idea he'd done so. He wasn't the kind of DCI who wanted to know every last detail of what was going on in an investigation and micromanaged the process, which was why Brian had got on with him for so long. So either Brian really wasn't doing the bang-up job he thought he was when it came to hiding his true state, or McGillivray had put on a bravura performance.

'Fine,' Brian growled.

'I'll hold you to it,' Lowe said. 'Email me when you book the appointment.'

Brian wanted to tell Lowe he was a man approaching middle age, not a fucking ten-year-old. But he held his tongue. 'Aye,' he replied.

'Good man.' Lowe turned his attention to the computer and started painstakingly picking at the keys with his index fingers. 'Catch up soon.'

It was amazing, Brian seethed as he walked out of Lowe's office, how somebody's purported concern for his welfare could sound so threatening.

Chapter Sixty

It took Brian twenty minutes to return to a state where he could trust himself to face his team without blowing a gasket at any minor annoyance. He'd lean forward, head down, white-knuckling the lavvy sink, his lungs working overtime and his brain straining to empty itself of negative thoughts. But, the second he managed to lower his emotional temperature by a few degrees, Lowe's voice, thick with faux fatherly concern, would float into his consciousness, followed by McGillivray's scornful smirk; a sight that blotted out everything else, making his chest burn and his hands ball into fists of their own accord.

Bastards. All of them. Fucking. Bastards.

He could tell himself it wasn't personal until he was blue in the face. But it didn't make it feel any less personal. Like the world was out to get him. Sure, all Lowe was interested in was keeping his higher-ups happy so he could have an easy ride. Same with McGillivray. The prick had skated by on the bare minimum most of his sorry excuse for a career. No wonder he hated having a mirror held up to him.

But, Jesus fucking Christ, he was—

Trying. Trying so hard. So, so hard to keep it together.

—working all hours to solve two murders. Was it too much to expect that everyone else would pull their own weight so he could get on with his job?

Eventually, Brian composed himself enough to tiptoe into his office and sneak a healthy gulp of Monkey Shoulder from the bottle stashed in his desk drawer. The liquid irritated his already tender stomach, and he dry-heaved over his desk. He grimaced, contracting his neck muscles and grinding his teeth, swallowing down the sour bile that had trickled up his throat. Another two smaller, more judicious sips warmed his chest and quelled the internal monologue. He walked back to the lavvy, splashed his face with cold water and rinsed out his mouth. Then, feeling as composed as he probably ever could, given the circumstances, he gathered the team in the incident room for an update.

As it happened, he didn't have to worry about confronting McGillivray. The bloke had begged off. Ostensibly working on a lead. *More like trying out a new curry place*, Brian guessed. Or whatever it was he got up to. The annoyance Brian struggled to shut down threatened to bubble up again. But he pinched his thighs through his trouser pockets, twisting the flesh anticlockwise as hard as he could, and rode the twin waves of tender pain. He'd have to have a sit-down with McGillivray. Sooner, rather than later. But it would probably be best to wait until he was on a more even keel, or it might escalate their cold war into open conflict.

When Brian turned his laptop around so the team could see the photos the blackmailer had sent Bidmead, there was a collective gasp, followed by stunned silence, followed by an explosion of excited chatter that crashed against the room's four walls.

'Quiet!' Brian shouted, rapping his knuckles uselessly on the conference table for emphasis, a hapless teacher who'd lost control of the classroom and knew it. 'Quiet. Please. Have some respect.'

It took several more stern words before the team had calmed down enough for him to continue. Even then, irregular bursts of muttered excitement and consternation punctuated his voice.

And so Brian outlined his suspicions, trying to be as detailed as he could, without tipping his hand that he was leaning toward Shawcross. Somebody might tell Lowe and he wasn't ready for that yet. Plus, he didn't want to influence anyone. Let the evidence lead where it would. Then he assigned tasks. Tracking down the cam model, for starters. Redoubling their efforts to access Higgins's external hard drive. Sifting through Higgins's cryptocurrency wallet to find out who he'd been transacting with. Taking a closer look at Bidmead's laptop and email correspondence. Brian himself, in need of air, headed down to the riverfront in search of CCTV footage that might shed light on who Bidmead had met with.

Riverfront Gate had got its name for the unexciting reason that, up until the early 1900s, there had been an actual gate leading to the riverfront. At the time, this particular stretch of the Strath's banks had been lined with factories, not high-end eateries and entertainment venues. Workers would walk through the gate in the mornings, and then the gate would be shut behind them again when the whistle signalled their work day was over and they left.

Frustratingly, there were no CCTV cameras trained on the expanse of benches where people tended to congregate when they didn't have set plans or just wanted to mill about and take in the views of the Strath snaking below them. Not willing to give up before he'd even started despite the nausea and pounding headache, Brian climbed up the concrete steps and began canvassing the various coffee kiosks and food stalls that dotted the area.

It was a bitterly cold evening, but there were several groups of people who, undeterred, had made their way there for after-work drinks and snacks. Brian picked the kiosk with the smallest queue, then worked his way methodically around them in a rough semi-circle, each time showing the person behind the counter a snap of Bidmead he'd downloaded to his phone – his Twitter profile pic, in which he was staring pensively into the distance like a modern-day philosopher – and asking whether they'd seen him on Wednesday, 10 January.

He struck lucky with the third stall owner he spoke to, a dreadlocked woman with a septum piercing and colourful hand tattoos peeking out from beneath the sleeves of her puffer jacket, who was selling artisanal macarons.

'Aye, that was definitely him,' she said without hesitation, when Brian asked her to take another look at the pic on his phone. 'He's whatshisface. That right-wing troll, isn't he? I recognise him.'

It was sad, Brian reflected, that this would be Bidmead's legacy – spreading hatred – when the company he'd helped found had – at least outwardly – the diametrically opposed ethos of inclusion. But here they were. If you didn't want to sleep in the bed you'd made for yourself, it was on you to change the sheets. In Bidmead's case, there would never be an opportunity to do so.

With a trembling finger, Brian swiped right to the photo he'd brought of Shawcross. It was a full-length shot of her he'd screenshotted from an interview she'd given a trade magazine, which he'd found online. In it, she stood in a power pose in front of a background with Mango Bank's brand colours: legs shoulder-width apart, hands on hips, chin thrust imperiously forward and eyes bright with superiority.

'Was it this person you saw with him, by any chance?' Brian said, thrusting his phone toward the stall owner.

His arm shook slightly, and he gripped his wrist with his free hand to steady it. His internal monologue – the voice that berated him for not living up to impossible standards and, at the same time, whispered discouragements in a misguided effort to shield him from disappointment – began its—

It wasn't her. It wasn't her. It wasn't her.

—management-expectation mantra. But the lively background chatter on the concrete walkway had lowered its volume, replaced by the whooshing of blood in his ears. A vein in his neck pulsed rhythmically, and he realised he was holding his breath in anticipation.

The woman brushed her dreadlocks aside and leaned forward, squinting at the screen. She studied the picture, her brow furrowed in concentration, teeth nibbling absently at her lower lip.

'It ...' She hesitated. '... It could be.'

Brian's heart leaped in spite of the voice telling him to—

Calm down, she's not sure.

—not get carried away.

'She looked different,' the woman elaborated. 'But it could be her, aye.'

'Different?' Brian asked. 'In what way?'

'Well, she was wearing a heavy coat, for one,' the woman said. 'So, she looked a bit bigger than she does in this photo. And she had a wool cap. But the hair was more or less the same colour. Em. Aye, I think it was her.'

'Are you sure?' Brian said, with barely suppressed frustration. It was promising, but it wasn't the clear-cut result he was after. Bringing Shawcross in for a formal interview on the basis of a theory and a dithering witness's statement would be tricky, especially if she brought along her solicitor. The whole thing risked blowing up in his face and pissing Lowe off even further.

The woman took another look. Taking her time. 'Aye, I think it was her,' she said. 'I mean, I was pretty busy with customers. But it was hard not to gawk.'

'How do you mean?' Brian said, tightening his grip on the phone, which he was still brandishing in front of her. He pulled his hand away.

'They were having a loud argument,' she said. 'Made quite the scene.'

Brian's ears pricked up. 'What kind of argument?'

The woman stood up straight and closed her eyes briefly, trying to remember. 'Hard to say,' she said. 'They were all up in each other's faces, and she was waving her hands about. I didn't catch much of what they were actually telling each other, though.'

'What *did* you catch?' Brian asked. He'd been holding his breath again, and his chest ached. 'Anything you can remember would help.'

'She said something like, "Won't forget this," before she stormed off,' the stall owner said. 'I'm not one hundred per cent sure, though.'

She paused.

'Wait. Or maybe it was: "You'll regret this."'

Chapter Sixty-One

Brian power-walked to the car, calling Fiona on the way.

'She goes by Madam Riv—' Fiona said.

The line went silent for a few seconds. Then Fiona's voice returned, her usual contralto replaced by an unintelligible gargle.

'Madam what, sorry?' Brian said, shifting his phone from his left ear to his right to shield it from the blustering wind headed at him from the river. 'You're breaking up.'

He pulled his coat tighter across his shoulders with his free hand and bent forward against the chill.

'Is this better?' Fiona asked. There was a faint buzz of static, but her voice was clearer.

'Aye, go on,' Brian said, fishing his car key from his front trouser pocket and pressing the fob.

'Madam Raven,' Fiona said, repeating the cam model's stage name. 'Legal name, Valerie Brown.'

'And?' Brian eased himself into the driver's seat and

leaned back heavily. 'What did she have to say for herself?'

'Well, I was careful how to word it, but she seemed genuinely affronted I'd think she might be involved in hacking Bidmead's webcam. Said her business depends on trust, and if she broke it, word would spread and she'd be finished.'

'And what do *you* think?' Brian asked.

On the other end of the line, he heard the unmistakable crackling of a packet of crisps being opened, followed by crunching as Fiona helped herself. He hoped for her sake she'd go home soon. Have a proper dinner and a good night's sleep. If she kept driving herself like this, she'd—

End up like me.

—burn out. Did she even have a partner to go home to? Weans, or a dog? He'd have to make it a point to ask.

'I believe her,' Fiona said around a mouthful of crisps. 'Her body language seemed genuine. And she does make a compelling argument. Nobody'd book a cam model with a reputation for taking compromising screenshots of her clients without their consent and selling them to blackmailers.'

Brian mulled this over. It wasn't necessarily bad news. In fact, it might even be good news. If Brown hadn't been involved in gaining illicit access to Bidmead's laptop, the obvious alternative was that it had been a professional who'd done it; somebody with the means, know-how, and opportunity. And, with his skills, his relationship with Mango Bank, and the access that relationship afforded him, Higgins fit the bill to a T.

The circle was closing. They were getting somewhere at last.

' ... next?'

'Eh?' Brian asked. He'd heard the words, but their meaning hadn't registered.

'What are we going to do next?' Fiona repeated.

'I want to see what Digital Forensics find on Bidmead's laptop. I'm guessing he downloaded malicious software somehow. Perhaps it might give us a trail to follow. Did we hear anything from Adams yet?'

There was more munching. 'No. But the blackmailer emailed again Thursday morning. Simply: "Tick-tock."'

Thursday was when Mango Bank had made the news of the Settl deal public, Brian reflected. 'And Higgins's cryptocurrency transactions?'

'Still looking into that,' Fiona said. 'It's a bit fiddly, not at all like going through a typical bank statement.'

Brian blew out his cheeks. 'I think it's worth bringing Shawcross in, given what the witness told me. See what she has to say for herself.'

Not today, though. It was late, and all the excitement had worn Brian out. His brain felt foggy. His head and stomach hurt. He was exhausted. Wiped. And that was no fit state to be in if he was going to interview the person who was increasingly looking like their prime suspect in one, possibly two murders, and a blackmail plot that had ended in suicide. He needed to be at the top of his game.

'I'll get on to—'

'Tomorrow,' Brian said firmly, cutting her off. 'Och. And Fiona. Have a rest, won't you? Go home at a decent hour today.'

Chapter Sixty-Two

Brian's advice to Fiona was a case of 'do as I say, not as I do'. As tired as he was, he doubted sleep would come easily. More likely, the minute he slid between the sheets, his synapses would come alive, his thoughts coalescing into a supernova of negativity that would drive his brain into overdrive and keep him awake. Which meant he'd probably end up doing more drinking in an effort to force it to catch up with his body. So, instead, he grabbed an XXL Bacon Double Cheese from the Burger King in town, washed that down with two pints of Blue Moon and a couple of whisky chasers from the pub next door, then drove aimlessly around Strathburgh, enjoying the temporary respite this gave him from his spinning thoughts.

It was 9:30, and the streets were mostly empty. The yellow light from the lantern-style street lamps reflected off the mud-and-grime-streaked puddles on the pavement into Brian's eyes, making him squint. A small, turned-up corner of newspaper, miraculously dry even though the rest of it was a sopping mess, billowed with every irregular gust of wind. In the park to his right, a couple that were too lithe, unconventionally dressed, and unselfconscious to be older than their early twenties, were going at it with wild abandon on a bench under a large, leafless sycamore, tongues down each other's throats, oblivious to the cold, wind, or rain.

Brian drove on. First down Strathburgh Way and its frustratingly stop-start agglomeration of traffic lights, then north-east, past the Sainsbury's two miles away from his flat. Next thing he knew, he was parked on the side of a quiet, tree-lined cul-de-sac, engine idling, phone in hand open to the messaging app. His thumb hovered over his chat with Pam. Made as if to press on it. Stopped. Pressed.

Got back-to-back post-mortems this afternoon :(

Her last message, which she'd sent at 11:15 that morning, said.

One of them's been in since Friday. A child, so that will be fun.

He pressed the text box. Began to type. Then deleted everything. Was he really going to booty call the forensic pathologist? Well, booty *text*, if you were going to be pedantic about it?

He sighed.

The alternative was going back home and sitting with his thoughts. Probably with a soundtrack of sad Elvis songs drifting lazily under his front door from the flat across the hall. How many plays of *Always On My Mind* and *Love Letters* would it take before he cracked? How much whisky before Liam came round to keep him company, reminding him of how, the one time it really mattered, his instincts had failed him and he'd proved himself to be completely and utterly—

Useless.

—clueless?

What are you up to?

He'd sent the text before he realised he was doing it. He killed the engine and turned off the headlights. Leaned back. The phone pinged. It was a snap of a generous glass of red wine, with just enough tantalising cleavage behind it to make his groin tighten.

That looks delicious

Three seconds later, she replied.

Join me? :)

He didn't have to think twice.

Love to. I'm in the neigh—

No, that was fucking stalkery. For God's sake. He pressed the back button. His finger had a slight tremble that made the process more fiddly than usual.

There in 15.

By the time he'd finished his second round of the cycle paths around Pam's house, his stomach was in knots and he was as oblivious to the weather as those two horny youngsters he'd clocked in the park. And when Pam greeted him in an open robe that revealed the lacy black bra and panty combo beneath, he almost threw up with excitement. Anything that had this effect on him, that made his body react in ways he'd never even known it was capable of reacting, couldn't be good for him, could it? It wasn't possible. But neither was alcohol. Or too much coffee. Or bacon, or crisps, or anything enjoyable in life, really. To hell with it.

'Brian,' she purred, opening her front door wider. 'Come in.'

And he did.

Three times in two hours.

Two hours in which he savoured every twitch and tingle that flooded his senses. Revelled in the slow build-up of pressure and its intense release.

Chapter Sixty-Three

Lying in bed, with Pam's head nestled on his chest and the post-coital glow fading away, Brian stared at the angular shapes the weak light from the street lamps was throwing onto the wallpaper. His thoughts inevitably turned back to the case. And, more specifically, to Shawcross.

The macaron stall owner's words rang in his ears. '*You won't forget this.*'

Or were they *I won't forget this*?

In the context of a heated argument, the latter made much more sense, didn't it?

No. They had to have said, '*You'll regret this.*'

Outdoors, in a relatively confined and notoriously busy area, from a distance, and while focused on other things, it would be easy to mishear *regret* as *forget*. But mishearing *you won't* as *you'll* was a harder sell. Or was he rationalising the evidence so it would fit his theory?

Christ. What *did* he know?

Well, Shawcross had a business relationship with both Higgins and Bidmead. She was in Stringbell right around the time of Walton's murder for that grand opening, which gave her the opportunity to kill him. Though, how she'd have gone in and out of his flat undetected, given the press were in attendance, was a pretty big hole in his theory that he'd have to fill in sooner, rather than later. She'd met with Bidmead at the exact place and time his blackmailer had proposed. They'd been in violent disagreement about an important business deal, and she'd ultimately had her way. And there was at least one prior report of her engaging in this kind of behaviour: when she'd blackmailed the still elusive Priya Singh.

Aye. As far as he was concerned, she was looking good for it. Really good. The problem was that the Procurator Fiscal might not agree. If only he had some actual physical evidence connecting her to the scenes, instead of his own internal – albeit solid – logic...

He fired up his phone and googled Shawcross, hoping that learning more about her background might spark an idea ... or three. Page one of the search results consisted of her LinkedIn, Twitter, and Crunchbase profiles, Mango Bank's 'About' and 'Meet the CEO' pages, several online articles that parroted back the same narrative about what an extraordinary and transformational achievement the deal with Settl was ... She even had her own Wikipedia page. The latter informed him she'd been born on 22 July 1979, the second daughter of oil and gas magnate Sir Robert Shawcross and his third wife Philippa Braxton, and grew up at The Barrows, their five-acre Shropshire estate. The rest of it was a bone-dry rundown of her career. Her business degree at King James University in Strathburgh. The fateful meeting with Russ Bidmead. Founding Mango Bank. No mention of her brief stint in medical school, he noted. Or of how her father had been sentenced to prison for—

'Penny for your thoughts?' Pam murmured, her breath tickling the soft flesh where his right arm connected with his chest. She stretched luxuriously, revealing her nakedness beneath. A sight that caused another faint stirring in Brian. Then she turned back on her side, draping her free arm around his midsection and nuzzled into his chest.

'Och, nothing,' he said. 'Just thinking about the case.'

'How's that going?' she asked.

'Eh. Nothing concrete yet. But I have a theory,' he said. A thought struck him. 'Hey, you must've been studying at King James around the same time as Angela Shawcross, right?'

'Angela who?' Pam asked, raising her right eyebrow.

'Mango Bank. The co-founder and CEO? She's all over the news lately.'

'Ah, yes,' Pam said. Her tone was noncommittal, but her lips curled in distaste.

'Not a fan, I gather?' he asked, his interest piqued.

'You could say that,' Pam replied.

'How so?' he pressed.

She shrugged. Her hair, still dishevelled, framed her face in a way that squeezed Brian's heart pleasantly and uncomfortably at the same time. Pleasantly uncomfortable ... Was that a thing? What the hell was happening to him?

'Just another entitled rich kid,' she said. 'Which I don't consider to be a particularly controversial opinion. Do you?'

Brian gestured with his head, as if to say 'Eh.' Based on the one interaction he'd had with Shawcross, he couldn't disagree.

'Do you remember her at uni at all? I think she'd have been at medical school around the same time as you.'

'Medical schoo— Ah. So you've heard about the prank?' she said.

'Prank?' Brian said, placing his phone on the bedside table and turning around to face her. 'The people I spoke to made it sound like it was much more than that.'

Pam gave another shrug. Moved closer. 'It was a long time ago. Plus, she was two years ahead of me, and we didn't really run in the same circles. I seem to remember a rumour going around she'd been expelled because of some prank gone wrong, but she was still hanging about at uni at the end of the year, so maybe I misheard, or the rumour was wrong.'

'I'm trying to get hold of the student on the receiving end of this ... prank or whatever it was, to get her side of the story. Priya Singh. I don't suppose you know her?' Then he chuckled sheepishly. 'Sorry, again with the interrogation.'

Pam traced a finger lightly from Brian's nipple down to his thigh. 'It's fine,' she said. Then, whispering in his ear, 'I don't mind being interrogated, if it's done the right way.'

'Define right?' Brian said. His voice had gone hoarse, and the tightness in his groin, as if his skin no longer fit him, had returned.

'Let me show you.'

Chapter Sixty-Four

You know what? I resent that you'd think that. I really do.

And, for the record, you couldn't be more wrong.

This was never about greed, or revenge, or whatever negative way you want to frame it so your narrow, blinkered mind can make sense of it. It's always been about one thing and one thing only.

Justice.

Balancing the scales.

As much as people like to think God, or karma, or whatever you want to call it is inevitable, it's, at best, a lucky accident, and, at worst, a lie we tell ourselves so we can sleep at night. The truth is that you can't trust the universe will make things right on your behalf, because life is inherently unfair. Most of the time, if you want to fix an injustice, whether it's against you or against somebody else, you have to take matters into your own hands.

You, of all people, should understand that.

I think it's partly why I do the work that I do. And it's

probably why you've chosen your career path too, isn't it? It feels good to know that, in some small way, you can contribute to making the world, if not less miserable, at least more bearable for those who've been dealt a bad hand. Doesn't it?

I don't want you to think I'm losing sight of that. I don't want you to think that for one second. Higgins. Walton. What's happening here, it's regrettable, but necessary. All in service of the greater good.

Besides, it's not like it's been all bad, has it?

Take Russ. That horrid, horrid man. All that testosterone splashing about, and in the end he couldn't handle being confronted with the reality of who he really was. So fragile. So pathetic. I'd say the world's a better place without a puerile hate-monger like that in it. Don't you?

And, as for you.

Well, think about it. And I mean that in its most literal sense. Genuinely take the time to consider this situation objectively. No more guilt. No more pain. No more sleepless nights. No more ... anything. And all you have to do is close your eyes. Right here, right now. Close your eyes and accept it.

Come on. You know you want to.

You know you don't have any more fight left in you, and that this is for the best.

What do you have to look forward to, anyway?

Doesn't everything you touch turn to shit, eh ... B?

Chapter Sixty-Five

Tuesday, 16 January 2024

'Tuesday, the sixteenth of January, 2024. Eleven thirty-four a.m.,' Brian said, aiming his voice at the recorder. 'Present for the interview, DI Brian Brandon and Ms Angela Shawcross, assisted by her solicitor Ms Gillian Laird-Heriot. Ms Shawcross has been cautioned and informed of her rights.'

He sat back in his chair, loosened his tie, and undid the top button of his shirt. Once he'd made the decision to bring Shawcross in for a formal interview, there had been no question in his mind that they'd conduct it here, in The Airing Cupboard. The room – which had earned its nickname because, at a puny seven feet by four, it was the smallest one in the building, windowless, and sandwiched between a south-facing office and the closet that housed the station's creaky, well-past-its-use-by-date heating system – had been tailor-made for exactly this kind of occasion: turning up the temperature on a suspect in the most literal way possible. The idea being that the discomfort would make their mask slip. But, now that they were gathered here around the chipped melamine table – which, despite being a relatively small fifty inches by thirty, took up most of the room's scarce floor space – Brian was regretting his choice. His shirt stuck to his back, and the air felt like steam in his nasal passageways.

Shawcross, on the other hand, seemed completely unfazed. She sat straight, hands neatly folded in front of her on the table, not one hair out of place, as if this were just another business meeting in a day jam-packed full of them, not a formal police interview. If she was torn up about her business partner's suicide, she wasn't showing it. Her brow was unlined, her face expressionless. Her eyes twinkling with ... Was that curiosity? A touch of playfulness?

Brian sipped water from a plastic cup and cleared his throat. Shuffled through the papers in his file. Next to the door, Liam leaned against the wall, hands crossed, smiling his encouragement. His presence was comforting, but also slightly unnerving. What if Shawcross or, worse, her solicitor caught on he was seeing people who weren't really there? He fought the urge to nod to him. Won.

'Ms Shawcross,' he began. 'How did you meet Sir Russ?'

'We met at uni,' Shawcross said, her posture relaxing. 'We were assigned to the same group for a project and enjoyed working together, so we stayed in touch. Eventually, we got to talking, found out we shared similar opinions about the state of banking in this country, and we came up with the idea for Mango Bank.'

'When was this?' Brian asked.

Shawcross scrunched her face. Her eyes took a faraway look. 'This would've been …' she hesitated. 'Our third year of uni, I think?'

The solicitor, Laird-Heriot, scratched a note on her pad with a gold fountain pen.

'Third year of uni' was an interesting choice of words. It implied she'd been studying business from the get-go, not switched from medicine after a …

But they'd get to that.

'So you'd say you were friends?' Brian asked.

Shawcross took a breath. Held it. Pressed her lips into a line. 'We went back,' she said noncommittally.

Not good enough, Brian thought. *Did you always see yourselves as just collaborators? Or were you friends whose relationship caved under the pressures of running a successful business, and, perhaps, diverging politics, worldviews, and attitudes?* The bitterest enemies often started out that way.

'What do you mean by that?' he asked.

Shawcross looked him up and down, her chin thrust imperiously forward. Her gaze defiant. 'Look, Inspector,' she said. 'Russ and I have a shared history. We started working together straight out of uni. But no, we weren't bosom buddies, if that's what you're asking.'

So they were just collaborators then. The question was, how far had that working relationship deteriorated? Bidmead's ex had made it sound like their disagreements were causing major friction. But had things reached the point where they were openly hostile to each other? And, if the latter, would Shawcross admit to it? She probably wouldn't if she had something on her conscience. Blackmail, for instance.

'OK,' Brian told her, his shoulders squaring. This was going better than he'd anticipated so far. While he was addressing Shawcross, Liam had even left the room. 'Is there any particular reason for that? Were you not on good terms?'

'No,' she replied straight away. 'As in, no, there wasn't any particular reason for that.'

Brian drummed his fingers lightly on the table. Waited. They made a hollow thudding sound that filled the room with nervous energy. *Tadadamm. Tadadamm. Tadadamm damm damm.*

'I mean ... I think I've made it very clear over the years through my community work that I don't share his views, if that's what you're asking,' she said, when he didn't say anything further. 'And yes, it bothered me that he never thought of the repercussions that airing them so publicly had on the company. We've spent way more money on crisis comms than we would've had to if he'd kept his opinions to himself.'

A shadow passed over her face.

'But we drifted apart a long time ago,' she said. 'You know how it is. Life ... happens.'

Brian thought back to what Hamilton-Baynes had told them. '*The difference between Russ Bidmead and Angela Shawcross is that Bidmead says the quiet part out loud.*' The earnestness of her delivery seemed at odds with the picture of calculation Hamilton-Baynes had painted for them. Plus, from a business perspective, having to spend money for avoidable reasons must've stung. Then again, Hamilton-Baynes's faux bonhomie and roundabout way of saying things had given him the impression of somebody with an axe to grind. While his story of blackmail had checked out, Brian couldn't rule out the possibility he'd embellished some of the details for his own reasons. Maybe there was history there, too.

'When's the last time you spoke with Sir Russ?' Brian asked, deciding to up the ante.

'It must've been ...' She bit the inside of her cheek. 'Last Tuesday, I think. I'd need to check. But it was a board meeting.'

Laird-Heriot scribbled more notes; the large-carat diamond jutting out of the ring on her finger glinted as her hand moved across the page. Brian had to work hard not to let his triumph show. He had a witness who said Shawcross and Bidmead had met on Wednesday, a day later. But even leaving that aside, her wording would've still put him on alert. She was hedging. Giving herself room to manoeuvre in case he confronted her with evidence that didn't look good for her. At least, that's what it sounded like to him.

'What was the meeting about? Do you remember?' he asked.

'DI Brandon,' Laird-Heriot said without looking up from her notepad in a tone that could cut through glass. 'As far as I'm aware, there's no indication of foul play in Sir Russ's death.'

'Well, that's just it, you see?' Brian said, letting a brief smile touch his lips.

'I ... don't?' Laird-Heriot scowled. 'If you have

evidence that his death might be suspicious, and you think my client was involved, by all means, let's see it.'

Brian flipped the file open. He wet his thumb and forefinger with his tongue, then flipped through the pages with deliberation. Selected four photos which he slapped down on the table. In the weak light of the LEDs, Bidmead looked even younger and more defenceless than the first time Brian had seen the photos.

Shawcross gave them a brief glance and gasped. Her hands flew to her mouth.

'For the benefit of the recording,' Brian said, 'I'm showing Ms Shawcross documents RB2, RB5, RB7, and RB8. Candid snaps, likely obtained illegally, of her business partner Sir Russ Bidmead in a compromising sexual position.'

His voice cracked slightly, because Shawcross's reaction had taken the wind out of his sails. He'd expected her to flush, a telltale sign she knew she'd been caught red-handed. Or double down and strenuously deny any knowledge of the photos. Be snarky, even. Not genuinely shocked. This was the reaction he'd expect from somebody who hadn't seen the photos before, not somebody who'd paid a professional to procure them, then proceeded to use them for personal gain. Nonetheless, he persevered.

'We retrieved these photos from Sir Russ's laptop,' he said. 'Any idea how they got there?'

In the meantime, Shawcross had recovered her composure to an extent. Her hands were once again folded on the table in front of her. But her left leg was jumping nervously beneath the table, her shoe's kitten heel clacking, typewriter-like, on the vinyl.

'What if I told you that *you* emailed them to him?' Brian said, going in for the kill. 'Would that jog your memory?'

'No!' Shawcross said. 'No, it wouldn't.'

'But you did, didn't you?' Brian said. 'You emailed them to Sir Russ. We know, because the email also requested a meeting. And guess who turned up for the meeting, at the appointed time and place?'

Shawcross paled.

'DI Brandon!' Laird-Heriot thundered. 'Let's not speak in riddles. If you're accusing my client of something, come out and say it so she can defend herself.'

'Very well,' Brian said, no longer trying to conceal his triumph. 'Where were you on Wednesday the tenth of January at seven p.m.?'

'Don't answer that,' Laird-Heriot snapped.

Shawcross's mouth was half-open. Instead of waiting, Brian pressed his advantage.

'We know you met Sir Russ at Riverfront Gate,' he said. 'We have a witness who puts you there. Said you had one hell of an argument. Was it because of the photos?'

'I,' Shawcross managed. 'I ... no, I'

He'd thoroughly wrong-footed her. He could see it in the way she avoided his gaze.

'DI Brandon. I must—'

'Why did you tell him "You'll regret this"? What was he going to regret?' Brian pressed, cutting Laird-Heriot off. He'd leaned forward, inches from Shawcross, grabbing the edge of the table with both hands. 'Was it about the Settl deal? He didn't want it to happen, so you used the photos to make sure he'd agree to it? Is that it?'

'Don't answer that,' Laird-Heriot repeated. 'DI Brandon, I need time to confer with my client.'

Shawcross sighed. Her shoulders slumped. But it was weariness, not defeat, that Brian read in her face.

'It's OK, Gillian,' she said, stilling the solicitor with a placating hand. 'Fine, DI Brandon. You win. Yes, I met Russ at Riverfront Gate on Wednesday. But ... that's not what I said."

'What did you say, Ms Shawcross?' Brian said, curious to see what kind of bullshit excuse she'd try to sell him.

'I said, "I won't forget this." He *accused* me of blackmail,' she said, her words dripping with outrage. 'After all I've endured on his behalf because he couldn't keep his mouth shut.'

Ah. There it was. *The truth comes out at last.* Brian leaned back in his chair. Sipped more water. Drummed his fingers on the table.

'But, I'd never do such a thing,' she continued. 'The board has floated the idea of removing him, I've lost count how many times at this point. And, every time, *I*' – she pointed toward herself with a manicured finger. A spray of spittle wet the table's surface – 'I defended him. Out of loyalty. Because Mango Bank is as much his as it is mine.'

Now Brian was confused. Was she confessing to blackmailing Bidmead, or denying it?

'Did you or did you not send Sir Russ these photos?' Brian said.

'No!' she snapped. There was colour in her cheeks and a thin film of sweat sheening her forehead.

'You deny it?'

'Asked and answered, DI Brandon. Move along,' Laird-Heriot said.

'So how did you come to meet Sir Russ at the time and place his blackmailer—?'

Shawcross recoiled as if he'd backhanded her across the face.

'How did you come to be at the exact place and at the exact time that the blackmailer specified to meet Sir Russ?' he repeated.

'I ... I received an email,' she said flatly. 'From Russ. Said we should talk and suggested we meet at Riverfront Gate.'

'That's convenient, isn't it?' Brian said.

'And true,' Shawcross shot back. 'I think I still have the email. I can show you.'

If this was true, could she have sent the email to herself? A double bluff she could fall back on for exactly this kind of situation? It had to be, didn't it? Otherwise, it would mean there was somebody else behind it all and they'd be back to square one.

'Except, you've done this before, haven't you, Ms Shawcross?' he said, deciding to show his hand.

'I'm sorry, what?'

Her eyes darted around the room. The typewriter-like clacking of her kitten heels turned to machine-gun fire. Brian suppressed a smile of pleasure at her reaction. He produced a tissue from his trouser pocket. Mopped his brow. God, the heat in here was getting unbearable.

'We spoke to Mr McCabe. He's—'

'From the student conduct team at King James,' Shawcross finished flatly.

Taptaptaptaptaptaptaptaptap. Taptaptap. Taptap.

'That's right. And he told us you've done this before. Haven't you?' he continued, implacable. 'You blackmailed a fellow student, Priya Singh. And now you blackmailed your business partner, Sir Russ.'

'That was—'

'Don't answer, Angela!'

'It was a long time ago,' Shawcross finished. She tucked a strand of hair that had come loose from her normally immaculate coiffure. 'I don't even—'

'Sir?'

Fiona's head appeared from behind the crack in the interview room door like a jack-in-the-box. Her face was flushed and her eyes twinkled.

Brian's face clouded. He turned around and gave her a questioning look.

'I'm sorry, sir, but you really have to see this,' Fiona said. Her head disappeared behind the door just as quickly as it had appeared.

Brian sucked his teeth, annoyed. 'Interview paused at twelve twenty p.m.,' he said, pressing the pause button on the recording system. 'If you'll excuse me, I'll be right back.'

Chapter Sixty-Six

'What is it, Fiona?' Brian hissed, once he'd closed the interview room door behind him. 'I was getting somewhere with—'

'I know. And I'm terribly sorry, sir. But this is really important,' she cut him off without breaking stride.

He followed her to the incident room, the annoyance at the interruption fading to curiosity. Fiona was always unfailingly correct and deferential. She'd never barged in on him like this while he was in the middle of interviewing a suspect. So why had she done so now? What was so important?

If he was honest, he was also happy to get away from The Airing Cupboard, even if just for a brief respite. The stuffiness in the room had become almost unbearable. His throat was dry and his shirt was sodden. Front *and* back. It would be good to take a break. Meanwhile, Shawcross was still in there, stewing. Which would work to his advantage.

Fiona rushed to the spot at the conference table

where she'd spread out to work. Her open laptop was surrounded by stacks of papers, some of them in thin piles and others fanned out to take advantage of the free desk space. Across from her, Frank Adams from Digital Forensics was glued to his laptop, his fingers tap-dancing on the trackpad. Fiona shuffled through the papers and handed two of them to Brian. They were printouts with several long strings of letters and numbers listed under each other. Next to each string was a shorter string of numbers followed by the same three letters: BTC. Fiona had highlighted several of them with yellow marker.

'What am I looking at?' Brian asked. He leaned against the edge of the conference table and scanned the papers. None of what was written on them meant anything to him.

'A sample of Ray Higgins's transaction history. From his cryptocurrency wallet,' Fiona said, the words coming out in a jumble. 'Frankie, er... Frank here has been tracking down who sent the money using their public keys.'

What she'd just said didn't make the letters and numbers any more intelligible. But he understood its significance loud and clear: they'd learned or were about to learn who'd been paying Higgins in cryptocurrency. Could it be ...?

'Who's the sender in these transactions?' he asked, pointing at the papers. 'The highlighted ones?'

'We've managed to track those down to a single crypto wallet,' Fiona said.

'And you're sure it's the right one?' he asked, daring to hope, but not wanting to be disappointed.

Adams cleared his throat. 'Sorry, Fi— er, DS Atwood, if I may,' he said. He blushed slightly and looked down at his laptop. 'So there's a common misconception that cryptocurrency transactions are anonymous. But that isn't the case. They're pseudonymous. That means—'

'You still leave a trail?' Brian cut in, willing Adams to get to the point.

'Aye,' Adams said. 'Something like that. The transactions are all public. Anyone can access the blockchain and view them if they have the right software. And if you know what kind of patterns you're looking for and manage to find them, you can link the transactions to the sender and recipient.'

'And you were able to do that?' Brian asked. He'd been gripping the printouts so tightly he'd crushed their edges. He smoothed them out and placed them on the table. 'So who is it?' His whole body was itching. Why couldn't Adams just come out with it?

'Well, normally, when there's something nefarious going on, the transactions tend to be convoluted to make them harder to track. There's nothing like that here. It's quite straightforward, which tells me the sender assumed anonymity was a given, so—' Adams must've seen the impatience on Brian's face, because he stopped. 'Aye. I'm as certain as I can reasonably be that I've— We've tracked down the right person.'

'And?' Brian pressed. 'Who's been paying Higgins in cryptocurrency?'

'The wallet the highlighted transactions originated from is registered to Angela Shawcross.'

Chapter Sixty-Seven

Brian took several deep breaths to compose himself. Here, in his hands, was cold, hard proof there'd been more to Shawcross's relationship with Higgins than she'd let on, and, possibly, the key to the whole tangled, murderous mess. Would it be enough to make Shawcross cave and confess everything? He'd do his best to pitch it right, and, hopefully, it would work.

He stretched his neck. First one side, then the other, feeling the pull of the tendons. Something cracked. His heart thudded relentlessly, the backbeat of a high-octane dance tune. He wished he could have a dram or two to take the edge off. But that was a risk he couldn't afford to take at this stage of the game. Not in front of Shawcross and her high-powered solicitor. They'd eat him for breakfast and get the whole investigation thrown out if they so much as scented the faintest whiff of marmalade, vanilla, and winter-spice notes on his breath. So he tightened his grip on the file in his hand, cleared his throat, and re-entered The Airing Cupboard. All being well, he'd reward himself later for a job well done.

The heat hit him straight away; it was like walking into a human-sized oven that had been running at full whack. At the table, Laird-Heriot and Shawcross had turned to face each other and were talking animatedly. When they heard the creak of the door hinges, they stopped, Laird-Heriot's hands frozen in mid-air, and turned toward him.

'All good to continue, or do you need a few more minutes?' he asked.

Laird-Heriot looked at Shawcross, who gave an invisible nod. 'We're OK to continue,' Laird-Heriot said. 'The sooner we finish, the better. I think you've taken up more than enough of Ms Shawcross's valuable time.'

Brian was about to remind her he could hold Shawcross for up to twelve hours if he suspected her of a crime. But he decided it wouldn't serve his purpose. It was better if Shawcross thought she could still talk her way out of the situation. That way, her reaction when he hit her with the cryptocurrency transactions would be genuine, and he'd get a more accurate read on her.

'Smashing,' he said, pulling out a chair and sitting across from Shawcross. He placed the file on the table in front of him, then pressed play on the recorder. 'Interview resumed at' – he glanced at the plastic clock on the wall – 'Twelve thirty-one p.m.'

He looked directly at Shawcross. The sheen of sweat on her forehead had beaded at her temples. At the corner of her right eye, there was a small black streak where her mascara had smudged, probably when she'd wiped sweat away. The first cracks in her seemingly impregnable façade.

'Ms Shawcross, what was the nature of your relationship with Ray Higgins?' Brian began.

'I believe Ms Shawcross has already comprehensively answered that question last time you spoke with her, DI Brandon,' Laird-Heriot interjected.

'And I'd like her to answer again under caution,' Brian said.

Laird-Heriot shot him a contemptuous look. Turned to Shawcross. 'You don't have to answer that, Angela,' she said.

'It's fine, Gillian,' Shawcross replied. 'As I've already explained, DI Brandon, my company, Mango Bank, engaged Mr Higgins to perform a cybersecurity audit. We terminated that relationship.'

'Due to misconduct?' Brian said.

'That's correct.'

'And you've never engaged Mr Higgins in your personal capacity?' Brian asked, leaning forward.

Shawcross licked her lips. 'No.'

'Can you confirm that?' Brian repeated.

'Asked and answered,' Laird-Heriot said.

Brian turned to Laird-Heriot, tapped his fingers twice on the table with a flourish, and flashed her a disarming smile. *Time to end this fucking pain.*

'You see, Ms Laird-Heriot,' he said. 'That's the thing. I'm confused.'

Laird-Heriot raised a silver eyebrow.

'Your client denies a personal relationship with Mr Higgins. And yet ...' Brian opened the file in front of him with the care a librarian would afford a rare medieval manuscript that might disintegrate if they handled it too roughly, and flipped through the pages. He picked out the printouts, one after the other, with his thumb and forefinger, and slapped them on the table facing Shawcross. 'These records say she had one. So you see my dilemma?'

Laird-Heriot peered at the printouts over her half-moon reading glasses. Next to her, Shawcross's left heel jerked up and down rhythmically.

'What are all these letters and numbers supposed to mean?' Laird-Heriot asked.

'For the recording,' Brian said, 'I'm showing Ms Shawcross and her solicitor documents H1 and H2, statements taken from Ray Higgins's cryptocurrency wallet.' He pointed to the highlighted transactions with his forefinger. 'See? This, this, and this here? Our digital forensics team have identified these transactions as originating from a single cryptocurrency wallet.'

His eyes bored into Shawcross, who, except for the frenetic tap-tapping of her shoe against the vinyl, was giving away nothing.

'*Your* cryptocurrency wallet, Ms Shawcross.'

The silence dragged out, hanging heavily in the air. The room had become so hot Brian could almost see white wisps of vapour swirling around, licking the walls. The three of them stared each other down, gunslingers in a Mexican stand-off, the printouts, with their evidence of shady dealings between Shawcross and one of Brian's murder victims, burning a hole in the table. Then Shawcross barked laughter, breaking the spell. But there was no humour in it.

'I'm sure your digital forensics team are very capable, DI Brandon,' Shawcross said with a hint of irony. 'But I'm afraid they have it all wrong this time. I never gave Ray Higgins any money, and certainly not cryptocurrency. I don't *own* any cryptocurrency. Never have. I've always thought of it as a solution without a problem.'

So this was it? She was just going to flat out deny it was hers? It was her funeral, he supposed. Once they got copies of the account-opening paperwork from the crypto wallet company, she could say the money didn't belong to her until she was blue in the face if it made her feel better. It still wouldn't change the facts.

'So how do you explain this, then?' Brian said.

'How? ... How should I know?' Shawcross replied. Her voice had taken on a hysterical edge. Her heel jerked up and down faster, one tap almost indistinguishable from the next.

'You hired Mr Higgins to dig up dirt on Sir Russ, didn't you?' Brian pressed.

'No!'

'Because you wanted him to agree to the Settl deal even though he was against it.'

'That's not how it—' Shawcross tripped over her words. 'No!'

'And you paid Mr Higgins in cryptocurrency, so the engagement would stay under the radar,' he continued.

'No. No, that account's not mine. Someone must've ...' she trailed off.

'Must've what, Ms Shawcross?' Brian asked. He'd shot to his feet and was pacing the six or so steps from one side of the room to the other, unable to contain himself.

'Used a false name. I ...'

It was Brian's turn to laugh. 'Identify theft? *That's* your excuse?'

'It's not an excuse, it's the truth!' she snapped, slamming her open palm on the table. Colour rose in her cheeks. It was the petulance of somebody who was used to getting their way and couldn't understand why things weren't going like they were supposed to. She must've realised this was how she was coming across, because she caught herself and lowered her voice. 'Sorry, I ... I had nothing to do with Russ's death. I didn't blackmail him. I ... I wouldn't.'

'Except these transactions here say you did,' Brian said.

Shawcross shrugged and stared fixedly at the table. She was shutting down on him.

'Where were you on Monday, the eighth of January, between midnight and noon?' Brian asked.

'At home, DI Brandon,' she said flatly. 'Asleep.'

'And can anyone confirm this?' Brian asked.

'I was alone, so no,' she said. 'But there's CCTV everywhere. You can check it.'

Other than helping them track down Walton, the CCTV from around the area where the Higginses lived hadn't been of much use. But, on reflection, maybe that was because they hadn't been looking closely enough. Or maybe they needed to widen the parameters of their search. Shawcross lived in Craig Hills, right across town from the Higginses. There were plenty of alternative routes she could've used where she could take advantage of coverage blind spots, especially if she'd driven down before the morning rush.

'And what about Thursday, the eleventh of January, between eight and eleven pm, Ms Shawcross?' Brian continued. 'Were you at home, too?'

He knew the answer already, of course. But this was where his theory was on shakier ground, so he waited for her answer with trepidation.

'I was in Stringbell, inaugurating a financial wellness hub. It was in the news.'

'And can you account for your whereabouts before and after the event?' Brian asked. He'd stopped pacing and was standing behind his chair, hands on its back.

'Wait. What?' Shawcross gaped at him, incredulous.

'What are you asking, DI Brandon?' Laird-Heriot cut in.

'I'd have thought it a pretty straightforward question, Ms Laird-Heriot,' Brian replied without missing a beat. 'I'm asking your client to tell me exactly where she was at every point in those two hours.'

'That's ... I can't account for every—'

'That's impossible and you know it, DI Brandon,' Laird-Heriot said.

The fact Laird-Heriot was interjecting more frequently while the usually unflappable Shawcross was breaking down into a bumbling mess told Brian his questions were hitting home. 'Does the name Danny Walton ring a bell, Ms Shawcross?' he said.

'Danny who?' she blustered.

'Walton. He was murdered just round the corner from your brand spanking new financial wellness hub in Stringbell. The forensic pathologist says he died between eight and eleven p.m. on Thursday, the eleventh.'

A pause.

'He also happened to be at Mr Higgins's home on the day Mr Higgins was murdered. Monday, the eighth,' he continued, enunciating every word for emphasis. 'Quite the coincidence, don't you think?'

Comprehension dawned on Shawcross's face. Her eyes widened. 'Are you accusing me of two murders?'

'I'm saying events might've run away from you,' Brian said evenly. 'For some reason, you argued with Mr Higgins. Maybe he threatened to expose your plot to blackmail Sir Russ if you didn't pay him more money. Or maybe he had something else on you. Like the fact you were expelled from medical school for blackmailing your fellow student. We know he was in a difficult financial position, and desperate people do desperate things. Nobody'd blame you if—'

'No!' Shawcross said vehemently, shaking her head. 'Absolutely not!'

'Nobody'd blame you if you'd lost your temper,' Brian continued over her protests. 'And then Walton showed up while you were in the middle of it. Recognised you. And—'

'Surely, you don't believe I ... I could kill someone, let alone two people?' Shawcross said, outraged.

'Then you won't mind producing alibis for Monday the eighth and Thursday the eleventh,' Brian said.

'But I've already done so!' She was the one leaning

forward now, her eyes darting about the room as if looking for a means of escape. 'I was home on Monday, and with the press on Thursday. You have to believe me!'

The way this was turning out, especially the change in Shawcross's demeanour, was concerning. People reacted differently to being accused of the crimes they were actually guilty of. But, more often than not, their reactions followed a predictable path: they got aggressive, indignant, or displayed a mix of defensive behaviours, and, if that didn't work, they shut down. Shawcross's first instinct had been to go on the defensive. But now she was frantic and pleading, her eyes beseeching him to believe her innocence. And those were two things guilty people rarely did, if ever. *Shite*. If she wasn't going to confess, he needed to tie her to the scenes some other way. The circumstantial case was strong. But, in court, the standard of proof was beyond reasonable doubt. The Procurator Fiscal wouldn't touch Shawcross with a ten-foot pole unless the case was watertight.

He glanced at the wall clock. Just gone 1 p.m. They'd brought Shawcross in at 10:30 that morning. Should he release her pending further investigation? Or keep her a while longer?

She was a prominent, respected woman with significant financial resources and a well-oiled PR machine at her disposal. Bidmead's death was still all over the news, and it wouldn't be long until the press caught wind of Shawcross's presence at the station. If he released her now, she might use the attention to her advantage. Twist the narrative or interfere with the investigation in other ways. And then she'd slip through their fingers. Get away with this scot-free.

No. He'd keep her here, in the custody suite. They had about nine and a half hours to go before they had to charge or release her. Now that they had a clear way forward, it shouldn't take too long to gather the evidence they needed to wrap this up.

'Interview suspended at one oh two p.m.,' he said.

He paused the recording and rushed out of the interview room.

Chapter Sixty-Eight

'Can I get a DNA swab from Shawcross, please?' Brian said to a uniform who'd been walking past him with a thick pile of files under his arm. 'She's in The Airing Cupboard. I want to run a comparison with the knife in the Higgins case. High priority!'

He strode into the bullpen without waiting for a reply.

'Wouldn't have pegged you for an Aberdonian,' a young detective constable was telling McGillivray. 'You know, because of the—'

'The accent. Aye.' McGillivray was leaning back in his chair, feet crossed on the desk, cleaning his nails with one of the pointy ends of his staple remover. 'Da was in the army, so we lived all over. I spent most of my teens in Shropshire—'

'Murray!' Brian snapped.

McGillivray straightened, taking his feet off the desk so fast he sent several files and his pen holder clattering to the floor.

'What do you have for me?' he said. 'D'you speak with the Community Policing Team?'

McGillivray gave him a quizzical look. Jesus fucking Christ what a useless waste of space. He didn't have time for this.

'About Stringbell,' Brian clarified. 'What did they have to say?'

'Ah. Aye,' McGillivray said. 'No call-outs to Stringbell within the window Henderson gave us. But there was a bad accident on the Huckleberry Road. That's the—'

'The main thoroughfare into Stringbell,' Brian finished for him. 'Aye, I know the one.'

'A lorry lost control and tipped over. Crushed a Vauxhall Corsa with a family in it.'

'Christ,' Brian winced.

So maybe McGillivray hadn't been exaggerating about the extent of the traffic jam he'd been stuck in en route to surveilling Walton, after all. An accident like that would've caused significant delays, especially if there was also a diversion because of the financial wellness hub's opening. Which meant Walton's killer had either reached Stringbell on foot or been already there beforehand. And that put another check in Shawcross's guilty column, albeit still a circumstantial one. He needed the DNA to pan out. And, ideally—

'Where's DS Atwood?' he asked. 'Still in the incident room?'

'Aye,' McGillivray said. 'With her special friend, Frankie.'

Brian ignored the juvenile comment and left the room, filtering out the low chuckles behind him.

'Fiona,' he said from the doorway. 'Did you make any headway?'

Fiona looked up from her laptop. 'I'm waiting to hear back from the crypto wallet company.'

'What did they say?' Brian asked.

'How do you mean?'

'When you spoke,' Brian said. Fuck's sake. It was like everyone had waited for the time pressure to be on to send their brains away for a break.

Understanding dawned on her face. 'Ach. Sorry,' she said. 'They don't have a phone number. I had to email them.'

'Shite,' Brian hissed. 'We can only keep Shawcross for another nine hours before we have to release her. We need to tie her to the scene. What else do you have?'

'We heard back from the disposable email service,' Fiona said. 'The account is in Shawcross's name.'

That was good. It proved she'd been the one who'd emailed Bidmead. 'And Higgins's hard drive?'

'Still working on that,' Adams said, not lifting his gaze from his laptop.

Brian's mind scrambled to list everything else they could do to crack this fast. It was hard to think with a clock to his head. He snapped his fingers, as if this would conjure the words he was trying to say.

'Check with the DVLA,' he told Fiona. 'See whether Shawcross or Mango Bank are the registered keepers of any vehicles, get their plate numbers, and search for them on the

ANPR database. And let's widen the area we're checking for CCTV. We can already prove Shawcross was in Stringbell on the day of Walton's murder, so let's focus on the eighth for now. If any car registered to Shawcross or Mango Bank was within the vicinity of the Higginses', I want to know.'

'On it, sir.'

Brian pulled out a chair and slumped in it. Sighed. Ideally, they also needed a warrant to search Shawcross's home and office, and to go through her financial records. Would the sheriff agree there were reasonable grounds, given what they knew? He needed to— His phone buzzed against his thigh. He fished it out of his pocket and swiped right absently.

'Brandon,' he said.

'Hello. Yes. Is it *DI* Brandon?' the voice on the other end asked. It was a woman with a faint accent. A voice that was familiar, but which he couldn't quite place.

'Speaking. Who is this, please?' he said, his brow furrowed.

'It's Dr Priya Singh,' the caller said. 'You left me a message? Said to call you back?'

The pieces fell into place. It was the slight Scouse twang that had greeted him on voicemail yesterday, before Lowe had summoned him.

'Ah. Aye, Dr Singh,' Brian said. 'Aye. I did call. Thank you for calling me back.'

She cleared her throat.

'First of all, I apologise for not calling sooner,' she began. 'We're terribly short-staffed at the moment.'

'It's fine, not to worry,' he said, a tad impatiently.

If Singh confirmed what Hamilton-Baynes and

McCabe had told him, it would add further weight to their case against Shawcross. But, while helpful, it would be icing on the cake, not a core ingredient. Perhaps he could take the bare bones of her story now, and the PF could take it from there.

'So what is it you wanted to discuss about your murder investigation, DI Brandon?' she said, her tone faintly curious. 'How can I help?'

Brian decided it was best to be direct. 'It's about Angela Shawcross,' he said. 'I understand there was an incident back when you were in medical school?'

The line went quiet. Brian was about to check his phone to see if the call had dropped when he heard the faint clinking of crockery in the background.

'Dr Singh?' he said. 'Are you still there?'

There was an intake of breath. 'Ehm ... Yes. Yes, I'm here, sorry.'

'Would you mind if I asked you a few questions? Is this a good time?'

Singh emitted a sigh of resignation. 'Sure. Yes, of course.'

'Smashing,' Brian said. 'So could you walk me through—'

'Not on the phone, though,' Singh cut in. 'I'd rather do this in person, if you don't mind. I'm ... I'm still in Strathburgh, by the way.'

Shite. Today of all days, he did mind. 'Are you free tomorrow?' he said. 'Maybe we could—'

'I'm on shift tomorrow, I'm afraid,' Singh said.

'Ah. OK then. Well, maybe—'

'And then I'm going away,' she continued.

That was fine. He had more pressing priorities. 'When are you back?' he asked her. 'Maybe we could chat then?'

'Sorry if I wasn't clear,' she said. 'I'm moving permanently. To Australia.'

Ah, for fuck's sake. He glanced at his wristwatch. Two o'clock. Eight hours to go. His stomach grumbled faintly. Perhaps he could get the warrant paperwork sorted, then combine Singh with lunch. He'd have done his bit and it would be up to the PF to decide whether it was worth the hassle of flying her all the way from the other side of the world to put her in the witness box.

'Fair enough,' Brian said. 'In that case, I could meet you in an hour if that works for you?'

'Do you know Fellowship?' she said. 'It's a Chinese café. On Castle Street.'

'No, but I'll find it,' Brian said.

Chapter Sixty-Nine

FROM THE OUTSIDE, FELLOWSHIP LOOKED MORE LIKE a wellness centre than a café, so Brian spent five minutes adjusting and readjusting his map app and going around the block in circles before realising he'd been passing right next to it all along. He opened the aluminium door with a groan of frustration and scanned the room, while Siri loudly announced he'd reached his destination for the sixth time.

The interior – covered in faux-pine panelling; red, yellow, and white Chinese lanterns; and prints of stylised lotus flowers, landscapes, and seascapes in gleaming silver frames – looked like a time warp. Two blokes sat in a booth, munching contentedly from Styrofoam boxes piled high with noodles covered in black-bean sauce and stir-fried vegetables. Across from the door, the only other customer – a woman in blue jeans and a thick, red cable-knit sweater – daintily directed a forkful of egg fried rice toward her mouth.

Guessing that this must be Dr Priya Singh, Brian walked toward her, produced his warrant card, and introduced himself.

'Please, have a seat, DI Brandon,' Singh said, forking more rice into her mouth. 'Sorry. I'm starving. Long shift. Hope you don't mind.'

'No, of course not,' Brian said, draping his coat over the wooden back of a free chair and sitting down heavily. 'I'm sorry I'm late. Finding this place took some doing.'

'Yes, it's tucked away, isn't it?' Singh said around a mouthful of food. 'So—'

'Can I get you something?' a waitress that had appeared out of nowhere interrupted. She looked expectantly at Brian, Bic pen poised over her notepad.

'Coffee, please,' Brian said.

The waitress scrawled his order. 'Anything else?'

Singh's food looked good, and he hadn't eaten anything since the single piece of buttered toast he'd gobbled hastily at seven in the morning. But, at some point between leaving the station and entering Fellowship, the idea of having Chinese for lunch had lost its appeal, replaced by a laser focus on the job at hand: getting Singh's side of the story down as quickly as possible so he could go back to work looking for the evidence he needed to get Shawcross charged before his time was up and he had to release her.

'Just the coffee, please.'

'Very well,' the waitress replied in the same tone she might've used if he'd told her the place was a shitehole and he'd rather eat dog sick. She put the notepad away and vanished.

'Do you come here often?' Brian asked Singh, in an effort to smooth out the awkwardness.

'I probably leave half my paycheque here,' Singh said.

'Och, I can understand why,' Brian replied.

The waitress placed a white mug in front of him, full to the brim with deep black liquid. Some of it slopped onto the table.

'Sorry,' the waitress sniffed. She conjured a pile of paper napkins, deposited them on the table, and performed her disappearing act.

Brian picked the napkin at the top of the pile and mopped up the spillage. He sipped the coffee – it was strong, but good – and placed the mug back on the table with a thunk of ceramic on wood. Singh finished the last of her rice, put the fork down, and looked at Brian.

'So, DI Brandon,' Singh said when she'd finished chewing. 'What is it you want to know?' She closed her empty Styrofoam box, set it aside, and folded her hands in front of her.

'I was hoping to get your side of the story,' Brian began.

Singh's expression gave nothing away.

'Why don't you start by telling me about your relationship with Ms Shawcross?' Brian prodded. 'Were you close before the incident?'

Singh wrung her hands. The dark, bruise-like circles under her eyes screamed exhaustion.

'I understand it might be difficult to talk about, even after all these years,' Brian continued. 'But it would really help to hear about what happened directly from you. This is an active investigation, so I can't go into specifics, but we think Ms Shawcross might have done it again.'

He made eye contact and raised his eyebrows briefly, hoping she'd get the message to read between the lines. Singh's eyes widened. Then her shoulders slumped. She looked down at the table and sighed.

'This has gone on long enough,' she said in a barely audible whisper. 'It's been weighing down on me all these years, and I just—' Her voice choked on the last word.

It was Brian's turn to be confused.

'I'm sorry?' he said. 'How do you mean?'

'Look,' she said, brushing away a stray strand of jet-black hair. 'You have to understand.' She looked up at him with pleading eyes. 'I'm from a single-parent, working-class family, OK? I was the only child to go to uni, and we could ill afford it. I studied. I worked shifts at the library. And I'm still up to my neck in student debt, even though I haven't missed a single repayment since I started working full-time.'

The words came out in a torrent, like a dam had broken. Brian looked at her. He had no clue where this was coming from or where it was going. But it felt like something big.

'I'm sorry, Dr Singh,' he said, when she didn't say anything further. 'But I don't understand. What does this have to do with what happened between you and Ms Shawcross?'

'Everything,' Singh said. 'It has everything to do with it.'

Her eyes were red. A single tear ran down the rim,

but didn't spill over the edge. Brian made an enquiring gesture with his head. Singh made as if to continue. Hesitated. Then she nodded to herself. Looked him straight in the eye.

'The dissection room ...' she said. 'Angela had nothing to do with that. She was never there.'

Chapter Seventy

'I don't ... I don't understand,' Brian said, clutching his mug and spilling more hot coffee on the table.

How could Shawcross have been expelled from medical school over an incident she hadn't been involved in? Surely, her father – still an influential figure, yet to be arrested – wouldn't have stood for it?

'It never sat right with me,' Singh continued. 'What I did. Even though it worked out for her in the end. But murder ... that's another story.' She toyed absently with her sweater's elasticised hem. 'I'm sorry,' she said, shaking her head and chuckling ruefully. 'This is all going over your head, isn't it?'

'I'm afraid it is,' Brian said. 'Why don't you start from the beginning?'

Singh nodded.

'The incident itself,' she said. 'It's ... It's a bit blurry, to be honest.'

She pushed the Styrofoam box toward her. Opened

it. Broke off a small piece from one of the corners and began shredding it into confetti.

'I remember ...' she continued. 'At the time, I was completely overwhelmed. My life was a constant game of addition and subtraction to make my student loan stretch. And in between lectures, coursework, and my part-time job, I was barely getting any sleep. I was one test away from failing pharmacology ... I had no idea where I'd find the money to pay off my credit card ... It was— It was a struggle.'

Her gaze was intent on the piece of Styrofoam between her fingers. 'My roommate kept insisting I go to this house party with her. She said it would be good for me. Take my mind off things.'

She dug her thumbnail into the soft material. Gripped it from beneath with her index finger, pincer-like, and tore off a minuscule piece. Then another. And another. Slowly. Methodically. Brian was about to prod her, but bit back the question and waited.

'She was going on and on about it,' Singh resumed. 'So I went. Just to get her off my back. It wasn't my crowd at all. Mostly spoiled posh kids. I reckoned I'd stay for an hour or so, and slip out once everyone was too drunk to notice.'

The tear that had collected in the corner of her eye spilled over the rim and trickled down her cheek. Brian's hands moved to the inside pocket of his suit jacket, but Singh beat him to it, producing her own packet of tissues from the leather handbag she'd slung across the back of her chair. She dabbed at her eyes, then blew her nose.

'Sorry, I—' She snorted laughter. 'It's just ... it's painful, even all these years later.'

'It's fine,' Brian said gently. 'Please. Take your time.'

She folded the tissue. Placed it on top of the growing pile of Styrofoam confetti.

'So we were in Angela's flat. Only it's not fair to call it a flat. It was a duplex in this lavish period building with a view of St Kentigern's Cathedral. High ceilings. Crown mouldings. The works. You get the picture.'

'Who was at the party, Dr Singh?' Brian asked.

'My roommate Sacha. Sacha Hollyoak. I think she's married now, so her surname might be different. Angela. A few other people I'd seen around. I think we were twenty in all.'

'OK. So how'd you end up in the dissection room?' he said, trying to restrain his impatience.

Singh opened the Styrofoam box, and brushed the used tissue and the pile of confetti she'd produced into it.

'I'm not exactly sure,' she said slowly. 'I was feeling pretty wasted by then. I've never been a big drinker, but that night ...' She trailed off. Focused on tearing off another section of Styrofoam from the box. 'I'd never been to a party like that – well, I'd never socialised much at uni before then. I suppose I got caught up in the moment and let my guard down. Sacha got me a drink, and then somebody else did, and before I knew it I'd had too much.'

Brian nodded. He'd lost count of the times he'd been in the same position. Only, in his case, the drink was less social lubricant and more emotional crutch.

'What happened next?' he said.

'I remember somebody saying they'd stolen the dissection-room key and made a copy, and then somebody else suggested we should go,' she said. 'The reason escapes me, but it made sense at the time.'

'And you're certain Shawcross didn't join you?' Brian asked, still half-hoping she'd change tack.

'Not absolutely certain,' she said. 'But I remember her at the door, waving us away. Anyway. The dissection room's a blank. Next thing I know ...'

She covered her face with her hands. Her shoulders shook. Brian squirmed. He could see how distressed she was, and it pained him. But he needed her to finish the story. He needed to know.

Before he could say anything, Singh produced another tissue from the packet, dried her eyes, and composed herself. 'Next thing I know, I'm given these photos and told they'll be released on the university's online forum unless I do what I'm asked.'

'And what were you asked to do?' Brian said, on the edge of his seat.

'To report the incident and blame it on Angela.'

'Who?' Brian said, his voice shaking. 'Who threatened you? Do you know their name?'

Singh looked up at him, eyes red-rimmed and raw, but steely.

'Yes. Yes, I do.'

Chapter Seventy-One

Brian didn't finish his coffee, which had gone cold, anyway. He mumbled a barely audible 'Thank you' to Singh and raced out of Fellowship, his mind reeling, his stomach clenching. Bitterness coating the back of his throat. He paced in front of the driver's side of his car with his nostrils flared and his eyes darting everywhere at once, a captive animal who'd been released back into the wild and had no idea what the hell to do with itself now that the savannah was stretching in front of it for miles in every direction.

What Singh had just told him. It changed. Everything.

If it was true, that is.

But why would Singh lie? She had every reason to perpetuate the narrative that Shawcross had been responsible for the dissection-room incident. If it ever became public knowledge that what had ended Shawcross's medical career before it even started was made up, a fabrication, Singh would be in the press's crosshairs and, potentially, the defendant in a very expensive lawsuit from somebody for whom a Magic Circle firm's fees were pocket change. Besides, given the rawness of Singh's emotions, even all these years later, could he, hand on heart, say he genuinely believed her confession to be false? And that Shawcross was indeed her blackmailer, Bidmead's blackmailer, and Higgins's and Walton's killer?

Except the alternative ... It didn't bear thinking about.

How could've he—

Not have seen it.

—got it so spectacularly wrong? Again?

How could he have been so completely, so utterly fucking ... stupid?

What was it he'd said?

'Traffic. It was chock-a-block.'

'A bad accident on the Huckleberry Road.'

The more he thought about it, the more it made sense. The more he realised the evidence had been all there, all along. He'd just been too busy getting trollied and arguing with ghosts to see what was staring him right in the face. If there were an idiocy Olympics, they'd ban him for having an unfair advantage over the other participants. Christ on a mountain bike.

He snatched his phone from his trouser pocket. Keyed in the station number from memory. And then his thumb stopped a bawhair away from the dial button. He couldn't just barge in like a bull in a china shop and start hurling accusations based on a single person's testimony of what had happened over twenty years ago in an incident whose relevance was, at best, adjacent.

Especially when—

You're snappy. Distracted. You don't look too good.

—he'd been putting himself in a position that might call his judgement into question.

'*I* will *bench you if I have to. Get it together.*'

No. First, he had to see for himself. Make absolutely sure. If he didn't find anything, great. He'd go back to the station and double down on putting together the missing pieces that would prove Shawcross's guilt beyond reasonable doubt.

And if he did find something ...?

Well, then he'd have to regroup, wouldn't he? Have a think about how best to navigate the situation.

But that was a bridge he'd cross later. When— No. *If.*

A humongously large *if.* In bold, eighty-two point font.

The loud blaring of a car's horn brought him back from his reverie. He looked around him, disoriented. Saw his hands at ten to ten on the steering wheel, and his seat belt snaking down his torso into its buckle. In front of him, a roundabout. To his right, a man in a black Audi sedan smiling ironically and giving him two thumbs-up.

Where the fuck was he?

Somehow, he'd got into the car and driven off without realising it, only to be brought back to the moment because he hadn't stopped on the give-way sign.

The Audi driver blared his horn a second time – a longer blast that hurt his ears – and gestured for him to pass, muttering something under his breath. Brian raised his hand in a feeble thank-you, crossed the roundabout, and drove on, one hand on the steering wheel and the other on his thigh, twisting the flesh relentlessly to keep himself present.

Brian could deny it as much as he wanted to, but he knew exactly where he was headed and what he'd do once he got there. The question was, what was he hoping to achieve? What kind of evidence – disproving or proving his new theory – did he think he was going to find?

If he was honest, he had no clue what to look for. Or where he'd even start looking for it.

Chapter Seventy-Two

By the time Brian realised he'd misjudged the climb, it was almost too late to course correct. The tree branch he was standing on – which had felt thick and solid when he'd tested his weight on it – jiggled, then shook alarmingly. An ominous crackling sound filled his ears, followed by a dropping sensation in his stomach as something gave way under his feet.

For an excruciatingly long millisecond, his left leg was suspended in mid-air, and he could feel gravity's irresistible pull beckoning him onto the box hedge twenty-two feet below. He grabbed the nearest overhead branch, his hands scrabbling for purchase, praying to the universe that it would hold. A sharp pain shot up his thumb as a wayward splinter pierced the fleshy web of nerves and muscles where the ball connected with his palm. He ignored it, holding on for dear life. There was more cracking beneath him. And then the branch held, though it now had a pronounced downward lean where it had weakened from bearing his weight.

If breaking and entering into a colleague's flat hadn't been a bad enough idea, he'd raised the stakes by deciding to do so through a second-floor window he could only reach by climbing up a tree. From the ground, it had looked reasonably straightforward. Test a branch to make sure it could bear his weight, pull himself up, repeat the testing process, and climb onto the next one. And on and on and on until he was close enough to reach the window that had been left slightly ajar despite the cold, presumably to air out the bathroom and prevent mould. Except, he'd never climbed a tree in his life. Ever. So, after an easy climb up the first two branches, he'd ended up stuck like the proverbial cat whose curiosity would be the death of it: too scared to look down, let alone attempt a descent so he could try entering some other way, and unsure whether he could get close enough to the wall to reach the ledge, open the window wide enough for him to pass through it, and hoist himself in.

If he'd been loath to call this in before he'd driven here in a muddled haze, it was even less of an option now. Not only would his—

index finger gesture at his temple.

—reputation take a further nosedive. He'd also be in a world of trouble. And there'd be no way he'd be able to talk himself out of it if they had to get him down from a tree in front of a crowd of onlookers. He was as committed as he could possibly be. There was no going back.

Brian sidestepped toward the wall, inch by excruciating inch. First his left foot, then his left hand, still gripping the branch overhead, then his right foot, then his right hand. There was more splintering beneath him. The tendons that connected his arms to his chest pulled as they bore more of his weight. His muscles tightened painfully. The branch held.

The windowsill was about two feet away. He stretched, trying to grab it, one foot in the air and one extending as far up as it would go with the tips of his toes still touching the branch. His fingertips brushed the rough, weatherbeaten material. Tantalisingly close but not close enough for him to get a solid grip. Beneath him, the branch shook. There was a loud cracking sound. This time, it didn't come from below, but from above him. The branch he was holding on to with his hands – and which was bearing most of his weight – was buckling under the pressure.

He made a sort of half-leap. It wasn't enough. The branch beneath him sloped further, its end touching the branch below it and resting there. His muscles strained, his chest on fire. He reached for the sill. Missed.

Shite.

Sweat, freezing in the cold air, beaded his temples, making him shiver. The overhead branch was the only thing standing between him and a head-first collision with the hedges. His fingers, numb from the chill and lack of circulation, were losing their grip. He tried again. This time, he caught the sill and held on to it, but bent a nail backward in the process. He bit down hard on his lip so he wouldn't cry out. Barely felt the trickle of blood down his frozen chin. Let go of the other branch so he could grip the sill with both hands, then stepped onto the razor-thin concrete ledge beneath. His foot slipped. And then he regained his footing. He paused for a brief respite. Breathing hard. Hands gripping the edge of the sill, and body pressed against the rough brick of the building's façade. There was a slight tremor in his right Achilles' heel, and the muscles in both his calves felt hard and tight.

When he thought he could trust himself to move without losing his balance and taking a dive, he studied the window. It was a bog-standard UPVC casement that opened outward. He slid his fingers into the gap and pulled toward him. It wouldn't budge.

'Fuck!' he hissed, trying not to think about the mounting frustration that was threatening to send him into a panicked tailspin. 'Of course it's not opening. What was I thinking?'

There was nothing beneath him except for a row of wheelie bins standing sentry next to each other. If he slipped and fell, he'd make a godawful racket. But alerting the neighbours would be the least of his problems. If it didn't kill him, a drop like that would—

Put him in a bed next to Liam's.

—require an extended hospital stay.

Gritting his teeth, Brian tried again, to no avail. And then he saw why the window wasn't budging. There was a restrictor attached to it from inside. He needed to get it off, or this was where he'd have to end this—

Madness.

—horribly misguided idea.

He squeezed his hand through the two-inch gap in the window. The UPVC's sharp edges peeled off several thin strips of skin. The back of his hand was so numb he wouldn't have noticed if he hadn't seen the swell of lurid red droplets. He felt around, probing the restrictor with his fingers. The arm was plastic. It was attached to another rectangular piece of plastic that had been stuck to the window with ...

Och. Hello ... The restrictor hadn't been screwed into the window frame, but attached with Command strips. He karate-chopped the restrictor's arm a few times to loosen it, then made a fist and hit it again. The adhesive was no match for the repeated blows, and the restrictor came loose.

With a flood of relief washing through him, Brian opened the window wide enough for him to squeeze through and scrambled into the dead silence inside the flat.

Chapter Seventy-Three

3:52 P.M.

Time was slipping slowly but inexorably away.

'Think. Think!' Brian muttered to himself.

What might he find that would—

No, I'm way off, aren't I? It can't be. Can it?

—prove his theory?

Bloodstained clothes? A journal or a notebook, perhaps? A scrawled piece of paper with Higgins's public cryptocurrency key, details of transactions or meetings, or both? Items from the scenes? Maybe even Higgins's missing laptop and phone? Brian scoffed, in spite of himself. Far, far too easy. But one could hope, right? Failing that, he'd need to check texts, emails, and other data. And that wasn't a possibility. Not yet.

He placed his hand on the bathroom doorknob. Except for the smarting pain where he'd injured himself on the window frame, his hands were still numb from the cold and the strain of clambering up the tree and holding on to a ledge, and he barely felt the smooth metal as he turned it. The hinges creaked open, letting him out into the hallway. Outside, it was getting dark, but weak light still filtered through from the living room, illuminating the two identical doors – standard six-panel models from B&Q, painted white – next to the bathroom.

He opened the first one. A washing machine. A box of Daz washing powder. A laundry basket. One of the cheap, circular ones from Ikea.

The clothes, which he fished out in three handfuls, had the stale, musty smell clothes get when they're left in the laundry basket for too long. But none of them had a stain that came even remotely close to the maroon of dried blood. Then again, it had been eight days since Higgins's murder and almost four days since Walton's. If not washed, his—

Would-be.

—suspect—

Killer. Killer, killer, killer.

—might have disposed of them.

He checked inside the washing machine – empty – and the cupboard next to it. There was a broom, a mop, a Henry vacuum cleaner, floor detergent, and the combi boiler. Nothing else. No pile of bloodstained clothes. No deadly souvenirs. No hastily scrawled confession.

A hysterical bray of laughter reverberated around the small room, making him jump. Then he realised it had come from his mouth. He ran his hands through his hair. Christ, what a mess. This room was a washout.

He tried the bedroom next, but there was nothing there either. Not among the stack of clothes – already worn, but not dirty enough for the laundry basket – piled on the chair across from the bed. Not in the built-in closet, under the bed – which was empty except for a farm of dust bunnies – or in the drawers of the single end table. Using a plastic storage box as a step stool, he scoured the built-in closet's overhead shelf, careful not to disturb anything. It was full of the odds and ends you'd expect on an overhead closet shelf, none of them incriminating: a suitcase (empty except for the empty hand luggage stowed inside it) and a pile of summer clothes that, judging by their musty smell, hadn't been worn in a long time.

There was no telltale pile of bloodstained clothes in the kitchen, either. The bins were full of standard-issue domestic waste: plastic bottles and containers, a couple of corks, drinks cans, tuna and tomato-sauce tins, crumpled bits of tissue and kitchen roll, wipes, fruit nets, dirty bits of cling film, biscuit wrappers, crisp packets, peel and vegetable offcuts. The cupboards and drawers were similarly full of the kind of equipment, neatly organised, you'd find in any kitchen: crockery, cutlery, cups, mugs, and glasses, a blender, and several other small appliances.

4:06 p.m.

He probably had more time, but best not risk it. Just the living room left to check, and he'd leave. A prospect he was unsure how to feel about. Frustrated, or relieved?

He walked through the doorway that led into the living room, and scanned it. On one side, a well-worn grey three-seater sofa and two armchairs placed strategically in front of a pine TV unit. On the other, a dining area and four chairs. Nestled in a corner between the two sections of the room, a small office nook. A square desk with a single drawer and a swivel chair in front of it.

The drawer's contents had settled in accordance with the fundamental rules of drawerology: the most useless bits and bobs piled on top, with the rest of the stuff in layers beneath it in chronological order of being stashed away 'just in case'. Half-used packets of A4- and letter-sized envelopes. Instruction manuals (including one for an Aiwa boombox that would've been well past its prime in 1996), an unopened set of coasters, and a package of what – according to the sticker attached to them – were cat water-fountain filters. A bit of trivia that came as a complete surprise to Brian. But, then again. Let's be honest here. What did he really know about this person?

The second layer consisted of a stack of greeting cards still in their plastic sleeves. *Happy Birthday!* one of them said in bright, rainbow-coloured lettering, with a festival of polka-dotted balloons floating around it. *Hello, little one!* said another, the grey elephant next to the *H* spouting heart-shaped bubbles from its trunk. Brian took them out, placed them on the desk and had a rummage underneath. A fresh pack of Duracell AAA batteries. Two empty boxes that had, at one time or another, probably housed chargers. For what kind of devices, it wasn't clear. A large cloth-bound scrapbook. He heard a soft thump. Looked down. Several Polaroid photos had fallen out of the scrapbook onto the floor.

Placing the scrapbook carefully on the desk, so as not to dislodge more of the photos it was holding inside it, he squatted down and retrieved them. Turned them face up and sifted through them. Judging by the subjects' hairstyles and clothes, they'd been taken in the eighties. In the top one, a woman with a dark brown perm and a bloke with a mullet and friendly mutton chops that would've put Lemmy Kilmister to shame were smiling at the camera. A baby with a perfectly round, bald head was sitting in the bloke's lap.

In the next one, the baby, head now covered in hair, was blowing five candles on a cake covered in blue frosting, while the bloke, sans mullet and with the friendly mutton chops replaced by a Tom Selleck moustache, looked on and cheered.

In another one, the child, possibly seven or eight years old, was standing astride a bike with a wide gap-toothed smile.

And then, the child was gone. Replaced by a gangly teenager leaning moodily against a wall next to—

Holy shite.

Could it really be?

No, it couldn't. Surely not.

Could it?

Brian looked again, his eyes scouring every square inch of the photo. Studying every detail. Then he set the whole pile aside and opened the scrapbook, undoing the old-fashioned ribbon that held it together with trembling hands, his heart racing a mile a minute.

He flicked through the thick cardboard pages.

More childhood snaps, interspersed with gaps where Polaroids had slid out onto the floor. Bath time in an avocado tub, a rubber duck floating nonchalantly next to a foaming sponge. A toddler taking tentative steps. The head covered in hair, but still with two big bald patches at the temples. The local playground. The baby, bald again, sitting in a swing and not looking especially keen on the whole experience.

Brian flipped the pages. Scanning quickly. Stopped.

No. There was no doubt about what he was seeing.

It was a big step from this to proving blackmail and murder beyond reasonable doubt. But it was evidence of a long-standing connection.

A connection that had been flat out denied.

Why, if not for fear he'd join the dots?

He stared down at the photos.

Two teenagers standing together in front of a large oak tree, their arms slung around each other's shoulders, grinning widely.

A candid snap at a house party. The photographer had caught one of the teens in the middle of handing the other a plastic cup. The teen receiving the cup had her nose turned up and her tongue sticking out in mock disgust.

But it didn't matter.

Even over twenty years ago, and while goofing about, she still had the unfuckwithable poise. The air of imperiousness that had made an impression on him from the get-go.

That the two of them might have crossed paths some time in their late teens or early twenties made sense.

But this was more than that. Much, much more.

From the looks of it, they'd been close friends.

And yet, when he'd asked –*'We didn't really run in the same circles'*—

'Brian? What are you doing?'

Chapter Seventy-Four

'Pam?'

'Brian?' Dr Pam Grace repeated. 'What— How'd you get in?'

She was standing in the hallway, her coat still on, her face partially obscured by the lengthening shadows. But he didn't need to see her features to understand he was in deep, deep shite. She'd caught him red-handed inside her flat – the flat he'd broken into – going through her things. And she knew exactly why he was there. He could tell from her voice. Icily flat. So frosty it had lowered the room's temperature by ten degrees and made his arms break out in gooseflesh.

'I— I know how it looks,' he said, the understatement of the decade. 'But it's not what you think.'

Really, Brian? That's the best you can come up with?

He took a tentative step toward her. Raised his hands, palms outward, chest height, in a placating gesture. Tried to make himself look smaller. Non-threatening.

'How does it look?' Pam said, again in that unnerving

monotone. 'What do I think this is? Enlighten me. Please. Since you seem to have the inside track into my innermost thoughts.'

She took another step into the living room. Looked him up and down with eyes that were blazing with fury and something else … Fear? Resolve?

Fucking hell. Instead of de-escalating the situation, he'd made things worse. The no-nonsense attitude was still there, bursting from every fibre of her being. But gone was any pretence – because their dalliance had to be a pretence, didn't it? A way of keeping tabs on the investigation so she could get in front of developments that might leave her exposed – of empathy or concern. She was all business. Her face had 'OK, this is a setback, but I can deal with it' written all over it.

'Sorry, I …' he blustered. 'The front door was open, and I'—

Shut up. Shut up. Stop digging yourself deeper into the hole you're already in.

—'came in to check if you were all right. I—'

'Was it now?' Pam said, taking another step forward. 'So how is it that I've just unlocked it to get in? Or did you lock it and then decide to have a nosey around? Is that it?'

'No. No, I—'

What the fuck was he doing? She was the one who'd threatened and murdered. Who'd abused her position to stay under the radar and, in the case of Walton—

'A lorry crushed a Vauxhall Corsa with a family in it.'

'One of them's been in since Friday. A child.'

—to get in and out of Stringbell undetected. Lying. Lies upon lies upon lies.

And he, always half-drunk and too happy to let his cock do his thinking for him to notice.

Ach. FUCK!

And here he was, letting her make him feel like a four-year-old who'd been caught with his hand in the cookie jar.

'I thought you said you didn't know Angela Shaw-cross?' he said, keeping his voice neutral.

'I don't,' she snapped. 'We moved in different circles. I told you that.'

'Those Polaroids beg to differ,' Brian said, pointing automatically at the scrapbook, which was lying open on the desk behind him, a silent scream of accusation. 'I'd say you very much moved in the same circles. Enough that you partied together as teens.'

Her lips curled into a snarl that gave her face a predatory cast. A wolf that had shed its sheep's clothing and was getting ready to make short work of every living being in the henhouse.

'Really, Brian? You're going to turn this on me?' she said, letting her arms drop to her sides. 'You've got some brass neck, when you were the one rifling through my drawers. In my *house*!'

The last word echoed around the room like a gunshot. If this were a different situation, it would've taken all of Brian's self-control not to wince. But he was too deep down the rabbit hole of recrimination, so the mega-decibel level barely registered. Now that he had all the pieces, the picture had materialised in front of him, fully formed. The cryptocurrency transactions and hidden email address pointing to Shawcross. The threats to Bidmead, timed to coincide with the Settl deal. The—

'Probably why he'd quit running.'

How ... how the fuck did that not raise the alarm?

There was no way she'd have known that unless she'd been in Higgins's office and ...

'Why did you kill Ray Higgins?' he said. 'In fact, why go to all this trouble just to frame Shawcross? That was your endgame, wasn't it?'

Pam said nothing, but her face told its own story. Her eyes were like flint. Her jaws clenched shut. Her expression etched out of steel.

'Why, Pam?' Brian said. 'Help me understand. What happened?'

'Do me a favour and shut the fuck up, will you, Brian?' she snapped. 'Your snivelling's setting my teeth on edge.'

The words were like a slap in the face.

'You should've left well enough alone. A love triangle gone horribly wrong,' she continued. 'Now look at this mess.'

Brian scoffed.

'Let it go, Pam?' he said. 'Three people are dead. Two of them brutally murdered. And one of them ... Well, you might as well have put the noose around Bidmead's neck.'

'He did it to himself!' she said, stamping her foot on the floor. The heel left a divot in the wood. 'They *all* did it to themselves!'

'Pam. If you give yourself up now, I—'

'You don't get it, do you?' she said, taking another step forward. 'This isn't your concern anymore.'

Pam's hand, which, at some point, had disappeared into her coat pocket, shot out in front of her. The hiss of a spray can filled Brian's ears. His hands flew to his eyes, which felt like they'd burst into flames.

'Ugh!' he moaned, the pain doubling him over. 'Pam! What did you do? This isn't you!'

Pam barked laughter. 'What would you know about me?' she hissed. 'Eh? We fuck a few times and, what? You're suddenly an authority on my character? Wonders never cease.'

Brian tried to get his bearings. To turn around so he could face her. But, with his eyes closed against the searing pain, he was completely disoriented. The sound of her heels, impossibly loud on the wood floor, seemed to be coming from everywhere at once, punctuating the whooshing of blood in his ears.

He opened his eyes. Tried to focus on some point in the room so he could orient himself. A dining chair. A snatch of sofa. But all he could see was a prism of colours, blending together into vague shapes, refracted by his tears. If only he could get to the kitchen sink, rinse his eyes under the tap. But how the fuck was he going to get there? He had no clue where he was in the room or even which way he was facing.

'Pam!' he shouted, flailing around blindly, arms outstretched. 'Pam!'

He took several steps forward. Crashed into something solid and angular. Pointy. The desk? An armchair? The dining table? Whatever it was hit him just below the breastbone, winding him. He tried to catch his breath and couldn't. He'd lost control of his lungs. He was panting. His chest heaving in shallow gasps, trying and failing to suck in enough air so his body could function. His world spun, a centrifuge of blurred colours. His head felt weightless. His brain told him to run. Get away. But his body had no clue how to even begin following that instruction. There were too many stimuli, assaulting him. Too many misfiring synapses, and too few of his senses working properly. His thoughts were an impossible tangle.

Click, click. Click, click.

Pam's heels, moving toward him.

Click, click. Click, click.

Another step. But now the sound was further away. What was happening? His throat constricted. White dots danced in front of his burning eyes, unbearably bright in the blackness.

Click, click. Click, click.

A thump and the sound of something heavy being dragged across the room. A piece of furniture? A—

Hockey stick.

—chair or an end table?

He stepped sideways, away from the sound. Only it was more like a lumbering shamble, and he crashed into something solid. The wall? He took several steps the opposite way. The smooth, unyielding barrier blocked his way again, sending a bolt of pain up his shoulder.

Shite. He'd cornered himself.

'Pam?' he said, hating the choked tremble that came out in place of his usual voice.

Oh God. Oh God. Oh God

WATCH OUT!

'Pam—'

The blow to Brian's head came out of nowhere, unbalancing him. He crashed to the floor, his left shoulder taking the full force of the impact. A stab of exquisite pain shot up and down his arm, resolving into pins and needles.

Another blow landed on his right shoulder. He lifted his good arm to protect himself. Made a blind grab for whatever Pam was hitting him with. But he was too discombobulated. His slow and clumsy movements were no match for her. The blows rained down, thick and fast. All Brian could do was curl into a foetal position, his free arm braced protectively in front of him, straining his ears. Listening intently for the next swish of air in a fruitless attempt to anticipate when the next blow would land.

Swish.

Pain flared up his shoulder.

Swish.

A hot, dull throbbing in his kidneys.

Swish.

Something cracked in his ribs.

'Pam!' he cried. 'Pam, stop. Please.'

But his voice was too weak, drowned by the sound of solid wood on crunching bone and Pam's heavy breathing.

Swish.

Another blow to his shoulder.

Swish.

A switch flicked in Brian's head, turning the lights off.

Chapter Seventy-Five

THE INTENSE BURNING IN HIS SHOULDERS, LIKE somebody was holding a naked flame to his bare skin, broke through the nothingness, thrusting Brian back into groggy semi-consciousness. He tried to shift the position of his arms to relieve the pressure, but they wouldn't budge. There was more burning, this time around his wrists, as something stiff and smooth dug into the tender skin. Plastic cable ties? No, the material felt too thin. Clothesline?

Ah, fuck.

Whatever it was, it was binding his wrists tight. So tight he couldn't move his hands apart. Not even a fraction of an inch. There was no give. So tight he couldn't feel his fingers anymore.

He turned onto his side. It made his head spin and the burning up and down his arms worse. He returned to his original position. Face down, flat on his stomach, waiting for the pain and dizziness to subside. His cheek rested on something cold and smooth.

Wood?

No.

Tile?

He opened one eye experimentally. It was too dark and he couldn't see anything. Everything hurt. And nobody had any idea where the hell he was, except for—

The realisation brought him back the rest of the way, shocking him into full consciousness, as if he'd been doused with a five-litre bucket of ice water. Christ alive. He'd literally —

How did I not see it? How? HOW?

—slept with the enemy. Shared a bed with a killer. And now she'd trussed him up and locked him away.

How long had he been out for? It was pitch dark, so it must've been a while.

More to the point, how the fuck was he going to get himself out of this? Jesus fucking wept. Why had he gone to Pam's flat by himself? What the fuck had he been thinking? How had he not realised the sheer, extraordinary depths of terribleness of the idea?

He closed his eyes. Tried to focus on his breathing.

Inhale.

Count to ten.

Exhale.

Count to ten.

Inhale.

The exercise barely made a dent in the rising tide of panic engulfing him. His head thudded like a rotten tooth. His arms burned. His *eyes* burned, still irritated from whatever Pam had sprayed him with so she could overpower him. He tried to wriggle his fingers to get some feeling back into them. Pins and needles shot up and down his arms, jolting him. The sudden movement sent more pain through his shoulders. He banged his temple on the floor. Saw stars.

'Some fucking predicament you're in,' Liam said from somewhere above him.

'Shut up, bud,' Brian hissed. 'Not now.'

'I'm just saying, if you'd got some hel—'

'This ... isn't ... helpful,' Brian groaned.

He squeezed his eyes shut. Grimaced. Reopened them.

His pupils had started adjusting to the darkness, and he could make out brief snatches of his surroundings. The bottom section of a washing machine, a small blossom of what had to be rust darkening the area around the filter. The plinth beneath a wooden cabinet. A circular Ikea laundry basket.

Pam's utility room. That's where he was.

What was her plan?

He was polis. She couldn't just make him disappear. There'd be questions. A thorough investigation with the full force of the department's resources behind it. Which was probably why she hadn't killed him.

Yet.

Because, there was no use making any bones about it. This wasn't the kind of situation you could chalk up to a misunderstanding and move forward from. She'd killed Higgins. She'd killed Walton. And, unless he came up with some way to get himself out of this, he was going to be next.

With an effort, Brian rolled first onto his side, and

then onto his back, crushing his hands beneath him. He arched his lower back. The bindings dug deeper into the raw skin. He breathed through the pain. Bent his legs toward him. Tried slipping his wrists over them. But there was no room to manoeuvre. Pam had tied his hands too high and too tight. Muscles straining, he turned back onto his side, then rolled face down. He tried to get up on his knees. But, without the use of his hands, his centre of gravity was off and he couldn't keep his balance. He fell face first onto the tiles, managing to turn left at the very last second and landing on his shoulder. Liquid fire shot up his neck and down his elbow.

'Och. God,' he moaned, writhing on the tiles. 'Fuck. Fuck. Fuck!'

If he could slip his hands over his legs, he'd be more mobile. Even if he couldn't unbind himself, he might still be able to attack, using his hands like a—

Hockey stick.

—club.

She wouldn't be expecting that, so he'd have the element of surprise.

He rolled onto his stomach. Counted down a full minute, second by second. Got up on one knee.

Smash.

He couldn't avoid it this time, and met the ceramic face first. An incisor tooth stabbed the inside of his lip. The coppery taste of blood flooded his mouth. He swallowed it down. Put his weight on one shaky knee. Overbalanced, landing awkwardly on his shoulder.

No. This was a non-starter. He'd have to think of another way to gain some leverage.

Except, there was no time. Footsteps, faint at first, and then a crescendo that ended right behind him, outside the door to the utility room. The doorknob turned. The door squeaked open. The light went on, blindingly white. He squeezed his eyes shut. Placed his forehead against the tiles to shield himself from the glare.

'You're up.'

A statement, not a question. Pam's voice had returned to the unnervingly flat, emotionless monotone she'd deployed when she'd surprised him going through the photos in her scrapbook. Brian used his legs to propel himself backward and turned on his side with a groan. Squinted up at her, a supplicant.

She'd changed out of her coat into an oversize hoodie and tracksuit bottoms. In her right hand, a knife he recognised from the block on her kitchen counter. In her left, a glass, full of water up to the rim.

'Don't move,' she said. As if he could do anything.

She stepped inside the small room. Squatted, the knife brandished in front of her, and placed the glass on the floor. It clinked against the tiles. A single bead of condensation trickled down one of the glass's grooves. She stood back up. Crossed the room toward Brian in slow, measured steps.

'You might not believe this,' Pam said. 'But I didn't plan' – she waved the knife from her to him in a wide arc – 'what happened between us. I really did like you. It's a shame it has to—'

Her voice shook.

'It doesn't have to end this way,' Brian said, trying to exploit the opening her unexpected slip of emotion had given him. 'You can stop at any point. And I'll do everything in my power to make sure you get a fair deal.'

She laughed then. A miserable sound, thick with regret.

'Oh, Brian,' she said. 'Did you really think that line would work? I'm not going to prison. Especially not for that *bitch*, Angela.' She spat the word out like a rotten piece of meat.

'What is this about?' Brian asked. 'Why try to frame her for blackmail?'

He still had no plan. No way out. But he reckoned the longer he kept her talking, the longer he'd stay alive.

Pam loomed over him, silent. Expressionless. The monster in a horror film, revealed at last, in all its ghastly glory. She squatted down to his level, inches away from his prostrate form. Light from the fluorescent bulb reflected off the stainless steel jutting out of her hand, making the knife look less like a utensil and more like an instrument of death. He squirmed. Tried to move further back. But there was nowhere left to go. Behind him was the unyielding solidity of the utility-room wall. In front of him, the merciless glint of the steak knife's blade.

Brian shivered. Was this it, then? The end?

A wave of despair gripped him. In spite of—

Liam is being felled in front me. And I can't stop it. No, no, no.

I'm helpless. Helpless. Helpless.

—everything he'd been through. In spite of the fact he'd been killing himself slowly, with whisky and with guilt, he realised he didn't want to die. Not really. Some primal instinct had taken over. Willing him to hang on. To stand his ground and fight.

'Pam,' he said, a slight tremble in his voice. 'Think this through. I'm polis. If you kill me, there's no going back.'

Pam scoffed. 'That ship sailed two people ago.'

'There's still—'

'Shut up, will you!' she snapped.

The knife's blade moved toward him, inch by excruciating inch. In real time, it couldn't have taken more than a few seconds to cross the space between them. But, in his mind, the moment stretched out, the march of time slowing down to a crawl.

He'd read that you never feel more alive than in the moments when you think you're about to die. And, it was true. He could attest to that, now. The cool yellow hue of the fluorescent bulb, the white of the washing machine ... Even the drab beige of the room's four walls felt vibrant. Bursting with energy and purpose. His ears had become more sensitive. More finely attuned to what was going around him. He could swear he could hear every single particle of air move aside as Pam thrust the blade forward. His nerve endings tingled in preparation for receiving the knife. Would it hurt when the blade pierced the skin and sliced through the layers of fat and muscle beneath, ripping his organs? Or would he just go cold as the darkness enveloped him, taking him away? Was it true what they said about the tunnel of light? And would there be something at the end of it, waiting for him? Or would it all be over like a plug being pulled, as if he'd never existed? He wasn't sure which option he preferred.

No, actually, he did. The third option. Staying alive.

Brian didn't want his life to end. Not now. Not here, in Pam's utility room, with his hands bound behind his back, stabbed repeatedly with a steak knife. Not yet.

He'd turn things around. Stop drinking. Go see the counsellor. And not just because Lowe had threatened to bench him if he didn't do it. He'd engage with the sessions. Do the work. Get better. Maybe even—

'Pam,' he begged. 'Pam, please.'

His brain caught up with events. The knife, whose motion he'd been seeing frame by frame, sped up, whooshing through the air. He tensed, anticipating the explosion of pain and wetness spreading through his body as he haemorrhaged. Held his breath. The muscles in his cheek trembled. The knife was half an inch away. A quarter of an inch. He closed his eyes. Steeled himself.

And then, the pain didn't come. His wrists tightened and came loose as Pam cut through the bindings with a smooth, practised movement, freeing him.

Chapter Seventy-Six

Brian was so surprised at the turn the situation had taken that he barely felt the wetness in his crotch as his bladder let go. One minute, he'd been hurtling toward certain death, courtesy of the business end of a knife. The next, he'd been given a reprieve.

He was cornered. Sitting in his own pish, with his back against a wall, trembling all over and cradling his flayed wrists in his lap. His mind whiplashed. Unable to keep up. But he was alive. Still alive against the odds. At least for the time being.

Pam had backed away, the knife in front of her, eyeing him from her spot next to the washing machine. He looked at her stupidly. What the hell was going on? What was her plan? She'd made it very clear he was a dead man, and he didn't doubt she meant every word. Not for a second. So, if she wasn't going to stab him, how was she going to do it? The uncertainty was worse than the anticipation. When he'd seen the knife coming toward him, he'd at least known what to expect. How could he prepare, let alone fight back, if he had no clue what was going to happen?

Wordlessly, Pam fished out a bunch of cable ties from the front pocket of her hoodie, and slid them across the tiles.

'Tie your hands together,' she said.

'Pam, what the—?'

'ENOUGH!' she screamed, spittle flying from her lips, eyes blazing. 'Shut up and tie your fucking hands, already.'

Brian bent forward and reached for the cable ties.

'And no funny business,' Pam warned.

Brian looped a cable tie around his left wrist and inserted the strap's tail into the head. Clenching the tail between his teeth, he inserted his right wrist into the loop, then pulled the tail to tighten the strap.

'Now, don't move,' Pam said, when he'd finished.

She squatted in front of him, placing the tip of the knife against his side. It felt cold and sharp, even through the cotton of his shirt.

'Try anything, and this goes in your kidney,' she said. 'You better believe me.'

She grabbed his wrists and tugged at the cable tie to check if there was any give. There wasn't.

'Good,' she said. 'Nice and tight.'

She picked another cable tie from the pile on the floor and looped it around his legs. Tightened. Brian winced.

'That's even better,' she said, surveying her work.

She stood up, stepped back. Brian wiped sweat from his forehead with his arm. Swallowed. Something stuck in his throat. It was becoming hard to breathe, and his field of vision was narrowing to a pinprick. What the hell was going on? Why untie him, then tie him again? What did it all mean?

The seconds ticked by. He licked his lips. They were rough and dry, like sandpaper. Blood rushed in his ears. From behind Pam, Liam stared blankly at him, motionless, arms by his sides. A mess of blood and gore coating the left side of his face and soaking his shirt. Brian's stomach lurched. He averted his eyes.

'What the hell are you thinking, Pam?' Brian said. His voice had a hysterical edge, but he was beyond caring whether she heard it or not. He'd do anything. Anything to get out of this mess in one piece. 'You killed two people and have an injured officer in your house. You do realise this won't end well, right?'

'Oh, it won't,' Pam replied. 'Not for you, anyway.'

She fished a small rectangular box out of the pocket of her hoodie and tossed it to Brian. It landed in his lap.

'Take them,' she ordered.

Brian picked up the box with trembling fingers. It was blue with a stylised white cloud in the middle. Inside the cloud, chunky blue letters spelled out *Nytol*. Beneath the cloud, the box said, *One-a-night 50 mg tablets*. And, in smaller print, *Twenty easy swallow tablets. Twenty-day supply. Clinically proven night-time sleep aid.*

'What's— What's this supposed to mean?' Brian asked.

But he feared he already knew. She was going to stage his suicide, wasn't she?

And, wasn't it funny? No … wasn't it absolutely gut-bustlingly hilarious that

You need help, bud.

—her plan might just work?

He'd set the scene with the way he'd behaved over the past week, and that bastard McGillivray had wrapped it up and bow-tied it with his complaint to Lowe.

Pam reached for the water glass. Placed it so it was within easy reach of his cable-tied hands.

'You're a troubled man,' Pam said, confirming his worst fears. To her credit, her voice thickened. But only ever so slightly. 'Your demons were bound to catch up with you sooner or later. Which suits me just fine.'

'Pam, no!' he protested. His voice sounded loud and frantic, even to his ears.

'Yes,' she replied. She turned the knife's handle around and around in her palms. The blade reflected light into his eyes. He squinted, narrowing them to slits. 'Or I could use the knife if you prefer,' she continued.

She turned the knife again, before looking directly into Brian's eyes. 'So here are your options. Do you want to slip peacefully away, or do you want to die slowly and very, *very* painfully?'

Her gaze burned a hole in his head.

Brian sized her up. Assessed his chances. By the time he managed to stand up and waddle toward her – if he didn't fall flat on his face for the millionth time first. And, given the way things were going and the state he was in, that was almost a certainty – the knife would be sticking out of his stomach. He didn't like it one bit. But the least worst— No, his only option was to play along. Bide his time and hope she lowered her guard once the pills kicked in. Hopefully, he'd still have enough energy to make his move.

'Go on, then,' Pam prodded. 'What's it going to be?'

Brian shook a blister pack out of the box.

'Just three of them for now,' Pam said. 'I don't want you taking too many at once and throwing them back up.'

Brian popped three tablets into his mouth. Reached for the water. Took a small sip. His Adam's apple bobbed up and down.

'Good,' Pam said. 'Now open wide. I want to make sure you've swallowed them.'

She squatted, just out of reach, and shone her phone torch into Brian's mouth in a dentist's pantomime.

'Wider,' she ordered. 'Lift your tongue up. Good. Now roll it to one side, and then the other.'

She turned the torch off and sat down in front of him, the knife in her lap.

'Now, we wait,' she said. 'It won't be so bad. You'll see.'

Brian leaned his head back, his stomach churning, his chest crushed under the weight of fear, his brain sifting through the various permutations of how this might turn out at warp speed. How long did he have before the tablets began to work? Ten minutes? Twenty, tops? And what would happen then? Shite, he should've just tried to attack. Taken his chances.

No. No. He couldn't rush this. He needed to have faith. Trust his instincts. But how could he do that when the last two times it had mattered, they'd failed him in such a spectacular fashion?

Be patient, Brian, he told himself. *Just get her talking.*

She'll do it now that she's killing time, waiting for the pills to do their number on you.

He swallowed. His throat clicked. 'Can you at least tell me why?' he managed, his voice choked with barely suppressed emotion.

'What does it matter?' Pam said. 'It's over. Well, it will be over soon.'

'It matters to me,' Brian said. 'I need to know.'

Pam considered this. She glanced at the knife in her lap. At the open box of Nytol in Brian's lap. At his trussed-up form, bound hands resting on his stomach, legs stretched out in front of him.

She sighed. Closed her eyes.

'I—'

She hesitated. Rubbed her eyes absently with her free hand. Looked back up at Brian, her face a mask of determination.

'I didn't mean to kill him. Honest,' she began. 'I genuinely thought I could make him see sense. Persuade him that it would be better for the both of us if he dropped it.'

She bowed her head. Sighed.

'More fool me.'

Chapter Seventy-Seven

When Dad told us we were moving to Shropshire, I gave it six months, tops. Maybe a year, if it went well.

After the colliery he'd worked in since the day he turned eighteen shut down, we were always moving around, depending on where he could find work. By the time I was seven, we'd lived in eight different houses in five different towns, and I'd given up on making friends. 'Why bother?' I'd tell myself. The second I bonded with anyone, we packed our bags and left. There was no point. It was a waste of energy.

And, it sounds horrible, but it became my norm. I was so used to it that I was already preparing myself for the following move before we'd even got there. And then six months passed. And then six months became twelve. And then eighteen. And then I started to believe that maybe, just maybe, this one was going to stick.

I suppose part of what made it different this time round was that the job wasn't too taxing compared to what Dad was used to, and came with rent-free accommodation in one of the cottages on the Shawcross estate. So Dad even laid off the drink for a while. He probably thought he was making a sacrifice. Doing his bit for the family. Ha. See how that worked out.

But the real turning point, for me, at least, was making friends with Angela. Becoming part of her gang.

Why? Why would she associate with the caretaker's daughter?

Tell you what. I've asked myself the very same question more times than I'd care to admit. After that party, when the shit had not just hit the fan, but flown across the room at hyper speed and splattered everywhere, coating all the available surfaces in thick layers that could never be completely cleaned off, it's a question that kept me awake most nights. A question I still can't find a satisfactory answer to even all these years later.

But I'm getting ahead of myself. I've told you about how Mum and Dad's arguments escalated to the point where he ended up in prison and she ended up in the morgue. And how it was all Angela's fault.

What I haven't told you, is why I blame Angela for it.

Well, it's because of the party.

You see. She's always talked a big game. But, for all her airs, she's really the worst kind of coward. At least where that spiteful bastard of a father was concerned.

This was Easter weekend of 1999. The year I turned seventeen.

Shawcross and his wife had jetted off to some private island. Angela had come down from Strathburgh for the

Easter break, and she'd decided to throw a party. It was all she'd talk about the whole week.

'Oh, it'll be fun, Pammy! You'll see!' she kept saying, her voice thrumming with excitement. 'Everyone will be there. We'll have food. We'll play drinking games. Theo and Harry might sleep over. Anything could happen!'

Theo was this guy she'd taken up with. He had a mate called Harry who Angela had got it into her head I should date, even though I told her a million times I wasn't the least bit interested. He had a large, hairy mole on his chin that made me want to throw up every time I looked at it. But that's Angela. She makes plans for you, and it doesn't matter if you aren't up for it. She keeps pushing. God forbid somebody gets in the way of her vision.

Anyway. The party was good. More than good. Pretty great, really. I remember sneaking back into my bedroom at 3 a.m., feeling exhilarated. Partly because I'd had a few drinks and got a good buzz going. But mostly because I relished feeling like I belonged. Like I'd found my tribe. The people for whom it didn't matter who I was and where I came from.

The post-party euphoria lasted all of three days, until Shawcross and his wife returned home from their jaunt to whatever exclusive resort for posh people they'd been to, and he realised there were two bottles missing from his whisky collection.

Bitch. Fucking BITCH.

I've gone over it again and again. And I'm positive – no, absolutely certain – it was her. It had to be. It's the kind of thing she'd do, suggesting raiding 'Daddy's' whisky collection and consequences be damned. What did it matter if she got caught? There were underlings she could blame it on.

I'll never forget it. Macallan in Lalique: Fifty Years Old. £240,000 a bottle. I looked it up, afterward, to understand why they were making such a huge fuss over them. The police came knocking just when we were about to sit down for dinner. With a search warrant. Can you believe it? A search warrant for two bottles of whisky. They turned the whole place upside down looking for them. The bins. Every single cupboard and storage closet. They even went through my underwear drawer. And when they didn't find them, they arrested Dad anyway. Claimed he'd drunk them and disposed of the bottles so there wouldn't be any evidence. Or sold them on.

They had to release Dad eventually, of course. It was Angela's word against his, and even the Shawcross name would only stretch so far. But we lost everything. Dad got fired, and we had to leave the cottage and move in with my aunt at Darlaston. He was never the same after that. By the time I left for uni, he'd be at the pub most days. He'd leave the house at eleven in the morning on the dot. Come back at ten at night or however long he managed to last before the landlord refused to serve him any more drinks. Have a godawful row with Mum. Sleep it off, wake up the next morning, rinse and repeat.

God, how I hated her. How I hate her.

Do you know what it's like to see your loved ones disappear in front of you, B? Killing themselves, little by little, every minute of every day?

Of course you do. It's what you've been doing to

yourself, isn't it? You understand. You know how it is. You get it.

And then, when we crossed paths again at King James, do you know what she did?

The bitch shrieked, ran toward me, and hugged me like a long-lost friend.

'Pammy! You got in! It's so nice to see you!'

As if nothing had happened.

As if she hadn't ruined Dad's life and cost Mum hers.

As if she hadn't ruined MY life.

It made my skin crawl. It was all I could do not to slap her silly right there, in the foyer.

And, before you ask. No, I didn't plan to blackmail Priya. That just happened. It was Priya's idea, actually, to pose with the cadavers. I'd had a few, too. But I'd never seen somebody get so utterly, uncontrollably, incoherently drunk as she did that night, except maybe for Dad.

This was around the time of Dad's murder trial. After the sentencing, I took the train back to Strathburgh, my rage eating at my insides the whole way. I don't think I'd ever been that angry. I ground my teeth so hard I ended up having to get work done on them.

That's when I got the idea. Sitting on the train with green hills passing me by, while Dad rotted in prison and Mum disintegrated into worm food. It wasn't fair, was it? So I decided I'd destroy Angela's life the same way she'd destroyed my family. Starting with her medical career. Priya's photos with the cadavers were lying around, so I used them. She was a means to an end, and, for that, I'm sorry. Truly. If anyone didn't deserve it, it was Priya.

But it worked out for everyone, didn't it? Well, except for me.

'Daddy' fixed it for Angela, and Priya's a hotshot cardiologist now.

So I finished my degree, moved to London, and that was the end of it.

Or so I thought.

Chapter Seventy-Eight

No. I had nothing to do with Angela's dad's embezzlement charge, either. He did that all by himself.

Incredible, isn't it? For somebody so posh, with his five-acre estate, and his oil rigs, and his luxury properties, and whatnot, he's always been tight-fisted. The filthy rich usually are. I suppose, once you get into a certain mind-set, once you get used to a certain standard of living, nothing is ever enough. You get consumed with accumulation for its own sake.

I read about the case in the canteen at work. And, I'm not going to lie. I almost sprang to my feet and jumped for joy, right there, in front of my colleagues. The bastard got what was coming to him in the end. And then – how long after was this? Three, four days maybe? – the same newspaper ran a puff piece about Mango Bank and how Angela had made her own way against all odds and in spite of everything. Ha. Please! Give me a break. She'd ridden 'Daddy's' coat-tails and trodden all over the rest of us her whole life, and she was making herself out to be the twenty-first century's answer to Ada Lovelace and Mother Teresa rolled into one?

Fuck. Off.

That rage I thought I'd managed to get past, to heal from, bubbled up all over again, as if everything had happened the day before, not almost twenty-four years ago. It was all I could think of. All day, every day. I couldn't eat. I couldn't sleep. And, eventually, I got pulled aside at work and bollocked for being 'inattentive'.

Inattentive. ME!

It didn't matter, though. I'd already decided I needed to do something about Angela. For my own sanity. To get some sense of resolution. Then Dad died. He'd graduated from alcohol to heroin in prison. So I applied for a position in Strathburgh, and when I got it, I saw it as a sign.

Except that bastard, Higgins, turned out to be just as bad as Angela. A loose cannon.

I should've expected that. He kept all our emails. Recorded our conversations! Threatened to send everything to the station if I didn't pay him stupid money.

'The terms have changed,' he'd said. 'You don't get to call the shots. Not anymore.'

And now look at this.

Look at us.

I didn't think things could get any worse than they already were. But here we are.

Chapter Seventy-Nine

Brian jerked back into wakefulness. It was a struggle to think straight from one second to the next. As she told him her story, Pam had made him work through a whole blister pack of Nytol one-a-days. Ten tablets. And, now that they'd kicked in, he could feel his consciousness, and, with it, his willpower, slipping.

His eyelids got heavier and heavier. His legs became restless. Jumpy. The way they sometimes got when he was so exhausted he fell into a fitful sleep in front of the telly. His tongue felt fuzzy, and he opened his mouth to ask Pam for some water. But talking required too much effort. He had to wrestle with every word. Even then, the sounds he managed to produce were an incoherent mumble.

Pam's face doubled. Trebled. Brian blinked until the image resolved into a single Pam. Each time he closed his eyes, it was harder to reopen them. He tried to sit up straight and couldn't. His head slumped against the wall with a soft thump.

'Sleepy, are we?' Pam said. 'You can drift off soon, promise. But you need to take a few more tablets first.'

The box was next to Brian's left thigh, but it might as well have been on another planet. He reached for it with hands that weighed a thousand tonnes. Couldn't get to it. The act of stretching, picking up the box, and moving it back toward him required too much effort. More than he could muster.

'Here,' Pam said, gently. Almost tenderly. 'Let me help you.'

She drew the box toward her with the pointy end of the knife and pushed five tablets out of the remaining blister pack. Holding the knife against Brian's side, she slid the tablets into his mouth, and held the glass so he could swallow them. Water dribbled down onto his chin.

Brian's head lolled. He stared at a spot on the wall behind Pam's head, breathing shallowly. Making his chest rise so his lungs could fill up with air was like pushing a boulder uphill. With every exhale, he drifted deeper and deeper toward unconsciousness. And it occurred to him that if he did let go, if he allowed himself to drift off, he'd never wake up again. He fought for control of his senses. But he was a man holding on to the edge of the precipice with his fingertips. Soon, he'd lose his grip and he wouldn't be able to avoid the drop.

With fingers so numb they felt alien, like they belonged to somebody else, he pinched the fleshy part of his right thigh. There was no pain. Or, if there was, it was too faint and far away for him to feel it. The drowsiness was all-encompassing. Overwhelming. A thick blanket that had been wrapped tight around him, cocooning him, making him feel like he was back inside his mother's womb. And as he felt its warmth course through his body, it struck him that, for all the fear humans have around death, this wasn't so bad. It wasn't bad at all. A long, restful sleep that nothing and nobody could ever interrupt. No more bad dreams. No more stress. No more guilt or shame. He wouldn't have to deal with the bottom of humanity's barrel any more. Just blessed oblivion. Forever.

What was there to fear about that?

It sounded quite lovely, actually.

Brian looked up through eyes that had become the narrowest of slits. Four Pams looked back at him. The urge to surrender, to give in, was irresistible. A high-pitched but melodious tone, like a siren's song, rang in his ears, lulling him into slumber.

Perhaps he should rest. Just for a brief minute. What harm could it do?

Aye. He'd rest a bit and everything would be much better.

His eyelids fluttered.

Red spots flashed over a black background. Five Pams hovered over him, their lips moving in sync, but their words not quite reaching his ears.

Another flutter of his eyelids. This time, he saw a golden circle, like a nebula, spiralling dizzily. Carrying him forward toward an unknown destination. The start of his greatest adventure.

One flutter. Two flutters.

He was on the move somehow. Tiles and a section of plinth passed him by in slow motion. There was a slight pressure where his arms and his shoulders connected. But it wasn't unpleasant. It felt almost like being rocked. Was he being dragged? Where? By whom?

Never mind. Why bother? He was so comfortable here.

Time stretched, Play-Doh in a toddler's hands. Flying by at warp speed and standing still at the same time. The nebula morphed into a series of hexagonal spots dancing across a dark blue background.

His eyelids closed. His chest hitched. His heart skipped a beat.

'B!'

The voice was crystal clear. But Brian wasn't hearing it with his ears. It was coming from the centre of his brain, as if somebody had beamed it into his auditory cortex.

'Liam?' Brian said. His tone was tentative, but his voice was loud and strong. Not the croak of someone halfway between wakefulness and the deepest of sleeps. 'Liam? Is that you? How'd you get here?'

'Aye, it's me,' the Liam voice said.

'Liam, I'm so sorry. I'm so sorry I couldn't—'

'It's not your fault, bud,' Liam said. 'I don't hold what happened to me against you, I need you to know that. There was nothing you could've done.'

'But there was! I could've—'

'Let it go, B.'

'I can't. How can you expect me to do that?'

'You have to. Now's not the time to argue,' Liam cut him off. 'You need to do something. Fast.'

Liam's voice was urgent, but Brian couldn't understand why. He seemed to remember being in some kind of tricky situation. But whatever had happened had happened a long time ago. Hadn't it? Everything was fine now. Wasn't it?

'B!' Liam prodded. 'You're running out of time. Wake up!'

The intensity stirred an emotion Brian couldn't quite describe.

Anxiety? Pressure? Focus?

But why? Why all the urgency? What was the rush?

In front of him, a three-lane highway narrowed into a tunnel with a pinprick of the whitest, brightest light he'd ever seen at the end. Behind him, wind was pushing him forward, gently but steadily. A firm, albeit invisible hand. But Brian didn't feel the least bit like he was being forced. He *wanted* to keep moving. He *wanted* to see what was on the other side of that pinprick. He wanted it more than anything in the world.

'B! You're not going to be able to come back if you keep moving. She'll get away with it. She'll—'

'Who? Who'll get away with what?' Brian's protested. A teenager complaining they needed five more minutes to the parent who was trying to rouse them for school.

'She killed Higgins. She killed Walton. And now she's going to kill you, B.'

The sense that he was in a bad situation solidified. It wasn't a while ago then, was it? Had it happened recently? How recently?

Wait.

Not recently. Now. He was in the middle of it. Right this minute.

A vision of Pam flashed before him. The knife in her hand, making a deft cutting motion. Throwing cable ties and a box of—

Monkey Shoulder.

—Nytol toward him.

Pam.

Pam.

Pam.

Aye. She'd done it. She'd killed them. And now she was going to kill *him*.

'But I—' he stammered weakly.

What could he do?

Here, in this world his fading consciousness had transported him to, he felt good. Vital. Full of purpose. At one with the universe. He was everything and nothing. Back in the real world, he was powerless. His body in the process of switching off, piece by piece.

'If you don't do something, you'll die and she'll get away with it,' Liam said. 'Do you want that to happen?'

Liam was right. Brian was dying. It wouldn't be long now. He could feel it in the stuttering pace at which his chest was rising and falling. In the erratic rhythm of his heart. But answering his question was proving harder than it should be.

Did he want it to happen? Did he want to die? Now? Like this?

'I—'

'You're going to give up?' Liam said, his voice rising in pitch. 'Just like that?'

Was he?

No.

No, he wasn't.

No, he wasn't going to.

If he was going to die, he was going to do it on his terms. At the very least, he was going to make sure Pam didn't get away with what she'd done.

'What was that?' Liam said.

'No!' Brian repeated vehemently. 'But what do I do? How? I ... I can't.'

'Just open your eyes, B,' Liam commanded.

In the depths of his unconscious mind, Brian stopped walking toward the light. Spread his legs wide to steel himself against the wind gusting behind him, pushing him forward. The pinprick, now only a short distance away, had grown into an orb. Its light, so white it was more accurate to describe it as the absence of blackness, had taken on a warmer hue. Enticing him to keep moving toward it. Beckoning him into its endless embrace.

He tore his gaze away with an effort that felt almost physical, like pulling off a piece of felt stuck to Velcro. Looked at the blackness at the other end. It stretched on and on and on, seemingly into the infinite. How had he moved so far away? Had he been out that long? Could he cross the distance back in time?

His brain ordered his eyelids to crack open. But the message didn't arrive; his neurons were too busy firing their last salvos. Pulling down his body's shutters. Turning off the lights. He stretched. Pulled. Strained. Mustering the last shreds of consciousness. Performing a mental chin-up to lift himself out of the dark liquid pool of warm nothingness into the cold unpredictability of the real world. He screamed. Inside his head, it sounded throat-shredding. Ordered his brain to lift up his eyelids. First one, then the other. Each time, he visualised the synapses firing – a bolt of light travelling through the snarl of neurons that led from his cerebral cortex to the muscles in his face. A crack of light split the darkness. His fingers and the tips of his toes tingled. He spied a sliver of coffee table. A TV unit's legs. A snatch of low-pile rug. Pam's living room.

The world spun. He squeezed his eyes shut.

'Do it, B!' Liam cajoled. 'Wake up! Stop her!'

More light seeped through the two slits below his forehead. Resting on the coffee table, he spied the knife, unattended, next to a bowl of soapy water and a sponge. What? Why? Was he being washed? Prepared for his final resting place?

He tried to move his arm toward the knife. It barely budged.

'Try again,' Liam said. 'It's only two inches away.'

To Brian, the distance, however short, was a chasm. How could he get to the knife when the different parts of his body were refusing to talk to each other?

He needed to focus. Squeeze his brain cells for all they were worth.

His hand moved. Made a faint grabbing motion. Caught air and ... nothing else.

The warmth was seeping away, a cold numbness creeping over him in its place. Soaking his muscles. Penetrating into his bones, down to the marrow. His thoughts drifted. To Laura, his ex, who was probably much better off without him, a man chronically incapable of letting things go. A man who'd made sweating the small stuff his whole personality. To Amelia and Matty, trying to pick up the pieces and move forward while Liam languished in hospital, the victim of a senseless tragedy that tore their family apart. To Lowe. To Fiona. How he'd let them down. How he'd let the whole team down. They'd counted on him, and he'd failed them.

To Pam. Consumed by anger and revenge. Rationalising grievance into a desire for justice. A vanity project that had led to the senseless deaths of three people.

And now, he was going to be the fourth death she'd add to her tally.

And she'd get away with it.

Because—

'B!'

Liam's voice brought Brian back, snapping him out of another downward spiral toward ultimate unconsciousness. Maybe that's how this would end, anyway. Maybe. No, probably, he'd die. But he'd finish this first. Or, at least, he'd try. He stretched his arm toward the coffee table, straining every muscle to its limits. Faintly, vaguely, he felt something stretch in his face. Muscles arranging themselves into a grimace of effort. And then, there it was. The knife's smooth rubberised handle in his hand. He curled his fingers around it. Pulled it toward him. It clattered to the floor. He reached for it, blindly, just as three Pam heads on a single, four-legged body loomed over him and uttered an angry alien warble that reverberated in his ears. Liquid, sticky warmth coated his wrist as the blade sliced painlessly through the skin, nerves, and muscle in his fingers. He let go of it and tried again, straining, his throat gurgling with effort, lifting the knife one inch of the floor. Then two. Then three.

And then, he couldn't lift the knife any further. Something solid, unyielding, was halting his progress. Pam gripping his wrist, knuckles white, trying to dislodge the knife from his grasp. He held on, his fingers a vice, pushing back. Trying to gain enough momentum to push through.

For a second, Pam almost got the upper hand. Her grip was too strong, and he was too weak. Almost completely spent. Then, a surge of electricity coursed through him, cutting through the fog. Clearing the way. His muscles didn't strain. His arm didn't push any harder. It couldn't. He'd reached the outer limits of his capacity. The last dregs of energy. But something ... somebody ... placed their arm on his. Liam, he was sure of it. Weren't those freckles that had suddenly appeared on the back of his hand. Wasn't there a hand over his, strengthening his grip, pushing forward, making Pam strain harder?

Aye, it was Liam. Lending him his energy from whichever limbo he was in while his body languished in the ICU. Helping him finish this once and for all.

Pam knelt. Bent forward in an attempt to use her body weight against him. Instinctively, Brian stopped struggling and thrust forward. The knife met a huge wall of resistance. Then the solidness yielded. The knife penetrated. More liquid warmth poured over his hand, coating it dark, venous red.

Pam's expression transformed. From a grimace of

effort and determination, her face rearranged itself into shock, and then into pain and fear. She let go of Brian's arm. Touched her side. Her hands came back covered in blood. Brian pulled. Felt the knife's blade yield and come free. Another thrust. Pam went slack-jawed. Slumped. Her head banged against the coffee table's edge. Faintly, he heard a sickening thud.

He sighed. A deep, rattling sound. His arm trailed to the floor. He'd given it everything. More than everything. Hand on heart, there was nothing else he could do. If the drowsiness had previously been irresistible, it had become completely unbearable. His eyes were still open, but his pupils were moving rapidly from side to side, making the room jerk spasmodically around him. His eyelids were so heavy it felt as if somebody were physically trying to push them down.

A white spiral circled in front of his eyes. Shrunk. Shrunk. Shrunk. Became a pinprick of dazzling brilliance.

'Sir?' the voice, as tinny is if it were being broadcast from a cheap AM radio in the other room, barely registered.

'Brian? Brian, hold on. An ambulance is on its way.'

With the last of his energy reserves, he looked up. Frowned.

'Fiona?' he mumbled.

And then the spiral shrunk into a microscopic pinprick that exploded like a supernova, then faded to black.

Chapter Eighty

Tuesday, 13 February 2024

THE OFFICE OF FERGUS CORRIGAN – WHO, THE BRASS plate outside the building helpfully advised anyone who passed by, was a qualified Gestalt psychotherapist – was a second-floor flat in a tenement located a gentle two-mile walk due south of East Strathburgh Police Station. A large one-bedroom with high ceilings, crown moulding, and other original period features, the flat had been reconfigured so that the living room worked as a reception area and the bedroom – presumably, Corrigan had chosen it because it was smaller and, so, provided a more intimate setting – served as his office.

The first time Brian had been here after being discharged from hospital, the off-white colour scheme, apple-green accent wall, and Japanese-inspired knick-knacks that were clearly meant to create a soothing, spa-like atmosphere had had the opposite effect on him. Probably because, aside from still being sore from the gastric lavage that had saved his life and not yet used to facing the day without leaning on alcohol to blunt its rougher edges, he'd been a bundle of nerves; unsure what to expect, and deeply uncomfortable with the idea of confessing his innermost thoughts to a complete stranger. But, three weeks later, going into his third session, Brian had to admit, he was starting to see how people might find it calming. He was even beginning to relish the few minutes he spent sitting on the squishy faux-leather sofa waiting for Corrigan to escort him into the office. Minutes which, increasingly, he was able to spend with a quiet mind, just feeling present. Savouring the room's zen-like silence.

'How are you feeling today, Brian?' Corrigan asked with trademark good cheer as he eased himself into his charcoal-grey Ikea wing chair and sipped tea from a red mug with *World's Best Therapist* emblazoned across it in white lettering.

Brian sat across from him in an identical grey wing chair. Not for the first time, he was struck by how different this short, rotund, unassuming man looked from the kind of person his rich, Morgan Freeman-esque baritone suggested.

'So?' Corrigan prodded. He placed his mug on a leather coaster, folded his pudgy hands in his lap, and studied Brian.

'Aside from this?' Brian said, waving his bandaged right hand. 'On the mend, I suppose.'

He put the hand back in his lap. He still had no sensation at all in his ring and pinky fingers. The orthopaedic surgeon had told him some of it would return over time as the nerves repaired themselves. But not completely. Nor would he regain his full range of motion. The knife had done too much damage.

Brian chuckled at the memory. He had to.

'What's funny, Brian?' Corrigan asked.

'No, nothing,' Brian replied. 'Just thinking about how things turned out. I ingest fuck knows how many sleeping pills, have to be shocked back to life and get my stomach pumped, and I'm none the worse for wear. But I accidentally grasp the business end of a knife, and my hand's out of commission forever. Got to appreciate the irony.'

'Well, it's good that you're seeing the humour in it,' Corrigan said. 'But I don't want you to minimise what happened. It's not—'

'It's how I got myself into all this trouble in the first place,' Brian finished. 'I know. And I'm going to do my very best to break the pattern. I'm doing the work, aren't I?'

Corrigan nodded. 'That you are. You're doing very well, all things considered.' He picked up his tea and sipped, smacking his lips. A drop of beige liquid landed on his dark blue sweater, and he dabbed at it with a bunched-up tissue. 'How are you doing with the meds? All good?'

'I ... I think they've started to kick in,' Brian said. 'I still get bad heartburn sometimes, but that might be the after-effects of the lavage. I feel much calmer. It's like everything was turned to eleven and somebody lowered the knob to a more sensible volume.'

'That's good,' Corrigan said. 'The side effects should

subside within a few weeks. But you can always ask your GP to—'

'No, this is fine,' Brian said. He moved aside the strategically placed box of tissues on the end table next to his wing chair, poured some water from the carafe, and sipped. 'It seems to be working, so I don't want to mess with it.'

Corrigan tented his fingers beneath his manscaped goatee and studied Brian.

'So how are you feeling, Brian? Really?'

Brian mulled this over, weighing how to answer with the care of someone about to share out the last slice of cake with a horde of sugar-starved weans. How *was* he feeling? He barely had any recollection of what had happened after the tablets Pam had forced him to take kicked in. Just random fragments, and what Fiona had told him when she'd visited him in the hospital. His stomach still felt so full from being pumped that he could barely manage half what he usually ate – and he wasn't a big eater to begin with. As for the way things had turned out with Pam ...

He pushed the thought away.

Despite what he'd just told Corrigan about doing the work, he wasn't ready to engage with the emotions her betrayal brought up for him. He would, eventually. He'd have no other choice, unless he wanted to jeopardise the fragile first shoots of his recovery. Just as Pam would have to deal with the consequences of what she'd done to fuel her misguided quest for justice.

But not yet.

There'd be a time for that. And, maybe it was the

meds evening him out, maybe it was personal growth, maybe it was something else he didn't even realise was going on inside him. Maybe it was all the above. But he wasn't dreading the moment when he'd have to confront it, because he knew that, when it came, he'd be ready. On surer footing. So aye, that was a long-winded way of saying he felt—

'Weirdly optimistic,' he told Corrigan. 'And grateful.'

He'd said as much to Fiona.

When he hadn't returned to the station two and a half hours after leaving to speak with Priya Singh, she'd tried calling him. And when her calls kept going to voicemail, she'd tried Singh, who hadn't answered either because, he'd found out later, she'd turned off her phone and gone to bed. That had made Fiona's spidey senses tingle, she'd told him; it was out-of-character for him to disappear without warning. So she'd called in a favour and tracked him down to Pam's house through his police phone.

Though, in itself, that hadn't rung any alarm bells; she'd thought it odd he'd visit the forensic pathologist at home in the middle of the day. But then the cryptocurrency wallet company had emailed back to say they didn't carry out formal identity checks on their customers. Which meant Shawcross might have told them the truth about it not being hers. Anyone could sign up for an account using a made-up name. At the same time, Adams had cracked the encryption on Higgins's external hard drive. Alongside more photos of Bidmead pleasuring himself on webcam and dirt on several other people that Higgins had most likely been using to extort payouts to fund his cancer treatment, there were also copies of several email and phone exchanges with an unknown person, who'd turned out to be Pam.

'Ten grand,' Higgins had said in one exchange, a phone conversation that had taken place just two days before he was stabbed to death. 'Or I'll tell your colleagues in the polis all about your extracurricular activities.'

Pam's voice was two octaves lower than usual, and thrumming with barely restrained rage. But McGillivray had recognised her straight away.

That was another ironic twist. The bloke who'd spent so much time living rent-free in Brian's head because of his slipshod work ethic had made the discovery that had solved the case and, quite possibly, saved Brian's life. If the cavalry had arrived at Pam's flat even two minutes later than they had, he might not have made it. He'd have permanently transferred to that great police station in the sky.

'That's really good, Brian,' Corrigan said, interrupting his reverie. 'I'm glad. But don't underestimate the impact this whole thing has had on you. Trauma leaves deep scars.'

'I'm not,' Brian said. 'I won't. I want to get better.'

Corrigan nodded. His eyes glinted. Was that ... Was that pride? Now, there was another unexpected twist, Brian reflected. Six weeks ago, wild horses couldn't have dragged him to Corrigan's office, even though Brian knew in his heart that he was skating very close to the edge. And now he was flushing with pleasure because the bloke was proud of his progress? Fucking hell.

'So when are you going back to work?' Corrigan asked.

'Next week,' Brian replied. 'Desk duty to start with.'

'And how do you feel about that?' Corrigan asked. 'Being out of action, I mean?'

Brian leaned back, spread his hands, and smiled. It was genuine. A smile that engaged his entire face and lit up his eyes.

'Honestly?' he said. 'It's fine. I'm fine with it.'

And it was true. To his surprise, he wasn't complaining about being benched. In fact, he was even looking forward to it. Sure, eventually, he'd get bored of pushing paper around and start yearning for the street. For the thrill of the chase. That was as certain as night follows day.

But, for once, he wasn't in a hurry to get back in the saddle.

He was happy to sit back and let others do the hard graft for a while – just until he'd recharged his batteries, mind.

Epilogue

'Craddock, please,' Brian told the receptionist.

'First floor, room one hundred and fifteen. On your left,' the receptionist, a fifty-something woman with short, blonde hair, chunky glasses, and a bright floral top, replied.

The *Mirror*'s distinctive white on red logo reflected on her lenses, which meant she was probably drinking up all the latest salacious details from the case of the forensic pathologist hell-bent on avenging her family. It was all the tabloids were talking about. They'd spilled gallons of ink and used up terabytes of space. And they'd probably still be milking the story for several weeks to come.

As Brian walked toward the stairs, he spied a pile of old newspapers on a moulded plastic chair next to the bins.

PATHOLOGIST'S REVENGE PLOT TURNS DEADLY, the newspaper on the top of the pile screamed in bold, black letters.

Brian thought of Pam, banged up in her cell with nothing to do except nurse the wounds he'd inflicted on her with her own knife and obsess over the headlines while she awaited trial.

His chest tightened.

What could they have been, if she hadn't turned out to be a cold-blooded murderer? What might've developed between them?

But the dominant emotion wasn't loss, though he did feel that. It was shame. Shame at not having seen through her mask. At having fallen for her act. Had what passed between them even been real? He remembered her insisting it was, back at the flat, when they'd confronted each other. Or maybe the memory wasn't real either? Maybe it was just his mind playing tricks on him to protect him from further heartache.

But there he was, ruminating, the same way he'd done in the aftermath of Roystonmuir. Meds or no meds, it was a very short leap from rumination to his local convenience shop and a fresh bottle of Monkey Shoulder. It had got him in trouble then, and, if he wasn't careful, it would get him in trouble this time round, too. Take him back to square one.

He took the stairs, climbing up to the first floor slowly. Step by painstaking step. His bandaged hand grazing the aluminium banister. With each step, his heart beat a little faster. Part of it was the old guilt resurfacing, even though, at last, he was starting to believe he wasn't to blame for what had happened. The Liam in his head, the one who'd come to his rescue when he'd needed him most, had been adamant about that.

'There was nothing you could've done.'

That much, he remembered as clearly as if it had just happened seconds ago.

But he was also afraid. Afraid of seeing Liam lying there, in his hospital bed, unresponsive, with a snare of wires and tubes snaking out of him, handling the vital functions his body couldn't perform by itself. Afraid of how he'd react to it. Would it send him into a panic-fuelled tailspin? Or would he be able to weather the distress and make a small but decisive step toward further progress? Toward – dare he say it? – healing?

He reached the first-floor landing. Opened the double doors onto the hallway that led to the ward. It was bright, airy, and tastefully decorated. But, despite the effort that had obviously been put into making the place feel homely, the smells of illness and disinfectant still lingered.

Brian walked along the corridor, his shoes clicking softly on the checked vinyl flooring, counting down the doors.

129. 127. 125.

An alcove with two battered blue chairs in front of a large sash window. Two older men, one of them missing an arm and another with deep, angry burn marks covering most of the right side of his face, were staring at the chessboard between them, considering their next moves.

123. 121. 119.

Brian's heart was a jackhammer. His hands were sweaty.

What would he find in Liam's room?

How would he look?

Would he even recognise his comatose form?

So many questions. And he'd soon be getting definitive answers. Whether he'd like them was another matter.

He walked the remaining ten or so steps that separated him from the blue door of room 115. Stopped in front of it with trepidation, staring at the stainless-steel knob with the interest of somebody who'd never seen one before and couldn't quite work out how to operate it. His arm stretched forward in front of him of its own accord, then stopped in mid-air and dropped back to his side.

Brian swallowed. Squared his shoulders. Nodded to himself. He turned the knob and crossed the threshold.

The scene that greeted him ... wasn't what he'd expected.

Walking in, he'd braced himself for the dark, dank atmosphere of a sickroom, his nose already wrinkled against the oversweet lemony smell that couldn't quite cover the acrid tang of ammonia. Instead, he found himself in a room that was bright and welcoming, if subdued and punctuated by the soft beeping of medical equipment.

Outside, the day was clear – the temperature a relatively balmy nine degrees. Somebody had opened the curtains to let the light in, and a wedge of sunlight had penetrated deep into the room, illuminating the side table, which was covered in get-well-soon cards, a child's stick drawings of a family of three standing next to each other on a bed of grass, holding hands – likely Matty's – and a vase of yellow and peach tulips. Lying on his back in the centre of the bed, noticeably thinner, his quiff longer and unstyled and what looked like at least two days' worth of thick ginger stubble colouring his cheeks, but still recognisable, was Liam. Eyes closed. Mouth slightly open. Cheeks drawn. Hands by his sides. Chest rising and falling rhythmically. His breathing like waves crashing at low tide.

Brian felt a catch in his throat. Cleared it. Eased himself into the armchair and leaned forward.

'Hiya, bud,' he said.

His voice was shaking slightly, but he felt more composed than he'd expected himself to be. This was fine. He and Liam would both be fine. Everything would turn out fine in the end. He could feel it in his bones.

'Nice rug you have there on your face.'

He removed the cushion from behind him, placing it on the floor, then turned back around, looking Liam up and down. In the time it had taken Brian to get comfortable – well, as comfortable as he could make himself while sitting in an unyielding hospital-issue armchair – Liam's body hadn't budged. But Brian could swear his right hand had rearranged itself so that it looked like he was giving him the finger.

THE END

23 March 2023, Edinburgh –
22 November 2024, Edinburgh

Afterword

Vanity Project was hard to write, partly because I was going through a difficult period, both personally and professionally, but mostly because I was suffering from a near-terminal case of self-comparisonitis.

When I wrote *Back From The Dead*, my first novel, I didn't have a frame of reference, so I just went for it and hoped for the best.

With *Vanity Project*, I had something to compare to, and the tiresome voice at the back of my head latched on to this and wouldn't let go. Was this story as good as the one I'd published? Or any good, really? What if I had just the one novel in me?

That it was so challenging to write makes me especially proud of the end result, and doubly grateful to the people who helped me along the way.

Craig Wright and Vicky Blunden read my excruciating first draft. Thank you for the valuable feedback and for delivering it gently. And sorry I made you read *that*.

Sam Davison answered my questions about Scottish

police procedure. Where I got it right, thank him. Where I got it wrong, it's my fault and mine alone.

My editor Rebecca Millar's input was instrumental. Her suggestions vastly improved the narrative, and her expert editorial eye made me look like a much better writer than I actually am.

Dom Forbes absolutely smashed the cover design brief. I love it, mate. Thank you.

And last but definitely first, I wouldn't be able to do this without the unconditional love and support of my wife Analise and my daughters Alicia and Adelaide. Thank you for being who you are, and for bringing joy to my life every single day.

About the Author

André Spiteri is the author of award-nominated crime thriller *Back From The Dead* and other novels featuring struggling characters with troubled pasts. He was born in Malta in 1982 and lives in Edinburgh with his wife, their two daughters, and two cats.

Stay up to date on andrespiteri.com

Printed in Great Britain
by Amazon

55106191R00280